PRAISE FOR TANKBREAD

"Paul Mannering's Tankbread is a guts and glory joyride into very dark territory. Very nasty and lots of fun!"

~ Jonathan Maberry, New York Times bestselling author of *Dead of Night and Dust and Decay*

"Mannering's take on the post-zombie apocalypse is scarifyingly real. Baked dog while you take orders from your zombie master anyone? Sink your teeth into an Australia where the zombies are in charge—you won't be disappointed."

~ Rocky Wood, author of *Stephen King: A Literary Companion and Horrors! Great Stories of Fear and Their Creators*

"Tankbread is a blast from start to finish. A breathless, country-crossing zombie epic—kind of like Mad Max colliding head on with Dawn of the Dead. Mixing great action scenes, laugh-out-loud moments, copious amounts of horror, and lead characters you really grow to give a damn about, Tankbread is a unique and very entertaining entry in the oversaturated zombie genre. Read it and enjoy it—I did."

~ David Moody, author of the *Autumn and Hater* series

PAUL MANNERING

A PERMUTED PRESS book

Trade Paper ISBN: 978-1-61868-122-5
eBook ISBN: 978-1-61868-123-2

Tankbread copyright © 2013
by Paul Mannering
All Rights Reserved.
Cover art by Alex Kranzusch.

PERMUTED
PRESS

DEDICATION

For Ash
"If I have a monument in this world, it is my son."
~ Maya Angelou

CHAPTER 1

The Asian across the table from me is tearing great gobs of warm flesh from his girlfriend's neck. Tendons and tissue hang from his mouth in bloody spaghetti strands while his jaw works tirelessly to consume. He chews her like gum.

The skull of the small dog, cooked and served on the plate between us, has me thinking the Asian is Korean. The crisped flesh with the dark ginger sauce and the crusty roasted eyes are probably a delicacy. I could be wrong or course; he might not be Korean. The cooked eyes might be garbage.

I look away from the dog head. It's making me salivate in a way I'm not comfortable with. The Asian casually pushes the girl away. She hasn't resisted him, cried out, or shown fear. She's Tankbread.

"You like dog?" The Asian's voice is thick with juice but eloquent for one of his kind.

"Reminds me of a pet I once had," I reply and let my right hand slide over the handgrip of the sawn-off shotgun holstered to my thigh.

"Ha-ha! You had good dog, yes? Now you good dog." Evol humor, I suppose. Maybe some geek has written a paper on it. Something for the other geeks to consider as they push out Tankbread and keep us from taking that final step into extinction. The Asian leans forward, his eyes clouded, like dead fish eyes, but I can feel his intelligence shining through.

"We do business now. You deal, you get dog."

As far as opening offers go, I've had worse. Usually of the Do what I say or get butt-fucked with a bayonet pedigree.

"I'm listening." It is true in the literal sense. I'm listening so hard I can barely think. The space behind us is filled with evols and the humans who serve them. Some of the walking dead are chowing down on Tankbread. The room echoes with the wet sound of living flesh being torn from bone, the low murmur of zombie growls muffled only by the thick wads of raw meat they are gorging on. And there's the smell. Slow decay, the nostril-clogging stink of flesh starting to rot. You get used to it. You become immune or your nose just gives up and says screw it, this stench is normal. Fresh air is what smells odd now.

"I'm listening." I'm listening for the one chance an outlaw like me can have. The early days of hunting these zombie pricks have long passed. It's a new world order, and each of us has to stake our claim and exercise our Darwinian right to exist.

"You go to Opera House, tell them Soo-Yong send you. Bring back what they give you. Bring to me here."

He knows I've understood. There is a change in his expression from the determined focus required for the formation of thought and words to the more basic recognition of meat emotions. His grey lips constrict into a grin that goes well beyond mere rictus.

"And what's in it for me?" I ask the age-old question that was yang to his yin. Judas would have asked the same thing.

"Passage, vehicle, supplies. You can run away like a bad dog."

I swallowed. I wasn't in a position to argue, but I could sure act like negotiating might be an option. "There's some wild turf between us and the house. Whatcha got to get me there?"

"Motorcycle, four liter fuel for bike. Two round for that shotgun. Fare for the boatman. House give you same for return. But must bring back what they give you or . . ." Soo-Yong didn't need to waste his rotting brains on spelling it out. Fuck it up, and I was worse than dead.

"Okay."

The evols do fine if they have time to marshal their thoughts, think things through, and arrive at the same conclusion that you or I could come to in seconds. Except with them, it can take hours.

How the hell did they end up ruling the world?

I ate the roast dog while I waited, crouched in the evening shade under a tattered canvas awning. The diner, in the Eastern Suburbs of Sydney, was run by meat — that's live folk like you and me. They were the people who'd gotten over the crawling revulsion that the living felt for our zombie masters and worked for them. Doing shit like cooking dogs in ginger sauce for the occasional living diner like me and tending the Tankbread.

All of us who are older than twenty-something still remember the war, the apocalypse, the end of the fucking world. Call it what you want, it all refers to when the dead started coming back to life and attacking the living. It's the sort of shit we used to go to the drive-in to see. We used to go see movies about all kinds of things back in the day. Now we live in a state of cold war. Some of us have gone crazy, some of us are holed up in secure compounds, and some of us are kissing dead arse. Yet we keep telling ourselves — at least we're alive, right?

Evols, zombies, the walking dead. Early on, when TV still worked and we thought we had a chance, some geek labeled the risen dead as Extremely Violent Lucid Organisms. Evol was easier to Tweet and the moniker caught on around the world. Almost as fast as the virus, or meteor, or toxic waste, or genetic engineering experiment. We still don't know what caused the mess. When someone dies you destroy their brain or they get up again and start trying to eat whoever is close. What the geeks call the infection factor is transmitted by undead body fluids in contact with open wounds. I've never seen anyone survive a zombie bite.

There was a little time between my accepting the job from Soo-Yong and sitting astride a beaten-up trail bike watching closely as exactly four liters of fuel was measured into the tank by one of Soo-Yong's mob. He must have been thinking about this for a while.

The bike took some starting, and evols don't like loud noises. When the engine backfired the bunch that were hanging around set to moaning and shuffling in that way they do when agitated. I was sweating ice water throughout the next three pumps on the kick-start before the bike came to life.

Soo-Yong handed over the two shotgun rounds last, carefully wrapped in a scrap of old tinfoil. The foil was a valuable item in itself. I hadn't seen tinfoil in I didn't know how long. The fare for the boatman was in a stained sack on a rope, which I looped and tied over my shoulder.

I didn't stop to wave or make a speech; they wouldn't have listened anyway. I tore out of the diner car park, past the burned-out shells of long abandoned cars and through the streets of the evol-controlled sector of the city. The dead were walking the streets; they had no concern for day or night, and it was now well dark. They just got out and wandered around, reliving some parody of their former lives. The geeks said it was part of their re-evolution. The walking dead were reinforcing synaptic links by repetition of learned behavior.

It still freaks me out to see them stumbling around, lining up for buses that will never come, wandering through decaying shops in silent malls, and no doubt when, whatever internal clock they are setting their time by tells them to, they go home and try to fuck their putrescent wives.

Meat live here too; the survivors who refuse to give up their nice north Sydney homes in suburbs like Roseville. They're usually in well-barricaded apartment buildings or parks. They keep some livestock, a sheep or a goat. I even saw a cow once, calmly chewing its cud in a rooftop garden, with no fence or tether to stop it stampeding over the edge and falling thirteen floors to the empty street below. The city-dwelling meat are hard-core survivalists and they tend to keep to themselves. I guess they know they are one failed crop away from cannibalism.

I rode through a silent city. Zombies, both solo and in small packs, caught on to the noise of the bike and started following. There was never enough Tankbread to go around and most of these were feral zeds. A steady diet of 'bread kept the evols who could get their hands on it intelligent and almost civil. Regardless, I usually walked, scuttled, or scurried from shadow to bolt-hole when I had to travel. The dead are everywhere and they have a taste for human flesh. There's been as much speculation as to why the dead attack the living as there has been about what caused them to get up in the first place. All I know for sure is that if they are eating Tankbread, they aren't eating me.

Many small communities in the great Sydney ruin would let me stay for a day or a night in exchange for some news or whatever job needed doing. Never longer; food was always a problem and they didn't like extra mouths to feed.

Crossing the Sydney harbor is always risky and I don't do it often. The bridge was blown back in the early days. No one thought ahead far enough to realize that evols don't need to breathe. Whatever need was driving them on would push them into the water, along the septic bottom, and up the other side.

They came out of the dark water, clambering and falling over the abandoned tables and chairs of the restaurants and cafes that lined the waterfront to scale the harbor side barricades.

I remember the screaming. It seemed constant; people just screamed and screamed during those dark times. We called it the Great Panic and I never got used to it, though I miss the noise now that the world is so quiet.

The dead got through all our defenses, of course. They always did. Every one of us that fell became another one of them. The siege mentality and a need to secure a large number of civilians made the Sydney Opera House an obvious choice. So it was there, at the living heart of the greatest city in Australia, that we made our final stand. The slaughter stopped at the barricades on those iconic steps.

Some survivors call it the War. It wasn't a war. It was a fight to survive. We haven't won it yet, and I don't see how we ever can. In time we will die out, Tankbread or no Tankbread. We have a limited usefulness, and if the evols haven't figured it out yet they will eventually. Like they seem to with everything else.

I rode down the Pacific Highway, passing empty shops and dead faces. There was nothing worth scrounging from here anymore; it had all been stripped years ago. First, anything that could be used as a weapon, then food and finally anything that would burn, could be used as shelter, or traded for food. The dead don't need to eat to survive like us living folk, but they have a hunger. Tankbread soothes that, like a nicotine patch for a heavy smoker.

At the corner of Pacific and Freeman I came up on a roadblock. There were no dead around and this wasn't their style. I stopped the bike, acting casual as I glanced around, looking for movement. The zombies following me hadn't caught up yet, but they were coming.

The intersection had been sealed off with wrecked cars. I waited, the bike idling away underneath me, burning through the precious few liters of fuel I had.

With a flash of movement he appeared first on a balcony of the apartment building on my left. I kept looking around because he might have had buddies lining me up for a shot. A minute later a thin figure with long grey hair and beard appeared on the other side of the cars. He wore a business shirt that might have been white once and a filth-encrusted tie. "Hey, mate," he said in greeting. I switched the bike off and stroked the butt of the shotgun on my thigh.

"Evening." I couldn't hear the evols coming up behind me yet, but I could feel the skin between my shoulder blades crawling in anticipation.

"Say," the guy wiped his matted hair back from his eyes. "Got any food to trade, mate?"

"Nope." It was true. I didn't have shit; the roast dog was the first decent meal I'd eaten in days. The man licked his lips and glanced back at the open doorway of the apartment building.

"You gotta have something." He paced up and down on the other side of the blockade. "We are dying here, man. Rats got into my supplies. There's no more cans, you know? No fucking cans!"

"It's hard all over. How about you shift this car and let me through?"

"Wait, wait, I got something you want. Yeah I got something every guy wants. Wait right there." He darted back into the shadows and reemerged with two kids in tow. One a girl, maybe fourteen years old, bone thin, small breasts, and long dreadlocked hair adorned with bottle caps and shards of shiny plastic. She wore a long singlet and her legs were pockmarked with sores and scabs. The other kid was an even younger boy. As thin as the girl, his hair hung down past his shoulders too. He wore nothing but a pair of stained underpants that he held up with one hand under his swollen belly.

"Gimme some food and you can fuck my girl. She's a great cock sucker. Just a can, some meat. Anything, man, and you can do her all night." He pulled the girl forward and swept her hair back, tilting her face up so I could get a clear look. "Maybe you like boys? You can fuck him too if you want. He kinda looks like a girl anyway."

"I told you, man, I don't have any food." Now I could hear them, the slow gait and moans of the dead. A whispering hiss of dry flesh shuffling down the street towards us. When the dead move they attract others, and crowds form quickly, which can mean certain death if they corner you.

"Listen," I hissed at the bearded man. "You hear that? There's a parade of evols coming up behind me, and if you don't clear the way they are going to be all over you and your kids and then food is going to be the least of your problems."

He started pawing the girl's breasts, doing the hard sell. I pushed the bike's kickstand down and climbed over the barricade.

The guy snatched at the sack over my shoulder. It had nothing for him in it, just my fare across the harbor. I pulled it out of his reach and yanked the car door open. Twisting the wheel I pushed back, rolling it slowly out of the blockade and opening up enough space to ride through.

"Please, we are fucked, completely fucked!" Shirt and Tie was crying, tears streaking white in the grime on his cheeks.

"Dance for the man, baby, show him you're sexy." He pushed his daughter at me. She started twisting and moving in a listless way. I got the car moved and jogged back to the bike. Dark silhouettes appeared from the darkness down the street. I kicked the bike to life and rolled through past the family. "You might want to get out of here," I called as I rode past. I didn't look back again and focused on putting distance between me and the following dead.

CHAPTER 2

I rolled the bike to a halt at the tip of the Blues Point Reserve before a floating dock that creaked and moaned as if it too were trapped in a rotting shell. A string of skulls hung on a rope. A festive banner perhaps? Or a warning? Like so many symbols and expressions these days, its meaning was as unclear as its nature was macabre.

To my relief I'd lost the trailing zombie crowd by getting off the highway and circling through back streets. I stood astride the bike, reached up, and pulled a rope so the summoning bell's tone struck out across the dark water. Turning off the bike engine was essential; the boat guy might be an hour away, getting his feed on. On the other hand, he might be at the bottom of the harbor in chunks. A wait was the only certainty.

Staring out across the harbor, I thought about how the nights in old Sydney town used to be a festival of lights, white and yellow like eyes shining in the darkness. Cars filled the streets, and people walked around in the open as if they didn't have a care in the world. Back then they didn't. Now they had plenty. They had the kind of cares that made eating a bullet a blessing. If only bullets weren't in such short supply and death was a guaranteed end.

I got off the bike and walked up and down the jetty, stretching my legs in the chill of the night. I didn't like to sit still for too long. I've always subscribed to a kind of law of averages which says that if you keep moving, the chances of getting jumped are reduced.

The water was oil-slick dark and decorated with the occasional piece of windblown trash floating past. The dead don't float. All that moving around pushed the gasses out of them and they decay so slowly. The why of stuff like that was for the geeks in the Opera House to wonder about. On the street you just stayed away from the dead and gave thanks for Tankbread.

When I heard the first creak and splash of an approach, I had the shotgun up and ready. The two cartridges were at home into the double breech, and the twin triggers were at half pull under my fingers. I had half a mind to run, but how far would the few liters of gas get me? Far enough to be in real trouble I guessed.

I waited; the echoing splash of torn water became more rhythmic as the boat approached. I hadn't traveled the harbor this way in a long time, mostly because I couldn't afford the fare. This time I was on evol business, and the expenses were not mine.

Leaving the bike, I crouched behind a jetty post as the harbor boat glided up to the dock. The watercraft was about twenty feet across and about twenty-five feet long. Little more than a raft, buoyed by the carcasses of small boats bound together under a flat deck. On the port and starboard sides was a mesh enclosure with nothing but a handrail and wooden slats. Here the crew hung, one man in each of the giant hamster wheels. Gripping the rail above their heads while their feet walked the slats. Stepping up and pushing down, driving the boat forward as they trod, rotating the wheel through the water. Now at rest they collapsed, kneeling in the water that stirred and slapped beneath them. The sound of their haggard breathing in the still night air indicated they were living meat. Evols were too slow for this kind of work.

In the center of the deck, resplendent on the frame of an old lifeguard's watch chair, sat a figure in a wide-brimmed hat and an old Snowy River oilskin. His hat and coat were stained black and foul by weather and guano from sea birds roosting on the boat. In each hand he held a thick cord, a leather rein that fed through a pulley. With these he could adjust the yaw of the rudders set at the rear and steer his boat like a great fish across the harbor.

The boatman had been doing this for a long time; repetition, the geeks said, was the key to the new evolution. The more times an evol did something the better they got at it. Like in the old days when they had the hunger and we hadn't figured out Tankbread, they had more than a passing skill at tearing fresh meat from screaming bones.

Standing up and facing the ferryman took more balls than I thought I had.

"Passage! Across the harbor! Got business with Opera House!" I called out, the shotgun casually hanging by my side.

"You got fare." There was no question in the boatman's voice. If I didn't have fare I wouldn't be standing there. The evols think like retards, but they have cunning.

"I have a head." A head, a fresh skull, encased in flesh. The brain still sealed inside. The sweetest meat, the price of passage. I swung the sack off my shoulder. The shotgun I holstered at my side and I opened the sack. Reaching in, I grabbed the hair and pulled the fare out. I waited while the boatman thought about what to say next.

"Come aboard."

I stuffed the head back into the sack and scrambling a little, half out of nerves and half . . . well shit, it was all nerves. I like the water, just not the walking dead, and I was going to spend some time with an evol who could just as easily decide that two heads were better than one.

I pushed the bike, rolling it down the trembling planks of the dock and then with a slight bump I was standing on the flat deck between the twin cages of the paddle wheels. The men on each side regarded me with a resigned loathing. No rest for them tonight. I parked the bike on its kickstand, feeling the boat move and settle under my feet.

The boatman watched as I repeated the ritual stripping of the sack cover. I held the head up to him; he reached down with a wet grey hand and snatched it up to his face.

My eyes adjust fast to dim light; it's a survival trait. Could be why I'm still alive and not some meat-munching evol. I could see well enough on the barge. Under that wide-brimmed hat, the dead eyes, and the torn flesh of an old injury that had left the boatman's right jawbone exposed. He sniffed the head, grunted in a satisfied way, and then slammed it neck first down onto a spiked pole next to his chair. The spike pierced the bone and burst out through the top. He slid his fingers up the exposed section of the spike and then licked the bits off them.

"Boat turn!" He spoke the way all evols do. Like they have a terminal case of snot on the lungs with some huge ball of thick soup waiting to be coughed up out of his throat. I swallowed hard. It reminds me that I'm alive and I can clear my damn throat anytime I want.

The men in the cages adjusted their grip on the rail overhead. First one drew his knees up and pushed down, his weight turning his wheel in a downward motion. The fellow on the other side of the barge also gripped his overhead rail and pushed down on the paddles behind him, driving them in the opposite direction. The barge spun on its own axis and without further orders from the boatman, the two paddle drivers got us going, slowly at first, and then up to a regular striding speed as they forced the paddles down and carried on thumping their feet in a sodden treadmill action.

I stood and looked ahead, one hand on the bike, staring out into the darkness and wishing I was anywhere else. Someplace where I could see the buildings or dirt would be nice.

Behind me the two boat drivers grunted and heaved. They stank, the harbor not so much. It's amazing how years after the collapse of modern civilization the ecology was coming back. Green things were pushing up through the concrete everywhere. Must have been all the blood on the ground.

The fog didn't roll in from the sea; the air ahead of us just started to get thick and pale. By my guess we were halfway across the water. Too far to swim either way, I thought as my palms started to sweat. If Soo-Yong screwed me and the shotgun shells turned out to be duds, I promised myself I would spend the rest of eternity getting enough dead-smarts to rip his head off.

"HUUUUUUUUUNNNNNNGHHH!"

I nearly shat my pants as the noise bellowed behind me. The boatman's head tilted back and he bellowed into the mist like a stag in rut. I slung a leg over the bike and clenched the handlebars. It felt better to be gripping something as he howled again, every undulating wail driving spikes into my skull. The meat treading the wheels didn't seem bothered by it. They just kept on plodding, driving the boat through the water.

The rest of the way through the fog the boatman kept howling into the sky while the meat kept trudging, turning the paddlewheels and pushing us ever closer to the shore.

Walsh Bay on the south side of the harbor used to be a trendy development of restaurants and office blocks, a thriving hub of humanity. Now the evols walked the streets, feral cats hissed from the shadows, and the occasional meat, driven out by hunger, scavenged and checked snares and cage traps for rats.

The boat slid to a halt against the lowest level of the Walsh Bay pier. I pushed the bike off and then ran it up the rough steps that took me to street level. You forget how dark it gets when there is no electricity. With the fog coming off the harbor, I couldn't see shit. The damp was seeping in through my clothes and I felt a moment of panic about the powder pressed into those precious shotgun shells soaking up the moisture and turning to clay.

Starting the bike, I rode down the pier, through the ruin of an old building and out onto Hickson Road. The harbor bridge, dark and broken, was out there somewhere. I rode across to Fort Street and down George; a few evols lost it as I roared past. By the time they had worked out how to respond, I was gone. I turned left into Alfred Street, the drifting trash mostly dirt and bits of tree now. In a thousand years this whole city would return to whatever it had been before people arrived. Left again onto Phillip Street, chunks of the Cahill Expressway like giant Lego blocks scattered around. Down to Bridge Street, riding around empty cars and buildings stained with faded graffiti and on to Macquarie. When I rode under the overpass evols peeled away from the walls and started following. Finally, the Sydney Opera House came into view, a grey-white cloud in the thinning mist.

I stopped halfway down Macquarie. An armored bus barricaded the street, with some kind of cannon and two guards peering over the corrugated iron battlements. Battery-powered torches mounted on their weapons flicked on and played over my face and bike.

"Fuck off!" one of them called by way of greeting.

"I got business inside!" I hissed back. Shouting isn't something we do. Like sharks smelling blood in the water, when evols hear screaming they get to thinking about eating someone.

"What kinda business, mate?" The other guy, sounded older.

"Message from the gook evol Soo-Yong, over on the north side."

"What's the message?" older asked, apparently not bothered about the idea of me sitting out here with my balls in hand waiting for the evols to come down and tear me a new one.

"Fuck man, let me in and I'll tell you all about it . . . but hurry up."

I could hear the evols behind me now, the groans, the slow stumbling steps, and the smell coming off a crowd of the dead gathering. They were drawn in by the noise of my bike and the chatter of human voices.

The old prick sat up there on the bus and thought about it like a damned evol trying to remember how to pick its nose. He waited for a good minute until I could see the shapes coming out of the dark. The sunken eyes, the withered flesh, the lips pulling back to reveal hungry teeth.

The dead stank. A smell of slow rot, old shit, and drying blood.

I stood astride the bike, ready to tear out through the gathering mob. There could have been hundreds of them behind me, maybe thousands, and more coming all the time. Like undead sheep, the evols tend to follow each other. Maybe they communicate in some way we don't understand, or maybe they were just bored and looking to party.

The young guy vanished and a few moments later the bus engine began to turn over, a slow grinding whine. I rolled the bike forward, as close to the sheet metal wall as I dared without being trapped by the advancing crowd.

The bus engine fired and the kid stirred the gear stick looking for reverse. The grinding noise was echoed by the moans of the dead; they were close. I pulled my shotgun and cracked it open, rechecking the load.

"Hurry it up!" I could barely hear myself over the revving of the bus and the growing agitation of the zombie horde.

A gap appeared and I dropped the clutch, punching the bike through just as the nearest evol was reaching out to tear me from the saddle. I skidded the bike on the other side, narrowly avoiding riding straight into another wall. Behind me the bus lurched forward and the cannon on the roof roared, spraying a jet of high-pressure water that knocked the advancing dead on their arses and gave many of them the first bath they'd had in years.

The gate closed again and the heavy engine shut off. The kid hopped out of the cab, all grinning and cocksure.

"Arsehole," I growled at him.

"Aww shit, mate, we let you in. But damn if you could have seen the look on yo—"

Leaping off the bike I slammed my fist into that shit-eating grin. The kid flew back and bounced off the side of the bus. He wasn't smiling now. He shrieked, an angry squealing sound like a rat in a snare trap. I stepped aside as he threw himself at me. He landed next to the bike, rolled, and came up with a knife in his hand.

"Cool!" the old guy above us on the bus roof shouted out and dropped down behind me. I moved to watch him and the kid. Both stood their ground and let me stand mine.

"Calm down, Cool," the older man said. So the kid's name was Cool. I could see the humor in that. Like calling a fat guy Slim.

"Sorry about that." The old man rolled a smoke and took his time. I guessed whatever he was smoking wasn't tobacco, though if he meant to impress me by showing he had skins to roll a smoke, it worked.

The final trick was the casual way he pulled a shiny chrome lighter from his pocket and lit up.

"You got business with the geeks?"

"Yeah." Giving information away free wouldn't get me anywhere except back out on the wrong side of the barricade.

"Leave your bike parked up over there. I'll walk you down."

I looked at Cool one more time. He seemed calmer. The blood on his face tracked through the grime but couldn't turn his frown upside down.

The old guy led me out through a well-lit maze of shipping containers stacked two high, switching back as we wound our way toward the Opera House.

"Name's Bert," he said, dragging on his limp cigarette.

I nodded, taking note of the drop gates hanging overhead, ready to slide down and block the narrow canyon between the steel walls. If the evols or some gang of meat got past the bus gate, they could be slowed down, boxed in, and exterminated here.

"You got yourself quite the entranceway here," I said.

"Sure," Bert said and we walked on in silence.

The Sydney Opera House gleamed in the damp night air, the tips of its roof rising above the fog. She'd always been an icon to Australians, a shining beacon of our culture, our can-do spirit, and since it all went to shit, it became a sanctuary for a chosen few of us too.

The ones who got into the house compound and stayed had the right skills, or the right connections. Scientists and military types, of course, and if the rumors were right the last prime minister was holed up in here somewhere. They said during the Great Panic things in Canberra went badly wrong. Most of the central government didn't make it out due to a screwup in the evacuation plan. The prime minister's helicopter crashed in the botanic gardens and the Opera House geeks rescued him. The story goes that he suffered brain damage in the crash, or just went nuts. Now they said he spends his days in a padded cell, jerking off and writing memoirs on the walls in his own shit. Not everyone survived the collapse of civilization with their minds intact.

We walked out into the open space beyond Macquarie Street, to our right the cliff that rose up to the Royal Botanic Gardens, to our left the decaying remains of the towers and shopping complex that overlooked the bay. People glanced up from small cooking fires; they lived in converted shipping containers and the lobbies of buildings. I could smell cooking meat, animal meat, and I mentally marked the rumor about the people inside the house compound being cannibals as bullshit.

"Where's it come from?" I asked. "The meat?"

"Botanic gardens, got a regular farm going on up there. Of course most of what these buggers out here get to eat is the usual, cats and rats and elephants, as sure as you were born." He sang the last bit.

"Elephants?" I said. I wouldn't have been surprised. We lived in strange times.

"Never mind." He might have been laughing; in the dark it was hard to tell.

The Opera House was huge close up, three buildings unlike any other on earth. One last barricade blocked our way, six-foot-long iron spikes set in concrete in front of a twelve-foot fence, topped by barbed wire and behind that, armed soldier types, watching and wary.

"I feel safer already," I said to Bert, who just smiled, pinched his cigarette out, and tucked the butt in his pocket.

"Just Bert, and a courier," he called out while we were well back from the fence. I could see sandbag machine gun nests dotted up the steps, and more bags were piled against the massive windows under the curving roofs I remembered from a lifetime ago.

We stopped at the mesh gate. Two guys with guns, wearing faded but proper army khakis, watched while a third unlocked the gate and let us through.

"What's the package?" the gate soldier asked.

"Message for the geeks, from Soo-Yong."

"What's the message?" They must get really bored out here night after night.

"Captain Kangaroo says fuck you," I said, forgetting to use what my mum always called my "inside head voice."

The three of them tensed up. I watched them until Bert stepped in between us waving his hands.

"Steady on, fellas. This bloke's come over from the north side. He's doing his job, so let him do it, eh?"

"Don't piss me off," the gate guy said.

Bert said something soothing and headed on up the steps. I followed him while staring back at the three of them for as long as I could.

"First time here?" Bert said as we neared the top of the stairs.

"Sure," I replied. Of course I had been here before, New Year's Eve shows and concerts mostly. On these very steps I got my hand up a girl's shirt and held bare tit for the first time. It was during a Crowded House concert one stinking-hot summer evening. It was also the first time I got drunk on a bottle of cheap vodka. I ended up puking my ring out in a rubbish bin and lost the girl in the crowd. I forget how many years ago that was.

"Evening, Bert. Courier is it?" A man stood in a doorway cut into the concrete barrier. This guy was clean shaven; his clothes were clean too, and I couldn't help but stare.

"Yes, sir. I'll leave him with you then?"

"Good as gold, Bert," he said.

"Well," Bert turned to me and seemed unsure of what to

say. "Good luck, mate." He hesitated a moment longer and then deciding there was nothing else to say, he trotted off down the stairs. I felt like a bride delivered to the sacrificial altar by her father and then abandoned.

"Well don't just stand there, come on in."

I glanced back at the dark city and stepped through the door into a different world.

CHAPTER 3

The guards inside the Opera House looked clean and polished too, as if the outside world didn't exist. Maybe for them it didn't. Everything I could see looked worn but maintained. Surfaces were free of dust and nothing looked abandoned. They stared at the sawn-off shotgun on my hip. I kept my thumbs hooked on my belt, nice and easy.

Some beavers had been busy in the house, tearing down anything unnecessary, replacing it with other things, the purpose of which made no sense to me. Like the prefab building with the two armed guards outside the door and the collection of potted plants huddled together like refugees from the end of the world.

It was bright inside, though; the place glowed with warm electric light. No sign of how they were generating the power, and I felt exposed without shadows to slip into.

"My name is Charlie Aston." The guy who invited me in didn't extend a hand. I pretended I didn't notice.

"Nice to meet you, Charlie. I like what you've done with the place." I'd never been so conscious of how badly I stank.

Charlie gave a short, polite laugh. "Yes, we work very hard to maintain our sanctuary. Without this operation the entire area would collapse into complete chaos and lawlessness."

It was my turn to stare at him. Exactly what the fuck did he think was going on outside the barricades?

"I have a message for the geeks," I said.

"Of course. Come with me; we will get you cleaned up and arrange an appointment."

I couldn't see a reason to argue with an offer of a wash. I followed Charlie across the floor and into a narrow corridor stacked with cardboard boxes.

"Baby food?" I said, reading a label as we passed.

"Essential for early development during the transition to more complex foods."

"I ate a box of baby food once, a year or so back. Mostly fruit. Shit myself blind for a week afterwards. My crap stank like bananas and peaches."

Charlie didn't laugh that time; I guessed my rough appearance and manner didn't sit well with his happy world.

We stopped at a bathroom, clean white tiles and actual working toilets. "Shower's at the end. Towels are on the shelf. I'll see if we can find you some fresh clothing."

I stood staring into the white room, waiting for the catch.

"Back in a bit," Charlie said and walked off down the corridor. I watched him go and then stepped into the bathroom. When was the last time I took a proper shower? Not in a few years. Stripping off in the rain or taking a swim in the ocean was how we did it now.

I stood under the shower with the heat turned all the way up. The drain ran black with filth and matted chunks of god knows what. I used soap for the first time in recent memory. When I stepped out of the shower my clothes were gone and in their place were the green scrubs that doctors used to wear and some slipper-like shoes. I dried off and dressed. I wanted my gear back; I sure as hell wasn't leaving this place without it. My gun especially.

Out in the corridor I turned and headed where I thought Charlie went. I passed a lot of doors, most of them locked. A few turns later the corridor ended in an unlocked door. In the room beyond were more boxes labeled as milk powder, baby food, and medical stuff. Rubber tubing, gloves, antiseptic, and swollen bags of saline were stacked on shelves and floor under harsh fluorescent lights. I wound my way through the stacks and opened another door where I could hear an English-sounding male voice and smell iodine.

"Hello?" I called out. You announce yourself or you get shot in my world. Unless you are stealing stuff; then the less said the better.

"Ah, hello." The English guy came into view, old enough to have white hair, his beard a choice, judging from its groomed state.

The room was like an operating theater, with big lights, a couple of tables, and benches in the background covered in bottles, tubes, and computers winking away.

"You a geek?" I said.

The old man laughed. "Why yes, I suppose I am. I am Doctor Haumann." He extended a hand and shook mine with a firm grip.

"Got a message from Soo-Yong. The evol out past Roseville."

"Yes," the old man looked grave. "I know of him."

"He said to come here and get what you gave me and take it back to him."

"He said all that?"

"Sure did."

"Did he say what it was that you should collect?"

"Nope." I hoped it would be something lightweight, and exactly what Soo-Yong wanted. Turning up with something in the wrong color or size would be a bad idea.

"What do you know about the work we do here?" Haumann asked.

I frowned and looked around; I didn't feel any need to engage in question time. "Just give me the shit and I'll be on my way. I need my clothes and gear back too."

Haumann carried on as if I had answered his question. "We are saving humanity. The risen dead are the single greatest threat to the existence of our species."

"True that," I said and idly wondered if he would notice if I walked out with some of the loose items in the room.

"Sacrifices were made, but only to give us time you see.

Time for a solution to be found! And we are close . . . so very close!" Haumann gave a little fist pump.

"Cool," I muttered and picked up a pair of chrome pliers with a spring handle. Might come in useful, except the green suit didn't have any pockets.

"Let me show you." Haumann opened a door on the right side of the room and the sound of pumps working and a deep humming came through the doorway. I followed him, wondering who I would have to talk to about getting something to eat.

Stairs led down into a massive chamber, pipes and cables ran everywhere, men and women in green jammies like mine moved around below us. They hunched over computer screens and walked around rows of glass and metal water tanks, like cylindrical aquariums. We stopped on a mezzanine floor high above the busy workshop.

"This is it," Haumann announced. "This is where we start the process. Here we make what you suburb dwellers call Tankbread."

"I knew that," I said. It was hard not to be impressed. I could see rows and rows of tanks, most of them full of a murky pink liquid, like clouds at sunset or cum leaking from a virgin after her first time.

"Did you now?" Haumann seemed amused. "What is it that you know then, young man?"

"Geeks make Tankbread, evols eat Tankbread so the rest of us have a chance."

"Succinctly put," Haumann smiled. "Yes, Tankbread appeases the dead. We give them what they want. With their limited intelligence they understand that we as a species are endangered. Therefore a viable alternative food supply must be maintained. Tankbread is that food supply."

"Good for the evols, not so good for those of us living out there." I had to get that in. Everyone on the outside hated and envied those who lived in the rumored luxury of the Opera House. I wasn't about to hold my tongue now that I had a chance to bitch about the injustice of it all.

"These tanks are used to grow the forms from zygotes to

full-sized specimens. The process takes about a month. Very energy intensive and highly complex. We are fortunate enough to have access to a nuclear reactor's output. Without it things would get very grim, very grim indeed."

"Guess you haven't been off the point in a long time then, huh Doc? Things are already grim, real fucking grim out there. Have been since day one."

Haumann had the decency to look regretful. "We do what we can, young man. Our resources are limited and sacrifices—"

"Fuck your sacrifices! A lot of people lost everything out there while you bastards—"

"Is everything alright, Doctor Haumann?" Charlie appeared behind us. He looked ready to throw me over the rail and onto the concrete floor below for speaking up against Haumann.

"Yes, yes, thank you, Charlie. Our friend here was simply expressing an opinion. Perhaps it would be best if you took him to the canteen, see he has a good meal and perhaps some coffee. Would you like that? A cup of real coffee?"

"Sure . . ." What else could I say?

The canteen was just that, a room full of chairs next to a kitchen, with a serving line. I followed Charlie's lead and got a tray and a plate. A sour-looking woman with a headscarf ladled it full. The coffee urn was at the end of the server line. I inhaled roasted beans all the way to an empty table, ignoring the pricks that stopped eating to stare.

I ate like I always do: quick, quiet, and like this may be the last meal I see in a long time. I glanced up to see Charlie watching me with apparent amusement. "Want seconds?"

I shook my head, patronizing arseholes like Haumann and now Charlie treating me like some kind of animal. I did not need this shit. Let one of them walk out there, see how long they survived without their air-conditioned comfort, hot canteen food, and fresh coffee.

I watched the women in the canteen while I shoveled food into my mouth. Some were young; they looked fresh and clean, as if they would smell great and feel even better up close.

"You'll be keen to get back on the road," Charlie said. A casual way of saying it was time for me to leave.

"No rush," I said and stood up. Leaving my licked-clean tray on the table, I walked over to where three girls were sitting together, chattering like birds in spring. "Hey," I said, sliding into an empty space next to a brunette with green eyes.

"Hi," they said, looking a little surprised. They did smell good, fresh like cut apples, with just a hint of that secret girl musk.

"How's it going?" asked the blonde one, hair pulled back in a loose ponytail from her narrow face.

"Not bad. So what do you ladies do around here?" I replied.

Again they exchanged looks, a smirk moving between them like a ball being passed around. "Well," said the brunette, "I work in administration. Mel," she indicated the blonde, "is a nurse, and Lisa," the third one, dark hair, olive skin, and large warm eyes, "is with compound security."

It had been so long since I had an opportunity to be close to three women who weren't waiting for me to lay enough in trade on the table for them to spread their legs, I realized that I didn't know what else to say.

"You from out there?" Mel indicated the general direction of dead Sydney.

"Yeah," I said and silence settled over us.

"What's it like?" Lisa's eyes were wide, and her lips parted slightly.

"It's . . . It's death, and starving, and shitting yourself every time an evol looks at you and watching your swag and creeping around and wondering why the fuck you bother . . ." I trailed off. My fists uncurled; they all looked a bit shocked.

"I . . . we don't hear much about it. We tend to stay inside the compound," Mel said, looking like she was going to cry. I swallowed hard and lifted my gaze to watch the rise and fall of her breasts against the soft, clinging cotton of her shirt.

"Haumann wants to see you," Charlie said. He stood at the end of the table looking pissed. The girls immediately pulled back and our moment passed like summer rain.

"Sure. Ladies, nice to meet you." I stood up. "You done my laundry yet, Charlie?" Something in his jaw twitched. I held his gaze until he moved past. "Follow me."

Inside the Opera House very little space was wasted. Crates and shelving were everywhere. We passed a giggling file of young women wrapped in towels, heading back to their dorm from the showers, and a file of men who weren't laughing heading toward the showers. We went down two flights of cold concrete stairs until Charlie unlocked a solid-looking door into another empty concrete space somewhere underneath the entertainment complex. The smell that wafted out was familiar; the stink of the walking dead. I stepped back. "What is this?"

"What you came for." Charlie stepped through and held the door open. "Come on, Haumann wants you to see this. Wants you to understand what it's all about."

"I don't need to know."

"Sure you do. Once you know, you will do what we tell you."

I went through the door. The smell of evol was strong here. Once the door closed and my eyes adjusted to the dim light, I could see more stairs leading down and evols shuffling around somewhere below us, down there in the gloom.

We headed down, feet quiet on the metal steps. Halfway down on a landing an armed guard stood waiting. "Hey, Johno," Charlie greeted him.

"Hi, Charlie."

"This is a courier from the north side. It's his first time inside." Johno nodded and seemed to relax slightly. "Well, take him on down then."

At ground level, I could now see a fence—panels of steel sheets welded against metal posts set in the concrete, large diamond shapes cut in to each panel. It gave the impression of a highly magnified wire-mesh fence. On the other side zombies, penned in and pacing up and down.

"Christ, if the other evols heard about this they would not be happy," I said.

Charlie gave a snort. "They're dead. Who gives a fuck what they think?" Above us, the door opened again and Haumann made his way down the stairs.

"Well, young man, has Charles explained everything to your satisfaction?"

Charlie stepped forward. "I was just about to start, sir."

"Very well, carry on." Haumann put his hands behind his back and beamed at us.

"Stop me if you've heard this one." Charlie had a practiced tone, like he gave this speech and tour every day. "We keep evols here for testing. We assess their development, the neural regeneration and retention of memory and cognitive function. We also test bioweapons against them, antivirals, genetically engineered toxins, and counteragents to the apoptosis inhibitor factors present in all evol cells."

"Does it work?" I asked, pretending I understood any of what Charlie had just said.

"Yes," Haumann said gravely. "But not fast enough and not with 100 percent effectiveness. We need a final solution to the evol menace. We need to destroy them, and inoculate humanity against future epidemics of the resurrection factor."

"So what's this got to do with me?"

"Soo-Yong is a well-advanced evol. He died very suddenly, and unlike many evols he resurrected with little loss of neurological function. We believe that Soo-Yong died of natural causes, probably in his sleep. Those who die under great stress, and resurrect after infection by body fluid contact through injuries such as bite trauma, seem to have less cognitive retention. The returned dead in these cases are more aggressive, but have reduced mental functioning capacity."

"So?" I yawned loudly. After the good food and the

shower I was looking forward to a good long sleep. Preferably with Mel, Lisa, and the brunette to keep me warm.

"Tankbread is the most advanced biotechnology we have, the only thing that has saved us from utter extinction. Here we created thousands of cloned humans, a direct copy of adult males and females. These living bags of nutrients supply the evols' needs," Haumann said and began to pace along the fence line. On the other side, the evols shuffled along beside him, moaning and wheezing. "Come over here. Let me show you some computer models."

Charlie hung back by the fence. I didn't give a damn about computer models, but that old lizard brain part of me, the bit that spoke up when danger threatened, was now saying give the old man some time to say his piece.

Haumann tapped keys, clicked the mouse, and made the screen show graphs, pages of text, and other stuff that meant nothing to me.

"There, you see." He stabbed a gnarled finger at a red line on a graph; it was going down. I guessed that meant something turning to shit for someone.

"Okay, what does it—?" Lizard brain started yelling. I spun around and saw the first of the evols stumbling through a gate on the fence that was swinging wide open, a mob of them on his heels.

"Motherfucker," summed it up pretty well I thought.

The door at the top of the stairs slammed shut. Johno the guard was standing at his post halfway up the stairs, mouth gaping, looking like he'd been slapped. Charlie had vanished.

"Get up the stairs, Doc!" I looked around. Other than Johno's shotgun and my dick, we were defenseless.

"Johno! Shoot!" I grabbed the Doc, who was standing there, mouth working like a dying fish, and pushed him toward the stairs.

"Johno! Shoot for fuck's sake!" Evols are like those old-world traffic signs. The ones that say walk, don't run. Evols don't run. They don't need to run. They don't stop either, not for anything, except to eat living human flesh, and that's why they are walking in the first place.

Haumann found his voice. "My research! It is very important we don't lose any data. Do not damage the test subjects!"

Johno still hadn't fired a shot. I was yelling at him to fuck some shit up, and he was looking from the zombies crossing the floor to Haumann. I was behind the doctor, closer to the open gate, and felt like I was literally pushing shit up hill.

"Move dammit! Get to the door! Get outta here!"

Johno led the way. He was whimpering, his gun forgotten as he headed up the stairs two at a time and fell on the door, shaking it and hammering at the solid steel. "Open the door! For godsake! Open the door!" he screamed.

The dead reached the bottom of the stairs behind us and started up. One slow stumbling step at a time. One walking corpse behind the other, up they came. Haumann shrank back, his lips curling in a grimace of loathing. Johno was still screaming and pounding on the door. I grabbed his shotgun, fighting to get him to let go. A swift head-butt stunned him and sealed the deal. Turning around, I flicked the safety off and squeezed the trigger. The first evol's head exploded in a stinking spray of grey-black ooze and bone fragments. I pumped the slide and fired again. Hot smoke filled the air between us and the worst way to die.

The more screaming and panic, the more aggressive evols get. They started moaning and reaching, clawing at us, probably trying to get us to shut up. It is like being dead means suffering the worst headache imaginable. I cured one at point-blank range, the shot tearing through the foul flesh and smashing the head behind him into pulp as well.

Six shots fired and seven evols were reduced to tottering headless lumps that collapsed and blocked the stairs for a few seconds. Then the pump-action slide fell dry.

"We can't get out! We can't get out!" Johno had totally lost his rag. Shrieking like a bitch he knocked me aside and made a jump for the rail, aiming to get to a clear space on the concrete floor below. The nearest evol snatched his wrist as he went. Johno howled and slammed against the stairs, his feet kicking in empty space as the other evols reached and latched on to his arm. Dead lips parted, peeling back from blackened gums and broken teeth. They bit hard and they bit deep. Johno screamed as his blood gushed, filling the air with a hot copper tang.

I laid into the nearest evols with the butt of the shotgun. Smashing faces, crushing skulls. The walking dead are strong, and in their blood frenzy they twisted Johno's arm until it popped at the shoulder and his screams went up so high only dogs could hear his final moments. The limb came out of his sleeve like a butcher-wrapped chunk of meat. The poor bastard fell to the concrete below, landing with a wet slap.

Evols started fighting over the arm. "Is there any other way out of here!?" I yelled at Haumann.

"Yes . . . yes . . . at the other end of the containment pen, there is a door but it is keypad locked."

"Jump! Over the side! I'll hold them off!" Haumann crawled to his feet and peered over the side of the rail. Maybe twelve feet to the concrete floor below. Maybe a broken leg or cracked skull for an old guy. Maybe enough of a distraction for the evols to give me a chance to get the hell out.

"Move, damn you!" I lashed out with the gun butt, smashing some dead girl in the face so hard her eyes popped out and dangled like earrings.

With a moan of fear Haumann clambered over the rail and dropped out of sight. I glanced over and saw him struggling to his feet, slipping in the spreading pool of Johno's blood. Evols snatched at the hot flesh of my face. Some grabbed at the gun, and being too far gone to know better they bit at the stock and barrel, pulling it out of my grasp. Zombie teeth then snapped at my fingers.

I ducked the searching hands with their claw-like nails. Johno's half-eaten arm had been dropped in the melee and I snatched it up and starting swinging it like a club. It didn't put any of them down, but I felt like I was at least making an effort.

With one last swing, I leapt over the railing. A fast drop and I landed in a crouch, Johno's blood soaking my slippers. I bolted after Haumann; he was the limping hunched figure in the white coat busting for the far end of the containment pen. I dashed across the floor and through the gate. Quickstepping to a halt, I sprang back and pulled the gate shut. It wouldn't hold them for long, but I'd be damned if I was going to make it too easy.

Catching up with Haumann took only a few moments. The containment area was littered with chewed bones, mostly human. No surprises there; I'd seen evol leftovers before. I looked back; some of the dead were feasting on Johno's remains. At least he wouldn't be coming back. There wasn't enough room at the table for all the diners, though. A bunch of them were pushing on the gate. They shook it until it popped open and they tumbled through and followed the scent of fresh blood.

Haumann let out a low cry when I swept him up, my arm around his waist as I half carried him, hurrying until we slapped against the back wall.

"What's the key code?" I demanded. The doctor was breathing hard; he pressed buttons. The glowing panel made a scolding beep. He grunted and with trembling fingers tried again with the same result.

"Fuck me, Doc, hurry it up," I hissed in his ear. Evols weren't coming up fast, but they were coming and I was all out of clever plans.

"Three . . . seven . . . nine . . . five . . ." Haumann said and pressed each button in turn and this time the door clicked. I gripped the handle and twisted, the doctor nearly collapsing as I dragged him across the threshold.

"Get up, old man!" I dropped his limp carcass on the floor of the corridor and threw my weight against the door as the evols started scrabbling on the other side. I didn't ease up until I was sure it had clicked shut and locked down tight.

The corridor was spartan, the exposed cables and naked

lights showing a dirt and stone floor and walls of raw rock. I leaned over Haumann and shook him. "Where are we?"

"Under . . . the Opera House. This tunnel connects to the harbor tunnel."

"They blew that road back in the war, same time the bridge got taken out."

"Yes . . . yes, but we opened up a tunnel you see. From here, the secret bunkers under the Opera House, they were never revealed to the public. We transport the Tankbread out through this tunnel, into the harbor road tunnel, onto trucks and out into the city for delivery. That's what Soo-Yong sent you here for. He wants you to take a delivery of Tankbread back to the north side."

About damn time, I thought. "Where do you keep them? Give me the zombie chow and I'll be on my way."

Haumann looked like he was about to cry. "I can't . . . not anymore . . . It's what I've been trying to tell you!"

I snarled and dragged him to his feet, throwing him back against the wall. "Well I don't speak your fucking language then!"

"You need to see. You need to see what I have seen. What I see every day. What I see in my nightmares."

He jerked away from my grip and left me feeling uneasy. Nightmares? What could be worse than the one we were living in?

We walked until the walls smoothed out from hewn rock to cement block and then doors on each side, steel doors like on a ship, each one with a glowing keypad lock. "The risen dead, do you know how they function?" Haumann asked between panting breaths.

"They have a virus or something. It keeps them ticking along." I glanced back down the narrow corridor. It was clear.

"Not quite." The doctor had that lecturing tone again. "The virus was genetically engineered. Like the Tankbread. Any organism needs an energy source to function. The walking dead, they are photosynthetic."

"They're what?"

"Like plants, the infected cells convert sunlight to energy and this gives them enough to function."

"You're serious?"

Haumann nodded. "Indeed. Higher brain function, however, requires a regular infusion of stem cells."

Haumann dialed open one of the locked doors, and with a pressurized hiss the door swung out into the corridor. "Tankbread are filled with stem cells." He stepped through and I followed, not having anything better to do.

"We keep the mature Tankbread sedated, otherwise they endanger themselves. If unmedicated they suffer psychoses, mental breakdowns, self-destructive behavior, and assault each other."

The room was warm, and dimly lit. Naked people lay on shelves. Plastic sheets hung down, hiding the details of features, but you could feel the life pulsing in this room.

I snorted. "Tankbread are brainless, and everyone knows that. They only move when they get moved. They're like dolls: they don't think, they don't feel, they sure as hell don't freak out."

"The only way to bring a viable clone, a Tankbread, to full systemic maturity is to allow it to fully develop. The human organism is a complex thing. We cannot retard their brain development without risking the rest of the system."

"So . . . you are growing real people for the evols?" I had a feeling right then, a worse than bad feeling. The kind of fuck-me feeling sensation you might get if someone turned around and said, Oh, by the way, cows can read and write.

"Only when they are ready . . . when they are fully developed, then we neutralize their higher functions. A selective lobotomy if you will. Reducing them to the mindless mannequins you see in evol-controlled areas."

"You . . . fuck . . . you can't . . ." I wrestled with what he was telling me, what I had seen out there. Haumann watched me calmly, letting it all sink in. Letting me stick my finger right into the electrical socket of this atrocity.

"You're no better than them. No better than the stinking dead," I said when I could finally give voice to my disgust.

"Perhaps. But what would you have us do? What alternative is there?"

"Anything. Tell them to go and fucking starve!" Somewhere in the room a living being moaned softly.

"The dead outnumber the living a hundred thousand to one, maybe a million to one. We must make these sacrifices. At least until we can perfect a solution to the evol factor." Haumann sounded like he might be trying to convince himself as much as me.

I pulled the plastic cover back on the nearest bunk. She was naked; tubes went in her nose and out her arse. Dark fluid seemed to be going in one end and out the other. From the color I couldn't tell which way it was flowing.

"Doc, we have a bigger problem. That motherfucker Charlie tried to feed us to the evols."

"It must be some kind of mistake. He would never try to kill anyone. Charles is my assistant; he has always supported my research. He runs this sanctuary."

"Yeah, well he tried to kill me and I take that personally."

Haumann coughed, the grey sheen on his face making the pink flush of his cheeks stand out. He looked like he was half rotten himself.

"Help me get back up to the surface. Charles will explain, you will see."

I went to drop the cover back when the babe on the deck grabbed my arm. I nearly pulled her off her bed in shock. With that tube going up her nose and down her throat, she wasn't talking. Instead she gurgled, her eyes staring as if she was trying to tell me something, and by the strength of her grip, she felt it was important.

"Christ! Get her off me!" I jerked my arm away, struggling to break her hold. Haumann snatched a steel syringe from the table and plunged it into the girl's neck. She quivered and lay still.

"You killed her?" I rubbed my wrist where bruises were rising.

"Of course not; she is simply sedated. We are seeing this more and more, I'm afraid. The Tankbread are growing more restless."

"You mean they know what you are doing."

"It . . . it is possible. Yes. You see, we have been making great improvements to them over the last few years. One of these specimens may be the magic bullet we need to restore humanity to the world."

I helped the old man out of the room and we closed the door on maybe a hundred warm bodies stacked on steel slab bunks three high. That was just one room. We passed many doors just like it on the way to the stairs that took us back up to the Opera House.

CHAPTER 4

Upstairs an alarm was making low groaning sounds. It seemed a shitstorm was brewing and we were without our coats. Those security personnel who weren't shouting were running. Some managed to do both at once. Haumann tried getting the attention of a soldier who dashed past us. He didn't stop. The second soldier running the other way only stopped after I stepped out into traffic and clotheslined him onto the floor.

"What is going on?" Haumann asked as I pulled the bleeding kid to his feet again.

"Whole bunch of evols are massing around the perimeter. The gardens have been breached. They're attacking the livestock. Last report I heard is that they're coming onto the concourse, out of the bay and everything."

Haumann looked stunned and then angry. "How dare they. How dare they breach the terms of our understanding."

"Listen, Doc." I had to shove the old man to get his attention. "Hey, Doc! I need guns, my gear, and a way out of here!"

"Leave? We can't leave . . . it isn't safe." Haumann blinked at me, his face a blanket of incomprehension.

"Fuck me . . . Okay, my gear. Show me where that is."

Doc looked at the soldier, who was still gingerly probing his nose for damage. "What quarters was the courier assigned?"

"Dorm seven, third cubicle. I think you boke by doze!"

"When the zombies get in here," I hissed through bared teeth, "they'll eat your fucking face."

We took off for dorm seven. Turns out that the sleeping arrangements were strictly boys in one wing, girls in another. No wonder the human race was on the verge of extinction.

My jeans were washed, folded, and stacked neatly on a freshly made bed. My shirt smelled strange, like soap. The color had changed from a nice camouflage grey mud to a soft blue. My boots shone with a high polish. I stripped off the bloodstained medical greens and slipped into the only clothes I felt close to normal in. Inside a tiny closet I found my jacket. They had just sprayed that with disinfectant by the smell of it.

"This scavenger hunt shit could get someone killed. Where are my weapons?"

Doc fluttered for a moment. "All weapons are held in secure storage and are only issued on a rostered basis to authorized personnel."

"Show me." I pushed him out of the tiny sleeping cubicle. Shame, it would have been a nice place to crash on any other day of my life.

Using the Doc as a human shield I got where I needed to go. He was wheezing hard by the time we came up on a couple of well-armed men in front of a steel hatch. It looked like the kind of door that wanted to secure a bank vault when it grew up.

"Open up!" I said. The two guards looked at Doc Haumann.

"Yes, yes, do as he says." Doc's wheezing had worsened and that healthy grey color he had before was now leeching out of his face.

The two stepped aside and unlocked the door. My heart skipped a beat. This was better than the hot chicks in the cafeteria, better than the soft sheets or the clean clothes. This was my kind of heaven. Every kind of thing that could kill people, living or dead, was here. Rifles, shotguns, grenades, support weapons, swords, even an umbrella stand full of baseball bats. I looked, touched, and tried everything on. It was the best five minutes of my life.

"You will need to sign for that!" One of the door guards finally found his voice.

"Put it on my tab." I slid the last knife into my boot and said good-bye to everything I couldn't carry out with me.

"Doc, what's the best way out of here?"

He started to speak, and then coughed. Blood, the kind that is so thick and bright red it makes you hungry to look at it, melted over his lips.

"Down . . . past . . . the . . . bread . . . shipping . . . tunnel . . ." Haumann gasped. "Wait . . . you must . . ." He paused to cough, spat a wad of bloody phlegm, and drew a deep breath that gave him the strength to continue. "The Tankbread, they are the key. Go to Moore Park, ask Josh Mollbrooke where to find Richard Wainright. Tell him I have found the answer. Tell him . . ." Haumann sagged under another coughing fit.

"Thanks, Doc. You guys, take care of him."

I ran back the way we came. People got out of my way without question. It's one of the advantages of being heavily armed and having a face on that says I am well prepared to kill anyone who gets in my way.

A decade spent running from one shit situation to another makes you fit, but it also makes you appreciate a ride. As I jogged down the corridor past the Tankbread storage, I found myself thinking about golf carts. I came to a stop when I saw the door to the evol pen was open. I had shut that door. Now it stood open, blood and stink smeared around it like evols had been chewing on the handle. Crazy dead bastards.

I lifted a submachine gun from around my neck and cocked it. The click sounded ominously loud in the barren corridor. The door to the Tankbread room also hung open and looked more ominous the closer I got. I inched towards it. Screams erupted from the inside. I ducked around and found myself staring at the back end of a zombie mob getting their munchies on the Tankbread who had crawled or been dragged from their benches and were now being pushed up against the back wall.

By reflex I squeezed the trigger. A solid stream of bullets scythed through the crowd. Dead guts and flesh sprayed, their blood, now semicongealed slime, splattered on the walls and ceiling. The SMG clicked empty. I tossed it and pumped the shotgun. Point-blank range, heads exploded; conserving ammunition meant trying to line them up. I pumped and fired, pumped and fired. A few of the evols were slipping on their own blood and trying to turn around. Most were too far gone in the feeding frenzy to notice me taking them from behind.

The shotgun ran out. I had a belt full of cartridges, but reloading would take time, so I pulled out the katana I had taken a shine to in the armory. I started by sticking an evol in the back; he never noticed. I pulled the blade out and tried to swing it in the confined space between the empty bunks. I couldn't get enough room to really swing until I tried going up from knee level. I cut some legs off and tore through a few midsections, dropping stinking black intestines out in a slithering mass.

The evols chomped and tore, ripping great chunks out of the Tankbread in their lust for blood and meat. A couple of pistol shots to the back of the head did for the last of them. I stood there in a slowly thinning cloud of smoke, panting and covered in six kinds of foulness. Something leapt at me from behind a bed rack, a savage howl erupting from its throat. I shot it in the face and then blinked as a Tankbread collapsed convulsing at my feet, his lifeblood spurting out of the back of his head.

I took stock. A shitload of zombies, all now perma-fucked. Bits of Tankbread everywhere, most of them torn to pieces by the evols. None of their faces looked like Tankbread after a chow session. They all looked like real people who had died in screaming agony.

"Fuck Haumann . . . fuck . . ." I wiped blood and sweat from my face. A slight movement had me on edge again. I crept forward, pistols ready, confident I had some shots left.

She had crawled under the beds, sliding through blood and death and horror until she reached the back wall. Then she tried to crawl through that. Even as I pulled the plastic sheeting aside she whimpered and tried to burrow into the blood-slick floor.

"Easy girl, easy . . ." I holstered my guns. Not sure what to do, I touched her lightly on the ankle. She screamed, a raw, primordial sound, like a baby's cry.

"Hey, quiet down . . . I'm not going to hurt you!" She kicked and thrashed, unable to stand but completely terrified. I waved my hands for a moment, then grabbed her by the ankle and pulled her out of the corner before she knocked herself stupid.

She went still. I thought she might have fainted, but she was just staring at me, her eyes the sharpest electric blue I had ever seen. Blood matted her short white-blonde hair, filth and zombie bits clung to her naked skin. She looked like she'd just been born, though her body was the mature figure of a young woman in her late teens or early twenties.

There was nothing I could wrap her in, no blankets here, no clothes. I carried her to the door and then checking the way was clear I set her on her feet. She took her own weight, the top of her head coming up to my chin. Swaying slightly, my arm around her waist, I smiled at her.

"You got it, now one foot forward . . ." I stepped back, drawing her after me. She swayed, her eyes going wide with alarm, and took a tottering step, and then another.

I walked backwards, giving the girl something to focus on and follow. I glanced over my shoulder constantly, looking for anything ready to take a bite out of us. By the time we reached the door labeled "Loading Dock" she was walking on her own with all the grace and confidence of a double amputee.

Moisture dripped down the walls of the old Sydney Harbour Bridge tunnel and the scent of brine rose strongly. By the light shining from the corridor I found a hurricane lantern hanging on a hook in the wall in the tunnel. I worked the pump a few times to prime it and then clicked the ignition. It flared into light. The girl stood unsteadily, leaning against the door and shivering, her eyes darting to each plunging shadow.

Holding the lantern up, I surveyed our surroundings. About a hundred feet to the right the tunnel had completely collapsed. Water trickled down amongst the rubble and gathered in stinking pools before draining away under the algae-clad concrete.

A truck stood in the tunnel, its rear end towards us. These trucks were common enough in the city. They delivered the fresh Tankbread. Canvas clad and armored steel over military green, they worked their way around the various drop-off points, Tankbread shuffling out of the back and into the waiting arms of the hungry dead.

I couldn't look the girl in the face, knowing what they were now, knowing what Haumann and his butchers did to make them. "You're never going to be Tankbread, girl, I can promise you that," I said, my voice echoing off the concrete walls.

The truck keys were nowhere to be found. The steering lock would have taken a week to cut through with a hacksaw. I rummaged in the cab, finding a pair of coveralls and a patched down jacket, both in faded orange.

"Here, get dressed." I offered the clothes to the girl. She just looked at them blankly and then, leaning forward from the waist, her hand still gripping the doorframe, she sniffed them curiously.

"Not for eating, for wearing." She pulled back as I waved the clothes again. "Here," I tossed the jacket aside and unzipped the coveralls. "Stand still, it's okay." I lifted her leg and slipped it into one of the leg holes, then the other, and then we did the arms, her looking at me intently the entire time and holding on to the doorframe for grim death until she was all tucked in and zipped up. The boiler suit was a snug fit, especially around her hips and chest. The weird thing was that even smeared in drying blood she looked hot, her womanly curves molded so nicely and her nipples pressing through the heavy cotton.

"We walk, that way." I pointed up the wide tunnel and hoisting the lantern I started off. After ten steps I looked back. She was still where I left her, swaying in the doorway, peering after me with a stricken look on her face.

"For fuck's sake." I went back and with some gentle coaxing and steady pulling on her hand I got her to start walking with me. We made slow progress, but she stuck close to me like a puppy and she didn't make a sound. Anyone who has spent time sneaking around zombies will tell you that's a great survival skill.

Walking up the tunnel road we passed half-built barricades; checkpoints I guess, or early attempts at blocking the entrance. I killed the lantern when I saw lights flickering ahead and the girl pressed closer in the dark.

Five of the house's finest were shitting themselves at the entrance to the tunnel road. We hung back, listening to them assessing the situation outside. It seemed that somewhere past their station all hell was breaking loose. Some of them wanted to get out there and join the fight; others wanted to stay at their post. I listened to them argue while I reloaded everything. That took awhile. I made keep down gestures at the girl and moved forward. She scampered after me on hands and feet, like a monkey.

I stepped out, turning the lantern up bright and holding it high. "Hello there!" I called out and stopped dead as the five of them turned their guns on me, the air crackling with the sounds of weapons being cocked. The girl crouched behind me, peering out past my knees to stare at them with wide-eyed surprise.

"Who the hell are you?"

"I'm a courier. I seem to have got caught in your shit, and I'm just looking for a way out of here."

"You can't go this way," one of them said. Jesus this kid was young. He would have been in nappies when the world went to hell. Now here he stood with a rifle and four arse-wipers jumping at every distant scream and gunshot.

"You in charge?" I asked.

"Fuckin' oath I am." Well, he sure talked big.

"Then you need to show me the way through to the outside." I took a step towards them. His gun came up to his shoulder.

"I said no. The door stays shut until the all clear sounds. If they get in here, it's my fault."

"Kid—"

"I am not a fucking kid!"

The girl gripped my legs tighter and growled around my knees. I wished she would let go. Diving for cover was going to be impossible with her hanging on like that.

"I am not part of this. I am not under your command. I need to get out there and get on with my own shit."

"What can you do? Go out there and die like everyone else?"

"I don't plan on dying but I sure as fuck ain't going to stand around in here holding my dick while people are getting killed out there!" It was a good speech. Complete bullshit, of course. As soon as I was free of this clusterfuck I was getting the hell out of Sydney.

"Moss, show the courier up to the door. As soon as he's out, you close it up tight, okay?"

"Yessir." One of the little punks snapped off a salute and hurried to a gap in the barricade. "This way, sir."

I set my shoulders and, feeling like a complete dick, I snapped a pretty good salute at the kid in charge. I could see his chest swell with pride as I strode past. Poor dumb bastard.

The girl scampered behind, like a dog. I let her; she didn't seem uncomfortable, and her keeping her head down like that would mean less chance of it getting shot off. From the sounds coming from outside, an awful lot of lead was being thrown around.

The Opera House command had sealed off the bridge tunnel exit and, using rubble, had built a ramp up to a couple of big roller doors overhead, like on a garage. These doors were shaking with repeated blows. Our kid escort stopped and stared upwards. My attention was taken by a motorbike parked up against the wall. Once probably someone's pride and joy, but now I thought a fair damn trade for the wheels I had left out by the main gate to get into this rathole.

"Open it up," I called. Kicking the bike into life, I readied my shotgun. The girl let out a wail and sprang onto the seat behind me. "Hang on!" I revved the bike and its engine sang.

The kid sidestepped towards a control box, never taking his eyes off the rattling metal overhead. With the push of a button the door started to roll back, showing the night sky and lots of meat fighting for their lives.

Outside it was hell on earth. Evols, mobs of them, tore into screaming flesh. Soldiers fired and howled, some pointing empty guns at the dead and shrieking in panic. They shook their weapons as if expecting some miracle to give them more ammunition. Some of them fought on, armed with clubs, bits of steel, anything that could be used as a weapon. The stench of hot blood and black zombie guts was thick in the air. Rotting fingers reached and tore. A naked boy, his skin grey with dirt, howled and latched on to a soldier's hand. The soldier fired, emptied his magazine, shattering the boy's face into a red-black mush before staggering back and staring in horror at his maimed hand. Bodies fell in an irregular rhythm over the edge of the ramp as I burned a crescent of hot rubber, spinning the bike around and lining up to ride out.

I twisted the bike's throttle, felt the girl's body cinch in tight against my back, and we blasted out of the underground tunnel like a duke of Hell risen victorious from the abyss. Bodies, dead and alive, scattered and were blasted aside. I started shooting with a sawn-off lever-action carbine, spinning the gun, ejecting hot shell casings, and firing again.

Evols snarled, frenzied with blood lust, tearing meat from screaming bodies, gorging on intestines and the soft organs of the living. I focused on shooting those who got in my way, the ones that watched with dead eyes and reached with black-clawed hands wanting to rip the girl and me off the bike.

"God help me please!" Pleading cries came from all sides. There was no time to stop, no time to save anyone.

Cooking fires had scattered in showers of sparks. Those who lived on the edge of the compound had fled, hidden, or died. A zombie on fire staggered towards us, blindly swinging. It stumbled into a rough shelter, which immediately erupted into flame; fresh screams of women and children hidden inside joined the cacophony of death's chorus.

I went the only way I knew, back towards the main gate, ready to navigate that narrow maze of stacked shipping containers. If Bert or Cool had gotten the gates down we were fucked.

We slid sideways around the first corner. The gate was still up. Bodies littered the way ahead, some blackened and smoldering, others still twitching, full body burns that hadn't killed them yet. Going evol would be a blessing compared to that final agony. Gunning the bike we got around the next corner, down a straight and around the next corner. All around us the walls were scorched and smoking, the acrid stink of burning fuel and flesh yelling in my nostrils. The second gate had come down but lay flat, twisted and buckled; the crushed dead lay still underneath it. Two zombies had only been amputated at the waist. They reached for us with desperate hands. The more fucked an evol gets the more they want to shit on someone else's day. I shot one in the head and rode the other down, black gore spraying as the soft tissue burst under our wheels.

We pulled up at the bus gate, the fire action finished here. A figure wearing a silver, full-body fire-resistant suit lay slumped against a wall with a sputtering flamethrower hissing in his lap. I rolled the bike close enough to see if he was still breathing.

"I need you to move the bus!" I put the kickstand down and nudged the fireman's boot with my foot. A hand rose, wavered, and then settled on his head covering. Pulling it aside, I saw the final moments of Bert's life flowing away.

"Sorry, cobber . . . I'm fucked. Need you to . . . need you to do me right. I don't wanna come back as one of them."

"You can't stay together long enough to shift the bus?"

"No, I bloody can't!" He started coughing blood. "Bloody gate nearly crushed me. I'm dying. I can feel it."

"Sorry, Bert."

"So am I, mate. Get the fuck out here. Just fucking run, get out of the city. Find some place, hide up there, and forget about us."

I reloaded the carbine with the last remaining round and then pointed it at the center of Bert's forehead.

"One more thing—" he started but I cut him off by blowing his head apart.

"Stay," I said to the girl and swung my leg over the bike. Cool had gone; I guessed he could now be counted among the dead littering the narrow way behind us.

Watching for trouble, my shotgun raised and ready, I reached up to open the bus door. The door flew open and with a bubbling howl Cool threw himself at me, knocking me on my arse and sending my gun sliding across the concrete.

Teeth snapped at my face, I threw a punch, felt it connect, and bloodstained hands tore at my throat. I threw my arm out to block Cool's savage attack. Kicking and struggling, we rolled around each other trying to get enough advantage to tear the other's throat out. "Motherfucker!" I snarled at that stinking dead face. Cool was too fresh to be thinking, too fresh to be doing anything but trying to feed.

His teeth crunched on my arm but the thick leather of the jacket sleeve held. I punched him in the head as he shook my arm like a dog with a bone. The little prick was strong. He lashed out, grabbing my fist, and I yelled as he began to squeeze. A throaty snarl and a blur of orange, the girl blasted across my vision. Striking Cool head on, she snapped his neck and left a few of his teeth in my jacket sleeve as she tore him off me. I scrambled for a gun, the barrel waved around, seeking a clean shot. The girl sprang back as Cool rolled up to his feet. I got to my knees and squeezed the trigger. The first shot shattered his cheek. Cool kept on coming, barely flinching. I fired again; this shot blasted through his nose and blew his brains into soup against the side of the bus.

"Fuck me . . . fuck me . . ." I stood up, the girl straightened, staring at Cool's still corpse. "Let's get the fuck out of here, eh?" I said, panting in panic.

She turned to face me, her lips spread in a wide, savage grin, and she howled in adulation at her first kill.

CHAPTER 5

We live in the cities with the dead. It's safer there; places to hide, food scraps to be scavenged, and a living of sorts to be made. Some do it for the community, some for the opportunity to make a better life for themselves. Others are just too pigheaded to give up what is theirs to the dead. Australians aren't known for admitting defeat, even against overwhelming odds.

We had stopped fighting this time, though. The enemy were legion and more came at our barricades every day. The smart dead started showing up, talking to the survivors. Promising us protection of a sort. I guess we were desperate enough to take any kind of salvation. The Tankbread weren't human. They seemed less alive than the evols. I felt the girl clinging to my back as we rode that motorbike through the dark city streets and my skin crawled at what that meant.

Dawn finally crept over the ruined city. My instinct when the haze of morning set the city line glowing red and gold was to find a place to hide. The girl at my back was still, warm and close. Maybe she was asleep; the events of last night would have been enough to exhaust anyone. Just how old was she, I wondered. Sure she'd the body of a grown woman, but if Haumann was to be believed, she'd lived barely a month.

I parked the bike on the street and the girl slithered off after me, her overalls darkening with a sudden stain in the crotch. She looked down, touching the wet cloth without understanding.

"Christ." I felt a flush of embarrassment. This, I told myself, is why I travel alone. I pulled her inside; the evols around were starting to pay attention, and standing in the street wasn't going to do us any favors.

Barricading doors is pretty straightforward. Evols tend to forget you unless you are making noise, standing where they can see you, or you are bleeding. I jammed a broken chair against the door and waited there until the two zombies motivated enough to follow pushed on it a few times and then went away.

Meanwhile my blonde companion had managed to get her coveralls zipper down and was squirming out of the tight outfit. Naked, she picked up the suit, sniffed it and with a grunt of disgust, tossed it aside.

"Yeah, you think that is bad, wait till you shit," I muttered, and scooping up the clothes I headed through the house doing all the standard checks. It was still dark, though a little morning light crept through the gaps in the boarded-up windows. No evols had managed to get inside and get stuck. It's a shit when they do. They get into a building and like fish in a trap they can never find their way out again. At least the ones not getting a regular feed of Tankbread couldn't. So you come stomping into a place, lock yourself in good and tight for the day, find a nice dry corner to sleep, and the next thing you know an evol is trying to eat your head. Happened to a mate of mine. I found his headless corpse rotting in a bathtub two weeks later. I guess my buddy's head was just the brain tonic the zombie needed to work out how to open the front door.

I found a copy of the white pages with some paper left in it. Using the toilet is just for form's sake; at least this one was clean and, of course, dry. The girl watched with interest as I took a crap and then wrinkled her nose violently when I tried to get her to sit and think for a while.

"Ya gotta learn how to do it like meat," I said. Fuck she'd a brain like a baby. I could not shake this nagging feeling that when things got really dangerous, I might end up dead because I couldn't drop her and run.

I held her down; she grunted and kicked up a fuss the whole time. She didn't do anything. I wondered if she was genetically engineered without an arsehole.

We settled in an upstairs bedroom. I secured the door and pulled a selection of clothes out of the wardrobe. Beating the dust out of them, I held them up against her. She made a hooting giggling sound when I pulled a shirt down over her head and ended up picking her up and dropping her on a filthy, stained mattress to get her legs in some pants.

She wasn't going to win any fashion awards, but she was going to be warm. There were even shoes in the wardrobe. That surprised me, because clothes you can pick up anywhere, but a decent pair of shoes are as hard to find as a vegan evol.

When I woke up it was late afternoon, the room warm and quiet. The girl had gotten naked again; she sat cross-legged on the mattress with her back to me, head tucked down in furious concentration.

I squirmed around to see what she was so absorbed in. She'd discovered the difference between boys and girls and with intense focus was exploring the patch of fur between her legs and the features beyond.

"Stay," I said. She gave a soft sigh and continued to explore. I slipped out of the room, listening and ready to shoot, but it seemed clear. My thoughts were now towards food and water. The pipes were all dry, but places like this often had rainwater tanks on the roof. Food was less likely to be found. I lived on rat meat and weeds. I'd heard that in Adelaide they just ate each other and claimed it was Tankbread. I'd also heard that there were safe havens in every conceivable place around the big country. Canberra, Melbourne, Ayers Rock, Tasmania. All bullshit. I have an idea, which sounds crazy, but it keeps me amused. I plan on getting a boat, finding somewhere safe like Hamilton Island and just fishing and eating coconuts for the rest of my life.

I found the rainwater tank, mounted on a concrete pad. It

stood about man height and was made of corrugated metal sheet. The outlet tap was clogged, rusted shut and useless. I licked my lips and heaved myself up to the edge of the tank. Pulling the old cover aside, I could see wet, green slime and the glint of tepid water in the bottom.

Wiggling and balancing on that tank edge, the surface remained just out of reach. I twitched a little closer, on the sharp edge of balance. One wrong move and I would plunge headfirst into the tank and probably break my damn neck.

I hung there, my legs waving in the air like some giant bug antenna, but that water, I just wanted to taste it, to wet my lips. Then the slime rippled and a putrid skull bobbed into view. I nearly deafened myself yelling in shock, my scream echoing off the iron sides of the tank.

Slapping my hands on the walls of the tank made it boom, and I struggled to push myself out while barely registering that the head wasn't moving. Whoever it was, they were really dead.

Dropping back to the ground, I crouched down and giggled like a lunatic for a while before picking myself up and going back inside. A food search of the house revealed a forgotten can that turned out to be pineapple pieces. The girl took some convincing, but once she started imitating me chewing she got the hang of it. I had to push her away pretty hard to make sure I got my share of the fruity golden treasure.

I dressed her again, said some bullshit about how she had to keep her clothes on or there would be no more pineapple. She got the message and I let her keep the empty can.

We headed out at sunset. She scooted up behind me on the bike and soon we were making our way cautiously along the streets, avoiding the evols who were stumbling around. These ones weren't getting a regular feed of Tankbread and they were looking worse for wear. The arrested decay was still working on grinding them down. They didn't speak, just moaned and shuffled and would swarm anything that smelled edible. The bike was the only reason I traveled so openly. On foot we could run, outpacing all of them, but if you run into enough of them coming the other way, you can get swarmed real quick. Once a swarm of evols has you surrounded, you're better to use the next round on yourself.

The Moore Park golf course was on our left, now home to thousands of civilians in a tent city they called Moore Park. On the west side it had a high fence that turned the evols back. On the Darcey Ave and Anzac Parade sides they had made their own barricades. Along the length of Anzac Parade they'd stacked up cars and turned them into palisades.

Historic battles had been fought along that fence line and legends were forged during the dark days of the Panic. Names like Jenny Scott, who sealed a breach by driving a school bus into a gap in the fence and died fighting the zombies who shattered the windscreen and tore her apart. Little Mickey Donaldson, who at age twelve ran along the line carrying messages in the dark when all other forms of communication were lost and the fighting was at its fiercest.

Little Mickey with his Aussie flag tied around his neck flying out behind him like a cape. He saved hundreds of lives during the war and then vanished. They said his family had escaped, but some of us figured he'd been done in by one of the sick bastards who even when the shit was coming apart all around them still had that burning urge to mess with kids. Other names and legends were bullshit, or just stories that might have happened, or didn't happen quite the way they were told now.

Without TV, books, movies, and the Internet we needed to make our own fun. We fell back on telling stories, and they gave us hope.

I barely stopped the bike at the steel and mesh gates at the entrance to Moore Park. The walls swung open immediately, winched back on a steel cable compressing the car-spring hinges. It was a good system; if anything went wrong, like evols surging through, they just needed to pull a lever and the gate would snap shut with about a hundred pounds per square inch of pressure. Enough to knock the most determined zombie on its arse.

We rode in and the gate closed behind us. A faded sign painted on a ten-foot corrugated iron fence declared we were welcome in Moore Park.

Park dwellers appeared all around us, most armed with pole-arms—curved blades on short handles salvaged from shovels and brooms. The metal came from cars, machetes, anything that would hold an edge and cut an evol's head off without getting you killed in the process.

"Hey, man." A crowd of almost familiar faces grinned at me through the dust and grime. I nodded in greeting. Parking the bike, we dismounted and I shook a lot of hands. The girl clung to my arm, watching with a protective glare every time someone touched me.

"Hungry?" one of them asked.

"Sure," I replied, not taking him seriously.

"Got any food then?" I didn't laugh, but they did. It was an old joke. These people mostly lived on the gravy they boiled out of their underwear and whatever they could raid out of the city. Unlike the residents of the Opera House sanctuary, they had nothing to give the evols except their own flesh. They did a lot of farming but without regular rain, crops were hard to maintain.

"Who's your missus?" That came from Katie; she'd lost a couple of kids during the war and I'd never seen her smile.

"Just a girl. I picked her up over at the Opera House."

That set them muttering, and they looked at the girl again more closely. The park people hated the Opera House. They resented their prestige and apparent luxury.

"Them Opera pricks never stick their noses out," Katie said and spat on the ground.

"Evols got in, tore the place up," I said. They all started talking and milling about.

"Anyone alive?"

"What happened?"

"Fuckers deserve everything they get!"

"What about the Tankbread?"

I realized that I didn't know anything and waved them

into silence.

"Fucked if I know. I got out when the shit hit and that was night before last," I shrugged helplessly.

They flexed their weapons and muttered darkly. "Those dead bastards know what'll happen if they try to get in here."

"Just thought you outta know," I said. I didn't expect them to do anything about the attack on the Opera House. If I thought something could be done, I would have been doing it.

"Come on in, we'll get a brew on and Josh will want to hear your story," Katie said, pushing the others back. We entered the tent city of Moore Park.

At its height they reckon over ten thousand people lived here. Terrified refugees from the horror erupting all around them gathered for a rumored evacuation that never came. Helicopters flew overhead almost constantly, but none landed. After frustrated survivors started taking shots at them, they stopped flying so close.

Left to their own devices, the desperate men, women, and children built the first fence of vehicles along Anzac Parade and stood against the evols who came at them.

Back then evols were just dead meat, corpses of all kinds crawling out of the ground and off the slabs of morgues. Mindless killing machines, puppets with no strings that only existed to feed and infect the living. Dismembered bodies stacked up until even the zombies couldn't crest the stinking stopbank of rotting flesh. The Moore Park people used fire and any weapons they could fashion or fake to keep the dead back.

For two months they fought day and night against the dead until the evols stopped coming. Word reached them that something had happened, on the very steps of the Opera House; the war had ended with meatkind's surrender and some kind of peace had been negotiated.

To most of the people living in the mud and filth of Moore Park the surrender was a betrayal. They vowed to keep fighting, to destroy every evol that tried to cross their fence. A lot did, and casualties were heavy on both sides. Over the next few years the evols stopped bothering, and the Moore Park tribe population went up and down depending on the number of refugees coming in and the number of people leaving. The only thing the new arrivals and the leavers had in common was that they had all heard stories of a sanctuary. For some that haven was meant to be Moore Park. For others it changed every day. The stories the newbies told were always the same: death, terror, and cannibalistic popsicle people from Hobart to Darwin.

We walked past rows of tents and scrap shacks. Stripped vehicles were home to entire families. Babies nursed at grime-streaked breasts; kids with swollen bellies and wide eyes huddled around tiny cooking fires. The place stank of shit, piss, and that weird sweet smell that rides on the breath of the starving.

Near the center of the camp stood Josh's house. It was the only place made of brick, and it would have taken a truckload of big bad wolves to blow it in. Josh was as thin as the rest of us, but he seemed okay with it. His hair was long and grey and he was fine with that too. He sat on an empty beer crate under a rough veranda as we approached, his long legs stretched out in front of him. His worn clothing hung loose and he looked normal until you saw his face. The mayor of Moore Park's tent city stood out in a crowd; he wore lipstick in a clown-like smear across his mouth. Sienna whorls patterned his cheeks and the dark eye shadow engulfed his sunken eye sockets and dribbled down to merge with the sienna patterns. You had to look him hard in the eye to see if he was awake or asleep.

"Josh, you gotta visitor." Katie wasn't Josh's woman. Josh had his pick of women and Katie didn't seem interested in men. I wondered if she considered us a distraction from her sole focus — hating evols.

Josh nodded. "Hey, stranger, you are looking stranger every day."

"Hey, Josh. I came from the Opera House. Some bad shit went down."

Josh stared at his feet, absorbed by the curling leather of his boots. "Bad shit is going down every day in every way, my friend. It was only a matter of time before the house got their share."

"True, I guess. Just thought you might like to know."

"Appreciate it, amigo. Anyone get out alive?"

"I dunno. We left before the party was over."

"Shame you finally got in there and then it all fell down."

"Yeah, I guess." I shuffled my feet. "Listen Josh, whatever peace treaty or arrangement or what the fuck they had with the evols, it's gone, man. It's all fucked."

Josh drew his legs up and slowly stood. He exhaled as he straightened and stepped out from under his little porch. Stretching in the open air, he could have been ten feet tall and able to see for a mile in any direction.

"Never counted on it lasting, man." Josh's makeup-smeared face shone in the last of the daylight. "Walk with me, brother, I need to take a piss."

I waited while Josh retrieved his piss bottle, a clear plastic tank half full of about two liters yellow water. We walked together, not speaking, except to reply to the greetings of those who passed. Everyone said hi to Josh. A lot of the people wanted to ask him things, to tell him things, and to take up his time. Getting to where we were going took awhile. The girl clung to my arm and walked on my heels.

Outside the camp the duck pond called Lake Kippax was their only source of fresh water, and there was barely enough for them all. Piss, on the other hand, holds many nutrients if you are a plant. So one of Josh's rules for his fellow campers was that you saved your piss and it went into a big tank. From here they hand pumped it out into irrigation ditches and they grew barely enough crops to survive. I didn't know shit about plants, but they seemed to be doing something right. Kids were strolling along between rows of six-foot-tall bushes, plucking heavy green buds. Past the fields, women toiled lifting long bunches of the buds around on drying racks.

"You can eat this shit?" I asked.

"No, but a smoke sure helps ease our troubles. We grow veggies between the dope rows."

They grew food in other patches too; it wasn't just piss that they used on the garden. Every kind of waste went into massive bins and turned into dirt; then they spread it around in big patches on the old golf course and grew food. The system was labor intensive but it worked. These people were starving but they weren't dead.

I waited, trying not to breathe while Josh emptied his takings into the tank. I kept my peace as we walked back to his house. I settled comfortably on the ground under Josh's porch roof and the girl pressed in tight beside me. I waited while Josh packed a homemade pipe with some dried bud and lit it with a stick from a cooking fire. Only when we had both toked up did I speak.

"Josh, what do you know about Tankbread?"

"Geeks make it to feed the evols, keeps them off our case."

"Yeah, but do you know where it comes from?"

"Geeks, they grow 'em in tanks. Some secret tech they were working on before the Panic."

"You ever seen Tankbread up close?"

Josh sighed and stretched his legs out, rocking back on his beer crate chair. "I seen it one time. Me and a crew were out picking up some things from the local store. A truck comes rolling up, and it's playing music, like one of them old ice-cream trucks. Evols start coming out of everywhere. And I mean everywhere. Man we nearly shit ourselves." Josh starting laughing, smoke jetting from his nose and mouth as he snorted and giggled.

"So we hunker down in the shop, you know. Hiding out and wondering what the fuck is going on. This truck was all plated up and the back drops down and Tankbreads start shuffling out. They were all linked by a thin string." Josh paused and stared out into the darkening sky. "Weirdest thing I ever saw. The evols started pulling them, not tearing into them but pulling them along like they were dogs on a big-arsed leash. The 'bread followed in a big long line and they disappeared around the corner. The ramp on the back of the truck got winched up and they drove off. Never saw anyone but the evols and the Tankbread."

"Where d'you think they take them?"

"Dunno. Say, why d'you care about this? It's just 'bread, right? Just evol Scooby Snacks."

"I seen how they make Tankbread. It's kinda fucked up, man. The girl, she's a Tankbread."

Josh leaned forward, his crate clicking on the ground. "Say what?" He peered closely at the girl, who was curled up against me where I sat on the dry ground.

"She ain't no 'bread, man. She got eyes that see and a mind that burns like fire behind them. She's knowing the truth and fully comprehending the circle of life, man." Josh leaned back and relit the pipe.

"They grow the 'bread in tanks, but they aren't brain-dead. They fuck them up before they ship them out. They lobotomize them. I heard it from the head geek. Some crazy old bastard called Haumann. It's been tearing him up, man. He knows that the 'bread are like you and me. Then they zap their brains, electro-fuck them into walking meat sticks and ship them out."

Josh's mouth dropped open, and I don't think the dazed look on his face came entirely from the dope.

"Man . . ." he said. "That's deeply fucking wrong. It's like that movie. Where they find out the green cookies are people."

"I dunno if she'll ever be normal, but I got the girl out of there before they could melt her brain."

"You did a good thing, brother, all life is sacred. We don't eat much around here, but we don't eat meat."

Katie turned up then, carrying a pot of vegetable stew. She gave us each a warm cup. The stew smelt like dirt, and didn't taste much better. The girl gulped hers down and made mm-mm noises, holding her cup out for seconds. Katie just gave a snort and walked away with the pot to serve others.

"You need a place to crash, man?" Josh scooped the last of the stew out with his fingers and licked them clean.

"Nah, I gotta keep moving, need to find a way back to north side and tell that fuckin' Soo-Yong that I did my best but the evols fucked it all up."

"Soo-Yong, he's that smart zombie who runs things up in Roseville, eh?"

"Yeah, that's him. He's king of North Sydney. Got every evol and meat running around after him, kissing his dead arse and cupping his shrivelled-up balls."

"You and the lady ride safe, my man. Wish we could do more than just wish you well. But with the gear you are packing I'd say you don't need any help from us."

"Appreciate it, mate. I'll come back this way sometime." I stood up, stamped the life back into my tingling feet, and readjusted my weapons into more comfortable hanging spots. I didn't feel any concern at not mentioning Doctor Haumann's last words to me about questioning Josh on the whereabouts of this Richard Wainright geek. The sooner I was out of this mess the better. Let them find their own damn cure.

"You're always welcome here, brother," Josh said.

I nodded and with the girl in tow I headed back to the bike. It hadn't been touched; the Moore Park crowd didn't have shit but they had pride, and that wouldn't let them steal anyone else's stuff.

"Sure you want to leave now?" a young girl at the gate asked me. She was maybe fifteen, belly heavily swollen with child and a shovel with a gleaming sharp edge hefted over her shoulder.

"Got places to go," I replied, kick-starting the bike.

"Big mob of evols gathering out there. Reckon they'd like a piece of you and your missus."

"She's not . . . Well they're going to have to try harder." The bike roared into life. "Open the gate!"

She waved to the guy on the winch and he set to cranking. The gate creaked and clicked, swinging open. I dropped the clutch and tore out of there. Leaving places in a hurry was becoming a habit of mine that I didn't like.The girl pressed up against my back, warm and somehow reassuring. Evols were everywhere. I didn't know how they communicated. No one ever saw evols standing around talking or picking up the phone for a chat. Not that the phones had worked since the end, but evols seemed to know. Somehow they picked up on things and they started moving together, coming to one place for reasons only they could fathom. It scared the shit out of me every time they did that.

I turned hard left onto South Dowling. The nearby evols wavered and started after us, but I opened the throttle and we were soon past them and tearing down the road, weaving between long abandoned cars and windblown dust and rubbish at the breakneck speed of fifty k's an hour.

The evols were streaming up the ramps from the Eastern Distributor, clogging the road ahead in a thickening mass of dead flesh and gnashing teeth that gleamed in the late afternoon light. I pulled the bike to a stop feeling the girl at my back whimper in fear.

"Shit," I said. There wasn't enough ammo left to fight our way through the mob. Even against a crowd like that we would be dragged down and eaten before we got very far.

"Shit, shit, shit!" I put a foot down and slid the bike around and pulled a wheelie getting us out of there.

The gate opened when we pulled up. "Yeah, us again!" I yelled as we tore through. The pregnant girl came waddling over.

"Told ya youse didn't want to leave."

"Got no fucking choice now have we?" I said, parking the bike. "You've got a shitload of dead coming this way. What's got them worked up, fucked if I know."

The pregnant girl exchanged glances with the man on the gate winch. She nodded and he ran off towards Josh's place.

"We don't ask why, mate, we just kill them that try and take what's ours."

Somewhere out in the rows of tents a bell started ringing, an urgent clanging alarm.

"You're here now. So you fight. Both of you." The pregnant chick went to the gate and slid a locking bar into place.

I unslung a baseball bat and handed it to the girl. She took it in hand, sniffed it, and wrinkled her nose.

"You hit with it," I said, moving her hands to the right position and swinging it lightly. "Hit really hard." I ducked as she took a swing. Hooting with delight, she smacked the bat into the ground with a childlike enthusiasm.

People came running, ready to fight for survival. They'd fought battles like this before, more than I had, which didn't make me feel ashamed at all. I just felt annoyed that I hadn't managed to get out of this scrap before it was too late. I didn't need to come here. I could be out there somewhere safe, heading up the coast looking for a patch of beach that wasn't ruined by leaking oil tankers.

The evols came in great numbers and we stood ready to receive them. Every man, woman, and child held a weapon. A club, a knife, a pole-arm, they stood shoulder to shoulder. No one spoke and no one showed any fear. They'd all been here before, except the youngest kids and even they were ready to fight. They'd trained for this in a fucked-up version of Stranger Danger, where instead of some creepy bastard offering you lollies, he would just tear your throat out.

A line of archers stepped forward and on command loosed a volley of burning shafts that arced into the darkness. Most of the shots found a target, and burning zombies lit up the crowd outside.

"Fuck me . . ." the pregnant girl muttered. The dead were legion, more than I had ever seen in one place. They were pressing forward, tumbling over the barriers between the different street levels and climbing over each other to tear at the high fence around the park.

The arrows flew again and rained fire down on the evols. They don't burn easily but their clothes, rags, and hair make great tinder. Zombies on fire can't see where they are going and they staggered into each other, setting their neighbors' clothing alight. The blaze spread until hundreds of burning bodies lit up the night, and still they came.

A shout relayed from down the fence. "Breach! Breaaaaaaaach!"

I ran down the line, past people ready to die for their patch of turf until I came to a surging mass of struggling fighters. The sheer weight of evol numbers had pushed the barricade down and toppled the wrecked cars. I could hear someone screaming as they were crushed beneath the weight of the collapsed wall of metal.

I worked the shotgun's pump action and waited for the first dead-head to make an appearance. I didn't have to wait long. I fired. His skull exploded in a black spray and the body slid down, to be replaced by two more. I fired again, while all around me voices shouted and weapons beat on metal as the defenders worked themselves up into a frenzy.

Evols poured into the gap, reaching and tearing at each other in their need to kill, to taste human flesh and to drag us down into their undying hell. We smashed them in their hundreds. Those with clubs crushed limbs and skulls. Those with blades swung and slashed, severing heads, arms, and legs. The ground grew slick with the black gore that poured from the dead. I emptied the shotgun, holstered it over my back, and drew pistols. I fired both at once, punching holes in rotting heads, screaming abuse at these things that would not stop crawling, reaching, and killing.

"Fall back! Fall back!" came the command and I slipped on the slick ground. The girl appeared beside me, teeth bared and grunting with a savage lust as she slammed the baseball bat down on evols in a furious rhythm.

I reloaded my pistols and we backed up, me firing, making each shot count, her swinging wildly with overhead strokes and hitting maybe every second swing.

"Get outta the way!" A cart was being pushed by six men, three on each side. Josh was on top manning a vintage fire hose, his lipstick warpaint fresh and gruesome. "Pump! Pump!" he roared at the two boys crouched underneath him. They heaved on the pump handles and a stinking liquid gushed out of the end of the hose, spraying the dead and the barricade. We kept retreating. Nothing happened for a moment until one of the burning ones fell down into a puddle of Josh's juice. The wall erupted in fire and we ran for our lives back towards the first row of tents. A moment later the trail of flammable liquid that led back to the cart went up in flames. First the pumpers ran and then in the final second Josh jumped clear. The fire cart exploded with a massive roar that knocked the wind out of us and seared our skin with the heat of the blast.

We regrouped as fresh evols came through the fire. This was insane; they should have given up—the fire should have stopped them. Fire would normally send them stumbling away seeking easier prey. Not this time; on they came, wave after wave. They burned and fell, snuffing out the flames that licked their scorched flesh until we were choked by the stench of burnt meat and our eyes streamed with the acrid smoke.

I drew my sword and started hacking. The pregnant girl, I never found out her name, came charging down from the gate. She had a squad with her and they hit the zombies on the flank. We rallied and pushed forward, chopping and smashing. Without warning a second section of the car wall creaked and toppled over, the breach widened, and more evols came over; slipping and stumbling, they fell down on us from above.

The pregnant girl swung her stick-blade, disemboweling an evol and spinning on the spot like a fancy dancer as she cut the next one down. Blades flew and caught on bone. Flesh parted, blood and black shit burst from bulging bags of grey skin.

"Look out!" I screamed and plunged forward. I missed and the pregnant chick went down, evols swarming on her. I saw her hand punch skyward, fist clenched in defiance as she aimed to knock one back. Instead her arm was grabbed and with growling savagery the zombie bit and tore at her wrist, ripping the hand off and covering itself in the arterial spray.

I swung and slashed with the katana, thinking I could

still save her, if I could just get there, I could save her. In the wavering darkness of the fires still burning an evol reared back, a squirming mass in its hands. I shrieked and cut a fat guy wearing a ragged suit in half. The evol sniffed and then bit into the wriggling thing, and maybe it screamed for the first and last time, or maybe that was me, as the zombie tore the unborn baby apart with its teeth.

The sun broke the horizon before the attack finally ended. The breach was clogged with bodies, some still writhing. A group of dull-eyed camp dwellers were moving amongst the dead, crushing skulls or separating them from the bodies.

My clothes were thick with blood and shit; none of it was mine and I couldn't understand why. I wondered if shock was keeping me alive, or I was dead and walking as an evol and this was what it was like—you get up and walk because you don't know you are dead. The girl found me, and moaning softly she sank to the ground tugging at my arm. I looked down and saw she was okay; her eyes were dry, but she whimpered with a pain that didn't seem physical. I took a deep breath and walked past her, back into the tent city, desperate for a drink of water and something to wash the worst of this shit off. Hell I'd even drink Josh's piss at this point.

CHAPTER 6

Josh and I sat in silence under his tiny lean-to porch roof with the girl in a blanket curled up and sleeping like a cat at my feet.

"They shouldn't have done that," Josh said.

"Ya think?" I get sarcastic when I'm tired. It's one of my few faults.

"They really shouldn't have done that. There is an agreement, an understanding. A peace treaty I guess you could call it." Josh wiped his hands over his face, smearing makeup and oily soot down his cheeks.

"Well yeah, I've heard of that. It's what stopped the war."

"Tankbread, the great salvation of mankind. D'you know what I did in the old world?" Josh shoved his hands in his filthy jeans pockets and clenched his fists until the seams came near to splitting.

"No idea, mate." I don't have much time for other people's problems, have too many of my own, but I'd listen to Josh.

"I was an engineer. Biochemical engineer. PhD in biochemistry and genetics."

"You were a geek, eh? Well I can understand why you'd keep that quiet. Doesn't really go with the whole hippy thing you have going on here."

"Man you need to stop listening to the words and hear the message," Josh sighed and leaned forward to pick up the cold pipe. I watched as he started to pack it with a fresh load of herb.

"We did it, we made the world end. Me, Richard Wainright, and fucking Abraham Haumann. We made Tankbread. We were working on a system for creating cloned organs, for transplant patients. Grow your own kidney, heart, liver, or even eyes. All genetically modified to be healthy."

"You made Tankbread?" There was a cold wind blowing from somewhere and it cut right through me.

"Combined project, US and Australian military. Man, the wars in Iraq and Afghanistan were never going to end, they were running out of troops. They came to us and said, if you can clone organs, why not an entire body? We said, sure we can do that. If you put aside the ethical considerations. Man they put so much money on the table we thought we were going to save the world. We finally got the funding we needed to make our theories on rapid growth real. We got to build the first grow tank and the first fully cloned human was lifted out twelve weeks after conception."

I looked to where Josh was staring, down at the girl still and quiet across my feet, her mess of filthy blonde hair sticking out of the blanket nest she'd made.

"The first one was male. The military owned it; they couldn't patent the technology because it was top secret. But they owned him like they owned everything else. They called him Adam, can you believe that bullshit? Adam lived for six days. We made seven more just like him before he died of organ failure. It took us thirty batches of up to a hundred clones each to get the formula right." Josh lit the pipe and took a deep drag; holding the smoke in he passed it over to me. I inhaled and sat feeling the blood pounding in my head.

Josh spoke, exhaling a white cloud that gave his words physical form. "We were insane. Zealots, drunk on the thrill of discovery. There was nothing we could not do. Man had become God and we looked upon our work and we rejoiced in the glory of our omnipotence."

My head was spinning. Josh's face seemed to split apart, a dozen mouths speaking at once in a mist that curled and made symbols in the air.

"But by creating the Alpha, we were bound to give life to the Omega. It came in the form of a mutation. Something we did in that lab, something made the first evol. Something that spread like a virus, like a fucking plague, man, raising the dead until they outnumbered the living and the plague had spread around the world." Josh shook his head against a swirl of painful memories.

"We could have stopped it, we could have been more careful. Haumann and I kept working, determined now to use our technology to find a cure. Wainright went off, some secret military base out in the desert. We holed up, treating the sick and doing our research in the Opera House basement. Then the evols offered us their devil's bargain. They evolved so quickly, they became so intelligent, beyond human capabilities."

"Josh, man . . . Most evols can't play tic-tac-toe without help, let alone be smarter than a geek."

"I can't explain it, man, but they're smart. Smarter than you think. Like the more of them come together with the same thing on their minds, the smarter they get."

"Huh?" I relit the pipe and puffed. It occurred to me that Josh might just be stoned out of his gourd and talking shit.

"It's like they are connected and together they form a massive hive mind. What one sees, they all see. What one knows, they all know."

"What one eats they all shit?" I giggled uncontrollably. It had been a long day.

"Listen, man, this is the important wisdom I am imparting here. This is a message not for the ears of the unwary." Josh's face wasn't made for anger; the best he managed was a sorrowful expression, like I had somehow disappointed him. He waited until I got control of myself before continuing.

"You can find the truth, man, the source and the cure. That's what Haumann is looking for in the Opera House, isn't it?"

I nodded. "Yeah, Josh, he said that he's real close to finding the magic bullet that is going to wipe out the evols. He said I had to ask you where I could find Wainright, said to tell Wainright that the Tankbread are the answer."

Josh spoke like a man lost in his memory. "Haumann and I came to a parting of the ways. He was the one who brokered the deal with the dead. Said we could buy ourselves time and save the world with Tankbread. Sure we had no fucking choice, right man? But it wasn't something I could stand there and be a part of. No way I could see people, tank grown or not, be handed over to a zombie buffet."

"Why does no one know this? Why do I know this?" I put the pipe down. I needed to clear my head and get some perspective. Currently my senses were telling me that the less I knew the happier I would be.

"Haumann is only part of the key. You have a long journey ahead of you and—"

"Whoa, I have a long journey ahead of me? I thought I might hang here for a while. Plant some veggies, put up a tent, you know?"

"No can do, amigo. There's space and what little we have we would share with you in an instant, you know that. But you have to do something great, man. The sort of thing that makes kings out of farm boys, and generals out of the little guys who dig the latrines."

"So . . . what exactly do you want me to do, man?" I could play along for now.

"You gotta get out of here, get out of Sydney, and get to Woomera. In the Prohibited Zone. It's where Wainright went and did dirty work for our government and the Americans. It's where the rest of the truth is, man."

"Really? Well that's good to know, but I'm going to pass. Thanks anyway."

Josh shook his head. "You don't get it, brother. I never want to be the one to lay a bad trip on a friend, but . . . The girl, that hot, sweet, fully kitted-out babe, with the brain of a newborn? She's on a timer. A countdown to perma-death. Tankbread ain't built to last, my friend. You got maybe a month, and then she'll just start shutting down. She'll get sick and then she'll die." Josh had the decency to look anguished.

"What . . . ? But . . . How can I stop that?" After all the work I had put in, it seemed like a waste of time to let her just die.

"Honestly? I don't know. If there are answers, you will find them in the Prohibited Zone, at Woomera," Josh shrugged.

"You're lying." That came out vicious and angry. I'd beg for forgiveness some other time.

"I don't lie. There's times when I'd really like to but I can't. Karma knows all, man." Josh calmly exhaled a long stream of smoke and leaned back on his crate.

"Fuck you and your fucking karma!" The girl stirred at my feet and sat up. Blinking, she yawned and then put her hands to her face, feeling the muscles move. Like everything else, that was a new experience for her too.

"I've got fuck-all gas left for the bike. I was hoping to get a few blocks, ride until the tank ran dry and then . . . Well . . . I don't know but I'll come up with something."

"I got gas, well not gas-gas but methanol. Won't take much to convert a simple engine like your bike to run on it."

"You make it all sound so damned easy." I put a hand out to stroke the girl's hair back from her face. It was matted and crusty with filth and blood. I ended up sort of patting her instead until I realized how weird that was and stopped.

"No, man, it's not going to be easy. It's going to be the hardest thing you've ever done in your life. But you're a fighter. The kind of crazy-arsed sonofabitch who survives. That's why karma is calling on you, man. You're going to put all the pieces together and save the fucking world, man!"

I started laughing and Josh joined in, laughing so hard the tears left pale streaks in his face paint. The girl looked from me to Josh, an expression of alarm on her face. Then she started laughing with us.

"You arsehole," I said when I could breathe again. Josh just grinned and shrugged.

CHAPTER 7

The bike conversion took a few days, which was fine with me. I got to sit around, smoke some weed, and teach the girl to survive in the real world. She seemed to understand language and started trying to imitate words and getting frustrated when she couldn't make herself understood. She got her hand slapped a lot because she wanted to touch everything. Like all of us she learned the hard way that fire is hot, knives are sharp, and food on someone else's plate isn't yours.

She fought back every time, a savage growl deep in her throat when scolded and pushed away. She followed me everywhere, even when Katie tried to take her away for a bath. Her howls of terror could be heard across the camp until she came back, sniffing her skin and pulling her loose blonde hair through her fingers to feel what clean was.

Josh found me helping out in the veggie gardens on the fourth day with the girl sulking behind me. Every potato I dug up she tried to eat, but they didn't taste like the cooked ones.

"Your bike's sorted," he said.

I sighed and straightened up. "Cheers," I dropped my last potato into the sack.

The Moore Park community had all chipped in; we had some clothes, food, water, methanol fuel, and a faded and water-stained map.

"The methanol will corrode the rubber seals and

generally screw the engine over time. But it'll get you where you need to go."

I nodded, my mind on the trip, no more eager to leave now than I had been four days ago.

"The girl, she needs to stay here. You lot can keep her safe, eh?"

Josh shook his head. "She's part of you now, man, you saved her life. She is yours to protect for evermore. Without you she's got no one else."

"I'm not worth it. If she comes with me, we're both going to end up dead."

Josh rested a hand on my shoulder. "Man, she's your responsibility. You need to accept that and give her a name."

Give her a name . . . ? I hadn't named anything since my goldfish when I was a kid. After Jaws passed away, I gave the aquarium to my sister and she used it to display her doll collection.

The bike started easy, the girl cinched in, and with a final wave to Josh and Katie and the watching crowd we headed out, kids yelling and running alongside all the way to the gate.

"Tell them we're here!" the gateman yelled and I waved an acknowledgment. The hope that somewhere out there someone was willing and able to rescue them would never die.

We headed south, winding our way down through Maroubra, around Port Botany, and back up past the asphalt wasteland of the airport, now a graveyard of abandoned planes and torn fences where the desperate had been trampled in their hundreds in the final stampede onto the runways for the last planes out. The Eastern Distributor could have been a faster route, but the tunnels and the sections blocked with abandoned cars made nothing easy. The dead were a constant presence. On foot we could have been in real trouble. On the bike we outran them, twisting and turning our way through the tangle of empty vehicles and blocked roads. We saw very few live people, and the ones we did see threw rocks and half bricks and shouted at us to stay away.

It took a few hours to make our way out onto the South-West Motorway, and as the last evols slipped away behind us I opened up the throttle. Sometime after midnight we made camp in an old truck cab, chewing cold baked potato and sipping water from our canteen. Out here, traveling by day was safer. There were few zombies, but the ones that did wander the highways were completely feral and always hungry. So we rode hard by day and slept locked in cars at night. We rode past a lot of small towns, abandoned houses, wild dogs and kangaroos running towards us or away, depending on what end of the food chain they thought we came from.

A couple of days later, when we hadn't seen an evol all morning, I took a break for lunch and we parked up in the middle of nowhere. The country around us was dry and looked barren. It'd never looked any other way, but we'd seen a flock of wild sheep, made huge and alien by their massive load of wool. They swept away over a low hill and I figured that meant there was no one, alive or dead, within an unsafe distance. The girl got excited, pointing at the sheep and then the few white clouds in the sky. It took me awhile to understand she thought the running flock were also clouds.

I couldn't forget what Josh said; the girl didn't have anyone but me, so I'd taken to calling her Else. Like I said, last thing I named was a goldfish that ended up in a matchbox coffin with "Jaws" written in pencil on the lid.

Else didn't seem to mind. I was grateful that no one could see me crouched there in the dust pointing to her chest and saying, "Else. You are Else."

She liked the game and her name was the second word she learned, "no" getting the gold medal. She learned fast and added to her words constantly. I scrounged some kid's books, the ones with pictures and few words. Else would barely sleep at night, pawing over them and making happy sounds as she touched the illustrations and the words over and over again.

We were on the Stuart Highway heading west and I'd relaxed for the first time in months. I kept an eye on the rain clouds darkening the southern horizon. Somewhere way out there, it was pissing down. Else chattered in my ear constantly, mostly simple questions and random-sounding sentences. We came thundering around a corner outside of a town called Mildura in time to see a power pole dropping in front of us. The bike hit and flipped. Else went flying. I rolled across the cracked asphalt. Our ride somersaulted down the road shedding bits and dying horribly.

I lay there for a while, trying to remember how many legs I was supposed to have and trying not to puke. When the ringing in my ears died down, I heard running feet. Evols don't run, so that meant meat. Meat could be worse than evols. Evols will just try and eat you. Meat will fuck you, or worse, first. I got off my back, my legs held me up, and I readied the shotgun.

Kids, an odd mix of scruffy faces and long hair. They were standing around the bike carcass poking it with sticks and jabbering away in shrill voices as they pillaged the saddlebags, snatching up the last of our food and the final canteen of water.

"Garn . . . fuck off!" I stumbled a bit, my insides still flipping over and blood seeping from my knuckles. The kids squinted in the sunlight, regarding me with curiosity but not fear as they clutched their booty. I waved the shotgun at them, trying to scare them as if they were carrion scavengers. I had to get a lot closer before they scattered like angry crows. They shook their sticks at me and hissed like big lizards as they ran.

I found Else on the side of the road. She was out cold, but all her limbs laid out straight and her head didn't seem bashed in. I carried her into the shade of a gum tree and then went and checked if they had stripped the bike clean. All our gear was gone, except for a water bag, which had ripped open in the crash. Else woke up when I squeezed the last few drops of water into her mouth. She coughed and jumped a bit. "Motherfucker," she groaned.

"Motherfucker," I agreed. "But at least we're alive."

"Alive," she replied. Leaving the bike in the middle of the road, there being no reason to try and shift it, we started walking towards town.

On the crest of the bridge over the Murray River, the residents of Mildura waited for us behind a corrugated iron fence that stretched from rail to rail. I picked out faces moving across holes, those feral kids, watching from shelter.

"Hey there!" I waved with my empty hand.

"Motherfucker!" Else yelled cheerfully, flapping her arms.

"Quiet down," I ordered. "You'll get us killed."

They watched us approach with that look in their eyes that people always have when strangers approach. You don't know what they want, what resources they have, and what they might try and con you out of. It's easier to throw a rock or yell a warning than let them get close enough to see that you don't have shit to steal or trade.

"Piss off!" came a woman's cry from the other side of the fence. I looked around. Where the hell were we supposed to piss off to?

"Just passing through, just two of us, not looking for trouble!" I called back, still walking towards that fence. I watched the quick flashes of movement as they shifted around back there. A fist-sized rock bounced off the road about a foot from my boot. I kept walking, smiling with my empty hands well visible.

"We had some trouble just up the road," my voice bounced off the corrugated iron sheets of the fence. It didn't make sense that they would need these sorts of defenses; there were no evols out here that I could see.

I stopped in front of the fence. Faces scowled down at me from holes cut in the metal. "We're just passing through," I said again.

"Where you headed?" The wall spoke with a woman's voice again.

"Perth," I lied.

"Perth's dead. Nothing for you in Perth. Where you

coming from?"

"Sydney."

"We heard Sydney was safe." She sounded sceptical.

"Sydney's just as fucked as the rest of the world."

With a scraping sound an iron sheet peeled open. A kid stood there, with a slingshot stretched back level with his ear. A fat woman in a floral-print dress motioned us forward.

"Try anything stupid and we'll kill you," she said calmly.

"You're welcome to try," I replied smiling.

Stepping through the door, I narrowed my eyes against the shadows and when they came at me, I was ready. A kid with a stick attacked first. I blocked his swing and then lashed out with a boot. It connected and the kid squealed.

Another lunged from the right. Else took him down with a double punch that I never taught her. She followed it up with a kick to the throat and his screaming downgraded to gurgles.

The woman yelled, and something snapped at my ear with the heat and speed of a bullet, but no shot sound. The kid with the slingshot. I pulled the pistols, fired and fired again. Two children flew back, crashing to the road. The gunshots flaring brighter than the sun.

"Next motherfucker to fucking move is gonna fucking die!" If I'd been thinking I would have said something worth writing down, but it did the trick. The woman crumpled, wailing and pulling some brat with half his skull missing into her lap. She rocked back and forth, scooping the bits that had fallen out back into his head. I didn't care, I'd seen worse.

"We just wanted to pass through. You understand? You did this. This is your fuckup!"

"Arsehole . . ." she hissed with pure hate rising up to me. "They are going to have you, and they are going to eat you and burn you and fucking impale you while you are still alive."

"Who?" I sneered. "Your dead brats?" I pushed her back and walked out of the narrow shade of the fence. Staring into the shimmering heat I could see movement coming along the road. Some kind of cars, blowing a lot of smoke, but coming our way fast. I ran to the edge of the bridge. The water was a long way down and a dull green, but it seemed to be moving and I looked back in the direction of the moving smoke.

"Else, today's lesson is about swimming."

"Swimming," she said and clapped in delight. "What is swimming?" she added, peering intently at the river far below.

"Lesson one, the high dive." I climbed up on the rail and offered her my hand. She took it and climbed up beside me, complete trust evident in her face.

"Hold your breath when we land," I said and jumped. Else screamed all the way down.

The water was deep enough to land in but hard enough to feel like we hit concrete. I burst back through the surface, gasping for air and shocked by the cold, Else's hand still in a death grip with mine. I looked around in a panic. She came up and her cheeks bulged with trapped air.

"Breathe!" I shouted and slapped at her face. She exploded and gasped, panting. With my gear dragging me down I started kicking for the nearest concrete bridge support. Overhead I could hear the rattle and clank of engines. They came to a wheezing halt and then the shouting started.

"They jumped in the river!" the woman was screeching. "They killed my babies and jumped in the river!" Some rocks got thrown, but we were out of sight under the bridge and they didn't even come close. After a while the engines started chugging again and they headed back across the bridge. Shivering with cold, I swam for the bank, pulling Else with me until we crawled out on the stinking mud on the Mildura side.

We kept low, drying out in the sun while I stripped the guns, cleaning and drying them. Else kept trying to take her wet clothes off and growled when I said no. The sun was low in the west when we moved on, creeping out of the shadow of the bridge and across a broken road strewn with flood jetsam and dried mud.

We crept along the ramped side of the bridge, and keeping low we made our way across the dusty ground to the edge of town. Where once a thriving community lived and grew now stood crumbling ruins. The wooden buildings had been stripped for fire fuel, and more than one place was now charred bricks and a smear of white ash on empty ground. There didn't seem to be much in the way of living meat around.

Else stayed close and we slipped from ruin to ruin, not finding anything of use in the buildings we went through.

"What—" Else asked and I shushed her. Going from house to empty shop and avoiding the clear areas of the street, we made good time across town. There seemed to be no one, only empty streets, some feral cats that fled before we knew they were there, and birds that watched silently from the dust-coated trees. Only when day settled into dusk did I let Else stop. She explored a trashed hotel room while I watched the street from a broken window. I could hear distant music approaching and then a short convoy of smoking vehicles rolled past. A pickup truck with a high-sided trailer rattled and banged up the street. Huddled in the trailer were figures that I thought might have been evols. They turned the corner up ahead and the engine noise faded. Else came bounding over to look and started asking questions.

"You gotta stay quiet. Ask questions later," I scolded.

We crept out, circling the intersection on the street where the truck had turned down. Keeping low we dropped into a burnt and broken foundation. The hole was deep enough to keep us out of sight, but still allowed me to see over the edge. Else explored again, feeling the textures of the charred wood and brick. At least she wasn't putting everything in her mouth anymore. I could see moving lights and hear voices. It sounded like they were shouting, or cheering, from a couple of blocks away. I glanced at Else and saw her holding a human skull in one hand while gently touching her own face with the other.

"Else, leave that, it's bad," I whispered. A scream pierced the night and we both ducked. Gesturing Else to keep quiet, I took a look. A naked woman came running down the street in a blind panic pursued by three laughing men, one of them armed with a hunting bow.

The guys whooped and howled. The woman came straight at us and was within twenty feet when an arrow shot her through the throat and she fell, sliding to a stop within arm's reach of our hiding place.

"Motherfucker," Else whispered wide eyed, her breath puffing ashes and dust.

"Fuck me!" one of the guys said, laughing and panting. "That bitch was fast!"

"Not as fast as you, Dingo!" one of his mates said with a drunken slur.

"Well go an' pick her up. No point lettin' her go to waste." That was number three.

Dingo swore and handing over the bow he came on down the road. I watched as the other two went back towards the party noise.

The archer walked right up to where we lay; the last thing Dingo saw was me reaching up and pulling him into the basement hole with us. I stabbed him deep and hard, right up under the ribs. The tip of the hunting knife split his heart in two.

With Else's help we dragged the two bodies into deeper shadows and I salvaged some electrical wire from the ruin and used that to bind the corpses' hands behind their backs.

"Remember how I told you that the dead come back to life?" I said to Else as I worked. She nodded.

"Evol," she intoned. "Motherfuckers."

"Yeah, evols are motherfuckers," I agreed.

The time to reanimation varies, but it's never more than an hour. These two came back less than twenty minutes after I finished binding their wrists. First Dingo and then the woman. Else growled and scurried back as they started to move and moan.

"It's okay, sweetheart, just get them on their feet while they're still groggy."

We got them out of the hole and pointed towards the distant lights and laughter. They focused on that and started moving. I stepped up behind them and cut the wire bindings.

"Why'd you do that?" Else watched the two shuffling away with an angry scowl.

"Because there's something going on around here, and those two are going to show us how well prepared this place is for a fuckup of evol proportions. Come on."

We followed them through the darkness, arriving in time to see the guy and then the woman reach the veranda of what might once have been a local pub of a quaint colonial style. Wide windows stood open in adobe walls, rough timber posts held up the roof. Now it looked more like a scene from a nightmare.

Human skulls hung like bunched strings of garlic from the roof. Torches burned and set the shadows dancing. The high-sided trailer with the people in it now stood empty in the car park. From inside we could hear laughter and shouting. The kind of shouting people make when they are watching a favorite team play and they have money on the outcome.

The two evols went straight up the low steps; a guy staggered out fumbling with his fly. He gave an audible sigh and pissed into the sand, only looking up when he heard a wheezing groan.

"Dingo? Who's that with you, mate? Ding—?" The recently dead Dingo stepped into the circle of light cast by the nearest torch and his mate leapt back in shock.

"Fuck me! Dingo!" he yelled and the crowd inside the pub roared. Dingo lunged forward, dead hands swinging and reaching for the throbbing warm meat. Dingo's mate ducked backwards and tripped over a chair. He twisted his knee and went down with a cry. The two evols were on him a moment later and his feet drummed out a convulsive tattoo on the plank floor as they tore his soft belly open and feasted on the pulsing meat they found inside.

Feral zombies, those who haven't been fed a steady diet of Tankbread, are like those sharks that get a taste for humans. Once they go that way, they don't seem to come around to a more civilized way of dining ever again. Their hunger becomes insatiable, and they kill without pause until someone puts them down.

Tottering away from Dingo's mate, who sat up as we watched from a safe distance, they pushed open the door and went inside the pub. No one noticed, their attention taken by the entertainment going on indoors. Dingo's mate got to his feet; his shirt was a torn bloodstain and only the drooping flesh of his belly remained, hanging down over his belt in wet clumps.

"He can still walk," I murmured to Else, "because his spine is intact. That long bone down the back. You have to cut that to stop them walking." I ran my finger down her spine and Else shivered.

"Tickles," she said.

The cheering inside changed to shouts of alarm and some screams. We listened to the crash of furniture, breaking glass, shouts of anger and then screams of pain. No gunshots, though; always a relief to have confirmation that the other side is at a disadvantage.

We gave Dingo, his mate, and the dead woman plenty of time to finish up. With Else tucked in behind me and the shotgun leading the way, I went into the pub. The risen dead were multiplying. I started shooting and Else yanked the sword off my back and went nuts whacking zombies on the head with it.

"Hit them with the sharp side! The sharp side!" I yelled. She soon got the hang of it and decapitated several men in faded denim and a couple of women with torn throats and ravaged chests. In no time at all we were done.

We'd done our killing in a large room, the original bar. Someone had built a small grandstand of seats at one end where they would have watched league games on TV back when there was still rugby league and TV. Now the grandstand overlooked a big cage of welded scrap metal. Inside the cage a small group of women were huddled in one corner. Chained at the other end and straining at the bit was an evol. Holstering the shotgun, I found the bolt on the door and opened the cage. Ducking inside, I punched the zombie in the face with the business end of my baseball bat until its skull caved in and it stopped twitching.

"Evening, ladies," I said. In response, they started shrieking and scrambling for the exit. Else slammed and bolted the cage gate in their faces and then stabbed at them with the sword.

"Else! Else! It's alright! Just step back! They're okay. Just a little freaked out."

"Motherfuckers!" she hissed a warning at them.

"Everyone just calm down and I'll get you out of here." I reached through the cage and unlocked the door. Holding it open, I indicated they could exit.

No one seemed keen to leave the pub; the unknown terrors of the dark outside bothered them more than the ankle-deep blood and gore inside.

"This is a pub, there must be something to drink," I said and went behind the bar. I found some bottles without labels. Cracking one open, I sniffed. It smelled like bad pussy, so I took a drink. It reminded me of what I remember beer tasting like.

I lined a half-dozen open bottles on the bar and raised one in salute. "Grab a beer and you can tell me your story," I said.

The women looked at each other, without speaking. The ones crying were sobbing quietly but no one said a word.

"Well just have a drink then," I indicated the bar.

"We do not drink alcohol." One of them stepped forward. Her hair was cut short, and even with half her shirt torn off, showing the sharp lines between tanned skin and pure white skin, she stood resolute and dignified.

"Neither do I. Usually don't get the chance." I took a long pull on the bottle. It was home brew but it had a nice kick to it.

"We never drink alcohol." The woman speaking had a determined expression on her face. They were all thin, some were just young teenagers, right up to a couple of grey-heads. Some had long hair and others went for the cropped look.

"We're from Sydney," I said, indicating Else who skirted around the group and joined me behind the bar.

"Sydney?" The woman looked surprised. "We thought that all Sydney was gone."

"No, it's not worth shit anymore. But the city is still there. Evols run things. The geeks give them Tankbread and they leave us alone. Mostly," I added after a moment.

"Tankbread?" she asked.

"Yeah, Tankbread. Zombie food?"

The woman shook her head. "We are the sisters of Saint Peter's Grace. I am Sister Mary."

"Hello. This is Else."

"Hello this is Else," echoed Else.

I took another drink. This stuff wasn't so bad once you got into it. "What brought you to Mildura? This is Mildura isn't it? The map said it was but the roads are shit."

"Yes," Mary nodded. "This is Mildura. A place gone to the devil, become Sodom and Gomorrah. What once was paradise is now the abyss."

"I thought that was Sydney," I said and let a rolling belch crack the air.

"In the months after the Rapture the townsfolk displayed Christian virtues. They took care of each other, aided those poor souls who had risen but could not ascend to Heaven, and laid them to final rest. My sisters and I gave them spiritual counsel through the teachings of our Lord. Then as time passed and more fell to God's wrath the survivors grew bitter and turned against us. We retreated to our compound. We welcomed all those who came to us, planted our crops, tended our sick, and flew far and wide in search of those who lacked the joy of our Lord's grace in their lives."

"Flew, eh? How did you do that? The Lord God give you angel wings?" I grinned at her over my bottle.

Sister Mary gave me a pitying look. "The Lord helps those who help themselves. Before the apocalypse, our missionary work took us to many far-flung communities of whites and encampments of Aboriginals. We were the humble recipients of a donation of a helicopter."

"Did they also donate a pilot?"

"As you were no doubt not born to this life of lawless murdering, I was also not born a nun, sir. I flew helicopters in Iraq and Afghanistan. It was there that God spoke to me and showed me the path my life must take."

"No shit?" I said, genuinely impressed with her for the first time.

"Now if you will excuse us, my sisters and I will seek shelter in the rooms above to pray and wait for morning, when we will return to our home and rebuild."

"What happened to your compound?"

"The savages of Mildura decided that we were holding out on them and thought to make sport of us. They came in the night and broke through our defenses, kidnapping us. They dragged us back here and . . ." She went silent, her eyes shifting to the cage.

"They put you in there for kicks?"

"It was only one of their games. They also attacked the girls, forced them to do unspeakable acts and—"

"Yeah okay you don't need to spell it out." I finished my drink.

"If you will excuse me, there are others held upstairs who may need medical attention."

I waved them away. Sure I'd done some shitty things in my time, but only when threatened. This town must have been a lot like hell if you weren't in charge.

"Else, you may not understand right now, but I think we did a good thing here tonight. We saved some people who needed saving, and killed some motherfuckers who needed killing."

"Motherfuckers," Else repeated solemnly. She took her first swig of bitter brew, which she then spat all over the bar and kept spitting and shuddering till her mouth was dry.

The nuns gathered in a couple of the rooms upstairs. They prayed quietly, which suited me fine. Else and I took an empty room down the hall; it stank but the mattress was comfortable after the hard dirt of the road. I slept until mid-morning and woke up to the sound of Else growling.

"Easy girl." I sat up. Someone was knocking on the door. I armed myself and then opened it wide. Sister Mary looked startled at my shirtless state and then cast her eyes to the floor.

"We are leaving. You are welcome to join us on our journey, it is but a half day's walk to the north," she said to the stained rug.

"Sure, ahh . . . give me a few minutes." I closed the door and found my shirt and boots. Dressed and armed, I led Else through the upstairs rooms of the pub. Some rifles, shotguns, but no ammunition. A few good quality hunting bows, though, and plenty of arrows, mostly recently made with flesh-tearing arrowheads fashioned from old tin cans. I took a bow and a bundle of arrows. Else needed to learn to kill from a safe distance.

The twenty surviving nuns had gathered outside. They were calm and kept their heads bowed, lips moving in silent prayer when we appeared.

"Sister Mary, I suggest we load up one of these trucks and make better time back to your compound."

"These vehicles are not ours, it is a sin to steal. Even from those who have falsely imprisoned us," she said.

I scratched my jaw. "Well how about I commit the sin of stealing, and you pray for my soul and then I invite you and your sisters to ride in my new truck?"

Sister Mary stared at me thin lipped for a long moment. "I am sure that the Lord has placed you in my path to test me."

"Amen," I said and went and got the nearest pickup started.

CHAPTER 8

We made good time going cross-country. The only things moving were feral sheep and a few cows. We stopped while a herd of kangaroos flowed across the grassland before heading for the horizon in a pulsing tide. Only drought and starvation kept the livestock in check now.

"Any men up your way?" I asked Sister Mary over the roar of the rattling engine.

"Father Toby died last year. I freed his soul from its mortal cage personally."

"Anyone else?"

"Not for very long. We are a religious order of charity, but we must rely on our own resources and God's mercy to survive. Those men who do come to us are in need of spiritual guidance or medical care. Once their wounds are healed and their souls are redeemed they leave again."

"Willingly?" I grinned.

"Not always," she said without trace of a smile.

The nun's compound stood on the edge of a lake she called Gol Gol. Whitewashed stone buildings rising out of a flat plain of red-gold dust. The fence around the area stood ten feet high in square mesh with barbed wire over the top. We drove over a wire gate that lay buckled from an earlier impact and up a long driveway between planted fields wilting in the heat. A white brick wall, at least twelve feet high, protected the inner compound. The gate in this wall had been pulled down and cast aside. We stopped in a courtyard covered with packed limestone gravel and everyone got out.

"I should take a look around, make sure there's no danger," I said, readying my guns.

"This is a house of God. We are under his protection," Sister Mary declared and swept past me leading a file of girls into the main building.

The sisters' compound would have been expensive to build. In front of me stood a long single-level building of white bricks with a large tiled dome rising out of the center of its roof. To the left and right of the parking area were more single-level buildings, also built with white painted bricks.

"C'mon, Else." We toured the outer buildings, finding a large washhouse with tubs and hand-cranked wringers. The other half of this building was a dry store filled with grain and seeds. The shelves were home to less than a dozen cans of tinned food. Under the shelves we found bins of fresh and dried vegetables. In a meat locker, strips of salt-dried flesh hung in abundance. The cured skins of kangaroo, sheep, and cow were stacked in orderly piles.

On the opposite side of the courtyard, the third building had cots and beds in it. An overpowering stench of rotting meat filled the room like a fog. A cloud of flies lifted listlessly from a swollen green corpse that squirmed with maggots and dripped rotting juices through the thin mattress to add to a spreading black stain on the concrete floor.

Else gave a disgusted snort and backed out of the hospital room. I stayed long enough to confirm that there was only one corpse and came out, leaving the door open to clear the air. The other half of the hospital building was a barn with racks of leather straps and harnesses for horses. They also had three hay bales and an old, empty bottle on a shelf. I carried the bales out and stacked them up against the wall. Teaching Else to shoot a bow and arrow was going to take awhile so it made sense to get her working on the basics. I took some leather strapping from the horse kit and wrapped it around her wrist and the heel of her hand. After I took a few shots to demonstrate,Else was jumping for her turn. By her third attempt the arrow was leaving the bow the right way. I slung the bag of arrows over her shoulder and told her to aim for the bottle on top of the bales.

In the main building the nuns were busy sweeping up and restoring order to their house. Girls squeezed buckets of water from a hand pump and set to scrubbing floors and walls.

Paintings that had been slashed and torn in the attack were commiserated over and then added to the kindling pile. I found Sister Mary supervising a cleaning crew scraping dried shit from the altar cross in their small chapel.

"Ahh Sister . . . ?"

"Yes, what is it?" She never took her eyes off the cross-cleaning maidens.

"Your patient, in the hospital. He died."

"Mister Tomlinson. We will pray for him. Has his soul been released?"

"Released? Yeah . . . he was perma-fu—" Sister Mary whirled and fixed me with a deadly gaze.

"This is a chapel of the Lord our God; you shall not use the language of the gutter in here."

"Sorry, Sister, I mean he was really dead when I found him."

"Very well." Sister Mary took me by the arm and walked me out of the chapel. "The girl who travels with you. What is the nature of your relationship?"

"Our relationship? We don't really have a relationship. She just follows me around."

"Is she developmentally challenged?" Sister Mary asked, the concern and sympathy thick in her voice.

"What? No, she's just learning is all."

"We have a place for her here. It is not appropriate for a girl of tender years to be out there in the world."

"Sister, you have no idea." I tried not to laugh, and ended up grinning instead.

"Young man, wipe that smirk off your face."

I did. "Sister, you don't understand. Else is with me because I'm all she's got. She may look like a young woman with around eighteen years on the clock, but she's only a few weeks old."

Now Sister Mary looked at me as if I might be the retarded one.

"What nonsense," she barked.

"Sister, I would not sh— I mean lie to you. Else is Tankbread."

"What in God's name does that mean?"

"Tankbread . . . well . . ." I looked into Sister Mary's hard grey eyes and started talking. It felt good to get it off my chest, and the whole story came out. I left bits out, messed some of it up, but she didn't interrupt much and by the time we were done she was looking thoughtful.

"Come and eat with us, I will pray for guidance."

I've never turned down an offer of a meal and went in search of Else to tell her to come eat. Out in the courtyard a row of broken glass pieces lay neatly arranged across the top of the bales. Else was nowhere to be seen.

"Else?!" I called, looking around. An arrow whizzed over my head and the left-most shard of glass exploded into fragments. I ducked as another arrow zipped past and the next small piece of glass shattered.

"Motherfucker!" Else yelled and waved from the chapel roof, a distance from her target of maybe sixty feet.

"Nice!" I yelled. "Now come on down before you injure yourself! It's time to eat!"

For dinner we sat at a long table on wooden benches and were served a thick meaty stew that smelled great. It took a lot of quiet effort for me to keep Else's fingers off her plate until the nuns had finished giving thanks for everything. I nudged Else and showed her how I was using a fork. She stared at me, her cheeks bulging with meat, and then she cast a slow look around the rest of the table. The women were all eating with the only table manners I'd seen in years.

Else chewed a little more, swallowed some of it, and then opened her mouth, letting the half-chewed mass drop out on her plate. She shrank back from her plate, her head bowed and a bright red flush rising on her face. Then with a sudden movement, she clambered away from the table.

"Where're you going?" I asked. Else punched me in the head hard enough to knock me into the neighboring nun and ran from the dining hall.

"What the fu—?" I caught Sister Mary's gaze boring into me. "Excuse me, Sister," I mumbled and wiping my mouth with my sleeve I got up from the table and went to look for Else.

I found her out in the courtyard, on her knees punching the shit out of the hay bales and crying fit to bust.

"Hey, Else, what's going on?"

She turned on me snarling and knocking me on my arse, slapping and scratching at my face while blubbering uncontrollably.

"Hey! Hey! Calm down!" I grabbed her wrists and flipped her onto her back with my weight pressing her down. She struggled and hissed and then shuddered, going limp and dissolving into tears.

"You . . . arse-arsehole . . . I'm a stu-stupid motherfucker."

I couldn't make out much more for a while, just a lot of anger directed at me and herself. I held her down until the rage passed. She finally quieted and I sat leaning against the wall with her in my lap, curled up against my chest, my arms wrapped around her shoulders.

"Now use your words, you tell me what's wrong."

Else sniffed and shivered. "I'm stupid. You never told me I was stupid."

"You aren't stupid. You learn things like no one I've ever known."

"No . . . I'm stupid. I don't know anything unless you show me. You know everything and I don't. Inside there, I didn't know how to eat right and they all stared at me! They look like me but they know how to eat right! They know everything. Why don't I know anything!?" Her anger was boiling up again, I could feel her muscles bunching under my hands.

"It's because you're new, all of this is new to you, Else."

"But why is it new? Why do the ones that look like me know everything?"

I took a deep breath. "Else, what do you remember of your life?"

She screwed up her nose in concentration. "I remember the evol motherfuckers, and you. I dreamed of you."

"You dreamed of me? When did you do that?"

"Before you came and took me away, I was in a warm place, sleeping, and I heard voices, you and father, you looked at me. Then I slept again until they came and you saved me from the motherfuckers."

"You were sleeping because you weren't ready to be born yet. Remember the little ones at Moore Park?"

Else nodded. She didn't have the language to ask about the kids and babies at the time, but she'd been fascinated by them, always trying to touch them and cooing over their tiny features.

"Well they were born really small, and they grow for a long time until they are big like us. They learn everything while they are growing up. You were born in a different way. You were born big and though you look like the sisters, you have to learn things like a baby does."

"Why?" Else asked.

"Because . . . you're special."

"What is special?"

"Well . . . special means you are valued, you are important. I would do anything to keep you safe and make sure you are happy and get a feed regularly, and I'll always teach you things until you know everything too."

"Why am I special?" Her breath was warm and distracting against my neck.

"Because I saved you from being Tankbread."

"What is Tankbread?" She yawned and snuggled her head tighter against my chest.

"It's a kind of meat that looks like people but isn't and we feed it to the evols so they leave us alone."

"I'm special . . ." she murmured, her voice soft.

"Yeah, you are," I whispered and kissed the top of her head. And I'm an arsehole.

CHAPTER 9

Else slept in a dorm with the other girls while I lay awake on a cot in the cleaned-out hospital. They held a burial service for the late Mister Tomlinson after dinner and I dug the grave deep enough to keep out the dingoes.

The next morning the sisters rose before dawn to gather in the chapel for prayers and giving thanks while I mumbled along in the back row. Else had jumped on that bandwagon with both feet. She quit swearing overnight and this morning she took to wearing a headscarf like the rest of the girls.

Sister Mary bailed me up after the service. "There are no free meals at the chapel house. If you wish to eat you must work."

"Happy to, Sister. What needs doing?"

She started by showing me their bore pump. It went down deep into the rock and drew fresh water up for their irrigation system and compound water supplies.

"You mentioned a lake? Why not just get your water from there?" I asked, eyeing the seized-up pump.

"The lake goes dry, it has never been a reliable water source. You had best get on with fixing the pump. I have other work for you to do."

The girls worked too and Else didn't seem to mind as she learned their songs and pulled weeds along with the rest of them. The nuns seemed to have put the horrors of their time at the Mildura pub behind them. By midday the pump was in pieces. Grit and corrosion had choked it, but I got it broken down and cleaned up.

Sister Mary came and offered a water bag, and I took a long drink. "She should stay here," Sister Mary said.

"That's not up to me and I don't think it's up to you either." I handed the water bag back, pulled my T-shirt off, and wiped my face with it.

"Clothes on if you please," Sister Mary said coldly. "We are not savages."

"Jesus Christ, Sister, it's damn hot out here."

"Do not blaspheme. The UV out here will give you skin cancer and the sunburn will be but a preview to the fires of Hell. Keep your shirt on."

I shrugged and dressed again. "I'll need some grease for the pump if you have it."

The sister walked off towards the girls plucking weeds from the distant rows. "I will see what I can find," she called over her shoulder.

She turned up an hour later with a tube of industrial gear grease. I smeared it onto the moving parts and got them working. By the time the pump was back together and the windmill was hooked up, the sun was setting in a searing red line across the far horizon. The sisters of Saint Peter's Grace gathered in the dusk like white moths around a flickering candlelight. They sang hymns when the water started gushing out along the irrigation lines. I picked out Else standing among them, her mouth making the words and her eyes shining with their faith.

After dinner, where Else sat with her new friends and used a fork with dainty precision, I cornered Sister Mary.

"Sister, we can't stay here."

"Of course, you are welcome to leave any time you wish with our thanks and blessing."

"Else needs to come with me." I could feel a weird blush rising in my cheeks. Sister Mary came up to my shoulder, yet the way she looked right into you made me nervous.

"Else has said she would like to join our order," Sister Mary said and folded her arms.

"Yeah? Well, less than a week ago she thought sheep were clouds. Look, what I'm saying is that everything is new to her, she doesn't understand the world."

"All the more reason why she should stay with us and receive a proper education and remain pure."

"Sorry, Sister, it's not going to happen."

"And what is that you offer her? Out there? In the heathen lands where the unrepentant souls walk trapped for eternity in the absence of God's love?"

"Like I told you yesterday, Sister, we have to get to Woomera. Else is on a countdown. She won't live long without getting help."

"She could find peace here. We would deliver her into God's grace." Sister Mary's eyes implored me to accept her offer.

"I understand what you believe, Sister, but I need to do more."

The light seemed to drain out of her face. "Woomera . . ."

"Sister, it's important that I get there. That Else gets there. Josh said that Tankbread don't live long. He said that the geeks out at Woomera might have the answer, might have something that will let her live."

Sister Mary's lip curled slightly. "Your very own Pinocchio? God help you then. May he forgive you for your sins, and the sins you propagate upon the world." She stormed off, heading for the chapel. Our conversation now ended, my questions would have to wait.

I went out to my bed in the clinic. Out here, far from the dust haze that kept the night sky hidden in the city, the stars shone bright and clear.

Now that the pump was drawing water again, Sister Mary set me to work repairing the gates. I spent the better part of the next day hammering the hinges on the ironbound doors back into shape and in an afternoon of sweat and effort I got them mounted back on the opening in the high brick wall.

The next day I packed pliers, a few scraps of wire, a hammer, and a canteen of fresh water, loaded up all my weapons, and took the long walk down the dusty driveway to the outer fence. The diamond mesh gate in its steel-pole frame lay buckled on the ground. I pulled it out of the dead grass and eyed it critically.

There was no way this gate was going to walk again. The Mildura bastards had driven a heavy vehicle right through the middle of it, bending the crossbar and turning it almost crescent shaped. I lifted it first on its end and then onto the hinge pegs in the deer-fence post of the fence. It slipped into place but didn't cross the gap anymore.

I stood there, thinking about driving something heavy over it to flatten it out again, when I saw the first one coming through the heat-shimmering distance. At first I thought it was wallabies; herds of the small grey cousins of the kangaroo flocked around here. I stood squinting into the glare and the mirages that quivered in a rolling boil across the land. More shapes appeared, dark silhouettes, shambling in a scattered line towards the fence. Evols, maybe a k away, but coming right at us.

By the time I had lashed the gate shut with a piece of wire they were thickening on the shimmering horizon like drops of rain falling on a dry road. First a scattering and then larger blobs, soon they would all be here.

I ran back to the compound and started yelling as I bolted the wall gate behind me.

Sister Mary's expression went grim when I told her what was coming.

"Maybe a hundred of them. Feral as fuck, rags and dust. Some of them have been dead for a while. They're all torn to shit."

"Girls!" Sister barked as they began to chatter and move on a current of nascent panic. At her voice they subsided, bowing their heads and clasping hands in prayer. Else just frowned and slipped in beside me.

"Mofos?" she whispered.

"What? Yeah. Maybe a hundred of them," I said. "That's more than all of us, more than everyone in Mildura the other night," I added, seeing her puzzled expression.

"We must release them from their mortal cage," Else said, quoting from some crap the sisters had been filling her head with.

"Sure. You go find the bow and arrows, okay?"

Else nodded and darted away. The other girls were taking orders from Sister Mary and scattering in an orderly fashion. It only took a few minutes before they regrouped armed with a mix of scrub slashers, machetes, and axes. They had armored themselves with motorbike helmets, heavy coats, and even sheets wound like desert nomads around their bodies, making thick padding against infectious zombie bites.

"Girls!" Sister Mary clapped her hands sharply and silenced them. "We remain inside the compound wall. They cannot get through. They will flow around us and go on their way. Like the Rock of Gibraltar we shall stand here. Our faith and the Lord's blessing shall sustain us!"

She said a lot more, but I went to the truck and drove it to the wall. From there I climbed up on the cab and peered over to see what was happening outside. The dead were gathering at the outer fence. The shimmering heat made it hard to tell their exact numbers. Else popped up beside me and with a casual nonchalance she lifted a pair of binoculars to her eyes and peered through them. I reached over and turned them around so the wide lens end was pointing away from her.

"Ahh!" Else squealed and stumbled back, flailing. I snatched the binoculars before she dropped them and took a good long look.

The wire fence was about half a kilometer away and it was buckling under the growing pressure from the dead pressing against it.

I moved the glasses down the line, checking the gate, which was moving but holding for now. A zombie was squeezing through the gap between the gate and the post. Skin and then flesh softened by slow decay tore and slid off his yellow bones. The flies swarmed among the mob. Flies were always around evols, but they never laid eggs on them and no maggots ever squirmed in that dead flesh. Must be something about the walking dead that acts as a fly repellent. Rats, cats, dogs, and birds never eat the dead either. Even after they are put down, scavengers don't eat zombie meat. I guess it's why most of the cats and dogs died out after the war. The ones that survived got mean and lived on rats and each other.

The evol that squeezed through the gap staggered; with torn muscles its arm hung useless and one leg dragged. What kept pushing them on? Why here? Why now?

Else's bow creaked beside me; she had a dead bead on the one making its slow way up the dusty track.

"You have to hit it in the head. Maybe more than once. Pretty big head on those arrows, so should do some damage. Wait until he is closer, you want to make every shot—"

She loosed her arrow and the shaft burst through the evol's skull, shattering it like a rotten egg.

". . . count," I finished.

Else put another arrow on the string and let it sit easy.

Out on the line the fence gave way. Evols tumbled forward, the ones in front fell and those pressing from behind walked right over them, trampling the fallen in a slow-motion stampede.

They came on up the driveway. A stinking fetid line of rotten carcasses with exposed bones bleached by the sun and gleaming where flesh had been shorn away. Out here when evols went feral, they went all the way.

"Don't fire again, let them go around us." We waited up there while the sun beat down on us and the sweat dripped in my eyes. Behind us, in the shade of the chapel entrance, the sisters stood with bowed heads praying in silence.

The first line of evols reached the wall. Ferals are stupid. They will walk until they hit something and then kind of bounce off and walk in a different direction. These ones shuffled right up to the white brick wall, and then to my surprise they looked up. I pulled Else back from the edge of the wall, my hands shaking.

"They looked up," I said, not quite believing it.

"So?" Else was straining to peer over and down at them again.

"So they're ferals. They should be stupider than a box of rocks. They should just shuffle on round the wall and stumble off across the paddocks and out of here."

Else got up and looked over the wall. "Whole lot of them now, all standing there, looking up at me," she reported.

I stood up on the truck roof again and looked for myself. More dead were arriving all the time. Each one of them reached the wall and then lifted their heads, not looking blankly into the sky, but twisting their necks until their gaze fixed on us.

We stood, staring at each other, the dead, Else and me. No one moved, nothing was said. It just seemed weird until Else drew back on the bowstring.

"Fuck you," she said and let fly. This arrow tore right through a female's head. The brain came out in chunks and the evol spun around, knocked off balance by the shot. The zombie woman stumbled, her jaw working until her legs gave way and she slowly sank to the ground and lay still.

A groaning murmur rippled through the rest of them, a voiceless muttering, a low throaty chanting of unease. They pressed forward, over a hundred evols raising their hands and slapping them against the white brick. The wooden gate to our right shuddered under the sudden assault. Behind us the nuns gasped and prayed louder. Else cycled through arrows, drawing and releasing, taking a zombie out every few seconds.

I started firing. Corpses broke under the assault. My shots tore off arms, popped heads, and smashed faces. The stink of corpse gasses clouded the air like a fog. Sister Mary led the nuns to form up in rows across the courtyard. Evols clambered over the crushed and broken bodies of their brethren to reach with blackened fingers for our warm, pale flesh.

Else ran out of arrows and slung her bow. I passed her the sword and left her severing any dead hands that reached over the edge while I dropped down and went to check on the gate.

The nuns were pushing on it while the evols on the other side were rocking back and forth, using their massed weight to slam the gate like a ram. The bar was cracking more each time they threw themselves against it.

"Get everyone inside. For some reason they want in here, and they're going to do it too!" I yelled at Sister Mary.

The nun turned and glared at me. "This is God's land. He will not tolerate these abominations in his house!"

I bit back on saying something about the chances of God turning up in person and laying his fucking wrath on the dead intent on getting in here to tear us all to pieces being fuck all.

"I heard once that God helps those that help themselves, Sister, so maybe it's time we gave him a break, eh?"

"Motherfuckers!" Else yelled from the top of the truck. The first of the evols were climbing over the wall. Else slashed down with her sword and zombie heads rolled across the compound, eyes rolling and blinking for a moment until the life went out of them.

"Else! Get down here!" She ignored me and kept swinging. Zombie parts rained down, gore and dark blood stained the wall, and still they came.

The gate beam broke and the nuns fell back as Sister Mary called on God to protect them and guide these lost souls to a final rest. The dead stumbled through the widening gap and the destruction started in earnest.

The sisters sang hymns and killed the walking dead with brutal efficiency. They decapitated if they could and hacked the rest into chunks.

I snatched up a shovel and crushed a skull with the flat of it, then swung it like a club until its edge sliced through rotten neck tissue and heads rolled. They kept on coming; those fuckers never quit. They have no reason to stop. They just press on, reaching, tearing, and biting. Gaping faces with shattered jaws and eye sockets crawling with flies drinking the foul moisture that weeps from somewhere inside. Their blackened tongues rasped over dead grey teeth ready to bite into the succulence of living meat.

A young nun fell, her screams choked off when the evols tore her throat out with their fingers. They ripped her apart as if she was a roast chicken. They stuffed chunks of dripping meat into their mouths and gulped them down. Fuck knows how they thought they would digest her. I've never seen a zombie take a shit.

The nuns kept up their singing, voices high and resolute amidst the dust and the moaning of the dead. Faith wasn't enough to hold the devil at bay, though; soon others were overwhelmed. Falling under a seething orgy of hungry dead, the rest of us fell back towards the main building.

"Else! Into the chapel!"

I didn't know if Else was going to make it, but that girl had a hate on for the dead like nothing I had ever seen. With an animal shriek she threw herself down on them from the roof of the truck. Slicing and hacking, swinging the sword around her head she smashed and cut.

I waited on the steps, pushing nuns in the door behind me and reloading the shotgun. A glistening length of steel burst through a shuffling chick; wrenching upwards, the blade cut her in two and Else sprang over the body. I raised the shotgun and took out two more reaching for her.

She leapt up the steps and her teeth were bared in what might have been a shit-eating grin as she dashed inside. I yanked the door shut and shot the bolts home, the dead thudding against the heavy panels on the other side.

"We can get them from the roof!" Else was jumping from foot to foot and panting like a dog.

"Sister!" I yelled over the chorus of hymns and the groans from outside.

"I'm right here." She passed through the crowd. Her clothes were drenched in filth and sweat, but her face remained as calm as a pond.

"We can't stay here. The place is fu—ahh . . . lost."

"Sisters, into the chapel. Seal the doors, and let God hear your prayers."

The singing girls moved without question. Their faces

shone brightly with a strange delight, like they knew they were being rescued. I wished I could share that enthusiasm. I reached out and grabbed Else by the shoulder as she went to follow them.

"Nuh-uh," I shook my head. "Remember, never get yourself trapped in a room with only one way out."

Else looked pained, torn between wanting to be with her friends and doing what I told her. Sister Mary didn't comment but murmured a few words to each nun that filed past. She stood with her head bowed until the chapel door closed and we heard the muffled thud of it being barred.

"This way," Sister Mary turned and marched towards the kitchen. Else and I looked at each other; I shrugged and we followed.

"Sister, we really need to break out some serious weapons or get the fuck out of here."

"And that is precisely what we are going to do." Sister Mary turned at the kitchen door and looked at me with that peculiar intensity. "I have prayed for hours for guidance, asked the Lord for understanding, begged him to share with me what purpose he has for you and Else."

"Yeah? What did he say?" I stood ready for her to say that God wanted us to be eaten by zombies. If it came to that, my shotgun would rewrite the Gospel according to Sister Mary right here in the kitchen doorway.

"He wants you to live. You have a purpose, and I must aid you."

"Fuckin' A," I said.

Sister Mary opened the door and led us through the empty kitchen and outside into the back paddock. The dead were still focused on the front door, trapped inside the courtyard, but it wouldn't be long before there was no more room and the overflow would slide around the outer walls and find their way into the back paddock. We didn't want to be out in the open when that happened.

We ran past the creaking water pump, down the rows of carefully tended plants, and vaulted over the low mesh fence that kept the feral sheep out of the veggies. Beyond that was a whispering line of gum trees; the sisters had cleared every scrap of deadfall from around them, burning it in the kitchen stoves, but they hadn't cut any trees down.

Sister Mary led us down a worn path, and there hidden on the other side of the trees, in the middle of a clearing of dry brown grass, under a weather canvas cover, stood a helicopter.

"You have got to be fucking kidding me?" I almost shouted aloud. Else grinned and clapped with no idea what all the excitement was about.

"The Lord's work requires us to travel over a great distance," Sister Mary said, striding towards the machine.

"Yeah, but I figured your chopper would have been scrapped years ago."

"Not bloody likely," Sister Mary said and moved around the craft, unhooking the tarpaulin ropes and sliding them off. "This is an A-S Five-Fifty Fennec helicopter. Originally designed for military use, but stripped of ordinance and modified with additional fuel tanks, I've got a service range of nine hundred klicks." Sister Mary patted the white flank of the chopper like it was a favorite horse.

In her experienced hands it took us only a few minutes to be ready to fly. Sister Mary left me to strap Else into a seat in the back while she flicked switches and pushed buttons. I stowed Else's bow under the seat and took a position next to her behind the pilot.

"Where are the wheels?" Else asked peering out the windows, a frown creasing her dusty brow.

"Ahh . . . Just close your eyes and trust Sister Mary, okay?" I had flown in a chopper once as a kid and I remembered it scared the shit out of me.

The heavy rotors began to whine and spin, rapidly increasing in speed until they vanished into a blurred disk and the grass around us lay flat.

"Let me out! Let me out!" Else started scrabbling at her seat belt. I grabbed her hands and wrestled with her while Sister Mary pulled back on the stick, or pressed the pedals or did whatever it is that makes a ton of plastic and steel forget that it's not meant to float through the air, and up we went.

Else moaned in fear, turned her head to see the ground falling away, and fainted with a soft sigh.

CHAPTER 10

Flying a helicopter seemed more complex than I thought. Sister Mary had one hand on a joystick, another on a handbrake-like handle, and her feet were working pedals like on a car. We roared low and angry over the convent courtyard, the dead stumbling and lurching below us. It didn't look like they had managed to get inside.

"What about the nuns?" I shouted over the noise of the rotors. The sister just tapped the big earmuffs she had on and jerked a finger at the set hanging next to me.

I put them on and fiddled with a switch. "What about the nuns?" I could hear my voice in my ears.

"The Lord will shield them," Sister Mary replied, her voice sounding tinny through the headphones.

"Will you go back?" I gripped the seat as we banked left and the ground and dust flashed beneath us.

"Of course, it is where I belong."

I couldn't argue with that so we sat in silence for maybe an hour.

"Where are we going?" Else had been awake for a while but seemed to prefer to keep her eyes tightly shut in case she saw how high up we were.

I repeated the question into the mic hanging in front of my mouth.

"Crystal Brook is still over an hour away." Sister Mary seemed a lot less like a middle-aged nun and more the war veteran chopper pilot with each passing minute.

"Not long now!" I shouted into Else's ear.

"What is this!?" Else waved a hand and then quickly clapped it back on to the seat, afraid she might fall out.

"It's a helicopter! We are flying! You know, like a bird!" I waved my hands in a fair impersonation of a bird in flight. Else cracked one eye open and gave me a withering look.

"Birds don't make this noise!"

"True, but they don't fly this fast either! Don't worry about it! Sister Mary is the best!" I gave an overly confident thumbs-up.

"Are we going to heaven?" A look of resolute calm had settled on Else's face and she looked ready to cash in her chips.

"Hell no!" The nuns' crash course in religion had some benefits, like teaching Else table manners, and how to make friends with other girls, even if they only looked her age. The more spiritual aspects were harder to explain, especially to someone with the brain of a two-year-old genius.

"Not even close," I added, letting Else sink into thoughtful silence.

Below us the ground went from burnt umber to grey and back again. Flocks of wild sheep swept across the ground like grey clouds and the wind blew dust over everything. Else curled up against me and slept. I'd almost switched off myself when a change in the engine noise and a sudden tilting jerked me awake.

"What the hell?" I muttered into the mic.

"Settle down, we are coming in to land." Sister Mary stirred the controls and the chopper sank like a feather. Dirt swirled and twisted around us, long curling trails of yellow smoke like ruffled feathers settling again only when we landed gently on the ground and the rotors wound down.

We stepped out, tottering on shaky legs, and looked around at a dry dust bowl that looked a lot like the dry dusty plain we had just left. This one had a long corrugated iron shed off to one side and the stripped shells of some small aircraft baking in the sun.

"Not heaven," Else said, squinting into the glare.

"Not even close," I muttered. We were exposed, and coming in as we did made noise, and that attracted attention. I could see no sign of life, or unlife.

"What now?" I asked Sister Mary, who was lifting a panel on the chopper's flank.

"I refuel and go home."

"But we just got here." I looked around. Here didn't amount to much.

"Yes, and from here you are in God's hands." She set the panel open and using some kind of small wrench she made an adjustment. "Make yourself useful; go into the hanger and roll the fuel hose out here."

I stared at the back of her head for a long moment and then shrugged and walked towards the shade of the hanger.

Inside the temperature doubled; it seemed that the day's heat got trapped inside and then the next day's heat just cooked it harder. I spat on a corrugated iron panel and watched it sizzle.

A heavy coil of woven black hose hung neatly looped on a large wheel against the wall. I checked my surroundings carefully. The dead can get trapped in some stupid places; you just have to open the wrong door without checking it first and—wham!—you're evol chow. The hanger showed signs of being stripped, scorch marks on the walls where people had camped or barricaded themselves in. Anything that would burn was gone to ashes. In piles of white cinders I saw cracked and dried bones.

"Is it safe?" Else's voice echoed from the doorway, her silhouette haloed by the daylight.

"It's okay, come in and give me a hand with this hose."

We pulled it out the door and it snaked along behind us all the way to the chopper, where Sister Mary took the nozzle and connected it to a fuel valve.

"Follow me," she ordered and we did. Back into the hanger, I helped her unearth a concrete tile about a foot across. Using our fingers we levered it up and she reached into a dark hole and twisted a tap open. Straightening up, the nun held a metal pole. She lowered this into the hole and started levering it back and forth.

"See this? Pump like this, as hard and fast as you can. All the way back and forth, okay?"

I stepped up and took over, working the lever until my arms ached and the dust on the ground turned black with my sweat.

"Sister Mary says you can stop now." Else trotted off as I sank to the floor gasping for breath.

Getting up took some concentrated effort on my part. Else dragged the hose nozzle back inside and hung it up on the wall before winding the long black snake of it back on to the wheel.

The fuel left in the pipe gurgled back into whatever underground tank kept it locked away all this time.

"Where are we?" I pulled my shirt up and wiped my steaming face as Sister Mary came into the hanger.

"Near Crystal Brook," she said.

"Do we want to go there?"

"Not much point, it's just another dead town. I would suggest you don't stick around here, though. The risen may be drawn in this direction by the sound of the helicopter."

"Well where are we flying to next?"

"I'm going back to the convent. You should head north and west. Woomera lies that way. If you make it, then the Lord truly guides your steps."

"You can't leave us here!"

"Of course I can; my sisters have suffered enough. We have sacrificed much to give you aid. Now we must pray and continue to rebuild."

"But what about Else?"

"She is an abomination!" Sister Mary exploded and then caught herself. Taking a deep breath she continued. "I am sorry, but I can do no more for you."

Else didn't react; abomination was a word she did not know.

We stood in the hanger doorway, the afternoon sun blistering the paint from the iron walls, and watched Sister Mary wind up and take off, never once looking at us.

Else tugged on my arm. "What is a . . . abomination . . . ?"

"You know what an angel is?" I asked and she nodded. "Same thing."

Else grinned and waved good-bye to the disappearing speck in the sky.

We had no food, no water, and the shotgun was low on ammo. We had the samurai sword and Else had her bow, but only four arrows. I've spent a lot of time close to completely fucked since the end of the world, but this was pushing it even for me.

I started walking, navigating by the sun, the flight of birds, and the trails left by sheep. At least that's what I told Else. Mostly I took a bearing by the direction Sister-fucking-Mary flew off in and then walked in the opposite direction.

Crystal Brook turned out to be an old farming town. A few wool-blind sheep crowded along shop fronts, panting in the evening heat. Else wanted to ride one, or pet it, or kill it and eat it. All good options, but not before we knew who else might be here.

It seemed to be clear of the dead. Evols like towns. For years afterwards some places had working lights and noise, even if the living had fled. Light and noise attracts zombies like giant flesh-eating moths. In Crystal Brook there were no lights—no amusement park rides ghosting in the night and no traffic signals blinking over abandoned street corners.

We peered through dusted-up windows and saw no signs of recent habitation. Like all small towns, plenty of places in Crystal Brook were boarded up long ago. You could always tell the early evacuees because they boarded their windows up on the outside. Those who stayed until it was too late boarded theirs up on the inside.

I led Else down streets lined with wilting trees and crumbling fences. The occasional sheep startled her, but we kept to the middle of the road and out of the shadows. I picked a house at random; it stood back from the road, a decent fence and mature trees shielding it. Else squirmed at having to stand still for so long; she dropped her pants and squatted to piss at one point. Other than that we didn't twitch until I was satisfied that nothing was moving in there.

Breaking in proved unnecessary, the front door wasn't locked. I stood in the kitchen, breathing the hot, stale air. No smell of rotting meat and no sounds. I moved around the room, opening cupboards and not believing how untouched everything was. In Sydney most places were stripped-out wrecks; here it could be that the owners were simply away for the weekend.

Else wandered off while I stacked cans of food on the bench next to a can opener.

"Uuuuuuuugh!" Else's choked scream sent me dashing through into the next room, where the sudden stink of rotting meat struck me like a hammer in the face. I bounded through the door before I remembered that I didn't have a weapon in my hand.

The girl had puked thin bile all down the edge of a chest freezer, grey with dust and smudged with her fingerprints. Now she was on her knees heaving her guts out.

"Ah shit. Did you open that?" I pointed.

"Unnghh . . ." Else groaned and dry retched again.

"Don't open those, just . . . don't." I helped her up and led her back to the kitchen. Cracking open a can of fruit juice, I had to hold her chin and pour it in; she kept turning her head away and whining.

Two cans of juice washed the puke taste away and she even managed half a can of pears for dessert.

After I locked the place up we slept in the master bedroom until well after dawn.

CHAPTER 11

Without Else I could have stayed in Crystal Brook, happily taking up sheep farming and probably sheep shagging too. But each new day brought her closer to her best-before date. Woomera might be a pipe dream, but getting her there and finding some answers was my only priority. We scoured other houses, found some well-gnawed skeletons and a few dried-up mummies, all of which fascinated Else. We found the biggest collection of the peaceful dead in a small church. Half the town seemed to have gathered here, a few hundred judging by the neat rows of skulls. I figured they got together and as a group they'd somehow punched their tickets, leaving a volunteer to cut their heads off before they got back up again. I found the short-straw holder sitting in a small room at the back of the church, the blasted remains of his skull still resting on the muzzle of the shotgun.

For the rest of the day we gathered supplies, pored over a map I found, and searched for fuel. Cars and trucks lined the streets, neatly parked in driveways and garages, but the faded signs on the petrol stations we found all declared NO GAS!

At one end of town we found the old sports field. The white Hs of the rugby posts at either end would never see a try scored under them again. Would the idea of the game be lost within a few generations?

So many things were extinct now. Weekend football

games, fast-food restaurants, supermarkets, radio, TV, movies, and the Internet. The entire world now stood as empty as that rugby field.

Else wandered over to a pit at the edge of the sports ground. The ditch digger they used to make it was still parked at one end.

The good people of Crystal Brook had taken the government's infection control instructions seriously: destroy the brain of infected persons and burn the remains. There must have been a hundred charred corpses twisted around each other and barely covered with dirt. Melted plastic fuel containers poked through the crust in places.

The sheer sides of the pit had been gouged smooth by the digger. The ash-blackened dirt showed marks where fingers had clawed in a desperate struggle to climb out of the pit. I'd seen this kind of thing before, infected people trying to escape the fire while the survivors smashed them down. I wondered how many of these people had turned, or were in fact infected when they were burned to death.

"Real dead?" Else whispered, looking into the hole.

"Real dead," I replied and led her away.

Heading west we found the railway line on the edge of town. Crystal Brook had a small station and the faded map showed the tracks headed towards Port Pirie northwest of town. Else and I both carried heavy packs, loaded with bottles of water, canned food, and books. We'd argued over those books. At least I'd argued; she'd just put them back in her bag when my back was turned even though she could barely read.

I'd found a couple of stockman's hats to protect us from the relentless sun. Else kept on taking hers off to look at it and then putting it on again.

When the sun sank low into the sky, we'd made good time. We kept an eye out for wandering ferals as we trudged across dusty fields between the rails and the highway. Else talked, asking questions constantly.

Most of her questions I could sort of answer. I told her the names of the constellations I could remember. We ate cold beans from cans sitting in the dirt before stretching out and trying to sleep. I could hear Else counting the stars until she drifted off.

Dawn came and we set out before it got too light. The walking dead seemed thin on the ground around here, and that freaked me out almost as much as a whole horde of them reaching for me. That day we were walking along the railway line again when one came at us — a woman. Naked, her skin red with dust and hair coming out in clumps. Flies buzzed around her, sipping the oozing moisture from a mass of small wounds on her legs and arms. Zombies don't heal. Once they get cut, they stay cut. Her lower jaw was gone, broken off somehow. It didn't stop her coming after us, though, gurgling in her throat, her blackened tongue lolling against her neck like a panting dog. We watched and waited. Putting her down would be a kindness.

"I'll take this one." I reached over and drew the sword from Else's back.

"What the fuck?" she said in her casual way of cursing. Sister Mary's influence on her had clearly faded.

"Been a few days, don't want to lose my edge," I said.

"Can you forget how to do something?" Else asked.

"Sure you can. If you don't do it regularly enough, you can forget how to do anything." I readied the weapon. I'd never taken a class in fencing, or kicking the crap out of people Bruce Lee style. But hacking up the dead was always an instinctive thing. Lizard brain thinking with a sword, a club, a chainsaw, or the butt of a gun.

Once, in those crazy months when the world was ending, I saw a guy in a business shirt and tie go down. He'd been holding his own in the street and then retreated into an alleyway. They could only come at him one way and they jammed that space with their squirming rot. He worked them with an axe, chopping like a man possessed. Zombie after zombie fell with its skull split wide open. Then the axe missed once and they had him. The first bite took three fingers off his right hand and he just went apeshit. Punching and kicking, he head-butted a dead guy so hard he crushed its skull. Must have concussed himself too. The last one he took out by simply ripping her head right off her dead shoulders. Then the dead tide swept over him and he was torn to pieces. I watched it all from the rooftops and nearly shit myself for the umpteenth time that week.

Miss Jawless arrived and I swung the sword with a strength born of a revulsion I just can't shake. The bitch ducked. Just like that she dipped her head and my swing went wide over her head. That had never happened before and my surprised momentum almost got me killed.

"Innnnghhh oooo," she gurgled and slashed at me with broken fingers. Else snarled and tackled her, knocking the feral off her feet.

"Else!" I yelled and jumped after them. The girl came up on her feet, quick as a cat, and scrambled up to stand beside me. The zombie, who'd rolled further down the slope, started crawling back up.

"Innnnnnggghhhh oooooooo!" she gurgled again. Else crouched, picked up a rock, and let fly. It missed by a mile. She picked up another one and this time hit the dead woman in the face.

"Go away! Leave us alone!" Else shrieked as she let loose a volley of stones. Each one struck the zombie in the head, splitting skin and bursting an eye so it oozed thick fluid down the torn cheek.

I didn't dare go down the shifting slope of loose stones to finish her off. She was coming up to us again, steadily crawling on hands and knees.

"Oooo!" she hissed again, her face twisted up to stare at me as she reached for my boot. I slammed the point of the sword down into her skull and twisted it. She shuddered and collapsed.

"Gaaaaaaaargh!" Else screamed in wordless fury at the corpse. Normally she smiled and chatted a lot. It wasn't until we ran into the walking dead that I was reminded just how much they messed her up. Everything was new to her. Everything created more questions and I kept giving half answers. Sometimes I think I could see her head filling up with new thoughts.

I handed the sword back to her. She wiped it clean and sheathed it.

"Lets go." I started walking up the track.

"She talked," Else said, hurrying after me.

"Air gets forced out of their lungs when they move. She wasn't really talking."

"Yeah, but she made words. She said 'Ing ooh.'"

"I couldn't tell what she said." I walked faster. The sun crawled over the sky and beat us with fists of fire. Later, when we stopped to drink water from the bottles we carried and take a toilet break, Else started in on it again.

"I don't think she said 'Ing ooh.' I think she was trying to say 'find you.'"

"You think so?" I got to my feet and tossed the empty water bottle down the railway line embankment.

"Why would she say that?" Else got up and shouldered her pack.

"How the hell would I know?"

Else met my glare with a steady gaze. "Why are they looking for you?"

I laughed, my dry throat making it sound shrill. "That's crazy talk, Else. Evols don't do shit like that. And a feral evol couldn't find their arse with both hands tied behind their back!"

"That one found you. She said she did."

"She didn't say a fucking word! Alright? Now quit it!" The idea of evols, especially ferals, getting personal freaked me out. I kept looking over my shoulder as we walked on.

CHAPTER 12

We felt the train long before we saw it. We'd left the railway line behind us and found the tracks again. From here the map said the line headed towards Port Germein. We'd seen empty houses, empty cars, animals, and flies. Lots of flies. The heat coming off the steel rails hammered my eyes. I squinted up the track when a slight vibration trembled through the sleepers underfoot. The way ahead was clear. I looked behind us and saw a black smear on the horizon, like a thin strip of grey cloud trailing down the line. Else grabbed my arm with both hands and clung to me as I stood in open-mouthed shock. Coming out of a shimmering mirage, forming into a solid black shape, spewing black smoke and puffing steam was a train. An actual, working steam train.

"Get down there! Behind that tree! Quick!" I tossed the shotgun to Else and sent her scurrying to cover behind an old dead tree at the bottom of the embankment. Then I started waving my arms for all I was worth.

The train hissed and belched a cloud of steam. Behind the old black engine rolled a single freight car. The squeal of metal on metal tore the air as the driver leaned on the brakes. I stepped off the track and away from Else as the train rolled slowly past and stopped with me standing next to the driver's cab.

Someone had welded a heavy steel mesh across the open windows and put in steel doors to protect the driver from evols and other travel hazards. I climbed up on the engine step, peering into the dark space inside. The firebox door was closed, but the heat coming off it was intense. The steel mesh draped down from the engine roof to the rear of the tender where the coal or wood or whatever you are burning to make steam is stored. The cab was empty. I heard a crunch in the gravel and went to step down, but a cold steel muzzle pressed into my neck.

"Careful, mate. I'm a crap shot but I'm pretty sure even I could blow your bloody head off at this range."

I gently turned my head and saw an old man in faded blue dungarees standing there. He had an old-fashioned engine driver's hat on his head and a massive mane of bushy white hair and beard. The end of his rifle jabbed me again in the neck.

"Step down, son, real easy," he said.

"No worries, mate." This is why I avoided most other survivors. You could never tell who had gone completely batshit crazy. Avoiding people reduced my chances of getting killed because I blinked at the wrong moment.

I kept my hands up and stood facing the train.

"You on your own?" the man asked.

"Yep, just me."

"What the hell are you doing out here?" He seemed genuinely surprised.

"Just wandering."

"Well there ain't much out here. Where'd you come from?"

"Sydney."

"Sydney?" He pulled the rifle back and kept it trained on me but leaned in to stare more closely.

"When's help coming?"

"There is no help. Sydney is dead. Just like the rest of the world."

The old man sagged. "I shoulda known. But you hear things, you know?"

I nodded. Sure you do. The Americans have a cure. The Russians are sending ships to evacuate survivors. New

Zealand is free of evols. There are no survivors in China, it's now a land of a billion zombies and they are migrating towards Europe.

"I heard Elvis was seen in Melbourne last week," I said.

"Elvis . . . ? Elvis?" The old man started laughing; he held the rifle in one hand and laughed till tears poured down his cheeks and he doubled over and slapped his thigh.

"That's what I heard," I grinned and started to lower my hands. Quick as anything he snapped the rifle up again.

"Keep your damn hands up."

I reached for the sky again and then a shadow fell over us from the top of the boiler.

"Put your gun down, motherfucker!" Else had the shotgun trained on him and I fervently hoped that she wouldn't pull the trigger. At this range, I'd be dead too.

"Jesus Christ!" The old man stomped his foot and turned in a circle. "Fine! You win! I don't have anything for you to steal anyway!"

"Else, come down here and don't shoot anyone." I dropped my hands and waited while Else jumped down.

Else clapped her hands in sudden delight. "We found Santa Claus!"

The old man looked at her, then back at me and I started laughing. He did too. I had no idea where in the last couple of weeks she'd picked up the idea of Santa Claus. But true enough, there he was, shaking his head and smiling at her.

"Where are you headed?" I asked.

"Tocolla's end of the line these days. Get some supplies and then trade 'em back down the line. Go as far as Crystal Brook." The engine driver waved a hand in a vaguely southward direction.

"You go anywhere near Woomera?"

"Closest I'd get would be Pimba. You got business in Woomera?"

"Yeah something like that."

"Well I guess I can take two passengers." He stepped past me and unlocked the heavy door.

The train started rolling with a hissing and wheezing and

a slow grinding creak. The driver said his name was Harris. He got me working on shoveling coal and wood into the open mouth of the firebox.

Else chose to ride on top of the tender. She stood up once we got moving and when Harris sounded the whistle she whooped in delight. When she sat down again her face was dark with soot and her eyes and teeth shone white. I shoveled coal and threw broken furniture on the fire until the firebox door glowed dull red and we tore down the track. We flashed past the miles of dry plains, panicking a few sheep and more grey-skinned ferals that gaped with dead eyes then turned to follow us as we flew by.

Else lay on her back on the mesh over the tender staring up at the cloudless sky.

"They give you much trouble?" I nodded at a trio of zombies, two women and a man tearing at a rotting sheep carcass beside the tracks.

"Nah, by the time they get their shit together I'm miles away. Sometimes I hit one with the train, though."

"What happens when you do that?" Else twisted around and stared down at us.

"They explode." Harris grinned and went back to staring up the line of the engine, watching the track ahead.

"Boom . . ." Else breathed and turned back to the sky.

CHAPTER 13

The smell of the sea came up on us faster than I expected. After our days on the road the cool breeze came as a welcome relief. Else stood up again and stared with her peculiar intensity at the sparkling water. The train slowed with a gush of steam and in case anyone had missed our arrival, Harris let out a blast of the whistle.

"You might wanna get your girl inside," he remarked casually.

I whistled. "Else! Inside, mate." She swung down and through the open door. I closed and bolted it behind her.

"So many of them," Else said, pressing against me and staring up the track.

Port Germein was under siege. Hundreds of zombies were pressing up against the walls and fences that surrounded the town. The roar of the train drew them away from the barricades and they shuffled towards the track. Harris didn't seem bothered. I guess he went through this regularly. Else shrank back and drew her sword as we slowed to a walking pace a hundred yards out from where the track went through the corrugated iron wall.

"Please keep your hands and feet inside the ride at all times," Harris said and let another blast of the steam whistle rip the air.

Evols reached for the train. The first ones lost arms as they grabbed hold and then got jerked off their feet.

"You don't have Tankbread out here?"

"Have what?" Harris barely glanced in my direction. Else bared her teeth and growled as a male evol managed to pull himself up onto the mesh. Broken teeth bared, he groaned and gnashed at us.

"What happens now?" I had a mental image of the train being derailed by the sheer weight of dead meat pressing against it.

"We wait for them to open the gate."

I could barely see the gate through the corpses that were climbing over the engine, the stink of seared flesh adding to the smell of burning. An evol wrapped its arms around the chimney and when he pulled them away, strips of melting flesh peeled off and fluttered like pennants. The mob surged forward and the lights went out as the windows were covered with the hungry dead. Else thrust her sword out through the gaps in the mesh, stabbing them through the eyes and destroying their brains.

"How can you see if the gate is open?!" I shouted over the noise of the moaning dead.

"I can't! But it's going to be open. It always is at the right moment!" The train rolled slowly on as Else continued to stab and destroy. The stench of decay and burst zombie guts clogged the stifling cabin until I thought I would pass out.

A wet scraping sound echoed through the engine cab. Harris didn't react, but I wondered what the hell had gone wrong. Daylight came through as the evols got scraped off the sides of the cab by metal spikes set in concrete. We slipped through a gap with maybe an inch to spare on each side.

The train stopped in a holding pen surrounded by high, corrugated iron fences. I heard a woman's voice yell, "Gates shut! Sweep it!"

We stood waiting as people dropped ladders from the top of the fence and clambered down into the pen. They were armed with sharpened shovels, homemade spiked clubs, and axes. In an organized way they passed down each side of the train. A few minutes later we heard a call of "All clear!" from behind us. Harris finished shutting things down and opened the door. I stepped out to meet the people of Port Germein.

CHAPTER 14

When the world fell apart and it became clear that help wasn't coming any time soon, the residents of the seaside town of Port Germein got down to the business of surviving. They built the temporary barricades that became the wall around the main blocks of town and lived quite well by fishing in the bay that bordered them on the southern side. When Harris and his train turned up a few years ago, they began bartering their excess catch for other supplies with the homesteads and communities along the line.

Else and I stepped out into a crowd who grinned and clapped us on the back. Questions came at us from all directions, the same ones I'd be asking if someone came out of nowhere and turned up on my turf.

I shook hands with a lot of people like some old-world politician. If someone had stuck a baby in my face I would have kissed it. Else pressed against my side, her hands curling around my arm.

"Alright you lot, move back." An older woman with a stained blue bandana covering her head pushed through the crowd until she stood in front of us, hands on hips, light blue eyes calculating and assessing.

"I'm Daisy-Mae Cartwright, mayor of Port Germein. You and your friend are welcome to stay as long as you do your share and follow our rules."

"Thanks," I smiled and nodded at her with my best "I'm harmless" face.

Harris finished shutting the engine down and dropped to the ground.

"G'day, Daze! Thanks for opening the gate."

"For you? Always." Daisy-Mae grinned at Harris, and he looked pleased to see her. I wondered if they had a thing for each other.

"Got some stuff for you to look over in the back." Harris indicated the freight wagon. Flies buzzed around us in a cloud as we followed Harris to the back of the train. He cracked the door and slid it open.

Daisy-Mae climbed inside and picked over the piles of skins, cans, books, and other salvaged junk.

"Didya get the spark plugs?"

"Yeah, got a dozen of them, here." Harris indicated a plastic bucket.

She nodded and stuck her head out the door.

"Crispy! Take these over to Mak!" she barked at the idle crowd and hefted the bucket. A young boy with bright ginger hair scampered forward, took the bucket, and ran like the undead were falling from the sky behind him.

Harris and Daisy-Mae negotiated for a selection of the remaining salvage. When they were finished I helped Harris pass the goods out to the crowd and make room for a load of dried fish. Else tried to help and then spent more time asking questions about each item she picked up than actually moving it.

"Guess they get tired of the taste of fish around here," I said.

"Yeah, and them out there get tired of eating beef and mutton every day."

"Why don't you bring some cows here then?" Else piped up from her corner of the freight car.

"And what would you feed 'em on?" Harris let Else think about this for a second. "Cows eat a lot of grass, girl. They need space to graze. Not much space around here."

"Ya know, I once saw a cow on top of a skyscraper in Sydney," I offered. Harris shot me a look.

"No shit, it was pretty thin, and I dunno what they fed

her, but she was up there."

"City people," Harris muttered, shaking his head.

Daisy-Mae stuck her head in the train car. "Smoko," she said.

We hopped down and I explained to Else what smoko was while we walked across the dusty ground of the train yard. A gate swung open and we went into town.

Most of Port Germein turned out to meet us, men, women, and lots of children, over a hundred people in all. Else relaxed and let go of me to talk to the kids who asked as many questions as she did.

We sat in the warm shade of a pub surrounded by watchful locals and drank fresh water that was almost cold. I felt weird being the center of such attention. Daisy-Mae waited till I'd drunk my fill and then she started the questioning.

"Where have you come from?"

"Sydney." A hopeful murmur went through the crowd and Daisy-Mae shut them up with a glance.

"What's it like over there?"

I took a deep breath. "It's okay. It's not easy. We scavenge what we can and do what we must to survive." I could feel the disappointment, the despair, and the hopelessness coming off the crowd in waves.

"Is there any government? Anyone running things?"

"Not really. The evols run things mostly. And they don't have any kind of government. There's a group based in the Opera House, they produce Tankbread and that keeps the dead happy so we get on with them okay."

"Tankbread?" Daisy-Mae asked.

"Yeah, uhh . . . like people, but bodies, grown in tanks. They feed them to the evols, and the evols don't eat us." The murmuring started up again, with a pissed-off tone to it.

"You're kidding?" Daisy-Mae said.

"Nope. Look, I don't know the high-tech details. But in Sydney the dead rule. They tell us what they want and we do it. Or we stay out of their way as much as possible." Someone in the crowd laughed. I looked them over and could see they weren't taking me seriously.

"The dead don't talk." Daisy-Mae spoke with authority.

"There's two types of walking corpse. There's your local kind, we call them ferals. They've been starved of human flesh for so long they've gone stupid. Turned into savage, mindless, shambling killers. Then there's the city evols. The ones who get a regular feed of Tankbread. They talk, think, and act like you and me. Only a bit slower and, well, they're dead."

The crowd erupted into angry accusations then. I'd been out in the sun too long. I was lying, crazy, fucked in the head. Daisy-Mae let them vent for a minute and then stood up and waved them to silence.

"You feed people to the zombies and they act like the living?" Daisy-Mae said, looking me right in the eye.

"Kinda. Tankbread aren't people. They're just mindless human bodies. Grown in big bottles near as I can tell."

"Growing people for zombie food like some kind of livestock?" Harris looked disgusted at the thought.

"Yeah, I guess." I'd never thought of it like that. Tankbread kept us alive, it saved humanity. Before the end of it all, I bet most of us never used to give much thought about where our T-bone steaks came from either.

The last hope faded from the faces around me. Way out here they had kept a dream alive, a wishful expectation that in a big city like Sydney things would be under control. Over there someone was in charge and in time, help would come as far west as their town. Instead they got me telling them about human sacrifices to undead overlords. I wondered if Daisy-Mae's next order would be to lynch me.

"Why did you leave?" Daisy-Mae sounded more like an interrogator than an interviewer now.

"I got in some trouble. We're heading towards Woomera."

"Nothing up there but desert and nutters." Daisy-Mae sat back and folded her arms, daring me to challenge her wisdom.

"I got told that's where Tankbread came from. The idea

of them anyway. There's an old military base up there."

"Well yeah," Harris scratched his Santa beard. "They used to test weapons out that way. Nukes and such."

"What do you want with Woomera?" Daisy-Mae's eyes stared hard into mine and I felt a warm blush creeping up my neck.

"If I don't get there soon, Else's gonna die."

"Why, is she sick?" This question sent the crowd pushing back and chattering in alarm.

"No! She's fine! We're both fine. But they are the only ones who can save her."

Daisy-Mae watched me for a long moment. "Any word on the rest of the world?"

"Nothing I can be sure of. Never met anyone who made it out of Asia, Europe, or the States."

Across from me Daisy-Mae nodded slowly. Turns out the great white hope was no help at all.

"You can stay here if you want, train leaves tomorrow morning. If you're on it, that's up to you and Bernie," she nodded at Harris.

"What happened in Crystal Brook?" I asked. "We saw a lot of real dead people."

"Killed themselves," Daisy-Mae scowled and the crowd muttered in a dark undertone. They saw the mass suicide as a weakness, and yet there was some envy in their eyes even while they shook their heads in disapproval.

"Alright you lot, enough of the questions. It's movie night and I don't wanna miss the coming attractions!" Daisy-Mae slapped her thigh and guffawed in time to the dry laughs of the crowd. I could see why she was the mayor. She had a way with people, like a mother. Comforting and caring, but also firm when they needed it.

We joined the procession of people going to the movies. The venue turned out to be an actual theater. Inside we stood in line with a short queue of kids and adults as each child was given a small plastic cup holding a single piece of canned peach and a spoonful of juice as a treat. The kids took the front two rows of the bench seats in front of a low stage hung with a curtain of blankets and lit by fish-oil lamps.

I let Else go and sit with the young ones while hanging back myself. The audience whispered, the kid's were chattering and looking forward to the show. What we were going to see, no one said.

Off stage someone beat a passable drum roll and the lights went out. Only the swish of hand-fans stirring the warm air and the hiss of children shushing each other broke the silence. We waited as two figures came on stage; they introduced themselves as the Port Germein Players. We applauded as they lit oil lamps over the stage and the kids in the audience went still in anticipation.

I recognized the film as soon as they started on the dialogue. Sure it wasn't an exact script, more a highlights reel, the remembered moments from a movie. The sort of thing we took for granted not so long ago. But not these kids. They were growing up in a world where real films were rare. The cast on stage changed roles with simple shifts in props and costumes. They used vacuum cleaners as Proton Packs and the ghosts were played by a third guy under a sheet. All of which had the audience screaming in mock terror. The kids laughed on cue, and I found myself grinning as I recognized moments I thought I'd forgotten.

As the show went on, I joined the kids in repeating the famous one-liners. By the climactic scene, when the demon Gozer asks Ray if he is a god, we shouted Winston's famous follow-on punch line as one. "Ray, when someone asks you if you're a god, you say YES!"

I glanced around the audience. Most of the adults were quiet; they'd seen this all before. One guy looked away from the stage, his face wet with tears. I stopped grinning. Seeing the anguish on his face reminded me of how much we had lost forever.

CHAPTER 15

Daisy-Mae organized Else and me a place to sleep, a room in a house occupied by a family of three women. Jen, her partner, Lynne, and Jen's daughter Lisa, who introduced herself by announcing she was four years old. We left our weapons outside, leaning against the wall next to a loose pile of discarded shoes.

Else didn't ask any questions about the two mums, which I appreciated. Each to their own, but having to explain their obvious relationship felt like too much work at this time of night. Harris didn't stay with us. I figured he had his own place to sleep, probably next to Daisy-Mae.

Jen left at dusk, heading out for a shift as a guard on the fences, leaving Lynne to prepare a meal from the supplies we provided.

Else and Lisa sat on the floor in the light of a fish-oil lamp and played with Lisa's doll, which fascinated Else. I lurked at the front-door step, dead tired, but too wired for sleep. "How old are you?" Lisa asked.

"I don't know. Younger than you, though," Else replied, stroking the impossible blonde hair of the doll in her lap.

"Nuh-uh," Lisa shot back. Else lifted her head and frowned.

"I wasn't born like you. I got born like this."

I readied myself to interrupt if the kid pushed it. Instead, Lisa changed the subject.

"Missus Wilson has kittens. I'll show them to you

tomorrow if you want."

"What's kittens?" Else asked.

"Baby cats. They grew in their mummy's tummy. Just like I did."

"Missus Wilson had baby cats in her tummy?" Else sounded startled.

"No, silly!" Lisa's laughter tinkled like the high end of a piano scale. "Her cat, Leo, had babies."

Else put the doll down and Lisa immediately picked it up, having her turn at fussing over the small figure.

"You grew in your mummy's tummy?" Else said quietly.

"Uh-huh," Lisa's attention now focused on changing the doll's outfit.

"I didn't have a mummy. I got grown," Else said and the sudden grief in her voice made me shiver.

"Everyone has a mummy," Lisa said firmly.

"Not me." Else gave a sigh.

"I have two mummies." Lisa put the doll down, stood up, and wrapped her arms around Else's neck in a gentle hug. "We can share."

Lynne came out of the kitchen, wiping her hands on a towel. "Lisa, time for bed, sweetheart."

Lisa gave an exaggerated sigh and pulled away from Else. "I have to go to bed now. It's the rules," she said.

Else nodded and wiped her face. I'd only seen her cry once before and I think it still freaked her out a little. Like maybe her sadness had caused a physical injury.

Lisa gathered her doll and Lynne swept them both up and carried her off to another room.

I took a deep breath. "How you doing, kid?"

Else sniffled and wiped her nose with the back of her hand.

"What?" She wouldn't look at me directly.

"You're crying," I said from the doorway.

"I don't like it. Make it stop!" Else snapped.

This felt like one of those times when I knew that anyone but me would have been a better choice to guide her through the world.

"You'll stop when you're done. Till then just let it happen."

"It . . . it hurts."

I stood up, came over, and got down on my knees. I hugged her like Lisa did. Else buried her face in my shoulder and cried. She wept in a different way than last time, when she'd cried like a baby with primal fury. This was a welling up of deep sadness from somewhere in her core and I didn't know what brought it on.

"Shhh," I soothed. "You'll be right."

"I don't know who I am," she cried into my shirt.

"Hell, none of us know who we are, girl. Some people go their whole lives trying to work that out."

Else lifted her head. Gripping my shirt, she shook me. "I'm not people!"

"You're as near as. Remember how I said you were special? I wouldn't bullshit you, Else."

She stared hard into my eyes, searching for deception. I didn't dare blink.

"Will I have babies? Like Lisa and Leo's kittens?"

"Sure, I guess. If you want. You just have to finish growing up and meet the right guy." The blush rising on my face reminded me we weren't so much straying into difficult-to-answer territory as hurtling into it with the same inevitable sense of catastrophe as an asteroid on a collision course with Earth.

Else sniffled. "Why aren't you the right guy?"

"Because you're just a kid." That came out sounding harsher than I meant. She got to her feet and glared at me, defiance flashing in her eyes.

"I'm just as grown as everyone else. And they can have babies."

"Yeah, you're physically a woman, but you've got a lot of growing to do in here." I tapped the side of my head.

"What does that mean!" Her hands curled into fists in frustration.

"Just that. You've only been out in the world for a couple of weeks. You don't know everything. You know a lot more than you did when we left Sydney, but having a kid is a big deal. It means being able to feed and take care of it until it's grown. And that takes a long time."

"You will help me," she said with complete conviction.

"Of course I will. But now, it's just not the right time. Trust me on that."

Else's face darkened and she clenched her fists so tight her arms curled up. "I could just take Lisa with us. You can teach me how to take care of her."

"Shit, Else! You can't do that! You can never take a kid away from their family. That's really fucked up."

"Well how do I learn then?"

"I dunno, I'll get you a baby doll or something."

"What about animals? If we had animals, they could have babies and I could help take care of them."

"Animals are for eating. There's no way we can take care of animals, not out there."

"We can stay here then. I want to stay here."

"We can't stay here. We have to get to Woomera."

"I hate you!" With that Else stormed out of the house and slammed the door. Lynne came out of Lisa's room and silently closed the bedroom door behind her.

"Trouble?" she asked.

"She wants to stay here and we can't." I got up from the floor.

"Like long term? Sure you can. We could use more help on the boats, there's always work for people with skills."

"We can't stay. We have places to go."

"Like Woomera? There really is nothing out there. Just the dead, and the desert."

"There has to be something."

"What is it you are looking for?" Lynne folded her arms and waited.

"A cure." It sounded crazy even as I said it.

"For what? The evol plague?"

"Sure, why not?"

Lynne laughed, a short sharp sound. "Because that's crazy. If there was a cure, they would have used it by now."

"Wouldn't you do anything you could if it meant that Lisa could grow up in a world where she didn't have the constant threat of zombies outside the walls? Always afraid that one day they would get in and tear her to bits, or worse?"

She stopped smiling. "Come with me, I want to show you something."

Lynne led me to the kitchen, a small room with bare shelves and carefully hoarded morsels of food in recycled containers. I waited while she opened a cupboard and lifted out a heavy-caliber rifle.

"There's one bullet left for this gun." She lifted a small jewelry box from inside the cupboard and opened it. The long brass cartridge gleamed with a dull polish in the lamplight.

"If all else is lost, that bullet is for Lisa. It will be quick, it will be painless, and she will never become like them or die at their hands."

"What about you and Jen?"

"We will take care of each other, if there is time, and if it comes to that," she said with a calm certainty.

"I'd better go find Else." I backed out of the kitchen and fled the house as Lynne put the weapon away.

CHAPTER 16

The streets of Port Germein were busy at night. People worked by lamplight and most were armed with sharpened blades on short poles. I'd seen a lot of variants on the sharp shovel as a weapon. It worked on one or two evols, but if a mob swarmed you—the calmness in Lynne's voice came back to me in a wave of chill. Saving a round for yourself made sense, and saving your last shot for your child didn't bear thinking about. The shotgun had its disadvantages too, but it would have to do as Else had taken the sword with her when she ran off.

I wandered the streets, nodding hello at everyone. They all knew each other, of course, and my celebrity status meant that I couldn't hide. I saw people working fish skin into leather. This stuff is soft and pliable, strong too. In a few years they'd be wearing it as the main material for their clothes. Some already were.

Two sounds filled the night and at first I thought they were the same noise. First the dull undulating moan of the massive evol horde at the walls, and then as I walked, I heard the distant hiss of the sea breaking in gentle waves on the beach, somewhere out beyond the barricade that ran along the Esplanade, parallel to the shore.

Port Germein's residents worked hard to keep themselves secure, and the mesh fence was reinforced with scraps of metal sheet, rusting car bodies, and building materials.

I asked if anyone had seen Else and got shrugs in return. The fence guards kept their gaze on the ground beyond the fence. Zombies stalked the sand and desert grass out there. The onshore breeze carried the smell of the sea, and the stink of their rot.

"Cute blonde chick?" A boy dressed in fish-leather pants and vest crouched on a ledge high up the wall. "I saw her running down that way." He pointed further along the line, almost to the edge of town. Out there no lamps hung on the fence posts. Only one or two guards patrolled along that section and the evols seemed to ignore it, probably in favor of the brighter distractions closer to the living heart of Port Germein.

"Else?" I called softly into the warm night as I walked into the gloom. "Else, it's me," I added, feeling a bit stupid.

"Go away," her voice came from somewhere ahead in the darkness. The shops along the Esplanade were stripped bare, being torn down one brick and beam at a time for shoring up the defenses and building homes as far away from the world outside as possible. Demolition in slow motion.

"Else, we can get a puppy or something. A baby dog, or maybe a rabbit." I stood listening to the whispering of the surf and the distant chorus of dead men's groans.

"That's bullshit." She'd moved. I followed the sound of her voice across the street and found her standing at the fence staring out towards the water.

"I can hear them," she whispered. Her fingers curled around the thick strands of wire. Layer upon layer of chicken wire and any other mesh fence they could find meant that even a snake couldn't get through.

"You'll get used to it. They'll bugger off in a few days. They get distracted and just shuffle away."

"It's not like that. I hear voices, all saying something, but I don't understand."

"What are they saying?" I stood back slightly, one eye on the fence. Any damned evol could come sneaking up and take a chunk out of her hand the way she stood there.

"I don't know."

I sighed; the onshore breeze was picking up and the night was getting colder. "Come on, let's get back."

She only moved when I took her by the arm and pulled her away. We walked back along the fenceline in silence. When we reached the point where the fence evolved into a sturdier barricade, the slow-moving crowd of walking corpses had spread around to the seaward side in greater numbers. I could hear the sentries on the ledges above us calling status updates to each other. They sounded nervous.

"I've got maybe a hundred of them down here."

"They're just sliding along the wall. I can hear them scratching at it."

"If they start pushing, we're fucked."

"Hold your positions. Tony, go tell Daisy-Mae."

We stopped as the kid in the fish-leather pants slid down a scaffolding pole and scampered off into town.

"I need to seem them." Else pulled her arm away and quickly flitted up the nearest ladder. I followed her with more care.

From the wall to the beach a large crowd of the dead pulsed and stirred below us.

"Something's got their attention," I said to an older guy wearing a policeman's hat.

"Must be a random bunch. The train doesn't usually attract this many. The ones that do show up wander off pretty much straight away. We don't give them any reason to stay."

"Why do they follow us?" Else asked, staring down into the sea of blank and worn faces.

"They're like a storm cloud. They just go where the wind blows them." The cop snorted deep in his throat and spat a thick wad of phlegm down into the moving mass.

"A storm . . ." Else whispered. She turned her head and looked at me. I felt a wash of cold dread flood my gut. Her eyes were lost, seeing a different view entirely. With a soft sigh they rolled up in her head and she spread her arms wide. I shoved the cop aside and lunged for her as Else took two quick steps forward and swan-dived into the necrotic surge below.

I leapt, grabbing at Else as she fell away. My hands closed on empty air and I barely had time to think ah shit! as I followed her down into the zombie crowd.

The stench hit me like a wall as I crashed down on the seething dead. I screamed for Else, saw her body, rising limp on a forest of dead arms. I punched and kicked, yelling in blind panic. Drawing the sawn-off shotgun, I fired point-blank into the nearest dead face and the second shell decapitated the fat bitch next to him. With no time to work the slide again, I used the gun like a club. Grey-skinned hands reached and grabbed at my clothes and flailing limbs. The air was thick with the stomach-churning smell of them. They pressed in on all sides, driving me to my knees, blinded by the tangle of reaching hands that clogged my mouth and nose.

Like a drowning swimmer breaking the surface, I felt my body gripped and lifted. I took a deep shuddering breath and shrieked as I saw the night sky again. Beneath me the mob shuddered and a hundred hands passed me over the surface of the crowd. I kicked and struggled, shouting abuse and empty threats. The few lights of Port Germein vanished behind us. The evol mob shuffled away, carrying us with them into the darkness.

CHAPTER 17

I've never made a study of the walking dead's habits. The city ones eat Tankbread and leave me alone. The ones that don't feed go feral and lose any intelligence and ability to function like the humans they once were. Yet we were being carried along, passed hand over hand by a nearly silent crowd of the foulest dead I'd ever seen.

The hands holding me were icy and I could feel the layers of skin sloughing off. The gel mush of their flesh smeared like cold snot against my clothes. The dead don't stop moving until something gets their attention, but outside of Sydney I'd never seen this many move with such purpose. The mob that turned up at the convent of the sisters of Saint Peter's Grace, they'd been fixated like this. Focused enough to turn up in large numbers and proceed to tear their way inside. Though what exactly was going on here was anyone's guess.

The evols holding us moved with certainty, but I could see others on the fringe stumbling around like real ferals.

"Else!" I bellowed into the night sky.

"Yeah?!" her shout came drifting back from somewhere ahead.

"You okay!?"

"No . . . !" She didn't sound like she was in pain, but honestly, there really was nothing okay about our predicament.

"Stay cool!" I yelled back. I experimented with pulling

my arm free of the two zombies holding it. Then the other. Finally I pushed myself up into a sitting position, my butt resting on two dead men's shoulders. From here I could see across the crowd. Else's blonde hair bobbed up and down a hundred meters away.

"See if you can sit up!" I called across to her. She struggled and got nowhere. "Pull your arms free. One at a time. Slowly!"

I watched while she did this and then sat up, dead fingers grasping at her back like giant Velcro hooks.

"Where are you!" she called, peering around.

"Back here!" I risked a wave. Else twisted until she was on her hands and knees. She grinned, waved, and then squealed as she lost her balance and vanished.

"Else!" I wrenched myself free and dropped to the ground. Pushing through the unresisting dead, I yelled and shoved. Else popped up again. "I'm over here!" In a few moments we were hugging each other and laughing in the middle of a mosh pit of the dead.

The press of them carried us onwards; they seemed okay as long as we kept moving in their direction. "Why aren't they trying to eat us?" Else asked.

"No idea. By all accounts we should be dead now. These ferals are acting more like city dead. Ones with a good amount of working brains."

"I want to get away from them," Else said with her typical objectivity.

"You and me both." As near as I could tell we were heading east. We needed to be heading west and north to get to Woomera.

"Follow me." I pushed to my left, cutting across a dead girl with skin as rough as sandpaper. By letting them flow around us, and moving steadily we soon reached the edge of the mob where the crowd thinned out. Here the zombies stumbled more, groaning and gnashing their blackened teeth against the air. I quietly slid my last two cartridges into the shotgun and gingerly worked the pump-action slide.

"I don't like this," Else whispered.

"Yeah, these bastards are for real." We compromised by going with the crowd for a few hundred meters, waiting for a chance to get a clear run at getting the hell away from them.

A dead tree split the crowd; we stepped around it, on the outside. A feral bumped off another, growled, and shuffled straight at us. I didn't dare fire, not this close to so many of his friends. His eyes widened with that slow realization of the really hungry dead. His crusted nostrils flared and with a snort that spat black ooze down his chin he lurched straight at me.

"Fuck," I muttered. "Run, I'll be right behind you."

Else ignored me, drawing her sword instead.

"I'm tired of running," she said and swung the business end of the blade down on the zombie's skull so hard it stopped between his eyes. With a gurgling sigh he sank to his knees and she jerked the blade free.

I stepped over the quivering corpse as another feral snapped his teeth at our scent. He jerked his head in our direction and then spasmed like he'd been tasered. I didn't stop to check what was wrong; a few more quick steps and we were out of the mob.

"They're coming," Else hissed behind me, and I ran without looking back.

We sprinted, then jogged, and finally wheezing and spitting dust from dry throats, we walked. I led Else in a wide circle away and around the back of the mob. They followed, of course, but we lost sight of them in the dark. We hit the railway line an hour before dawn and without comment we turned and followed it.

With the break of dawn we started jogging again. I needed to get back to Port Germein before the heat of the day sapped our strength and slowed us to a crawl.

Only a few evol stragglers remained around the walled town, zombies that just stood still like toys with flat batteries or shuffled against the wall in a never-ending cycle of steps.

From a safe distance I tried waving my shirt, but no one seemed to be paying attention. The train gate stood closed, though a pall of dark smoke smudged the morning sky. I really hoped that the dead hadn't gotten in and destroyed the town overnight.

With a nervous eye to the south, we marched through the dust by the railway line. I was about to pound on the railway gate when the hiss and grind of the steam engine driving itself forward broke the silence.

The dead responded by going into a lethargic frenzy, thrashing themselves against the wall and finally turning towards the massive gate as it swung open and Harris' train rolled out.

Else and I jumped up and down, waving and yelling. The train whistle shrieked and we ran to meet the slow-moving train even as the Port Germein gate swung closed behind it.

I pushed the girl up into the cab ahead of me and then swung up behind her. Else was already chattering away to Harris, telling him about our bizarre nighttime adventure in a torrent of words without seeming to take a breath.

I did a slow turn, showing Harris that other than dust and sweat I was clean and unbitten.

Harris grinned and clapped me on the shoulder. "You must be the luckiest bugger I've ever met! No one's ever gone into a mob like that and come out with out so much as a bite!"

"Yeah, it's some kind of bloody miracle, eh?"

"Too bloody right, mate. Someone up there really wants you two to get to Woomera, so let's not keep him waiting." Harris pushed a lever and the train picked up speed. Rolling off the side track and on to the main line, we puffed our way northwards.

CHAPTER 18

Harris gave me instructions on what not to touch, which seemed to be everything. I couldn't remember the last time I had slept, so I took a corner and a blanket. Else clambered out onto the mesh covering the back of the cab and lay there staring out at the countryside. Even though it was early morning I could hear her counting stars, picking up from where she started the other night from the sounds of it, and then she too was quiet and still.

It was afternoon when Harris nudged me with his foot.

"Whassa?" I mumbled and clambered to my feet.

"Dead ahead." He stepped out of the way and let me peer up the length of the engine.

"McIntyre's place." Harris pulled a lever and the train exhaled a gust of steam. The clatter of the wheels shifted its cadence and we began to slow down.

"What are you doing? Just drive through them."

"At this speed going through that many we could derail and then we'll be in real trouble."

I checked on Else. She was now crouched on the mesh peering into the shimmering heat of the day, watching the evols with the complete focus of a hunting dog on point.

"Evols, zombies, the fucking walking dead," I muttered. This group looked as big as the one that besieged Port Germein.

"Shit . . . I hope they're okay." Harris wiped his beard and squinted as we rolled on.

"Port Germein?" I said as I opened the cab door, pulled a growling Else inside, and bolted it shut behind her.

"No, some friends of mine live up this way." Harris slowed the train on the approach to a tiny train platform and a weatherboard-paneled shack. We hit the first evols head on. The warm air filled with the stink of ruptured guts and crushed bodies. Their moans surrounded us and the grey silhouettes moved in a dull monochrome as they pressed in on all sides.

"Jesus . . ." Harris spat through the bars of the window and with a final exhalation of steam the train creaked to a halt.

The dead surrounded us immediately. Harris and I stepped back, keeping a safe distance as blackened fingers curled through the heavy mesh and steel bars.

"Helluva lot of them for the middle of fucking nowhere," I commented as I pulled Else back against me.

"I've never seen anything like it away from a town. Sure maybe one or two. But this kind of mob?" Harris looked seriously freaked out.

"Maybe you should just get us the fuck out of here?" I said as Else strained to get free.

Harris turned some levers and the train started to wind up again. Deep under the boiler, pistons pumped and pressure built. The dead pressed against each other and crawled over the engine. We stood in our metal box and breathed the stink of them.

"Now would be a great time to get moving!" I would have started shooting, but there were so many of them, it wouldn't have helped.

"Haaaaaaaaaaaaaris!" Somewhere, out there, a woman screamed.

"Eh?" Harris looked up.

"It's nothing." I didn't give a fuck. Anyone out there was on their own.

"Harris!" she yelled again. Goddamnit!

"Lizzy! That's Lizzy McIntyre! Lizzy! Where are ya, love!?"

"On the shed roof! They started turning up this afternoon. Bunches of the buggers!"

We couldn't see her, but I guessed she was on top of the shed by the train platform. May as well have been Mars.

"Hang in there, Lizzy! We'll get you safe!" Harris' face lost that shit-scared look and he now moved with purpose.

"And just how are we going to do that?"

"I'm not leaving without Lizzy."

I lifted my shotgun into his face. Harris just shook his head. "Without me, mate, this train isn't going anywhere. And neither are you." He had a point. Harris pushed past me and yelled through the zombie-covered mesh.

"Lizzy! Can you get onto the carriage without them getting you?!"

"I think so! They're all over the engine! But none of them are around us!"

"Go for it, girl! You can do it!"

"Then what?!" Lizzy's voice cut over the groans of the dead all around us.

"Shout out and I'll get us moving quick-smart! Get in the car if you can! And close the bloody door!"

We waited for a few minutes in hot silence. Else wriggled free and drew her sword. With astonishing speed she thrust the blade through the gaps and plunged it into the eye of an evol. Twisting it, she pulled back and the body sagged into the press of zombies. Thrust, twist, and withdraw. She took out ten of them before we heard Lizzy calling us from somewhere down the train. "We're on board! Please go, Harris! Go!"

Harris leapt to his controls and heaved on a lever. The train shuddered and began to roll. Else kept on stabbing evols in the head, the dead weight falling away as we picked up speed.

The sun was setting before we dared stop again. Harris said he wanted to be sure the train was clear before we went much further. We stopped and crept out to stretch our legs. Other than a few stray limbs and other unidentifiable chunks caught on the train, there were no zombies to be seen. After the inspection Harris hurried down to the freight car.

"Lizzy!" he called out. "Open up, love, she's all right now!"

The freight car door cracked open and then slid back. The biggest fucking evol I've ever seen leapt out onto the track and grabbed Harris. My shotgun was up but I couldn't get a clear shot. "Harris! Fuck!" I yelled, but he just laughed and hugged the damn thing. Else was jumping around, looking to get in there with her sword.

"Steady on there, Gordon, steady on." Harris pried himself free and patted the thing on the shoulder.

"Lollies," it rumbled and started patting Harris down like he was searching him.

"In a sec, mate." Harris turned and waved me back. "It's okay, mate, this is Gordon. He's Lizzy's brother."

Lizzy emerged from the gloom of the freight car. She had the same dark hair and deep tan of her brother. Gordon was a grown man, built like a brick shithouse and clad in jeans and a blue T-shirt. Lizzy was long and thin like a strip of bark and looked like she couldn't be more than sixteen. She was wearing a faded halter top and loose skirt with a ragged hem that wrapped around her hips and floated over her knees. Gordon gave a rumbling guffaw and straightened up, clutching a deformed paper-wrapped toffee in one hand.

"Last one," Harris said.

"Nuh-huh," Gordon shook his head and worked on solving the riddle of getting the wrapper off his prize.

"Is he a big motherfucker?" Else said in an awed whisper.

"Don't think so. I think he's just . . . well, special," I said.

Lizzy rolled her eyes. "Shit, mister, nothing special about Gordy, he's just a retard."

"What the hell happened? Where's your mum and dad?" Harris asked.

Lizzy's expression darkened. "Dad was out somewhere on the farm, wasn't due back for a day or more yet. Mum . . . Mum told me to take Gordy and run like hell. Knew you'd be coming back along the line. Glad you didn't take too long. Gordon was getting upset."

"Traaaaain," Gordon gurgled with a mouth full of sticky brown toffee juice.

"He loves it when Harris comes to visit. You always bring him some kind of lollies." Lizzy looked at us a bit shyly. She seemed embarrassed by her brother, but protective of him at the same time.

"Glad we could help out." I had this crawling oh shit thought crawling up the back of my neck. That was three places so far we had run into big mobs of evols. They weren't supposed to be such a problem outside of the cities. So much empty land they could wander off into.

"Well we're heading up past Pimba, you kids are coming along. I'm not sending you home till I'm sure the place is clear." Harris would brook no argument, and while Lizzy seemed worried about her folks, Gordon got stuck on the idea of a train ride.

"Best get on; the fire's stoked and we have some miles to go." Harris swung the door open on the train cab and Gordon immediately clambered up hooting in delight. Else watched him suspiciously but climbed up to her spot on the mesh over the tender.

"I guess we're riding in the back," Lizzy smiled and led the way to the freight car. I gave a shout to let Harris know we were on board.

With the door closed the freight car was cool and shaded. Lizzy pushed some skins around and made a comfortable place to sit, so we did in silence for a while.

"Where you from?" she asked.

"Sydney," I said, trying to find somewhere safe to look between her thighs and her face.

"I went there once. When I was a kid." The skirt split when she crossed her legs, sliding like a caress up to one bare hip. No undies or tan lines. I felt my throat go dry.

"Yeah? How old are you then?"

"I was seven when it started, dunno now. Old enough, though." Lizzy slid forward, her knees parting as she lowered herself down in front of me. I stared down the dusky slope of her chest. Where the halter top bordered the swell of her tanned breasts a faint scatter of freckles lay like the first drops of rain on desert sand.

She opened my jeans and I lifted my hips, leaning back against the wooden side of the freight car. She pulled them down while I wiggled my feet and pushed my boots off. Lizzy slid a hand around me and squeezed up and down. I pulled her close, the musky smell of her skin intoxicating. Sliding my hands up under her top, I peeled it off over her head. She in turn pulled my shirt off, her skirt slipping away. The heat of her body intensified against mine as we kissed hard and hungry like evols. The last time I touched a girl like this it had cost me three cans of food, and I'm sure one of them was spaghetti. I stroked my hands down her back, her skin so smooth and trembling. My tongue stroked over her teeth, they parted slightly and hers touched mine. There was a wonderful naivety to her kissing, but a passionate need too. Drawing her knees up, she settled over me. Her hand slid down and with a slight gasp, she guided my cock into position. That intense enfolding heat made me groan. She sank down, clenching me as her head fell back and she cried out. "Ohhh fuck . . . yeah . . ." Her hair tickled my hands. I gripped her sides and drove into her, deeper and harder. My mouth slid down her neck, onto the firm swell of her breast and the warm hardness of her nipple. I sucked and flicked it. She whimpered, her head falling forward, draping us in the soft fronds of her hair. In the close heat we writhed and pressed against each other, thrusting and speaking in half words until our skin shone with sweat. In the final moment she bit down on my shoulder, screaming in muffled ecstasy and I came so hard I thought I might die.

We lay together afterwards, her head on my chest and my arm around her.

"That was nice," she murmured.

"Very nice," I agreed.

"I'd only seen mum and dad doing it before."

"They were okay with that?"

Lizzy giggled. "Hell no. If they'd known I was peeking they would have freaked. Gordy lets me watch him playing with himself all the time, though."

"That's not very nice, he's disabled. You should treat him with some respect."

Lizzy sat up and glared at me. "It's not like I fucked him or anything."

"Yeah but —"

"He's my brother. I look out for him and I don't need you telling me I'm doing it wrong."

I sat in silence for a moment; there were worse crimes being committed every day. "Do you think your mum and dad will be okay?" Lizzy lay down again, her fingers tracking through the grime on my chest.

"I don't know. If mum made it back inside she can lock herself in the cellar. If the Zeds can't get in they'll leave. Dad was out checking stock. They might have got him. Or a snake could have bit him, or his horse."

"Harris will take you back after he's dropped us off at Pimba."

Lizzy hesitated. "Is she your girlfriend?"

"Else? No. She's . . . No she's not my girlfriend."

"I could be your girlfriend. You could take me with you and we could be together all the time."

"I dunno. It's hard enough looking after me, let alone two girls."

"I can look after myself. I can shoot with a rifle and a bow. I can skin, and cook and fish and I'll let you fuck me whenever you want."

"What about Gordon?"

"What about Gordon? You want to fuck him too? Sure, he'd probably like it."

"No, I mean who's going to take care of him if you come with me and Else?"

"I don't care!" The anger in her voice was bitter and absolute. "I'm sick of having to look after him. I don't want to spend the rest of my life on the farm. I want to travel, see other places, meet people and see things."

"There's nothing to see out here. It's all gone."

"There is more out there than there is on the farm."

I sighed. We had a way to go, and I liked the idea of another round before we reached our destination.

"You can do whatever you want," I said and drew her tighter against me, laying kisses on her hair and face. We did it again and I hated myself for lying.

CHAPTER 19

The hiss and shudder of the train braking woke me up. I pulled my clothes and boots on while Lizzy stirred sleepily on the sheepskins. I peered out through the gaps in the wood, seeing only dry scrub and red sand. We were still in Australia then.

I pulled the door open, letting the hot smoke of the engine swirl in. I looked down past the long black chassis and saw we were rolling into a town. A battered sign said, "Welcome to Stirling North." The place seemed quiet.

Harris brought the train to a halt. I waited until he hopped down and started back towards us.

"Get up, Harris is coming," I said and jumped out, sliding the door shut behind me.

"Regular pit stop," Harris said with a casual glance around.

"No zombies here?"

"There's no one here. The few survivors buggered off to Port Augusta back in the Panic. The rumor was that there were UN ships coming and Port Augusta had boats to get you to Adelaide. The roads were choked, so for many folks it was the only option."

"And the boats?"

"Never came as far as I know."

"There were a lot of rumors, seemed everyone thought that someone had a cure, or an escape. They were dark times."

"Dark?" Harris snorted. "They were complete shit. The government lost control. People were in complete panic and everywhere you looked dead people were trying to kill you."

"You should have been in Sydney. What are we doing here?"

"Top up the boiler, and gather some supplies. People left pretty fast, and the Skipper doesn't let people out of Port Augusta without good reason. They reckon the dead plague is carried by the living."

"So they don't let anyone into the town?"

"Nope. I offload about half a klick out of town and run a flag up to let them know that supplies are there. They leave their barter goods for me and that's how we do business."

"More fish?"

"Sometimes. Mostly it's machine parts, hardware, lumber, fuel, that sort of thing."

"Where do they get it all from?"

"They're a port. I guess they trade it with other ports."

The idea of a working port, particularly one with some kind of working economy, immediately had me intrigued. "How can we get in there?" I asked.

"Like I said, you don't. Anyone gets within range their snipers shoot you in the head. There's a white line about four hundred meters out from the town wall. White from the bones of the walkers and the wanderers who got too close."

The door beside us slid back and Lizzy jumped down. "Stirling?" she asked.

"Yeah, how was the ride?" Harris asked blandly, and I nearly choked.

"Not bad, I slept for most of it. How's Gordy?" Lizzy said casually.

"Excited. You might want to talk to him about not touching things in the cab. He'll listen to you."

"Sure." Lizzy gave me a slow smoldering look as she brushed past.

Harris and I unloaded two wheelbarrows from the freight car and walked back along the train to where Else stood on the roof of the train cab. She climbed down and came to me, scowling at Lizzy who smirked harder while tossing her hair back.

"Harris says we need to get supplies. Water and stuff," Else said. "He says he needs to fill the train with water and we have to get the supplies from in there." She pointed vaguely at the deserted streets that stood next to the tracks.

"Sure thing, we can do that. There's no evols here. Harris says everyone left years ago," I said.

"I can't hear them," Else whispered.

"That's good though, right?" I put an arm around her and gave her a hug. Else tensed and then pressed against me, one arm folded up like a wing against her chest.

"Gordon, you can help me with the water, okay?" Harris clapped his hands and Gordon lumbered out of the cab, laughing like a child in his rumbling baritone.

"Whaddya want me to do?" Lizzy stretched and swept her dark hair back, exposing a good expanse of taut midriff as she did so.

"Give those two a hand. Collect anything that's not nailed down. But make sure it's stuff we can trade. Nothing broken or useless."

"Nothing broken or useless, got it."

"We can handle it, Harris. Lizzy should stay here and help with Gordon," I said. Putting the two girls together seemed as smart as looking for a gas leak with a flamethrower.

"Time's wasting and the boy is fine. Go on you lot. Use the wheelbarrows. Oh, and you'll need this. It'ss the places I've already stripped." With that he returned to unpacking a heavy hose from the train.

"Lizzy, grab a wheelbarrow. Ladies, this way." I pushed one of the barrows ahead of me and we went to town. The rough map Harris had sketched showed each street, the houses he'd already pillaged marked with an X. We walked through a ghost town. The occasional sheep panted in the shade, blinded by its heavy wool.

"So you from Sydney, too?" Lizzy piped up. Else ignored

her. "Hey, Blondie, I'm talking to you," she tried again. Else kept walking, scanning the houses to each side as she went. Expecting trouble because that's all she knew.

"What is she, deaf?" Lizzy carried on.

"Shut up, or they will hear you," Else said.

"Who will hear me? The zombies? There's no one here!" Lizzy twirled her arms flung wide, head back, mouth open with a joyful expression I knew intimately. "There's no one here! Just us!" She shouted it to the sky and laughed.

"Lizzy, quit it." The unnecessary noise made me nervous too. Else gave Lizzy a look that said what she was thinking.

Lizzy gave her the finger, which meant nothing to Else. Then she scowled hard when Lizzy laughed at her glancing upwards to see what the other girl was pointing at.

"I don't like you," Else said, which made Lizzy laugh in shocked surprise.

"Well fuck you too, bitch!"

"Whoa!" I grabbed Else's sword arm as her blade came out and she lunged at Lizzy. The black-haired girl stumbled back with a scream.

"She's crazy! She's fucking nuts!" Lizzy yelled from a safe distance.

I struggled with Else. Her teeth were bared and she snarled and spat.

"Liz, go down a block and start checking those houses."

"But—"

"Just go!" I didn't know how long I could hold Else for, or what she might do if I let go.

Lizzy stormed off, taking the wheelbarrow with her and marching away in a slighted fury. Else stopped struggling. "And don't come back!" she yelled at the other girl's back.

"Else, calm down. We need to work with other people to survive. You can't go around killing everyone who pisses you off."

"I don't want to kill everyone. Just her."

"Well you can't."

"Why not!?"

"Because . . . because you don't kill people."

"We kill people all the time."

"Well that's different. They're dead. Which means they aren't real people anymore."

"Do you want to make her a mummy?"

I blinked. That came out of left field. "What . . . ? No. Of course not."

"Why not? She looks at you like she wants to make babies with you and you look at her funny."

"I don't want to make babies with her."

"Why not?" Else stamped her foot in frustration.

"I don't want to make babies with anyone!" I knew as soon as I said it that it was a mistake. Else's face twisted in a sudden grimace of pain.

"Else . . . I didn't mean it like that. You know you're special to me."

Else threw her hands up in the air and walked off at a brisk pace.

"Else! For chrissakes!" I shouted after her.

"Just stop talking!" Else ran up the driveway of the nearest house. We searched it in silence, finding canned pet food and shelves full of books. We loaded the wheelbarrow, Else making room for new books to add to her collection. In a different world she would have loved libraries.

CHAPTER 20

With our barrow loaded to teetering we started back to the train. Else got halfway down the street when she froze and put a hand out to stop me.

"What?"

"Someone's there." She quivered like a hunting dog.

"Evols?"

"No, someone alive."

I set the barrow handles down and took a slow look around without being obvious about it. Else's senses were just another odd trait she had. If she somehow made it past her thirty-day life span, I wouldn't be surprised if she learned to read minds. We stood there, in the middle of the street, for a long minute.

"Lizzy? Or Harris?" I couldn't see any sign of anyone.

"No . . ." Else drew her sword. It glinted in the sun. She held it in a casual way, pointing off to one side, tip to the ground.

With a sudden whirring noise, kids on bicycles came at us from all directions. They were shirtless, filthy and bone thin. I stood there with my mouth open. "What the hell . . . ?" Each had little more than pants made from cast-off clothing. They wore helmets and masks made of grass, animal skulls, and bits of plastic.

Else watched them come, her sword ready but waiting to see what I did. "Don't move Else, we'll see what they want."

The worn rear tires of their bikes slid to a halt in front of us, a nicely synchronized power slide that raised dust and looked cool. None of them could have been over fifteen years old and most were younger. They dropped their bikes and jabbed at us with rough blades of sharpened metal beaten into crude sword shapes. Each homemade sword carried a jagged edge that could tear through flesh, living or dead, with ease.

"Hi," I said with my arms gently raised to chest height and a friendly grin on my face. One of the older kids with a dried carcass of a hawk woven into his bike helmet and a big sword got in my face.

"Whaddya doin' here? This is our place right?!"

"Sure," I smiled and nodded. "Your place right."

We weren't going to walk away from this one, these kids were wired. In the back row they crouched down in the dust and hopped from foot to foot. A gleeful chant of "Hawk-Head! Hawk-Head! Hawk-Head!" started, low and menacing. Those squatting down started drumming on the ground with cupped hands, the rest started fidgeting and dancing.

"We'd best move on then." I started to walk and was immediately blocked by Hawk-Head's buddies and their crude swords.

"Our place! Our stuff!" Hawk-Head barked, his voice breaking and going shrill.

"Your place, your stuff, I get it. Okay. No problem." My jaw was beginning to ache from the constant smiling. I tried not to blink when a scream ripped through the town air. Lizzy. Shit, had they gotten her too? The chant grew louder, each beat of those drumming hands adding authority to Hawk-Head. Each voice pushing him up, making him a big man. Telling him to do something really impressive, give them a reason to keep chanting his name.

Four boys dragged Lizzy out into the street. She kicked,swore, and clawed at them. A younger boy ran ahead, blowing across an open bottle, adding a dirge-like tone to the drumming rhythm of the group. They pushed Lizzy to her knees in front of Hawk-Head and the crowd went into a frenzy, leaping and shouting, slapping their chests and thighs. Hawk-Head stared at the girl at his feet and then raised his hands high, cutting the noise off like a switch.

"Our place! Our stuff!" he shouted and they roared their assent in shrill and cracking voices. I remember seeing a nature documentary years ago about hyenas. Half dog, half demon. Those animals scavenged the dead and the weak on the plains of Africa. These kids were hyenas.

Pushing us back, the howling crowd shed their few scraps of clothing. Naked, they surged forward and tore at Lizzy's clothes. We couldn't see what was happening but we could hear her screams. Hawk-Head stood above it all, bare arsed, erect, and panting with excitement as he watched his boys crawl, licking and writhing, over the helpless, shrieking girl.

"No! No, hey, leave her alone!" I reached out and grabbed the nearest kid, lifting him off his feet as I pulled him back from the pile. His teeth were stained with blood and he was chewing something. I stared in horror and then got stuck in and dragged them off until I could see Lizzy. Else stabbed at the ones who tried to get back in.

They'd stripped and bitten her. Face, arms, breasts, and legs mostly. Their teeth had torn her flesh. She was a rash of half-circle purple bruises, deep bites and thickly seeping blood. Thick smears of cum glistened on her belly and thighs. I smashed my fist in some giggling brat's bloodstained face and helped Lizzy to her feet.

She shuddered with wracking sobs and tears streaked the dust on her skin. The kids hung back, jeering silently with their eyes, some of them openly jerking themselves off in a distracted way.

"We are leaving. Okay?" I spoke to Hawk-Head, ignoring his little gang of rapist-cannibal monsters.

"Fuck you." Hawk-Head moved fast. The beaten metal cutlass he carried whistled through the air and caught Lizzy in the side of the head, burying itself in her face with a sound like an axe going into wood. She sighed and collapsed into dead weight as I caught and laid her down. Else didn't move.

"You little fucking shit!" I ripped the heavy blade from Lizzy's skull and came up with it in my hands. I screamed at them and started hacking. Hawk-Head tried to get away but tripped over his cohort. I sliced a long gash down his bare back and he screamed louder and higher than Lizzy.

"Fuckers!" Else joined in and we started killing.

Kids screamed. Shit and piss ran out of them in stinking rivers and in a few seconds the survivors had bolted. A boy of maybe twelve lay writhing and screaming among the dead and the dirt. Blood didn't just ooze through the fingers clenched against his leg, it jetted. I kicked him aside and found Hawk-Head trying to crawl away. I turned him on his back and knelt down, my knee pressing down on his chest.

"Her name was Lizzy. She has a mother and a father and a brother. She just wanted to get away from all of this!" I gestured at the sky and put the jagged point of the bloodstained steel to Hawk-Head's gut. Bloody spit bubbled through teeth clenched in agony as he whined, "Missah, I'm hurt. Help me . . . pleassse . . ."

"There is no help. Not for you. Not for any of us. We're all just doing what we can to survive." I felt cold. I'd plunged into the icy river of shock and come out the other side. Dived into dark waters only to emerge into some dark and barren place where the voice of reason was lost on the wind. I stood up pressing my weight down on the blade, feeling the serrated edge slice through the boy's heaving flesh until it stopped against the ground. Hawk-Head's back arched, his yellow teeth bared as he screamed in agony. With a wordless cry I twisted the wide blade, tearing him inside. The acrid stink of ruptured bowel filled the air.

I cried in fury at the silent houses. The flies came to the feast and I watched numbly as Else casually lopped off the corpses' heads.

"We should get back to the train. Harris will want his stuff," Else said and I nodded.

"Yeah sure, let's go." We left the bodies to rot. We had no

tools to bury them with, and the ground had dried to stone.

CHAPTER 21

The train steamed gently in the baking heat of the afternoon. The idea of climbing aboard and driving on almost made me puke. Every time I closed my eyes I saw visions of Lizzy. I could still taste her on my tongue and see her blood on my hands. Else set the wheelbarrow down and frowned. "Where is everyone?"

"Harris? Gordon?" I drew the shotgun. Only two shots left, I reminded myself. One for Else, and one for me. If it came to that could I take her life? Or my own?

Else bounded up to the train and yanked the door open. Harris lurched around and Else squealed, fallingback onto the platform. Harris stumbled against the door reaching for her.

"Harris . . . ?" I stood dumbstruck as Harris waved his dead arm, blindly exploring the space where Else had stood a moment before.

Else rolled to her feet; the long katana she carried slid from its sheath and she stood calm and ready.

"How the . . . ? There are no evols here. What the hell happened?"

"I have to kill him right? I have to do it?" Else stood ready but waiting for my confirmation. Harris' dead eyes focused on her and he half stepped, half fell onto the platform.

"Goddamnit! What happened!?" I demanded. Harris snorted and lurched in my direction.

"I'm sorry, I'm sorry." Else swung her sword. Congealed blood burst and dribbled from Harris' neck. She chopped at him again and he collapsed, his bloodstained beard painting a trail in the red dust as his head rolled to my feet. The eyes blinked and then went dull.

Else killed zombies with a passion, but killing one that she knew as a living, laughing human shook her to the core. She sank to her knees, vomiting and retching, the sword dropping with a clang on the station platform.

"Nugghh more, no more," she mumbled, spitting and wiping her mouth.

"First time killing a friend is always the hardest. We call that puking," I added helpfully.

"Don't like it," Else groaned. A scuffling sound behind me brought me to my feet. The snatched sword flashed in my hands. Gordon cowered, a dark piss stain spreading over his pants.

"Mamaaa . . ." he wailed. I lowered the sword.

"Fuck, Gordon, where were you? What happened to Harris?" I lowered the sword.

"Fell down! Fell down!" Gordon wailed and rocked.

"Harris had a heart attack or something? Is that what happened, Gordon?" I got in his face, demanding an explanation. Gordon cowered lower, hands coming up to cover his eyes, fingers waving like pale tentacles.

"Don't yell at Gordon. Don't yell at Gordon," he repeated until I patted him gently on the shoulder.

"It's alright, mate, not your fault. Just freaked me out is all. She'll be right."

"Want Lizzy. Wanna go home. Wanna go home! Maamaaaahh!" Gordon rocked back and forth, his fingers dancing against his face.

I stepped back, unsure how to explain Lizzy's absence to him. "Lizzy's gone, mate. She's gonna come along later. We have to get on the train now. We have to get on the train and go."

Gordon wailed again, his voice high and wavering, strangely childlike for such a big man. Else gathered herself up and came to investigate the noise.

"Make him shut up. Make him shut up," she insisted. I waved her down.

"Come one, Gordon, back to the train, mate," I coaxed and pleaded, speaking gently to him like a frightened animal. Gordon just dug in his heels and squatted down, covering his ears and drumming his fingertips on his temples.

"Evols are coming," Else announced and took the sword back from me.

"What?" I sprang up and scanned the nearby streets and open desert. The dead were coming towards us through the scrub and saltbush, a ragged crowd of dusty shufflers slowly turning towards the noise.

"It's that mob that carried us away from Port Germein. They're coming." I didn't argue with her. Else has a nose for zombies.

"We have to go now." Else darted back to the train and then returned. "Now!"

"Gordon! Come on!" I may as well have been tugging on a tree.

"Lizzy . . ." he moaned.

"Fuck. Fuck. Fuck." I let Gordon go. He immediately curled up in a fetal position, shuddering and moaning. Resisting the urge to kick the hell out of the intellectually handicapped, I paced up and down.

Up on the platform I could see the approaching zombies spread out across a wide horizon. We were out of time.

"Come on, Gordon, come on. Please mate. Please. Just get up and come on the train. Come on, mate, we're going on a train ride. You like to ride the train, doncha?"

Gordon wailed and shuddered. His massive hands blocked his ears, and his crying drowned me out. I had a sickening realization that he was going to be left behind.

"Now!" screamed Else from the train. I backed away from Gordon about to start shrieking myself.

"For fuck's sake, Gordon! Get up willya! You stay here you will die!"

Gordon grizzled in long lip-buzzing cries. Rivers of mucous streamed from his nose and bubbled on his lips. I took his hand and made a last attempt to pull him off the ground. The hungry moans of the approaching evols drowned out Else's shouts for me to hurry the fuck up. Gordon's hand slipped from my grasp and I fell back. I scrambled to my feet, my breath coming in panicked gasps. The stench of the long dead clouded the air with a foul haze. I ran for the train as the zombies reached it and started finding their way around the engine.

Ragged walkers, their skin peeling off in strips like old wallpaper. The more recently dead, or at least more recently feral, with clearer skin and less postmortem injuries. They moved with more purpose, their eyes still clear enough to see everything. Dead teeth bared and black tongues lolled. Strings of thick saliva stretched like tendons in their jaws. They all homed in on me. I drew the shotgun and smashed the butt into the side of a dead man's head. His skull cracked and black pus oozed out like a fancy chocolate with a crème center.

They tore at me with cracked hands, and as I jerked away from one, I stepped into the grasp of two more. I used the gun like a club, smashing and sweeping a space around me. They found Gordon and I heard him die, screaming for his mother until his voice cracked or the dead tore his chest open and ate his lungs.

There was no way these evols wanted to carry us away. These ones were hungry, blinded by a single driving need. They would tear us into bloody rags and gnaw on our bones.

Steel flashed and a head rolled. Else wielded her blade with a blinding speed. She overswung each time, but never missed.

I pushed through the last crowded yards of rotting flesh. I almost lost my grip on the shotgun, holding it aloft in one fist as I punched deep into a zombie girl's swollen belly. The taut flesh burst, thick grey slime and a slurry of necrotic organs spilled out at my feet. I knocked her back and as I stepped forward my boot crushed something in the gore that writhed and hissed.

Else backed up, fighting a retreat. She got to the train a few steps ahead of me, reached out, and pulled me into the engine cab. I yanked the steel door shut behind us against a forest of scrabbling hands and then stared helplessly at the wall of dials and levers. "I . . . don't know how to drive a fucking train." I pressed my fists to my forehead. "Shit, shit shit."

A chunk of wood hit me in the shoulder. "This goes in the fire," Else said, throwing more wood at me as she dug into the pile stacked in the tender like a dog on the scent of a rabbit.

I cracked the firebox open and soon a blaze was roaring. More evols were crawling out of the desert and over the train. Drawn by the noise and the motion, they came on—a legion of desiccated and broken corpses that walked and crawled, summoned by an insatiable need to make us like them. We made fire until the gauges in front of me were pulsing into the red.

"One of these levers. I'm sure it's one of these levers." I waved my hands over the mechanical arms in front of me. Nothing was labeled. Else shoved past me and pulled something. With a shuddering jerk, the train moved forward. She pulled on something else and the motion smoothed out. We started rolling down the track.

"You didn't learn that from a bloody book!" I grinned at Else over the noise.

"I watched Harris. He does the same thing every time." Else shrugged like it was obvious. I laughed again and hugged her. She gripped me as if she never wanted to let go. I stared back down the track, trying not to think about Harris, Lizzy, and poor, fucking fucking Gordon.

CHAPTER 22

The train rolled on, through the ember glow of sunset and into the night. The evols clinging to the train fell away. Those that managed to get close enough to reach at us through the heavy wire got a sword point through the head.

I sat with my back to the tender, trying to get comfortable against the wood and other burnable shit that kept the firebox sizzling.

Dreams are not something I remember often. At best I awaken with a vague sense of disquiet, an unease that fades as quickly as the vague details of the dream. That afternoon, with my back pressed against sharp corners of wood and hurtling down an unknown railway line with a girl less than three weeks old at the controls, I slept and I dreamed.

I dreamed of a cave made of flesh. A living cathedral that pulsed and writhed. I floated, or flew as you do in dreams, over a writhing landscape of half-formed or half-digested corpses that wallowed within the dark gunk and slime.

Ahead of me in the dim light I could make out something vast and tumorous in the gigantic shape of a terrible disease-ravaged heart. It hung suspended on great cables of pulsing flesh. Tentacles of grey intestinal color and shape waved and caressed the surface. These tendrils of dead flesh probed and tasted the air in a sickening parody of life. I could sense none of the warmth of life here; just this vast and horrific thing, throbbing and swollen with a black, stinking fluid that previously I had only seen oozing from the dead. Within the great cocoon there was no human shape, only a perfect alienness. My senses told me that this thing was utterly, perfectly wrong. In my dream I flew closer to it, unable to close my eyes until the squirming landscape filled my vision. In the final moment before impact the entire shape shuddered and the rank flesh split, parted, and lifted. An immense eye rolled yellow and bloodshot with black veins to fix its focus on me. I screamed and the million mouths of the corpses ensnared in the web of the cathedral's flesh whispered my name.

Else slapped me a second time. The blow shook my tongue loose from where it had cemented itself to the roof of my mouth.

"Gagh," I said, raising my hands to avoid another head-spinner.

"You made a loud noise. I didn't like it," she said, crouching down and peering carefully into my face.

"Bad dream," I muttered. "We're slowing down?" I pulled myself to my feet, feeling the train's motion changing.

"Town ahead. One with lights and everything." Else leaned past me as I stared out the narrow front window.

"How long was I asleep for?"

Else shrugged. "Long time."

"Any trouble?"

She gave me a withering look. "You had more trouble sleeping than I did getting us here."

"You shoulda woken me," I said. "You need to get some sleep too." Else shrugged. I caught a flicker of unpleasant emotion on her face.

"You don't like to sleep?"

"Gotta keep the train going. It's what Harris would do."

"Yeah, but Harris liked to sleep too. Are you having bad dreams, Else?" She wouldn't look me in the eye.

"Gotta stop the train." She shouldered me aside and heaved on a lever. The train snorted steam and the wheels locked and sparked. We slowly ground to a halt, the hot metal all around us ticking, the boiler valves hissing. Only the desert was quiet.

I cracked the door open and stepped down. Lights from a single house winked at us from nearby. I walked down to the front of the engine and stretched. Nobody and nothing could be seen in the emptiness around us.

"Did you love her?" Else said at my back, making me jump.

"Did I love who?"

"Lizzy." Else scraped a booted foot in the red sand.

"Nope." I couldn't get my head around why Lizzy bugged her so much. Else's stupid notion of wanting to have a baby and this fiery jealousy she had. I hoped we would both live long enough to work out what she was thinking.

"You can't love her anyway. She's dead." Else kicked a small stone.

"Do you know how far we are from Sydney?" I asked. Else shook her head.

"Over a thousand miles would be my guess. My life in the city was shit. But I did okay. Yet here I am, in the middle of fucking nowhere, with you."

Else glanced up, a flicker of uncertainty showing in her eyes. "Why did we come out here?"

"Like I told you, there are men out here. Really smart guys who can help us make sure you get to live as long as you want."

"If I live long enough, can I have babies?"

I sighed. "Sure, you can live long enough to learn enough to do whatever you want."

"How long is that?"

"Harris was old. Harris was really old. You could live long enough to be older than him."

"When I die, will you stop me coming back?"

I shivered in the stifling heat of the desert evening. "Yes. I will put you down because I will know it isn't you that gets back up again. It will be some empty, hungry thing. Everything that is you will be gone. Only a dead body will be left and that I will lay to rest." In the back of my mind faces rose unbidden. Those I'd cared about in the past, during the Panic and the plague. The ones who taught me that when they came back they were not mine to love any more.

Else tackled me in a bear hug. "You have to stay with me until I die, older than Harris, no one else. Just you."

"Always." I hugged her and scanned the horizon. No advancing line of evols. Maybe, finally we had gone beyond their determined reach.

"We should check out those houses. See if anyone's home."

Else hesitated and then pulled away. "Sure," she nodded and casually checked her sword was in place on her back.

We walked the short distance up the track to the first lights—a house surrounded by a stand of stubborn trees and a cluster of low shrubs pushed together in what could have been mistaken for a garden. Solar power generator panels on the roof gleamed in the moonlight. A dog started barking before we reached the gate. Else shrank back, her blade sliding half out of the scabbard.

"Best we wait here I reckon. Anyone home will come and check out the noise," I said. "Hello the house!" I called. "Just passing through. We're friends of Harris, the train driver."

"Where is Harris?" A voice in the darkness with a thick Greek accent. Somewhere by the trees, well beyond the reach of the house lights.

"He had a heart attack. He died peacefully and we were sorry to lose him. He was a nice guy."

"Did you bury him?" This wasn't the question I expected next. "No. No we didn't bury him. We didn't have time. A mob of evols came on us and we'd just gotten over putting Harris back down."

"There's no evols out here. That's a city problem. Where are you buggers from?"

"Sydney," I said into the darkness.

"Syd—?" A scuffling sound came from the darkness. A man came into view, struggling to pull off his harness of weapons. Knives, an axe, a heavy pistol, hunting bow and a quiver of brightly fletched metal-shafted arrows.

"I gotta cousin lives in Sydney. Maybe you know her?"

Silhouetted by the sickly glow of light from the house, he looked soft for someone living in a post-apocalyptic world, almost flabby.

"What's her name?"

"Julie. Julie Giannopoulos." His face glowed with a wet sheen and he actually looked hopeful.

"Don't know any Julies, sorry. I knew a Sarah once."

He looked thoughtful, scratching his swarthy, unshaven face with a soft hand. "Nah, I'm pretty sure her name was Julie." With a sudden smile he hurried to the gate and opened it. "Come on in, you must be hungry, thirsty, or tired. Probably all three, eh?"

"This is Else." I let her go first into the well-kept yard with its dry, rock-bordered garden.

"I am Leandro, you are welcome to my home." He opened his arms in greeting.

"Thanks, Leandro. How you all doing out here?" We followed him up the short path to the front door. A large dog went berserk behind a heavy screen door at the sound of our footsteps.

"Ulysses! Stamata!" The dog went still and I could hear his claws clicking as he padded around.

"In these times, a good guard dog is essential, no?" Leandro said with an apologetic smile.

"Must be hard to feed an animal that size these days," I replied. We were shown into a kitchen that shone with a polished neatness under the yellow glow of a chandelier of hurricane lanterns.

"Please sit, my table is yours." Leandro closed and locked the screen door; the bars on it were as thick as the grill welded over Harris' train.

"Serious door you have there, Leandro," I said, moving a chair to sit back from the table.

"Yes, well there are some rough people out there. Many come here thinking they can simply take what they want." Leandro fed wood into an old coal range firebox and oven and slid a kettle of water onto the hot plate.

"With the dog and that door you are well defended,"

Else piped up.

"Perhaps . . . perhaps. But enough of the woes of the world. We eat now." He left us waiting in the kitchen, returning a few minutes later with a fresh hunk of white-pink meat on the bone.

"I been hanging this in the cool room for a few days. Meat always tastes better when it has time to mature."

Sitting still for too long makes me nervous, strange places make me nervous, and a fat man in a time of famine . . . I stood up and covered it by stretching.

"What's on the menu?" I asked our host.

"Ahh is something special, you will like I think yes?" He had a sweat on. The heat from the day was still stifling inside and out and the oven didn't make things any less tropical, yet Leandro had been cool as a cucumber a few minutes ago. I watched him dress the meat, season it, and then slip the prepared roast into the coal range oven and slam the heavy door.

"I just go and put this back, for next time," he beamed, nodding and hurrying out of the room with the rest of the meat.

"Hear that?" said Else, rising up like a dog on point.

"It's just the dog."

"No, there's something else." She drew the sword and pointed with it deeper into the house. I listened, senses straining for the usual sounds of evols and got nothing.

We opened the kitchen door. A dark hallway ran to the back of the place, ending in a secure backdoor. Shadows recoiled from the light at our backs. I took a lantern and, holding it high, I followed Else into the passage.

The girl reached back and put a hand on my face, shushing me before I could say anything. "There," she whispered, nodding towards a door on our right. I could hear it now too; a shuffling sound and a muffled groan.

"Evols?" I whispered.

"Smells like something different." Else turned the blade, holding it in a position ready to strike and kill. I felt a cold shudder of real fear rising up my spine. Cannibals. You hear stories, but I'd never met anyone who knew of a real one. Or at least no one who had survived to talk about it. How to explain to Else that there are people who eat other people did not seem as important right now as, say, survival.

"We need to get out of here. Right—" I froze as something heavy thudded against the door and we heard a muffled scream. "Don't!" Else ignored my protest and twisted the door handle. With a hard shove she forced the door open. A sinus-burning stench of shit and moldering furnishings washed through the gap. A figure lunged at us from the room. Else gave a squeal and fell backwards as something huge barged through the door and, with a snuffling grunt, a wet pig's snout rummaged into the crotch of my jeans.

"Pigs? Pigs . . . It's okay Else, it's just pigs." I turned around, almost laughing. Else stood in the doorway opposite. I couldn't see the guy holding her, but his hand was clamped over her mouth and a wide-bladed skinning knife pricked at her throat.

"Easy pal," I raised my hands. It wasn't Leandro. This guy's arms were milk pale, lean and corded. I could see a flash of blond hair moving behind Else's bulging eyes.

"Who the fuck are you!?" His voice was high and shrill, like a girl's.

"Leandro invited us in. We came up on the train, with Harris."

"You're infected!" the guy screamed with hysterical tears in his voice.

"No, we're fine. No one's sick."

The front door opened and Leandro came bustling into the kitchen carrying a wilted selection of vegetables. He saw us standing in the hallway and dropped the lot. "No, Stefan! They are guests!" Leandro hurried forward and the blond man pushed Else away unharmed.

"They are infected!" Stefan screamed at Leandro, who raised his hands in a placating gesture.

"No my love, they are friends. Friends who bring news of the world beyond Port Germein. Come out of your room, eat with us. It is safe."

Stefan hesitated and then slammed the bedroom door in Leandro's face. He stood there for a moment, his shoulders slumping in defeat. "Forgive him. These difficult times have taken their toll on his heart." I nodded, not sure what I could say.

"Priscilla, my darling, you have escaped. Back in your room. It is time for you to sleep and tomorrow you can play. Shoo now." Leandro clapped his hands at the large sow who seemed intent on forcing her way into the crowded hall.

"She loves to play, and we recently butchered one of her brothers. She misses him."

"Pork is on the menu?" I almost laughed with relief.

"Of course," Leandro beamed. "Priscilla and her friends, they are special to me; without them we would find life here very hard. Come, back to the kitchen. We will eat and drink and then you will stay the night."

Else looked at the pig with a wary curiosity until I motioned for her to go back to the kitchen. She shrugged and with Leandro behind us, I never saw what he hit me with. But he did it right and everything went black.

CHAPTER 23

I woke up groaning. My head felt like a crushed eggshell with the yolk leaking out. I fumbled in the dark. My hands were free and I wasn't tied up.

"Else?" I mumbled.

"I'm here." She sounded like I felt.

"You okay?" I reached out and felt her leg, still intact but naked.

"They took our clothes," I said. Stating the obvious seemed to be a side effect of being knocked unconscious.

"Yes, and the dog is outside the room. I can hear it growling."

"Pigs," I said, that bad feeling coming back with a vengeance.

"Like sheep, but with flat noses and they have no hair," Else said from the darkness.

"Yes, but sheep only eat grass. Pigs eat anything. They're going to feed us to the pigs. I don't know if that makes them cannibals or not."

"It makes them fucking dead," Else growled.

"Maybe." My eyes adjusted to the gloom and I could see we were in a bedroom, no furniture and the same heavy grills on the windows, with boards on the outside. We'd been out most of the night, the orange glow of dawn now turning the air in the room grey.

I'd barely seen Else naked since the day we met, and even then she'd been wrapped in a plastic sheet and fighting for her life against hungry zombies. She didn't know to be self-conscious or modest, and as I blinked the haze away from my eyes she regarded me with raised eyebrows.

"Does that hurt?"

"Huh? Oh." I cupped my hands over my crotch. "Uhh, no." I could feel a red heat climbing my cheeks.

Else stood up, walked over, and bent down. Pulling at my hands she said, "I want to see. What is it?"

"It's just me," I said pulling away.

"It doesn't look like that when you pee out of it. Is it broken?"

"No, it's not broken." For a smart girl Else was really dumb sometimes.

She slid a hand down between her thighs and a sudden light went on in her eyes.

"It goes in here!" she grinned.

"Who told you? How do you know that?" I scanned the room and grabbed a blanket from the corner. I wrapped it round myself and thought hard about being eaten alive by pigs until my boner vanished.

"The girls at the convent had a magazine. With pictures of men and women in it. Putting those things in here," she gestured between her legs again. "It's naughty," she added with grave authority.

"Uh-huh." I tried the door handle; it wasn't locked. How stupid were these people? I cracked the door open and peeked out. Leandro's dog, Ulysses threw itself at my face, snarling and slavering. The foul, hot stink of its breath blasted over me as the beast crashed against the door, scratching and snapping. I leaned against the door and got it closed again. The sound of Ulysses pounding against the wood echoed in the room.

I motioned for Else to move. "Get behind me." She got into position and I took a deep breath before throwing the door wide open.

The dog leapt for my throat. I grabbed its front legs and jerked them apart, slamming us together like we were dancing a tango. His jaws snapped, drool splashing on my face as the crack of his ribs splintering twisted his snarl into a howl of agony. Long shards of bone drove deep into the dog's heart, killing him instantly. I dropped the twitching corpse and leaned against the doorframe panting in terror.

Else peered around the door and then stared at the dead dog. "We should go now, before Leandro finds out you hurt his dog."

"Yeah, good idea." I led Else up the hallway, my head still pounding from the adrenaline and the bashing that Greek prick gave it the night before.

The kitchen stood empty and the back door was locked. Our clothes had been neatly folded and left on a chair. Else's sword and our other weapons were stacked beside them. We dressed and I thought about creeping into Stefan's room and leaving Leandro a surprise for when he got home.

"We have to find another way out," I whispered to Else. She nodded and we crept back down the hall. I tried the door handle to Stefan's bedroom and it opened. The room stank with a dense, cloying reek and it took me a moment to realize it was the smell of air-freshener. I hadn't smelt anything like that in years. Else put a hand to her face and made muffled gagging noises.

The heavy curtains nailed over the windows kept the room nearly dark. In the dim light shining in from the hallway I could see hundreds of car air-fresheners hanging from the ceiling. Cans of sanitizing spray were stacked neatly against the walls. In one corner stood a dressing table with a large mirror, dead candles, and cases of colored makeup. A collection of various dresses and costumes hung from a string across another corner of the room.

Stefan liked to play dress-up. A large bed, draped with clear plastic sheeting and silk ribbons, stood in the center of the room, an isolated island of happy quarantine forever safe from the horrors that existed outside. The two men lay curled around each other on the bed, sleeping soundly, Leandro's dark and hairy belly rising and falling against Stefan's slim and pale boyish frame.

Leandro's clothes were draped over a chair, along with

his weapons. I searched the pockets, looking for the house keys and came up empty. Shaking my head at Else I moved around the room, searching for the damned keys. Else tore the sheeting back, exposing Stefan to the open air. He woke up screaming, clawing his way up the headboard as Leandro gave a snort like one of his pigs.

"Open the fucking door to outside!" Else threatened Stefan with the point of the katana. He wailed and pressed himself up against the wall, eyes closed and screaming red-faced in terror. Leandro rolled to his feet. I snatched up his pistol, cocked it at his head, and he froze, half off the bed.

"We are leaving," I said. "You can either open the door, or I can blow your head off and then feed you and your boyfriend to the pigs."

"Is no problem, no problem." Leandro showed his hands. "I open up for you, is no problem." He moved slowly, hands spread wide. I stepped back, gesturing him out of the room.

"Stefan! Shut the fuck up!" I yelled and he went silent. I thought Else might have killed him, but he'd gone white with shock and slumped down against the silk pillows.

"Else, let's go." We followed Leandro out to the kitchen. He took a key out of an old sugar container and with trembling hands opened the door. An evol loomed, dark against the bright morning sunlight, and ripped out the Greek's throat, spraying hot blood up the wall and spinning him round. Leandro gurgled and clawed at us as he sank to the floor. Else snarled and swung, her blade splitting the first zombie's head down to the neck.

I fired Leandro's pistol, bursting a dead woman's head. I fired again, yelling, "We gotta shut the door!"

Else stepped forward, hacking and slashing. Bodies fell in twitching lumps before us. I crashed against the door, using it as a shield against the mass of rotting meat pressing their way into the house.

A corpse burst, spilling foul entrails around our feet. Black putrescent juices sprayed as I crushed the squirming dead in the door until it clicked shut. Fumbling with the key, I locked it and backed away. Else growled at the shadows moving on the other side of the barred window.

"Out the other side, let's go." I led the way down the hall and paused at the back door. Cracking open the curtain that hung across the wood and stained-glass panel, I saw more evols shuffling around in the vegetable garden dirt between us and the tree-line fence.

"Can't go out that way." We both jumped when the pig-room door thudded. We were covered in gore, and the stench of meat hung thick in the air. I guess the hogs were hungry and getting restless. "Okay this is what we are going to do," I said, lowering my voice and pulling Else into a huddle.

I explained the plan to her twice. The first time she flatly refused to do what I asked. I told her if she didn't, we were going to die here.

Else took up her position in the kitchen next to the back door, her hand on the key. She nodded at me up the hall and I took a deep breath.

"Sook! Sook! Sook!" I yelled, a half-remembered pig-feeding call from summers spent on my grandparents' farm as a kid. The pigs in the room must have spent summer vacations on a farm too because they immediately went nuts, squealing and charging against the door. I mentally counted to three and then pushed the door open. The pigs pushing the other way made it hard, but they soon realized that the door opening meant food and backed up. I shoved the door open and leapt back as four of the biggest pigs I've ever seen charged at me. I turned and ran, yelling at Else to wait.

The pigs shrieked and fought their way through the door that was barely wide enough to fit one of them. They exploded into the kitchen and I leapt onto the table yelling. "Now!"

Else twisted the key and opened the back door. The pigs went straight for the spilled guts. One of them ran under the table I was crouched on and lifted the entire thing on its back. The stampeding hogs bulldozed their way into the evols milling about on the back porch. The kitchen table ran aground on the doorframe and the pig shot out from underneath it, squealing in outrage.

"Let's go!" I yelled. I leapt through the gap and Else jumped over the table behind me. We sprinted across the open veranda and into the yard. Behind us the pigs were feeding on the dead. Some of the zombies were struggling to fight back, but these pigs were frenzied with hunger and meat was back on the menu.

The wind had picked up; a dry, dust-laden storm was brewing, sending grit and sand to scour our skin. We ran around the house and out on to the road, where we turned west. Zombies were scattered around Leandro's house and more were milling about the train. We heard a shrill screaming from inside that could have been Stefan, but I never looked back. I pointed out a faded sign that said "PIMBA" as we jogged past, then another that said "WOOMERA 8KM" and an arrow pointing north on the road to our right. The burned-out shell of a building, probably a truck stop, marked the land to our left, corrugated iron banging in the wind like a dinner bell for the dead. I kept running, glancing back and being reassured that no shufflers were following. Else just loped along beside me, barely panting.

We stopped when it got too hot to breathe. My chest ached, and sweat stung my eyes. I wiped my face on my shirt and gave Else a sick grin. "Touch and go there for a bit I reckon, eh!?" I shouted over the wind.

Else nodded, looking over her shoulder. She seemed concerned that I had chosen now to stop running.

"What about the train?" she said.

"Pimba," I replied, waving a hand at the sign behind us. "Woomera," I waved in the other direction. "Walking, maybe take us an hour to get there."

"That means it'll take them about an hour too," Else said and set off up the road. I followed her. The sun pounded down on us; through the swirling dust clouds, it sucked the moisture out of my skin and mouth until even my eyes felt like they were filled with grit.

"Slow down, Else, you'll get heat stroke."

She turned without breaking her stride, said something I didn't catch, took two steps backwards, and then collapsed.

I didn't scream, didn't have the wind for it. But my throat choked up and I whined, a shrill sound of shock. Else wasn't moving. I fell beside her, pulling her up into my lap, cradling her head and feeling for a pulse. It was there, but it felt weird.

"C'mon Else, c'mon girl. Just a little further." Her eyes were half open, but the tiny delta of blood vessels across them had turned grey and her breathing was a shallow wheeze.

I didn't cry; there was no water left for tears. Instead I picked her up, carrying her in my arms like a child. I had never carried anyone this way before. The last thing you did was hold someone near death close to you. She was a complete deadweight but I didn't care. Together we were going to finish this journey, and if she died and turned then she could take me too. I'd had enough.

I stumbled on up the road in the dust and the wind. My lungs burned with a deep fire fueled by the ache in my arms and legs. Black spots danced in front of my eyes, clouds of grit and shimmering visions of silver flickered. With a roaring sound a deformed figure came up behind us, emerging out of the dust storm. Grey faced, with large black eyes, blank and alien. Its face was featureless, except for a bag-like jaw. I stumbled, my legs said fuck it, and I fell down. From my knees I watched the creature become a man wearing round, tinted goggles with a cloth wrapped around his face. Behind him an old white pickup emerged from the dust cloud. I heard other voices, guns were waved around, and then hands were lifting Else, carrying her away from me. I croaked and struggled, but they lifted me too. Laying us down in the back of the truck, we were covered with a tarpaulin and the wind cracked the heavy plastic like a whip.

CHAPTER 24

The wind-driven dust swirled like a reddish sea fog, and they kept the tarp over us as we hurtled up the road towards Woomera. I quit struggling when a boot pressed down on my chest and a gruff voice told me to lie still or they would toss me out. We skidded to a halt a few minutes later and I could hear the wind and the moans of the dead. Even out here, even in the place that I had finally allowed myself to believe might be a sanctuary, the dead still ruled. The boot lifted and I shuffled backwards. Pulling myself up into a sitting position, I took stock.

Three people, wrapped in ragged, dust-shielding cloth and carrying M16 automatic rifles, stood staring into the desert. I stood up, leaning against the back window of the truck's cab. I saw a familiar scene—the grey pulsating mass of a couple hundred zombies clawing at the fences and barricades of an island of humanity.

One of our captors turned around and, field glasses hanging from his neck, walked back to the pickup and lifted a dust-stained water bag from the front grill.

"Thirsty?" His accent was American.

I nodded and took the bag. The water tasted dirty, but it was wet. I drank more than my share and gasped for breath when I lowered the bag.

The other two observing the mob at the fence ahead of us came trotting back through the swirling dust storm.

"The signal light is flashing. Let's go!" They piled back

on board and the driver gunned the engine, sending us racing up the trail as the road ahead dissolved under the shifting sand. The madman behind the wheel kept us on the hard-packed dirt, or the remains of the asphalt under the drifting grit.

I couldn't see shit, my eyes gumming shut from dust. A plume of orange flame erupted ahead of us. I flinched and ducked. Staring forward through the windshield I could see gouts of flame pouring down from sentry towers along the fence line. Long pipe flamethrowers vomited thick burning oil down over the zombies crowding the fence. The blazing flow immolated the dead; they hissed and sizzled, skin crackling, their eyeballs swelling until they burst.

At the end of the road, heavy armored gates with dozer blades scraping the ground shuddered to life and began to open.

I saw a moment later that the gates were bulldozers, a pair of them, with welded plates armoring the driver's seat. In a lumbering ballet they turned outward in a synchronized fashion, each one pushing corpses back as the racing truck bore down on the slowly widening gap between the two gates.

At breakneck speed a tire blew on the pickup; the truck leapt like a dolphin and we twisted in the air. I fell hard, sliding in the loose sand as the vehicle crashed down, crushing the cab like a tin can. I crawled to my feet. Else lay facedown in the dust on the other side of the track. Evols stumbled away from the fiery onslaught and a man with half his face burned away shuffled towards her.

"Hey, arsehole!" I ran towards the zombie, waving my hands. He moaned and lurched, trying to see me through eyes that had melted down his face like ice cream. I snatched up a rock as I ran and slammed it into the evol's face. With a wet, crunching sound he went down. I followed the dead man to the ground, hitting him until his skull was a wet smear in the dirt. The driver had been killed in the crash, the other two were thrown clear. One staggered to his feet as I gathered Else up. "Hey!" I yelled. "Help me here!" He turned and stumbled towards us.

Evols were being ground to paste under the dozer tracks, some losing limbs, thrashing and reaching up from the ground, open mouthed and moaning. Fire sprayed out from the gate towers, burning more zombies and adding to the chaos. I stood with Else in my arms and the rock in my hand, ready to fight off the dead. Over the roar of burning oil and crackling of burning flesh I could hear the shouts of those inside the fence. Through the black and swirling smoke, men in faded khaki fatigues ran out to the wreck. They wore a mix of gas masks, grime-stained bandanas across their faces, goggles and sunglasses over their eyes. All favored a buzz-cut hair style.

With military precision the squad of seven fanned out. Four men dropped to one knee and covered the other three. Rifles came up and a steady smattering of gunshots rang out.

The man coming towards us off the back of the pickup reached up and yanked his cloth mask away. His mouth split open in a yawning moan. Blood, already turning black, drooled from his mouth. Behind those dark goggles his eyes would be clouding up and his brain was focusing on the new hunger that would drive him on until it was destroyed. I let Else slide to the ground at my feet and stepped over her still form. I swung my rock at the dead man's head. The zombie's arm came up and caught my fist. I twisted free and punched an uppercut to his jaw; it was my off hand so it barely staggered him. Groaning, he smashed his hands down on my shoulders, knocking me off my feet and coming down on top of me. The sudden weight pushed the wind out of my lungs with a grunt. Thick drool dripped down as his jaws opened wide. The remaining air in his lungs vibrated out of his throat in a gurgling moan. I punched and fought, tearing his goggles off and gouging out an eye that was still warm and soft with my thumb. The new zombie didn't care. He pressed down, his teeth clacking, snapping at my face. Then something hit him from behind. His good eye rolled up in his head and I pushed him aside.

The first of the soldiers to reach me aimed his automatic rifle again. "Are you bit?" he yelled from a safe distance, his voice strongly American.

"No!" I yelled back. Rolling to my feet I pulled up my shirt, turning around to let him take a good hard look. "Neither is she!"

He nodded and waved the two men behind him forward. They lifted Else and we started back towards the opening between the dozers. I ran with them.

The four men covering our retreat worked steadily and reloaded with calm professionalism. The third man from the truck hadn't made it either. The soldiers dropped him as soon as he started to crawl towards them.

As we ran past, the leader patted each of the four-man team providing covering fire on the head, and each in turn rose and jogged after us. We passed between the two dozers; they ground the gears into reverse and pulled back. Coughing and choking on the thick black smoke, gasping for breath, I dropped to the ground inside the compound. Else was dumped beside me.

Our noise and movement attracted the dead, and a thickening crowd of them came on through the smoke. The bulldozer on the left stopped moving. I stood up, yelling myself hoarse. The soldiers opened up with a volley of head shots that dropped the first six zombies with pinpoint accuracy. I ran at the machine. It was open at the back and protected at the front by a heavy steel plate, brown with rust and gore, welded to the chassis. The driver was muttering and working the starter. I clambered up behind him and snatched his M16 from its holster next to the driver's seat.

"Get out of here!" he yelled, his accent also American. I flicked the safety off and squeezed the trigger. A female zombie's skull exploded. A dead man with a dark cavity under his ribs where his gut used to sit lurched at us out of the smoke. The driver yelled and kicked out at gutless, who grabbed his boot and bit hard into his calf, growling and savaging it like a dog with a bone. The driver's voice rose to a scream as I fired again, tearing a chunk of bone and brains out of the top of the zombie's head. The rest of the soldiers reached us and we fired until the gap between the bulldozers filled with the broken corpses of the dead and the rifle in my hands clicked empty.

"Fall back! Close the second gate!" The squad leader barked his orders and the men moved quickly, dragging the wounded driver out of his seat and pushing me back with them. We abandoned the stalled dozer and they swung a high mesh gate across the empty space and sealed it with a heavy chain and padlock.

The squad leader tore the gas mask from his face and turned to the dozer driver who lay at my feet, his wound bleeding into the dirt.

A week's blond stubble, tinged with grey, framed the soldier's cold blue eyes. "Why has my secure perimeter been compromised?"

The driver grimaced. "It just died on me! It's been running like shit for weeks!"

The soldier standing over him spat a wad of yellow phlegm into the dust. "I do not need your fucking excuses. If you had not fucked up you would still be alive!"

The bulldozer driver's face, already grey with the blood loss, went white with shock. The squad leader stepped forward and shoved me aside. Drawing a pistol from his hip he fired once, blowing the wounded man's brains across the ground. No one said a word.

The flamethrowers shut down in their towers and now three more men, each black-faced with burnt oil, joined the group. The only sound was the moaning of the crowd outside the fence and the creak of the mesh being constantly tested.

As the smoke cleared I got a better look at my surroundings. The village of Woomera was littered with the rusting hulks of vehicles. Rockets and missiles of various shapes and sizes creaked in the wind on corroding metal stands—decade's worth of space and military junk, recovered from where they'd crashed in the desert and painted in their original livery, now scoured back to bare steel by wind and sand. The wrecks showed the way things used to be, when men were still masters of the world, still able to challenge the heavens and blow shit up for the sheer hell of it. In the background a grove of tall, white-shafted windmills, each topped with two massive blades, stood in the red sand, barely visible through the wind-blown dust and smoke.

I stepped around the body and checked on Else. She barely stirred when I lifted her head into my lap. The squad leader gave orders and the two men lifted the driver and dumped him by the fence. They made no effort to bury him.

"She needs a doctor!" I yelled. The squad leader spat into the dust again.

"Jenks, Madden, put them through decom and alert the fucking geeks."

Two soldiers slouched forward, slinging their rifles onto their shoulders. I staggered up, Else limp in my arms.

"This way." They also spoke with American accents, muffled by the gas masks they both wore.

I carried Else and they led us to a concrete block building with a steel door. A faded sign said "USAF/RAAF PROJECT LIBERTY." One of our escorts pushed a code into a keypad and the door clicked open. He vanished inside. I went in, maneuvering Else past the steel doorframe, and the second soldier followed, closing the door behind us.

The interior reminded me of a hospital: the same creamy green color scheme, the easy-to-clean cement walls and linoleum floor that was starting to show cracks.

"What happened to your woman?" the leading soldier asked.

"She's sick. Not bit, just sick."

"Well you came to the right place. We got a shitload of doctors around here."

"This is Woomera?"

"Indeed it is. Combined US and Australian air force operations center. The current seat of US military operations in Australia. Sergeant Thad Arbuckle commanding." We walked into a tiled shower room off the corridor. The first soldier gestured for me to stand against the wall. He unhooked a fire hose and the sudden gush of cold water knocked me off my feet. I couldn't hear the next command over the roar of the water filling my ears.

"Strip!" he bellowed again and I pulled at my sodden shirt with numb fingers. They shut the water off and stepped over us, undoing pants and boots and reducing us to bare flesh in seconds before turning the hose on again.

I covered Else, afraid she would drown in the deluge. She coughed a few times and groaned without opening her eyes. When it was over they lifted their gas masks off and clipped them onto their belts.

"Damn, Jenks," one of them grinned. "That's a fine piece of tail you've got there, mister."

"Don't touch her; you'll regret it." I felt numb with cold and bruised from the assault of water.

"You don't look like you've got the balls to stop us, man." Jenks didn't look old enough to shave. I wondered how he came to be here working as a US soldier. If that's what they actually were.

"Not me." I shook the water out of my ears and lifted Else as I got to my feet. "She on the other hand will kill you with her bare hands if you touch her."

They laughed at that, no surprise. Else lay in my arms shivering like a child with a high fever. Madden picked up the Japanese sword that Else had carried all this time and unsheathed it a few inches. "Wow, this is really cool," he said and shoved the scabbard into his belt.

"I'll need that back," I said, my eyes steady on his.

The soldier shrugged. "Sure, maybe when I'm done with it."

"Move out." Jenks pointed with his M16 and I carried Else, naked and dripping, out into the empty corridor. We walked down to a set of doors that hissed and puffed high-pressure air when they were unlocked with a keypad code. Behind the doors, a lift and another keypad needing a code. Finally we started to descend. I realized I stood under an electric light, something I hadn't seen since the Opera

House.

By the time the lift stopped, my arms ached with the strain of holding Else. We stepped out into more bright lights and a security station, with television monitors and another soldier watching from behind thick glass.

"Got two walk-ins," Madden said to the glass window. The soldier on the other side nodded in acknowledgment and with a buzzing sound a door clicked open. Jenks and Madden nudged me forward with their gun butts. I found myself in a room that could have been an office. Worn carpet and plastic pot plants joined furniture that could have been fashionable thirty years ago. Soft music flowed from hidden speakers in the ceiling and I stood dumbfounded until Madden opened a door into a room no bigger than a closet.

"There's a gown in there," he said. "Put it on. We'll get a gurney for the lady."

I gently lay Else down on the carpeted floor. Stepping into the closet I slipped into something less comfortable; a paper-thin cotton hospital gown in a wraparound style.

When I emerged they had Else on a hospital stretcher under a thin sheet. An Indian-looking guy in a white coat stood bending over her, shining a light into her eyes.

"She's sick, you have to help her." I took Else's hand and it felt painfully cold.

"A remarkable specimen. Where did you find her?" The Indian straightened up and regarded me with genuine interest.

"Sydney," I said.

"You came all the way out here from Sydney? I must commend you, sir. Quite the hazardous journey."

"You need anything else from us, Doctor Singh?" Jenks looked bored now that Else was covered with a sheet.

"No, no, return to your posts." The doctor waved my escort away with barely a glance.

"You're a geek? Her name is Else, she's Tankbread, but she's smart Tankbread, you know?"

"Fascinating." Doctor Singh seized the end of the gurney and pushed it out of the room. I hurried along beside him and we entered another corridor. The piped music played on until Singh swiped a card over a door panel and led me into a room with beds.

"Donna, come and see this," Singh called to another white coat. This geek had a pale complexion and an attractive face backed by dark hair tied back in a braided ponytail. She strode down the ward, sliding a pair of glasses into her coat pocket as she came.

"Walk-ins?" she asked, regarding me curiously.

"Indeed, and he claims the girl is a clone."

She seemed surprised. "Where the hell did they come from?"

"He says Sydney." Singh didn't seem convinced either.

"It's true," I announced. "Her name is Else, I got her out of the Sydney Opera House . . . about a month ago."

"A month?" That peaked Donna's interest and she bent over Else, peeling her eyes back and staring into them.

"I guess. I've lost track of the days."

Donna and Singh pushed the gurney into an empty space along the wall. Moving quickly, they connected adhesive pads to Else's chest and forehead. IV lines went into her arms and clear fluid began to drip from hanging bags.

"Get Wainright down here," Donna ordered and Singh left us alone.

"It's been a long time since we have seen a fully functioning clone around here." Donna pressed a stethoscope against Else's chest and moved the silver cup around, listening intently.

"Her name is Else, she's Tankbread. But she's smart and she's one helluva fighter." I felt stupid explaining this to a geek. "She's important. Josh sent us, told us to come here."

"I don't know any Josh. Why did he tell you to come here?"

"Because she'll die."

"Of course she'll die. She's a clone." Donna slipped the stethoscope out of her ears.

I reached out and grabbed the geek's arm. "She can't die."

Donna stopped and regarded me with her full attention for the first time.

"You need to understand she was designed to fail. Thirty days is the best you can hope for. Then its systems shut down. Renal and hepatic failure, neurophysiologic degeneration. Internal tissue breaks down, the immune system turns on the host, she slips into a coma and death occurs within twelve hours."

My grip on Donna's arm tightened. "Not this time."

The ward door opened and a white-coated bald man with a hippy-length beard to compensate strode into the room. Singh hurried along behind him.

"Doctor Preston, where is the subject?" the new arrival asked.

"Right here, Doctor Wainright." Donna stepped back, pulling her arm out of my grip with a smirk that said she was going to tell.

Wainright probed and pressed with his fingertips up and down the length of Else's body. He opened her mouth, peering into her eyes. He listened to her chest with a stethoscope. He lifted and then tapped her knee and elbow for reflexes before stepping back and regarding her thoughtfully. We waited in silence for him to speak.

"Malnourished, dehydrated, and in late-phase multiple system failure, but an otherwise perfect example of my work," Wainright announced. "How did she get out here?"

"This man carried her in." Donna made it sound like an accusation.

"Explain yourself." Wainright seemed to notice me for the first time. I took a deep breath. "We came from Sydney. I met a Doctor Haumann at the Opera House, right before they were attacked by a big mob of evols. I took her to Josh at Moore Park. Told him about how the peace treaty we had with the dead was gone. Then a big mob of zeds arrived and tore up the place. Josh told me to take Else and head for Woomera. Find Wainright, he said. Said if she could be saved, you could do it."

Wainright folded his arms and tapped his hairy lip with

a long index finger. "Notify me when she has expired. I'll be interested in a postmortem examination." He dropped his arms and started out of the room. Singh and Donna accepted this decree and relaxed.

"Wait." I don't think anyone had ever questioned Wainright before because he didn't stop until I ran after him.

"Josh told me you could save her. That you could save all of us. The evols have been following us. All the way from Sydney, more and more dead. Something's making them hunt us down. If you don't help me then they are going to come here in numbers like you have never seen. They are going to tear through your fence, through your steel doors. They'll come straight down the lift shaft and they'll chew your fucking face off."

Wainright blinked. I guess he didn't hear threats very often.

"The evol threat is minimal. There are a few scattered individuals out here. We have thousands of square miles of desert and wilderness. The dead congregate in urban centers; it's where their food supply is. Their reduced neurological function guides them through familiar routines and patterns."

I got up in Wainright's face. "Don't lecture me. You've been buried a mile underground for so long you haven't got a fucking clue of what is happening out there. When did you last go up and take a look outside?"

Wainright actually flinched, a crack in that cool intellectual facade. "My work has kept my busy. I haven't had an opportunity to go to the surface in some time."

"So you really don't know?"

"I receive regular reports from Sergeant Arbuckle. I am quite confident that he is maintaining a secure facility."

I laughed. "The zombies got through today. Arbuckle lost three of his men. Two of them in a crash, and one who got bit when the bulldozer stalled and the dead came through the gate." I watched his face, seeing the color drain out of it as I leaned in until I could smell the minty freshness of his breath. "You came this close. This close to having a full-blown security breach. You want to know the worst thing? There are over a hundred walking corpses pushing against that fence. How long can Arbuckle and his men keep them back? How much ammunition do they have? There are no reinforcements coming. There is no resupply, no relief. No cavalry coming over the goddamn hill!"

Wainright jerked back when I yelled, flecks of my spit hitting him in the face. He wiped his cheek with a bleached white handkerchief.

"We must maintain our research protocols. We have an obligation, a duty to mankind and to the advancement of science." Wainright spoke like a man convincing himself of an uncertain truth. He mopped his brow with the handkerchief.

"You might want to start by doing everything you can to keep that girl alive. Doc Haumann and Josh said she was important. They told me to come to Woomera and tell them that she's your answer."

"The answer?"

"Haumann said the Tankbread are the cure, the way to destroy the evols."

Wainright looked past me and studied Else's still form. "I will need to do some tests," he said and walked back to her bedside.

"Preston, Singh, take blood and tissue samples. I need a full workup and DNA analysis as soon as possible. Oh and get a sperm sample from him too."

"How much do you want?" I said.

CHAPTER 25

Doctor Donna Preston woke me on the morning of the fourth day. "Doctor Wainright will see you now," she said. I grunted and rolled over, slipping an arm over her smooth hip and pressing against the moist warmth between her thighs. "And I have to go to work," she murmured and kissed me on the head before slipping out of her bed.

I dressed and stumbled out into the glaring fluorescent light of the corridor, following her crisp, white-coated back down to the hospital section. Donna had followed orders, obtaining a sperm sample from me as she'd explained that fresh genetic material was essential for both their ongoing research and for the continuation of the human race. After she got her specimen jar load, we had a lot of sex. Donna explained this matter-of-fact seduction by saying she was at the right time of her cycle; if I had turned up a few days later I would have gone to bed with another woman. She showed me a round adhesive patch she wore, stuck to her ribs near her armpit, with a green-colored disc on it.

"This is an invention of Doctor Wainright's. It measures hormone changes through the skin. Right now it's green because I'm fertile. If I get pregnant, it changes color."

We met Doctor Wainright outside the ward. He looked tired and irritatingly pleased with himself. I wondered if he was also contributing to the facility's fertility program. Pulling me aside he said, "We took some valuable samples from the girl. She really is quite the prize for our bioengineers. Quite the prize indeed."

"Is she alive?" I hadn't seen my weapons since we arrived, but my hands felt plenty strong.

"Yes, and she is going to be just fine. We have been feeding her some genetically engineered stem cells. Tankbread are made of highly active cells, a furnace of stem cells, burning brightly. When the evols eat the clones you call Tankbread, they replace much of what is lost to the trauma of reanimation. Think of Tankbread as being like a protein shake for the dead." Wainright smiled at his little analogy. My scowl deepened.

"She's going to live? A normal life?"

"Normal? Hardly. We had to remove all the terminator sequences on her DNA. She should outlive all of us, barring accidents. However, in all other respects she is a normal human female."

"When can she travel?" I asked.

"Today, tomorrow, whenever you like. But I would like to request you display some restraint."

"Restraint?" I almost grinned. "In case you haven't noticed there is very little use for restraint out there."

"I have a proposition for you, a you scratch my back, I scratch yours. And trust me, I have scratched yours long and hard already." Wainright smiled with a confidence I didn't share.

"What do you want?" Walking out into the desert without supplies and Else in an unknown state would be suicide.

"I want you to go back to Sydney. There is one thing you need to do."

Then I did grin. "Sydney? Back to that shithole? You've got to be kidding!"

Wainright barely shrugged. "Why did you come out here? It wasn't because of any sense of duty, was it?"

"I came out here for her. Because Haumann said Tankbread were the answer and Josh said I needed to find you. You would know what to do to help Else."

"I have helped Else. Now you need to help her too. Take

her back to Sydney. Take her back to Haumann, tell him she is ready. Tell him she is the cure."

"Haumann is dead. The evols attacked the Opera House. We barely got out alive ourselves."

"Did you see him die?" Wainright's hands gripped my arm. "Did you see him die!?"

"No! But it was all going to hell. The evols were breaking in all over. We got out while we still could. I didn't look back. I just took Else and ran."

"So he might be alive . . . ? You mentioned a Josh. Who is he?"

"Josh, he used to be a scientist, said he worked with you and Haumann."

"Joshua Mollbrooke?"

"I guess. PhD in genetics and biochemistry he said."

"If Haumann is dead, you can take her to Mollbrooke. Mollbrooke will know what to do."

"And what if Josh is dead? Moore Park was getting hammered when we left. They might not have survived."

"Then goddamnit you do what you must! Get the girl back to Sydney! She knows what she must do!" Wainright's entire head turned bright pink when he lost his temper.

Else stirred when I came into the ward. Singh was making notes and taking readings from the various sensors hooked up to her.

"Hey!" she squealed in delight when she saw me, and ignoring Singh's protests, she tossed the covers aside and leapt out of the bed. Wires went taut, machines teetered, and electronic alarms beeped. I hugged Else tight, feeling my ribs creaking under the strain of her embrace. "I felt sad when you were not with me," she said.

"I missed you too, Else." I smiled at her, a sick feeling growing in the pit of my stomach.

"I missed you too." She smiled at the new phrase. "I'm hungry," she announced.

"Yeah, how about some food?" I asked the two doctors.

Donna and Singh looked at each other and then started unclipping the cables from Else's forehead, chest, and arms.

They dressed her in a thin robe and we ate in the facility cafeteria with the rest of the population.

Scientists, technicians, engineers. Only the soldiers who lived topside, tasked with keeping those that dwelled below secure, were absent. Breakfast was fresh eggs, toasted bread, and some kind of tea.

While Else was being worked on, I'd explored the underground base and found hydroponics and a working farmyard. Under lights they grew everything from wheat and rice to potatoes, lettuce, and apples. Chickens, goats, pigs, and an aquarium provided meat protein. Else cleaned her plate and then politely asked for more. I stood up, took her tray and the lights went out. I froze. Else growled at my elbow. "It's okay," I said gently. "The lights go out sometimes. It's okay." The place always stopped when the lights went out; the first time I nearly climbed the walls until they explained that the generators sometimes failed. The power came back on after ten minutes that time. Donna told me it could have been hours.

"I can't see . . . where are the stars?" Else's voice cracked slightly. I felt her next to me and slid back down into my seat. "It's okay, Else, we are inside. There are no stars inside. It's why we have the lights on."

"I want to go outside," Else said, the crack in her voice widening.

"Hey does anyone have a torch?"

"Hang on, there's a lantern here . . ."

I sat in the dark, surrounded by invisible people who were used to long periods of complete darkness. No one said a word or sniggered. If they had, I would have tried to kick the shit out of them, pitch-dark or not.

A glow flared at the end of the table, casting shadow puppets of our faces along the wall.

"I want to go outside." Else found my hand, her grip cinching in tight. "Sure," I said, keeping my voice calm. "Let's go. Donna? Doctor Singh? Can we get out of here now?"

Donna sighed and stood up, dropping her napkin over

her unfinished breakfast. "Sure, I'll tell Wainright and we'll get your escort down here."

I borrowed the lantern as Donna walked off into the dark corridor without hesitation. Leading Else back to the room I had been sleeping in, I gathered the last of my clothes.

"You cut your hair." Else ran her hands through it. It was still down past my ears, but now it was about as long as hers. "You look like me," she said smiling.

"Partners in crime," I said and led her back to the ward. Else dressed. The quartermaster stores of the station had allocated her two pairs of khaki cargo pants, four T-shirts, two pairs of socks, canvas-top sneakers, cotton underwear, a light jacket, and a knapsack to carry it in. All of it in the same shade of faded military green. The underwear allocation included a sports bra. Else amused herself by tucking her breasts away and then jiggling them up and down while admiring her enhanced cleavage. Five minutes later Donna returned and guided us through the dark corridors to where Doctor Wainright waited by the security station at the bottom of the elevator shaft.

"Well I guess this is good-bye," I said to Donna while Doctor Wainright cranked the handle of an old-style telephone mounted on the wall.

"Sure," Donna said. "I'll name it after you," she added suddenly.

"What?" She couldn't know already, we'd only been doing it for four days. I glanced at her flat belly, an eyebrow raised.

"Don't be stupid. The batch."

"The batch?" I echoed.

"Yes, your gene sample. It's going into a new round of cloning experiments. With your genetic material and the data we have gathered from her, we are going to commence a full body cloning program. What did you think it was for?"

"Well I kinda thought you might make babies with it."

Donna smiled at me gently and put a soft hand to my cheek. "We are going to make babies with it, silly, hundreds of them."

Wainright hung up the phone. "Something is wrong. I can't raise Arbuckle or his men on the phone."

"We can activate the lift from down here though, right?" I stepped past Wainright and pushed the up-down button.

"Yes, but it's an electric elevator. So it requires electricity to make the car go up and down." Wainright had a way of explaining obvious things that made me feel stupid. I went and tried the door next to the security station window. It was locked. Peering into the glass, I couldn't see if the guard was still inside.

"We'll take the stairs," I said.

The stairs turned out to be thick with dust. The metal door took some opening. It had a large wheel on it and the hinges had stiffened from disuse.

I never step straight into the unknown, so I paused a moment and sniffed the stale air on the other side of the door. It smelt of dust.

"Okay," I said softly. "Let's go." Else followed at my heels, and to my surprise Donna and Wainright brought up the rear. "What are you doing?" I hissed.

"I haven't seen sunlight in so long, I've almost forgotten what it feels like," Donna responded.

"We need a status report from Arbuckle. It is unacceptable that he allow communications to break down." The geek found his courage when he had something to be incensed about. I gestured for Wainright to close the door behind us. He wound it shut, good and tight.

"Stay behind me, keep quiet and . . . just keep quiet." I went up the concrete stairs. Looking upwards, the flights crossed over each other, rising at least a hundred feet to the surface. There was no sound, until we were five flights from the surface. Then I heard the wind and the soft whistle of sand whispering across the roof high above us. I paused at the bottom of the last flight. From there I could see a door similar to the one we had come through down below, except that this one had a porthole window.

"Wait here," I whispered. Keeping low, I moved up to

the door. The wind was blowing hard outside, visibility was low, the sand and dust coated everything. I peered out the thick glass of the small window, barely able to see through the patina of fine desert silt over it. The Woomera compound appeared deserted.

"Okay, come on up." I kept my voice soft; nothing out there seemed right. They all took turns looking through the window. Wainright quickly got his bearings and sketched a map in the dust of where he wanted to go—the power generator building, which was in front of us and diagonally to the right.

"Ready?" They all nodded. I twisted the stiff wheel and with an ear-shattering squeak, the door pulled inwards.

Donna gave a small scream and stumbled backwards. I stepped around and saw a fresh arm hanging on the outside of the door, the hand still clinging to the outside door wheel.

"Shit," I muttered and scanned the dusty compound outside, but nothing moved except the wind and swirls of dust. I thought about pushing the door shut, spinning the wheel until it locked, and going back down. Except down there we would be trapped. If the evols had broken in through the fence and overrun Arbuckle and his troops, down below was a good place to die. Or at least go crazy in the eternal darkness.

"I'm going for the power station. The rest of you stay here."

Else immediately shook her head. "Not without me."

"Assuming you get to the power station, what are you going to do when you get there?" Wainright had that lecturing tone again.

"You need our help, and I'm sure as hell not waiting here on my own," Donna said, lifting her chin just a little higher than usual.

"Stay close, and keep quiet. If I say run, then follow me. Wainright, get up here. Is the power station going to be locked?"

"I don't know." Wainright's bald pate was glistening already.

"Okay, stay close. Here we go." I stepped out into the wind and fog-like dust. With the others treading on my heels I moved towards our target. The first dismembered corpse lay less than ten meters away from the stairway entrance. One of Arbuckle's men. I liberated his M16 and found his last full magazine on the ground next to him. The final zombies he killed were a few steps further on. We kept walking, heads down, trying to see through the flying grit. I stopped and waved the others to a halt. An evol wandered aimlessly past, less than ten feet from where we crouched. I counted to twenty after it vanished into the yellow gloom and then we moved again. Reaching the edge of a building, I pulled Wainright forward by his sweat-stained shirt and hissed in his ear, "Is this it?" He nodded, his heart thudding so hard I could feel it.

With my back to the wall and the M16 a comforting weight in my hand, I edged up to the door. To my relief it hung open. A dark stain flowed across the threshold and dripped into a sticky pool on the ground.

I glanced inside; a half-dozen corpses—all of them still, already stinking and bloating in the heat. The bad news was that the equipment in the room had been hit hard by panicked gunfire. Nothing even sparked with short circuits.

I waved everyone inside. Donna pressed her sleeve to her mouth and coughed, not looking at the bullet-ravaged dead. Else, ever practical, collected weapons. Only one rifle still carried ammunition and she handed it to Wainright, who held it as if it were a live grenade with a missing pin. Else heaved one of the dead soldiers aside and pulled her sword scabbard from the tangle of his webbing belt. The blade had been buried in an evol woman's head as she'd bitten Madden's throat out. "My sword," Else grinned at Donna, who looked somewhat horrified and then turned back to crouch by the doorway. Else yanked the blade out and wiped it clean.

I consulted with Wainright, who agreed that the power station was beyond repair. Clearly, the security of the compound had been compromised. He expressed regret and told me that Arbuckle would be receiving a very stern lecture on security protocols when Wainright found him.

"Chances are he'll want a big piece of your mind, Doc. He'll eat it right out of your skull given half the chance. We cannot stay here. Once the wind dies down we can be seen, heard, or smelt. Whatever it is they do." Wainright opened his mouth to give me a lecture on the sensory biology of the dead, but I waved him to silence.

"We need a reliable vehicle. Something that can get us out of here and can drive a long way, off road at times."

"The Americans, they brought Humvees. They were so proud of them. They used to drive them everywhere."

"Where would they keep them now?" I waited while Wainright thought for a long moment.

"In the vehicle storage shed? It's on the western side of the compound. About four hundred meters that way."

"Okay, ladies, same drill as before. We are going to the vehicle storage shed. It is four hundred meters away. Stay close, don't make any noise. Wainright, do not shoot anything unless I do. Even then, do not waste your ammo shooting the same target."

Wainright nodded and helped Donna to her feet. She looked trapped between her eagerness to get away from the stench of the rotting bodies and her terror at being outside.

I looked both ways, just like crossing the street, and then stepped out into the compound. We stayed close to buildings, backtracking a couple of times when we saw silhouettes moving in the gloom. Once we almost stepped right on a pair that were feeding. Else bounced past me and stabbed them both in the back of the neck with her sword. With a twist of the wrists she cut their spines and they crumpled face-first into their bloody meal. Wainright had an arm around Donna and supported her as we crept along. I could hear muffled sobs squeezing out through her hands, which she kept pressed against her mouth. We reached a large shed, with two fuel tankers standing sentry out front. The hose for one lay on the ground. I couldn't tell if the other one had anything left in its underground tank, but it did have a manual pump handle. Along the front of the building hung large sliding doors of corrugated steel, tightly closed against the wind and intruders.

Wainright tapped me on the shoulder and I jumped so hard I nearly knocked him down. "Side entrance," he whispered and I followed his finger. The door was ajar, swinging in the wind, which seemed to be lessening. Another corpse, this one naked and missing a good portion of its head, lay outside the door. We stepped over it and slipped inside.

CHAPTER 26

The vehicle storage facility was a concrete block and iron-roofed shed about the size of a small airplane hanger. There were no aircraft here, just a line of Humvees and most of them were stripped to the chassis. A steel frame and a few wires sticking out like frayed threads on the edge of torn cloth was all that remained.

"Someone's in here." Else held her sword out at arm's length, turning slowly in a full circle. I sighted down the M16 pressed to my shoulder and did a slow pirouette. There were birds roosting high up in the rafters and the place stank of their guano. The few streaks of dusty sunlight streaming in from high windows made it hard to see anything clearly.

"Else, go around that way." I waved her around to the front of the line of vehicles. I moved to the back. One of us would get the jump on whoever was in here.

I found a splash of blood on the concrete, then a trail of large, dark drops. Blood dried fast in the desert heat but the trail felt sticky to the touch. I moved carefully, leading with the rifle, seeing Else slip across the aisles between the trucks in synch with me.

The fifth Humvee in line appeared unscathed. My nose wrinkled at the smell of shit, piss, and fresh blood. I stepped around the corner of the fourth truck with my finger tightening on the trigger. A soldier lay panting like a dog with his head against the running board of the last Humvee. His dark skin now turned grey with blood loss and shock.

Sweat oozed out of him, adding a musky stink to the cloying odor of his own filth. He had a pistol in his right hand, and he raised it with a grunt of effort. His left arm lay between his legs, the neatly severed stump above the elbow tied off tight with wire. An axe lay across his lap, the head of it dark with blood.

"Easy, man," I said, slowly stepping forward and putting Else on hold with a warning gesture. I crouched down on the edge of the pool of blood. The soldier was dying; I could see the chunk of flesh missing from his severed hand. The semicircular bite had almost taken off his pinky finger. After being bitten, he managed to get to a safe place, tied a wire tourniquet around his arm, and then hacked off the infected limb.

"Man . . . You have balls of steel." I meant it too. I don't think I would ever be able to do that to myself.

"Oo . . . rah," he managed between fast and shallow breaths.

"Semper Fi, motherfucker." I think that was a marine thing; I vaguely recalled it from a movie once.

The black soldier managed to smile. "Semper . . . Fi . . . Momma . . . Semper Fi . . ." His voice trailed off into a whisper as his breathing slowed. I picked up the axe that lay across his lap, waited until his eyes fully closed and the last of the air sighed out of him. Then I stepped back, raised the bloodstained weapon, and split his head like firewood.

"Else, give me a hand." She came over immediately. We took a leg each and dragged the dead soldier away from the Humvee.

"Anyone else here, you think?" I asked.

Else's head turned slowly, like a dog listening for a distant bark. "No, they are all outside, lost in the wind."

Else waited by the Humvee while I went and gathered up Wainright and Donna. We checked the rest of the shed for useful supplies and found nothing except a stash of well-thumbed girlie magazines. The back of the Humvee contained carefully sealed packs of dried food, some full water containers, and a spare fuel tank. Semper Fi, fellas, I thanked Arbuckle and his men silently.

Else rode shotgun and I took the driving position while the others loaded themselves in the backseat. The keys were in the ignition. I sat in the driver's seat and stared at them for a good ten seconds. These rare moments of good luck are worth savoring.

"What are you waiting for? Get us out of here," Wainright interrupted my moment.

"One problem." I pointed to the hanger door. "Someone has to open that." Wainright and I got out and inspected the door mechanism. There were two parts to it: a heavy grease- and dirt-encrusted electric motor that ran a chain loop which pulled the door open along a track, then pulled it back the other way to close. The other option was to unbolt the door and slide it down the rail by hand. That meant someone standing out there exposed to whatever came at him, or her, until we had enough space to drive the Humvee through.

We reconvened in the truck and I explained our situation.

"The thing is that, before the door is opened, we need to get the truck started. The engine noise is going to attract whatever is outside and they are going to come."

"We have weapons, we will fight them!" Else jabbed the air with her sword.

"When we came in here, I saw over a hundred zombies piled up against that fence. I don't know where they are now, but I know where they are going to be." Else pondered my meaning for a second and sat back frowning. "Any of you drive?" I asked and they each shook their heads. One day I would have to teach Else to drive.

"I will do it." Wainright's hands clenched between his thighs. He stared down at them. "I'll open the door, but you have to be ready, you have to get out as soon as there is enough room."

"I'll be ready."

Wainright opened the passenger door and slid out of the truck. He looked a little unsteady on his feet as he went around the front. We watched as he worked the stiff bolt on the hanger door. It slid free and he looked back and gave a half wave, not quite good-bye. I took a deep breath and turned the ignition key. The big 6.2 liter engine caught and roared. I guess Arbuckle's boys knew to keep the escape pods fueled and tuned up.

I revved the engine and Wainright put his weight into pushing the door back along its rail. Slowly overcoming inertia and the hanging weight of the heavy steel, he got it moving. The twelve-foot-high sheet metal and steel frame slid along the track with Wainright bent at the waist, digging his feet into the concrete and heaving with all his might. I started to roll forward. The sky outside had cleared; a thick patina of dust covered everything, but the wind was no longer blowing. Evols lurched into view, some rising from the fresh corpses they were feasting on while others just turned in their aimless wandering and homed in on us.

Donna readied the passenger door. Wainright gave one last push and we had a clear run. I pressed the accelerator and the nose of the truck slipped out of the shed. Donna threw open the back door and yelled for Wainright to get in. He let go of the door, grinning in triumph. The first evol stepped around the gaping doorway and slashed at him with ragged fingernails.

Wainright yelped and tumbled forward. I threw open my door and fired the M16 through the gap, the explosive noise in the confined space of the Humvee cab was deafening. Donna screamed and another evol staggered into the shed. Wainright tried to get to his feet, but the second zombie dropped her arms around his neck and bit into his shoulder. The bald geek screamed in agonized terror and his blood sprayed upwards in a dark jet.

I slammed my door shut and floored it. The rear passenger door hit Wainright and the zombie, knocking them both flying as we shot past. All around us, evols were closing in and the truck jumped and rolled on its suspension as we hit and drove over a wall of bodies.

"Go back! We have to go back!" Donna was screaming hysterically.

"Shut the fucking door!" I yelled and Else climbed over from the front passenger seat and pulled the rear door shut.

Corpses reached and slapped at the thick glass windows, grabbing hold of the mirrors and door handles, more by reflex than conscious thought. I sped up, driving the Humvee across the open compound, barely able to see over the dead people crawling up the hood. Donna was still screaming in the backseat. "Oh my god! You left him to die! You piece of shit! You left him to die!"

Else growled, disturbed by the woman's freak-out. Desperate to get out of the moving truck, Donna started slapping at Else, who took that for about half a second and then punched the young doctor in the jaw, knocking her senseless.

CHAPTER 27

I found a hole in the fence and we drove through it, scraping the festering dead off our fender against the ragged mesh, like dog shit coming off a shoe. Once we were out into the open desert I veered back towards the road. In less than ten minutes we were back on the highway. I swerved to avoid a trio of pigs rooting in the dirt by the road near Leandro's house. With so many evols scattered around I wondered how long the porkers would last.

I sped up to around seventy k's an hour on the highway. Any faster and we might hit something, and then it would be all over. The Humvee purred along the old asphalt under a cobalt blue sky. A few clouds hovered to the south. All around us the flat scrub-and-sand wasteland stretched out to the horizon.

Else got comfortable in the passenger seat beside me, her feet resting up on the dash. She watched the passing landscape with her usual wide-eyed interest. Donna lay in the back. I could hear her crying, but she didn't make a fuss.

In the late afternoon I stopped in the middle of the road. A town lay ahead of us, a shimmering mirage in the heat. Else and I sat on the hood of the Humvee. We drank water from a canteen and ate dried fruit from the supplies loaded in the rear. Donna stayed in the back. She drank a little water but wouldn't speak to us.

"I like it out here," Else said.

"Yeah?" I kept looking around, no zombies in sight, and

I'd checked under the truck thoroughly before letting anyone else out. "Why?"

"It's quiet," Else said after a moment.

"Sure, but there are no people and nothing to do. It's hot and it's dry."

"I would have you, and you would have me. We could live in a small house and drink orange juice. I would read."

I stared out into the burning horizon. Sometimes it seemed like I'd known Else for longer than a month—a lifetime longer, but for her kind a month was a lifetime.

"Plenty of places to choose from," I said, painfully aware that I couldn't look at her right then.

Else sighed and stretched back on the hot glass of the windshield, her eyes closed. "We would have babies. I would make you have babies with me."

"Okay, okay, we can have babies." I'd meant it as an offhand comment, something to appease her in the moment. Instead she sat up and then flipped over to sit astride my lap.

"Now?" her eyes as wide and intense as I'd ever seen.

"Not right now, no. First we have to find a place, and make sure there's no evols trying to eat us."

"We have to go back to Sydney, to the Opera House." The light in her eyes faded, the way a storm front darkens the green-blue of the ocean.

"Yeah," I said, putting my arms around her. "Back to Sydney, to the Opera House and then somewhere quiet to make babies and drink orange juice and read for the rest of our days."

"Can we get a move on? I don't want to be stuck out here at night." Donna had climbed out of her self-imposed exile in the back of the Humvee.

* * *

The Stuart Highway is the only direct route from Woomera to anywhere. We followed the road south and east. What used to be a major link across the country was now a rough track of broken asphalt and abandoned vehicles. It was slow going. At best, the run from Woomera to Port Augusta at the tip of the Spencer Gulf should have taken about three hours; now it took all day. Else found a road atlas of Australia in the glove box. With some brief instruction and a lot of questions, she soon mastered the basics of navigation.

No zombies marched around the walls of Port Augusta. I stopped the Humvee a good distance back and, telling the girls to wait in the truck, I continued on foot. The sun was setting now, long waves of brilliant red light turning the air to gold.

My boot crunched on a bleached pile of bones and I stopped, Harris' warning about Port Augusta coming back to me like a slap. In a rough circle around Port Augusta lay a tangled heap of bones and abandoned supplies—the four-hundred-meter mark that the Port Augusta snipers used to drop anyone, living or dead who came too close. I raised my hands and took a large step backwards. The bullet spanged off the ground a half second before I heard the shot. I didn't wait to see if it was a warning or just a near miss. I bolted back into the rising darkness and we gave Port Augusta a wide berth.

We camped that first night on the highway. There is no way to sleep comfortably in a Humvee. Even with the windows open a crack to let in air, it got stuffy. You can't stretch out and I woke up stiff, tired, and thirsty. Taking stock of our inventory I found we had plenty of food: some unidentifiable jerked meat, dried fruit, and a large jar of roughly ground flour. All we lacked was water, only two canteens full remained. Two full jerry cans of whatever home-brew methanol fuel we were burning, plus the three-quarters-full tank meant we had plenty of range. We could probably drive all the way to Sydney.

After breakfast and a stretch we loaded up again. Donna went for the shotgun seat and Else growled until the doctor threw her hands up in the air and said, "Whatever!" before retreating to the backseat again. As I drove Else explored a first aid manual she'd found under the map in the glove box. She read it while tracing the various parts of her body shown in the anatomy diagrams with a finger.

"Next stop, Port Germein," I said.

"Lisa and the kittens!" Else leaned forward grinning. "This time we should try and stay long enough to actually see Leo's babies. They probably think we're dead now."

"Sure, and we need to tell them about Harris," I said. Else sat back, her smile evaporating.

The home of Daisy-Mae, Lynne, Jen, and little Lisa had changed a lot since we last visited. High walls and strong fences still surrounded the fortified town, and they still had a major zombie problem. I stood on the roof of the Humvee, looking through a fine pair of military-grade binoculars at the siege of Port Germein. The zombies outside the fences were thin on the ground, but smoke rose from various out-of-control fires inside the perimeter. From this distance I couldn't hear gunfire or any sounds of life.

"Where is that?" Donna stood looking across the desert at the town.

"Port Germein. We have friends there," I said.

Donna didn't say a word; she'd lost a lot of her friends recently. She just folded her arms, hugged herself, and stared.

"Okay, what we are going to do is lock up tight, drive in slowly, see if there is anyone left alive in there, and then drive out again. We do not leave the vehicle. We do not stop. We go in, we get out. Understand?"

"But Lisa?" Else said.

"We do not stop," I repeated.

"I don't know why we're even getting that close," Donna said.

"Because I need to know what happened. I need to see it for myself," I said. "Now let's go."

We crossed the railway line, the heavy train entrance gates still closed. We drove down the eastern perimeter until we found the breach. A light plane had crashed, coming down only a few meters from the fence and then sliding right through the barrier. I drove slowly up to the hole. The plane, a single-engine thing of fiberglass and aluminium, had burned down to ashes; only the twisted propeller and a bit of wing frame remained. The dead now walked the streets of Port Germein. The only corpses we saw that weren't moving had been skeletonized, pulled down by the tide of evols washing over the defenders. The Humvee rolled quietly along the streets and like flypaper we gathered a sticky line of undead vermin behind us.

I circled a few blocks. The theater where I watched the Port Germein Players performing highlights from one of my favorite childhood movies was a smoldering ruin. We drove past Lynne's house; the front door stood open and I hoped they made it out okay.

The growing mob of evols pressing in around us couldn't block the Humvee. I gunned the engine slightly and we bumped forward, crushing at least three of them under our fat tires.

"Fuckers," I hissed. Then in a moment of savage fury I slammed on the brakes. The dead clustered around us, slapping and moaning. They scratched at the armored glass and scrabbled to open the locked doors, desperate to crack open the hard shell and feast on the soft meat inside. I waited, my teeth bared, breathing in an angry hiss.

"What are you doing?! You said we don't stop!" Donna twisted in the backseat, checking all the doors and windows around her, seeing nothing but vacant, feral hunger in the dozens of faces only a few feet away.

Taking a deep breath I dropped the Humvee into reverse and dropped the clutch. The engine roared as the truck leapt backwards, Donna bouncing off the rear of the front seat, Else hanging on, her face pale. We plowed through the dead, necrotic flesh splattering up the windows as we crushed them. I drove backwards until the road was clear. Here I paused again. The remaining zombies muddled forward. I noticed one, a woman with fresh blood staining her face and clothes. She pushed at her dead brethren, driving them back, herding them out of harm's way. She couldn't have been dead long and she'd recently been feeding well. Her brain was still firing enough to know what the older, hungrier, feral dead could not see coming. I engaged the gears and floored the accelerator. At fifty k's an hour we hit them again. Blood and visceral shit sprayed up as the Humvee bounced and rocked. The smart woman's severed head, eyes closing at last, bounced off the windscreen.

I laughed maniacally. Skidding to a halt I looked back, judging my next pass.

"People!" Else shouted, pointing to the roof of a nearby building.

I craned forward, activating the windscreen wipers to clear some of the caked shit and see where Else pointed. On top of the pub someone waved a towel. It wasn't white, so I guessed it wasn't the evols attempting to surrender. I drove forward. "Else, open the top hatch, give them a shout."

She did, standing up in the top gunner's position, waving and yelling, "Hello! We're not dead!"

"Come round the back!" the towel waver yelled back. I drove around the corner. A corrugated iron gate swung open beside us and I drove in, ordering Else to come down and close the hatch.

We waited while the gate closed and a young man with long red hair dropped down from the fire escape on the side of the building. I cautiously cracked open a window.

"Nice work," the redhead said.

"Thanks. Where's Daisy-Mae?" I asked.

"You ran her over about two minutes ago. Come on up, I'll buy you a beer." He stepped back and I took the M16 in hand and exited the Humvee. Else and Donna followed and we climbed up the fire escape to the first level. Our host pulled the ladder up after us before leading the way to the roof-top beer garden.

CHAPTER 28

"About a week ago, middle of the night, we hear this noise, like a fly with engine trouble. Too late we realize it's a plane coming down, right on top of us!" Martin paused to take a drink from his can of beer. "Then all hell broke loose! People are yelling, 'Fire! Fire!' And zombies! People are running for the fences, others are running for shelter. The fire really messed things up. The evols smartened up and came over the fence on the other side of town. We were all watching the plane burn and arguing about how we were going to fill the hole in the fence when the fire went out. By the time we realized the entire zombie nation of Australia was climbing up our arses, it was too late."

I recognized Martin as one of the actors from movie night. Else watched entranced as he told his tale of the fall of Port Germein, with full sound effects, actions, and constant switching between key characters.

I stood on the edge of the roof, looking down at the carnage on the street below. We'd made a dent in the local evol population, but more kept coming. They paraded listlessly up and down the street, tripping over the fallen and wandering off out of sight.

"There was a woman called Lynne and her partner, Jen. They had a little girl, Lisa. What happened to them?" I asked.

"I think Lynne's alive. There's some live locals upstairs at Nancy's place. About a block that way," Martin waved at the street. "She might be with them."

"I'll need to get down there," I said.

"Knock yourself out, mate. I'll close the gate after you."

I regarded Martin for a moment. "If you can shoot you could come with us. We could use you."

"Nuh, got everything I need right here. They locked the beer up, locked it up and had an armed guard on it. Not anymore. I'm going to drink myself to death and then worry about what happens next."

"You said we weren't going to stop," Donna reminded me again.

"I know what I said. C'mon Else, it's time to go."

We loaded up and waved to Martin, who saluted us with a fresh can of beer and pulled the rope to unlatch the gate.

I pulled out into the street. The beer had been warm, but there's nothing like it when you're really thirsty. I crawled the Humvee down the street, heading towards the sign marked "Nancy's Café."

Else climbed up through the hatch and yelled, "Hello! We're alive!" A second-floor window over the café veranda opened and a grey head popped out. "Who the hell are you?" the woman called down.

"I'm Else! We came back, but not like zombies. We came back like live people!" The head disappeared and a moment later a man with a rifle appeared at the window.

"Whaddya want?" he shouted.

"We want to see Leo's kittens!" Else called back. I had to tug on her pant leg to get her to come down from the hatch.

Taking her place, I explained who we were and that we were looking for Lynne and her family.

"Yeah, she's here. Can you come up on the veranda?"

With helping hands pulling us up we climbed from the roof of the Humvee onto the veranda and then in through the second-level window.

The man with the rifle introduced himself as Colin. The grey-headed woman closed the window once we were all inside. "Keep watch, Colin. Some of those buggers might get crafty and try to climb up the same way," she said. "I'm

Nancy by the way."

The stairs down to the ground floor of Nancy's café were blocked off and another armed guard stood on the landing.

"Is Lynne here?" I asked. I didn't see any faces I recognized among the few survivors.

"Lynne is in here," Nancy said and took me through to a small sitting room. Lynne sat under a window, her knees drawn up to her chin, her hands curled into tight fists against her chest and a cold look of complete emptiness on her face.

"Lynne, some friends here to see you," Nancy said gently and patted me on the arm. "She could use the company. Poor dear has had quite a shock."

I swallowed hard; no sign of Jen, no sign of little Lisa. I crouched down in front of the woman. "Hey Lynne. It's me." She didn't respond. I reached out and touched her knee. Lynne's head jerked slightly and she finally made eye contact. "Hey you," I said. No response. "Lynne, where's Lisa?" Lynne blinked and slowly unclenched one fist, her fingers uncurling as she raised her hand into the light. Resting in the palm of her hand was a single, spent rifle bullet casing.

CHAPTER 29

It took some time to convince Else that Leo, her kittens, and Lisa were not in residence. After that, she lost interest in Nancy's. They were surviving here, mostly on a mix of Nancy's cheerful can-do attitude and a willful ignorance of the trouble they were in.

We attended an impromptu meeting in the living room. I explained where we had come from and where we were going, but left out the details of why. No one begged to join us—our destination was just as dangerous as their current situation.

There was no exchange of supplies, just good wishes and some half-hearted good-byes between strangers. Colin, the man watching the window, stepped aside.

"They like your ride," he said. I looked—evols were crawling up over the Humvee cab, slapping their hands against the locked hatch and generally leaving greasy marks on the paintwork.

I climbed out onto the veranda roof and Colin followed. "How much ammo do you have?" I asked.

"Enough," he replied and worked the bolt action on his .303. "I'll take the thousand on the left, you take the thousand on the right," he added. Yeah it was an old joke, but I half laughed. It seemed like there might be a thousand evols below us, all trying to reach up and claim the prize.

We started killing. The M16 on single shot at close range was devastating. Colin and his heavy rifle on my right blew smoke and fire and we brought death from above to a number of them. I counted close to twenty fallen bodies around the Humvee when we stopped. More came from both ends of the street, the sound of gunfire drawing them in. Else came out through the window, gripping her sword.

"Thanks, man," I said to Colin and jumped from the veranda down to the roof of the Humvee. Unlocking the hatch, I called Else and Donna down. Else slipped inside like Alice going down the rabbit hole. Donna hesitated on the veranda roof as the next wave of dead arrived. I had to use my boot to push Else back down inside the truck.

Colin reloaded and fired into their midst, making each shot count, steady as a heartbeat. I emptied my second magazine, kicking the last zombie hard enough in the face to rip his lower jaw off his stinking face.

"Donna! Get down here or stay and rot!" I bellowed at the sky and she thudded down on the roof beside me.

"We don't stop!" she yelled and jumped down to me. Evols reached and clawed at her clothes as she went headfirst through the hatch.

I clubbed a few dead-heads and got ready to get inside. Someone dropped from the veranda to land beside me. Lynne, armed with an axe. She swung it round. I threw myself flat and she buried it in the neck of an evol rising up behind me.

"What are you doing!?" I yelled. Stupid questions take precedence when you are in shock.

She ignored me and jumped down to the hood of the Humvee. From there she dropped to the ground. The dead swarmed forward and Lynne stood ready, the axe hanging from her hands. The first one reached out to claw at her face and she brought the axe up, knocked the zombie back, and chopped the axe head deep into its shoulder.

"Else! The other gun! Get it!" A moment later the second M16 popped up through the hatch. I dropped the empty one down the hole and flicked the safety off. Lynne spun like a dervish. The axe crashed down, severing limbs, cutting chunks from heads, and disembowelling evols on all sides.

She never said a word, never howled a battle cry, and never screamed. The grieving woman just killed. I fired, trying to keep her safe, picking off the ones coming up behind her as she worked her way forward. The zombies didn't come fast enough so she strode out to meet them, swinging the axe and decapitating a naked woman. Colin covered my back from the café, picking off any who got close enough to come up the back of the Humvee.

Soon Lynne stood on a slick mound of torn and crushed bodies. Like some ancient goddess of war she stood on the killing pile and surveyed the slaughter around her.

Port Germein's zombie population had been decimated and the surviving meat might have a chance after all. With someone like Lynne on our side, the future looked bright.

The cold anger flowed out of her shoulders and I watched as she sagged, sinking to her knees amidst the bloodshed. A small child, her lips chewed off, exposing ragged teeth, stumbled out of the shadows of a building. This girl was older than Lisa, maybe seven, born after the end of the world, and still one of its casualties.

Lynne saw the child. The girl tottered forward, one leg trailing, the flesh eaten off her calf. She reached out to Lynne. I raised the M16 and sighted down the barrel. The girl got close, Lynne blocked my view. I lowered the rifle and yelled a warning, but the woman took the dead child in her arms and held her as the little girl bit deep into her throat. Lynne's blood gushed, dousing the kid in a red torrent. The zombie girl gulped it down and Lynne slowly toppled over, pulling the evol into a tight embrace with her as she fell.

By the time I got myself inside, the truck was covered with the dead again. I closed the hatch, crushing fingers. The press of bodies trying to get inside blocked our view on all sides. The interior went dark and hot as I started the engine. We slowly rolled backwards. Bodies crushed and burst under our wheels, guts and visceral mucous spurting in all directions.

I reversed to the end of the block, then spun the wheel

and pointed us towards the road out of town. We ran evols down, and scraped a few off by driving close to buildings and cars. Only when we had passed through the ruptured fence did I let Else climb up and hack the leftovers off with her sword from the gunner's position in the hatch.

CHAPTER 30

The drive through the countryside of South Australia took us through the hills and forestlands of the Murray Town Road. I drove carefully; the myriad twists and turns of the two-lane highway hid fallen trees, crashed vehicles, and once an evol who splattered through the Humvee's bull bars.

When we first passed this way, we rode in Harris' train following the line along the flatter land to the south. Else climbed up and stared in wonder at the trees. Donna turned out to know a gum from a pine tree, so when Else started asking what the trees were called, Donna started giving answers, common and Latin names for everything Else could see.

I didn't feel like talking; that look in Lynne's eyes as she went out to avenge her loss still gnawed at me. After an hour Donna squeezed up beside Else in the gun hatch and they were soon chatting away like old girlfriends.

After the hills and the scrubby forest came rolling hills of dry grassland. The road hazards here were the wandering stock, sheep so laden with wool they could barely move. Cattle roamed too, grazing along the road and moving in giant herds. If you could find a way to transport them back safely to populated areas, you'd make a killing in the fresh meat market.

Turning right onto B82, the Main North Road, I eased us into a herd of milling cows. Most of them moved out of the way, but a few big steers, with horns and balls that had never been clipped or truly tested, pawed the ground. I resisted the urge to lean on the horn or fire a shot. Stampeding cattle would run right over the top of us, and that could cause real problems.

We eased through, the stink of fresh cow shit adding to the other aromas of the great outdoors.

Night fell as we reached the village of Wirrabara. A sign at the border proudly proclaimed, "127 Days Without Infection," a bloody handprint smeared across the 7.

In the center of town we passed the usual collection of boarded-up shops and houses, bones scattered across the streets, and the occasional zombie. The dead were so starved they barely registered our passing, shuffling in a daze or just standing lost and forever alone in the baking summer heat.

We camped in Wirrabara for the night, stopping in an open park of long dead grass and concrete hard earth. We planned to sleep in the Humvee with the windows cracked for air.

I went scouting, finding a good supply of canned food, a shotgun, and some cartridges that didn't crumble in my fingers. I even found sodas and beer in one of the houses I visited. Else and Donna stayed with the truck, Donna teaching Else by answering her endless flow of increasingly complex questions.

Coming back, I found an old evol making his way towards the Humvee. A slow shuffler, so thin his spine and ribs jutted out against the leathery skin of his back. The pants he wore flapped like sails and his hair had come out in clumps. The last few wisps of it were white long before he died and his beard was long and ragged. He shambled along, hunched over and attracted by the lilting sound of Else's laughter. He must have been deaf before he died, because he didn't hear me coming up behind him. I used the solid walnut stock of my new shotgun to smash his knee in, dropping him with a grunt that almost sounded surprised.

The zombie groaned and rolled onto his back in the sunburnt grass, clutching at his shattered leg. I hesitated, the gun raised and ready to smash the foul creature's brains out. The evol had pink gums and no teeth. His lips peeled back in a grimace of agony. This man was alive.

"Whaddya do that for?" he moaned. "Shonnofabish."

"Shit, sorry man, I thought you were dead."

"I am dead, you shtupid bashtard, you've fushing killed me." He slurred his words with no teeth. His moans got louder and I heard Else's distant laughter go still.

"I'm really sorry." I raised the gun and smashed it into his throat, crushing the fine ringbones of his trachea. He started gurgling, eyes bulging as he drowned in his own blood. A few well-placed blows broke his skull open and ensured he wouldn't have enough brain left intact to get up again and bother us during the night.

Else met me near the Humvee. "What was that noise?" she asked.

"Just an evol, I took care of it. Hey, I found some fruit juice and some soda. You'll like this." We feasted pretty well that night, and I tried to ignore the sound of wild dogs snarling and tearing at the old man's body that lay less than a hundred yards away.

CHAPTER 31

In the morning all that remained of the dead man were a few chewed bones and a smear of blood on the grass. Dingoes and dogs were mostly extinct in Sydney; the living ate them all. Out here, though, they hunted the wild sheep and scavenged. A man would have to be sick, injured, or dead to go down to them, and I wondered how the old man survived as long as he did.

We left town at dawn. It was still cool enough to be pleasant driving, and I wanted to get as much distance between Wirrabara and myself as possible. Else read her road atlas and called out names of towns as we drove along. She took delight in seeing the names on the yellow page and then seeing the actual place a few minutes later. The road had always been dotted with small towns, the rural communities that are the foundation of any great nation. Since the Great Panic, these communities had shattered or died out. We drove through ghost towns, as dead and bordered up as Wirrabara and Crystal Brook. We drove for four days, averaging a little over a hundred k's a day and passing through empty shells of towns like Laura, Mount Bryan, Morgan, Taylorville, Renmark, and Yamba.

The dead were less common than the animals. Kangaroos thundered in herds across the road and Else yelled things from the gunners hatch like "Macropus giganteus!" and "Macropus rufus!" at them, casting her words like a wrathful spell.

Kangaroos, wallabies, koalas, and wombats, none of them cared that humankind was dying out. They were here before us, and would be long after. Thinking like that is enough to drive you to drink, and we were running low on everything. Else's navigation skills had proved accurate. According to her map we were within twenty kilometers of one of the last places I wanted to return to: Mildura and the nearby convent of Saint Peter's Grace.

Our journey took us straight east along the Stuart Highway again, that long line of road, twisting and turning like a trapped snake across South Australia and then lying flat and straight from the state border into Victoria before tangling up in Mildura again.

Else guided me through side roads, skirting the town and bringing us up on the outer fence of the convent. Their efforts in rebuilding after our departure showed in the new gates with firmly grounded posts set in concrete and the double mesh and barbed wire–topped fencing. Homemade road spikes waited to catch the unwary on the other side of the gate. It seemed that the lost and injured were no longer welcome at Saint Peter's Grace.

I stood on the roof of the Humvee, scanning the area with the binoculars. The fields were looking fresh and green, benefiting from the water brought up by the irrigation pump I had fixed. I waited while Else and Donna walked along the fence line. Sooner or later one of the nuns had to come out and investigate, either to offer aid or tell us to piss off.

It took until dusk for someone to come down the road, a woman on horseback, arrows in a quiver on her back, a homemade zombie scythe glinting over her shoulder. She did not wear the carefully mended habit of the sisters; she wore men's trousers, boots, a denim shirt, and a stockman's hat.

She reigned her horse in far enough away to be heard but out of melee range. "There is nothing for you here!" she called, ignoring the horse as it stamped and snorted, twisting under her.

"I'm here to see Sister Mary. Tell her the courier and Else

have come back. Tell her we got to Woomera, and we have news."

"You come on foot, leave your weapons in your vehicle!" She lifted the bow from her saddle hook and notched an arrow to the string, not aiming at me but at the two women jogging back along the fence line towards us.

"That's Else; Sister Mary should remember her. She's your goddamned miracle."

"Step away from your vehicle, hands behind your head, turn around." The nun didn't care to be argued with, so I did as she asked, slowly spinning so she could see I wasn't carrying anything deadly behind my back. Disarming her bow and holding the reins, she unlocked the gate. "Come through, slowly and in single file."

We did that, and she locked the gate again before swinging back up into the saddle. "Start walking," she said, backing the horse up to watch over us as we marched.

"Can I put my hands down now?" I asked.

"Just move," she replied. We walked up the long driveway to the walls of Saint Peter's. Here, maybe a month ago at most we had fought for our very lives against an onslaught of the undead. Coming back, I had expected this place to be dead, every last holy virgin torn asunder or infected and reborn as a cannibalistic, animated corpse. The heavy doors in the whitewashed walls swung open as we approached. Four girls, two with bows and two with rifles, covered us as we entered. None of them were dressed like nuns either.

"Did Sister Mary make it back here okay?" I felt a sudden twinge that she might have never returned, and I would be held responsible for her disappearance.

"We have chosen to separate ourselves from our Godly work for now," Sister Mary said, stepping out of the main building. Standing on those steps looking down at us, she looked every inch the military veteran she claimed to be rather than a middle-aged nun. "The Lord spared our lives, but taught us a valuable lesson. Faith must be accompanied by action. I will not allow my girls to come to harm ever again."

"I'm glad to see you're alive, Sister. We've come from Woomera. This is Donna. She's a geek," I added.

"Come in and explain yourself." Sister Mary vanished inside and we went up the steps and into the cool interior of the convent.

They gave us food and water. Grace was still said with a fervent solemnity over the meal, and Else ate daintily using her correct utensils. After dinner she went to reacquaint herself with her friends among the young nuns.

The Mother Superior ordered Donna and I to her office for a chat. I gave Sister Mary the highlights of our trip west and explaining honestly the situation we found in Woomera. To explain our return journey I only said that we had an important message for the geeks at the Opera House on a possible cure for the evol epidemic.

She listened and asked Donna questions, which the doctor answered truthfully. The shudder in Donna's voice as she described our escape from the Woomera compound and the horrors she had witnessed since then did not move Sister Mary.

"I told you that the Lord had a purpose for you," she said eventually. I half shrugged. My feeling had always been that if there ever was a God he'd long since buggered off to some other project.

"I guess," I said.

"You will not stay here," Sister Mary announced.

"Well, no," I said. "We have to get back to Sydney."

She carried on as if I had not spoken. "After I returned we were contacted by a small community who saw the chopper flying over. Two young men volunteered to follow my path and with God's guiding love, they found us. It falls upon us to restore the world to his grace. To do so we must fill the earth again with his chosen."

"Uh huh," I said.

"One of the young men died of injuries sustained during their journey here. The other has returned to his people. He will gather them and they will make a pilgrimage to this holy site. From here we shall repopulate the earth."

"Okay . . ." I'd seen this kind of plan before.

"How many of them are there?" Donna asked.

"By the account of Thomas, the last woman who lived among them died six months ago during childbirth, leaving twelve men of marriageable age."

"Marriageable age?" I said, only to be ignored by both women.

"They are genetically diverse?" Donna leaned forward, her gaze intensely interested.

"They come from three separate families." Sister Mary's nostrils flared slightly, unsure whether to be offended at this line of questioning.

"To ensure the survival of a species you need a minimum of four adults. The entire world once reduced to a population of less than five thousand humans, and before all this happened we numbered in the billions," Donna said.

"There shall be no debauchery in God's new world," Sister Mary declared.

"Of course not," Donna said immediately, "but there is so much work to be done, so much genetic cross-matching, selective trait breeding—or marrying the right man with the right woman to ensure viable and, uh, truly Christian offspring."

"What do you know of such things?" Sister Mary didn't glare so I spoke up.

"I told you she's a geek. Donna does this sort of thing."

"I can help you build the community. I can help make your divine vision a reality." Donna reached out and gently laid her hand over Sister Mary's. "I am here for a reason, Sister," she said.

Sister Mary announced that she would pray on the matter. Duly dismissed, we went outside.

"You didn't tell me you were religious."

Donna snorted and gave me a withering look. "Of course I'm not. That woman is completely deluded. However she does present a unique opportunity. I can launch my own eugenics program that will last thousands of years. An entire new race of people will be born from this genetic stock. I can shape the genetic future of humankind from right here. You have no idea what an amazing project this is going to be."

"You sure Sister Mary is the one with the delusions?" I quickly grinned. Donna didn't react like I'd hoped.

"I'm not pregnant," she said. I stopped grinning.

CHAPTER 32

Since Sister Mary's return, the convent had been transformed into something more akin to a military base. The girls still prayed and worked the farm, but they also went out in armed groups, returning with animals, tools, building materials, food, and books. The chapel had become a library, books stacked on the floor and against the walls. I found Else here, surrounded by volumes and reading three at once.

"You should get some sleep," I said.

"Not tired," she replied without looking up.

"Whatcha reading?" I scanned the titles of a stack that included medical texts, autobiographies, and car workshop manuals.

"Everything," she said.

I left her to it. After the long days of driving and sleeping in the Humvee, I needed sleep. I slept hard until the bell calling the faithful to morning devotions woke me up again.

Else and Donna joined me for breakfast and Sister Mary scolded Else for reading at the table while we ate porridge drowned in fresh milk.

"We have no wish to keep you any longer than necessary," Sister Mary announced over a strong cup of bush tea.

"I understand, Sister. Else and I will be out of your hair by the end of the day."

"I was speaking to you specifically. The young lady is

welcome to stay with us."

I put my spoon down and looked the nun in the eye. "We've had this discussion before. You know she goes with me."

"She goes with you into a world of sin and the wrath of God. That is no place for one so innocent."

I held back on filling Sister Mary in on some of the things Else had seen and done during our time together. She'd order us both burned at the stake if I told her the whole truth.

"An early start will see you well on the road," Sister Mary said, her final word on the matter.

"Yeah about that, Sister, I have a proposition for you . . ."

After breakfast they gave me permission to bring the Humvee in and Else learned the fine art of bartering. We traded the vehicle and everything in it for a helicopter ride.

Farewells are something I've never been good at, and saying good-bye to Donna proved harder than I thought. I found her in the chapel library writing up lists of things she needed to ensure the creation of a new master race.

"We're heading out," I said from the doorway.

She glanced up. "You're not coming back." There was no question in her voice.

"No, I guess not. At least not for a while." I didn't walk out then. It would have been easier to just tip my hat and stride out into the sunset. Instead, I stood there in the doorway and took a deep breath. "I'm sorry we didn't work out, with the baby thing I mean," I said.

She stopped writing her notes and, tucking her pencil in her shirt pocket, she stood up. "Yes, the hormone patch hasn't changed color, see." She lifted her shirt, twisting to show the round patch near her armpit to me. The patch glowed a dull red.

"We could try again?"

Donna snorted. "I'm now menstruating, you idiot. Safer this way I guess. Back at the lab I could tell you the sex, screen for any genetic disorders," she gave me an appraising look. "But here . . ." she looked around the white stone chapel. "Here I'd be lucky to survive childbirth if there were any complications."

"Sister Mary and the nuns, they'd look after you."

"Sure, they would pray for my health and the health of my baby. How reassuring. Besides, I'm going to be busy with my eugenics program. If a suitable sperm donor turns up in the screening process, I may try again."

It was my turn to shrug. "I have to get going. I hope it works out okay. If I can, I'll come back and help."

Donna had gone back to her note taking. I waited a moment longer while she ignored me and then I left.

Else carried her sword, I carried an M16 with two spare magazines. The weapons, a backpack full of books, and the clothes on our backs were all we took away from Saint Peter's Grace convent.

Sister Mary led us to the helicopter beyond the line of gum trees. "You okay with this?" I asked Else.

"Sure," she said. "This is going to be fun."

"Well okay, if you're sure," I said.

"Stop treating me like a child," Else scolded. "Life can only be understood backwards; but it must be lived forwards."

"What?"

"Søren Kierkegaard. Nineteenth-century Danish philosopher, 1813 to 1855," Sister Mary said from ahead of us without breaking her stride.

"He thought a lot about God and life and wrote it all down," Else explained.

"Kierkegaard wrote extensively on Christian theology. He was a devout man and an instrument of God's will," Sister Mary added with a hint of admonishment in her voice.

We reached the helicopter and got settled in. Sister Mary did her preflight checks, the engine whined, and the rotors began to spin. Else took a deep breath and as the turbine above us began to wind up, she reached out and silently took my hand, squeezing it hard and closing her eyes.

The dropped-gut feeling of takeoff soon passed and we turned towards the east, flying at two thousand feet. Below us I could see lines of roads, small gatherings of buildings, and small gatherings of the undead moving around them. Rooftops marked with faded signs of SOS! and HELP! passed underneath us. Sister Mary's community of men were just one more group of survivors who still held out hope for salvation.

The sound of our helicopter flying overhead drew the few remaining living souls out of their holes. Tiny figures ran about waving sheets, burning torches, and flashing sunlight off mirrors. Sister Mary ignored them all and we flew on to land before dark at a small airfield outside Goulburn.

CHAPTER 33

Goulburn—once home to over twenty thousand people—survived well into the apocalypse. Host to the New South Wales police college, the city found itself with a ready supply of cops-in-training who assisted the town fathers in keeping the infected quarantined and the uninfected under control. I'd been there twice since it all went shit, but found the martial law they used to justify punishing the few remaining civilians more dangerous than reassuring.

The sun set over the horizon as we climbed out of the chopper and stretched our legs. A fire had burned through the dry grass of the plain recently, leaving the ground charred and shedding flakes of burnt grass like black dandruff. We were only a few kilometers from town and other than the birds coming in to roost in the empty hanger, we saw nothing moving.

"You can give me a hand with the refueling," Sister Mary announced and trudged off through the ash towards a concrete shed. Soon enough she set me to working a hand pump, drawing fuel up from somewhere deep under ground where a precious few gallons remained untouched.

"Sister," I called to her, "I gotta ask. How the hell do you keep doing this? Finding gas for your bird, I mean."

The nun drew her shoulders back and stared coldly down her nose at me. "The wise and the faithful do not question the Lord's providence."

"That another Keer-guard saying?"

"Kierkegaard, and no. If you had faith, you might have a future." Sister Mary walked away, speaking to Else who was crouched in the dust drawing with a stick. I couldn't tell what she said but Else stood up abruptly, casting her stick aside and looking chastised. I worked the pump handle until it sucked air and the pump shuddered,the flow becoming a trickle.

"That's it, she's done." I walked out of the shed. The night sky glistened overhead like a spray of broken glass and the blackened ground just made the evening seem darker.

Sister Mary sealed the fuel tanks on the helicopter and we stood next to it for a moment.

"Good luck, may God be with you," she said.

"Yeah, see you around, Sister, and thanks." I stepped back, swinging the M16 onto my shoulder and making ready to head out and find shelter for the night.

Else hesitated and then engulfed Sister Mary in a hug. "Thank you," she said, speaking earnestly in the older woman's ear. "Your belief system is fundamentally flawed in ways I can't begin to describe. But I see that it gives you a sense of security and absolves you of the guilt you feel for the traumas of your past." Else relaxed and held the nun at arm's length. "So God go with you too, Sister, because that's your paradigm."

Else smiled warmly until Sister Mary blinked, and when the nun spoke her words came out in an angry hiss. "He that believeth and is baptized shall be saved; but he that believeth not shall be damned."

Else flinched like she'd been struck. Sister Mary's words didn't bother her, but the venom behind them and the look in her eyes were a harsh lesson.

The girl dropped her hands and moved back. "I don't . . ." she shook her head.

"Else, we need to go," I said. Else nodded and we walked together across the burnt plain, leaving Sister Mary to fire up her helicopter and vanish into the darkness for the last time.

"Can we get another Humvee?" Else asked as we

walked.

"Doubt it. Maybe a pickup, or a car, or a motorbike. Gonna have to walk tonight, though."

Else nodded. "I think we should run," she said.

"Run? In the dark, why would you want to do that?"

"Because there are at least a thousand dead people coming up behind us."

I twisted round; the shadows just got darker the harder I stared into them. "How can you tell?" I asked, walking faster.

"I hear them."

"You mean like moaning and walking and stuff?" Our walking broke into a trot and the grass whipped under our feet.

"No." Else ran easily, her long legs reaching out in a ground-eating stride. "I mean I can hear them. Not what they are saying. What they are sensing and responding to."

"Assuming you are right, and I'm not saying you are, but if you are, what the hell are you talking about?"

"I'm not sure." Else managed a half shrug as she ran. "You'll think I'm crazy."

"Well if you are crazy I won't tell anyone." We ran on into the night, reaching the Hume Highway where we slowed down and started walking. "Are they still coming?" I asked. I couldn't see a damn thing in the dark.

"Some came as far as the airfield. Then they got confused by the helicopter flying the other way. They don't like noise, it distresses them. They hear everything. They see everything. Lights are too bright, the rasp of living breath is too loud."

"They have like super hearing and vision?"

"No," Else scowled, her lack of knowledge causing her deep annoyance. "We hear things, we see things. We smell, taste, and feel. But we don't see and hear and feel everything."

"Well no, of course not."

Else stopped walking, her face tense with concentration. "Imagine if you couldn't filter it all out. The sounds and the smells and the sights of the world. If everything just came straight in. No way to ignore it."

I couldn't imagine it and said as much.

"It would be the worst thing in the world. I think the genetically engineered virus that reanimates the dead tissue, it destroys those filters in the brain. The body functions but the mind is ripped open."

"How do you know this?"

"I read books. I asked Donna lots of questions, and when I was asleep in the hospital underground, I could hear the scientists talking. They know so much and they were making more evols. Trying to make them safe."

"Safe? How the fuck do they think they can make them safe?!" I shouted, making Else wince and shy away.

"The idea was soldiers! Soldiers who don't die! They can get up again and keep killing!"

"Well they sure got that right! They get right back up again and they keep right on killing!"

Else started crying, great wracking sobs that shook her frame, tears welling in her eyes. "It's not my fault!" she screamed, loud enough to raise the galahs from the nearby trees.

I watched her cry, thinking about the hundreds of miles we'd traveled together, the shit we'd been through, the times we'd fought and killed and kept fighting.

"What are we supposed to do in Sydney? We go to the Opera House? What if they're all gone?" It felt weird to be asking Else questions for once.

"It doesn't matter. We can still stop them." Else walked off, winding her way among the abandoned cars.

CHAPTER 34

From Goulburn to Sydney is a journey of nearly two hundred kilometers. We found shelter that night in an abandoned farmhouse. The skeletal remains of a dog lay on the porch, the collar and chain still around its neck. We went in through the front door, the shriek of the rusted hinges making us both freeze and listen intently for a long minute.

After barricading a bedroom door and stripping the dust-filled bedding onto the floor, we slept until late the next afternoon. I woke up and rolled onto my back, listening to the rats and possums in the walls and roof—slowly becoming aware of an Else-shaped emptiness on the bed next to me.

With a sigh I rolled off the bed and stretched. We had no food or water and only limited ammunition. Gunshots would attract unwelcome attention and we were without vehicles or any easy means of escape.

I wandered the upper level of the house and saw no sign of Else's passing in the unbroken carpets of dust. Only the stairs to the ground floor showed our footprints so I headed down and into the kitchen.

Else sat cross-legged on the floor surrounded by books. Two of them lay open in her lap and she held two more in place under her feet. I watched as she absently dipped her fingers into a large tin of dog food, scooped out the rich meat paste, and ate it. Her eyes scanned a sheet before flicking to the next book while she turned the pages with wet fingers between mouthfuls.

"What flavor you got there?" I asked, announcing my presence.

"Some kind of meat," she said. Picking up the can she deciphered the faded label. "Dog, I think."

"Care to share?" I opened kitchen drawers and collected cutlery. Sitting down next to Else on the cool tiles of the floor, I took the can she offered. "It's not dog meat, it's what people used to feed to their dogs," I explained.

"Lucky dogs." Else grinned and picked up one of her books. "History, science, poetry, religion, politics, economics, engineering. How the fuck are we supposed to learn it all in one lifetime?"

"Most people didn't. Instead you focus on one thing. You learn a little bit about lots of things and a lot about something specific. Some people learned all about science, like Donna. She might know about Shakespeare" — I picked up the collected works of the Bard from the floor and hefted it for emphasis — "but she probably doesn't know everything there is to know about what he wrote."

Else sucked her fingers clean. "How do you know what to learn and what to ignore?"

"Some people decide what they want to do pretty young. Others never really work it out and just do whatever."

"I'm young, I can still decide, right?"

"Sure." I finished the spoonful of meaty dog chow and rested my head against the cupboard with a sigh.

"Do you know how old you are?" I asked.

"Thirty-seven days," she said promptly. "How old are you?"

I had to think about it. "I was twenty-nine the year of the Panic. I think it's been at least ten years since then."

"You could live to be eighty. Or older," Else said, eyeing me critically.

"Sure. I don't smoke, I eat healthy, and I get regular exercise. I could live to be a hundred."

Else nodded. "I'd like that." She stood up and offered me a hand. "Come on, old man, we have a long way to go."

We filled my pack with tins of dog food and canned fruit.

Clouds had gathered, a heavy storm front pushing in from the south. The parched ground seemed almost expectant—we hadn't seen real rain for months.

"Is that rain?" Else asked, shielding her eyes and staring.

"Yup. May come to nothing, though. It hasn't rained for ages."

The sky grew dark and the smell of wet earth came on the rising breeze. Chilled by the southerly damp, we walked on until the rain burst down on us. It fell roaring on the rusting steel shells of the empty cars and drumming on the long blacktop of the highway.

"Will it flood?" Else yelled, staring around in the darkness.

"Probably," I said, shivering in the deluge. We trudged on, splashing in puddles now and blind to anything that might be lurking or hunting us in the growing darkness.

After an hour in the rain even Else stopped talking. She walked now, arms wrapped around herself, head down and trembling with bone-deep cold.

"Ma-Marulan . . ." Else said and waved at a sign. The town of Marulan, another of those small satellite towns that dotted the Australian countryside.

"Shelter." I had to physically guide Else off the highway, across the rough ground to a side road and into an old petrol station. Feral evols don't care if it's night or day. They don't seem to care about anything except eating. Else didn't have a theory on why they ate the living. Maybe we just pissed them off somehow.

We crossed the forecourt, where a car had driven into the gas pumps, shearing one of them right off the concrete island. The car doors stood open and a suitcase hung half out of the car, the lid open and the clothing inside scattered like spilt guts. Years of weather had faded the fabric to grey-brown rags. I went around the car, watching for zombies in the store. Nothing moved inside and motioning Else to keep silent I opened the door. The stale air inside puffed out in a fetid gust like a dry fart. We waited a moment, listening hard, then went inside and let the door sigh shut behind us.

Like most shops on highways near major urban centers, this one had been stripped early on. People fought to the death over fuel, food, and anything they considered to be emergency supplies. I remember seeing a guy being knifed to death over a twin pack of AA batteries. He bled out on the floor of a petrol station like this one, coming back a few minutes later and taking three others out before we hacked them down. I left the scene after we cleaned up and saw his wife and three children outside in their overloaded station wagon, her face ashen with the realization that daddy wasn't going to get them to safety.

Else's teeth chattered and she grabbed my arm, her face twisting in panic. "Wh-wha-what's wrong with me?" she managed to blurt.

"You're cold, your body shakes to try and warm you up. We need to get you dry and warm. It'll stop then."

She looked at me hard, seeing if I were bullshitting her in some way. I walked across the dark and empty aisles. Trash, windblown dirt and leaves, no fresh footprints or smears in the grime. I found the bathroom; it had one of those roller towels that hadn't rotted away completely. I tore some long sections and showed Else how to rub herself down and then clean her sword to make sure it didn't rust. Her shivering eased and we scrounged for any overlooked food. I found a chocolate bar, kicked under the counter. Tearing the wrapper open, the chocolate had gone dry and faded but it smelled okay. I broke it up and offered a chunk to Else. She sniffed it like I had. "It looks like shit," she said.

"Yeah but it tastes like heaven," I grinned through sticky brown teeth. She ate her share, took the rest of mine, and crawled around on the floor peering under every shelf for more.

The window in the small office out the back had bars over it. The glass lay in shards on the floor and thick mold grew up the walls. Mushrooms grew out of a mound of something dead in the corner. Sleeping in here wasn't going to be an option.

I opened the door to the workshop. The rain thundered on the roof out here and an SUV sat right over the pit. I walked around the perimeter of the room. Tools, rat-chewed paper, and spray cans were scattered on benches and the floor. In the back corner I found a forty-four-gallon drum with a hand pump attached. I unscrewed the cap and took a careful sniff of the contents. Petrol. More than enough to fill that SUV tank by the weight of the drum. Grinning to myself I checked another bench, finding a set of keys that looked like they might fit the truck parked right behind me. I opened the door and yelled, "Hey Else, come check this out." She got up from where she'd been poring over maps and I stepped aside. "Your carriage awaits."

"Cool. I have maps," she announced.

"Great, grab them and get in."

Else shook her head. "I have them, in here," she tapped her temple. I didn't argue; thinking about how this girl's mind worked was pointless.

The key fit and I pulled the fuel drum on its trolley close enough to pump the tank full. I opened up the hood and checked the wiring. The battery terminals were crusted with green corrosion but the engine was in remarkable condition for an abandoned vehicle. I hunted around the workbench and found a wire brush and cleaned the crap off the battery. I checked the oil and water; both were fine. Climbing into the cab, I took a deep breath and turned the key. The engine turned over; it didn't start, but it did turn over. I pumped the gas pedal and tried again. The engine coughed, whined, and then caught. Leaving it idling, I slid out and trotted back to the garage door. Pulling on a chain pulley I started winding the door up. It had been so long since we had seen evols that I got sloppy. As the garage door rolled up, I looked back to give Else a thumbs-up. The rain still poured down outside, and as I yanked again on the chain, the door slid up past my head and I came face to face with an evol. With a snarl his bottom jaw clicked wide. His black tongue lolled out and I leapt back with a yell. Dead hands snatched at my shirt and I dragged the dead man with me.

"Fuck!" I screamed in shock. Grey teeth lunged for my neck. I punched him in the throat. His head cracked back as he thrashed and growled.

Struggling to keep my footing on the concrete floor, I shoved back. The evol's teeth snapped an inch from my arm and I got a clear foot of space between us. Snatching up a wrench, I swung it and smashed the dead bastard's nose right off his face. He didn't stop. Instead he gurgled and lunged at me. I took the wrench in both hands and smashed it down on his head. The evol staggered, his legs spasmed and jerked, sending him crashing to the floor.

Breathing hard, I saw more of them coming across the forecourt. In ones and twos they stumbled in out of the rain. A woman staggered into view, a small naked toddler waddling after her, its tiny arms held up, making a plaintive mewling sound that she ignored.

I threw open the car door and leapt in behind the wheel. "I could have used some help there, you know," I said to Else as I dropped the SUV into reverse and ran it straight back. We hit the end of the crashed car and sent it spinning into the woman with the toddler. The woman went flying and the kid splattered under our wheels.

We ran a half-dozen zombies down getting onto the highway. This truck had not been there since the Panic, and I hoped whoever parked it up was now too dead to care we had taken it. The wheels spun in the wet as I slammed it into drive and we fishtailed, wiping out two more of the hungry dead before swerving through the lines of empty cars and getting underway.

CHAPTER 35

I took us off the road when I had to, keeping our nose pointed east and skirting around the regular traffic jams. Evols patrolled along the road, climbing over cars and reaching out to us as we drove past. I tried not to think about what would happen if we ran out of gas, or broke down, or stopped to ask for directions.

We drove on until the rain stopped and I pulled up in the middle of the road. The Hume Highway ran to four lanes here, and with no evols in sight we made ourselves look like any other abandoned vehicle. Else settled in the backseat; I hunkered down behind the wheel and tried to sleep. Every time I closed my eyes I saw the face of the zombie from the garage an inch from my own, those blackened teeth bared and lunging for my face. I sat there in the dark watching through the tinted glass as silhouettes of the moving dead passed aimlessly among the cars ahead. A world without the walking dead seemed like a dream, but maybe a dream worth giving everything for. To dismiss any possibility for an end to this horror would be to give up on life itself. The survivors didn't fight and hide and keep fighting for nothing. We were the ones who did whatever it took to get through each day. Knowing that Else sleeping behind me might have an answer, the secret to some kind of cure, that gave me hope. It was precious little, but it was enough.

My eyes were closing when I saw something larger than a man moving through the cars. I blinked, staring hard into the dark; it could be a cow, or a 'roo. Something washed down from the thin pine forest around us.

I straightened up, leaning forward onto the dashboard. Out of the dark came a man on a horse. I blinked. Riding towards me was a knight. Dressed head to toe in plate armor and riding a horse. He seemed to be in no hurry, letting the horse pick its own way through the tangle of cars. I checked my mirrors and, M16 in hand, I carefully stepped out into the road. Raising a hand, I waved. The rider pulled the horse up and checked his surroundings, looking for an ambush.

"Hey," I said, doing my own look around. The dead were gathering. A mob of them were strung out and following the horse's trail. "We've got company," I said.

The knight twisted in his saddle and then turned the horse around and flicked his heels, goading it into a trot. I closed the car door and went after him on foot. The first evols found a way through the cars that blocked their way and hurried forward with renewed bloodlust. The rider dropped a length of chain with a jagged metal weight, about the size of a softball, on the end. Swinging the chain in a circle parallel to the horse, he rode down on the advancing dead. The heavy metal ball whirred through the air and cleanly tore the head off a naked male. The horse reared back and the guy kept his seat, swinging his weapon over his head and crushing skulls left and right. I caught up and braced myself on a car hood, sighting down the barrel of the automatic rifle and squeezing the trigger until it spat fire and blinded my night vision. "Shit," I swore and straightened up. Somewhere beyond the spots dancing in front of my eyes I could hear the horse whinnying and striking its hooves on the hard asphalt road. The moans of the dead were cut short by the whirring crack of the chain and the crash of the weapon tearing into dead flesh and bone.

I headed back to the car. Else popped up when I opened the door, her sword ready to run me through. "It's me!" I climbed in, closed the door, and locked it.

Else leaned over from the backseat and punched me in

the shoulder. "Don't go away with out telling me," she growled.

"Okay." I started the engine. Turning the headlights on, I let the SUV creep forward, easing around the traffic jam.

Our lights illuminated a pitched battle. The knight had dismounted and now smashed and hacked at the dead surrounding him. His horse screamed and pawed at the sodden ground nearby as if telling him to get the fuck out of there.

I hit the brakes. Opening the car door, I stood on the running board and, angling the M16 down from my higher position, I started dropping zombies with head shots, closing my eyes each time I fired to keep my night vision intact.

The knight didn't seem bothered by the evol that sank her teeth into his arm. He just reached over with one gauntlet-clad hand and jammed his fingers into her eyesuntil they popped and grey goop spurted out. With a yank he tore his arm free and drawing a sword he hacked the dead woman's head off.

Else left the car and, sword in hand, she joined the fight. Slicing the legs out from under a dead kid, she stamped her foot down on his neck, snapping it. From there she swung her blade, burying it in the oozing bulk of a zombie so obese his skin had split—great rolls of fat the color of rotting curds heaved and wobbled when he moved. She hacked at the fat man, carving chunks off him until she exposed the dull grey bones of his spine. A final chop and he broke in half like a felled tree.

We fought until the gun steamed and Else panted, twisting around seeking new enemies and finding none. I raised my rifle; only a precious few rounds remained. Being without a reliable weapon felt like being naked.

Else stared at the metal-clad man with open curiosity. He wiped his sword blade on the ragged remnants of a dead girl's dress before sheathing it. Then he reached up and unfastened a strap under his helmet, lifting it off to reveal a bearded face and long hair, greying at the temples. "Well met, m'lady," he said and bowed. "I beg your leave to recover my steed." He bowed again and went to the verge, whistling a sharp note that brought his horse at a brisk trot. Patting her on the neck, he spoke soothingly and then led the beast back to us.

"Body armor," I said. "Now that's cool."

"Thank you, sir. My weapons and those of the fair lady do not require ammunition, which I am sure you realize is going to become increasingly rare as we return to a more simple state of living."

Else reached out and tapped the greave on his arm. "They can't hurt you because you wear metal clothes," she said. Sometimes I could see her working things out.

"A knight of the realm wears his armor to fight for the honor of a beautiful lady," he said.

"And what do we call you, sir knight?" I didn't need to see a man wearing sheet metal and speaking like something out of an Arthurian legend to know he was either a genius or a complete nutter.

"Tristan, Sir Tristan of Penrose. I have a small holding in yonder forest land," he said, indicating the expanse of the Penrose State Forest to the south of the road.

"If we had metal clothes, we could be safe," Else said. She measured Sir Tristan with her eye. "He's about your size," she added glibly.

We all moved at once. Sir Tristan's sword came out, my rifle came up, but Else's blade was faster than both of us.

"Wait!" I yelled. Else's sword tip froze an inch from the knight's bare throat.

Tristan raised his hands slowly, letting his sword drop to the ground. "You have bested this humble warrior, m'lady, but I ask your mercy."

"Else," I warned. "We do not do this; we do not fuck with people!"

"Indeed, fucking with people is not an honorable pursuit," Tristan's voice cracked slightly.

"We can get further if we take his stuff," Else said.

"Yes we can," I agreed. Tristan blinked rapidly, his eyes

darting to me and back to Else. "But just because we can do something, it's no reason to do it."

"No reason not to either," Else the ever practical said, her arms tensing to deliver the killing blow.

"If I may offer a solution to our impasse?" Tristan didn't wait for permission. "If you accompany me to my castle, I can provide you with armor, weapons, and supplies, enough I am sure to see you on your way with good grace and enhanced safety."

"Sounds like a good deal, Else. Maybe we should see what he has up there?"

I waited while she thought about it. Tristan sweated until Else drew her sword back and then sheathed it. "Okay, but if it's shit I'm going to cut your head off."

Tristan breathed and lowered his hands. "Christ, you are one fucking hard-core chick," his noble accent evaporating as he deflated with relief.

"You don't know the half of it," I said, turning my rifle aside. "How far is your castle?"

"Not far; you'll have to walk, though. No vehicle access."

"Lead the way," I said and we headed up into rows of tall pines that whispered as we passed through them. Dirt tracks, some wide and smooth enough to drive a car or an SUV along with ease, crisscrossed the forest. The occasional felled tree across the track with side branches whittled back to sharp stakes, however, would stop any vehicle short of a tank.

Tristan's castle turned out to be a palisade wall of pine logs. More like a Wild West fort than a castle. The front wall ran a good hundred feet with a solid gate in the middle. The horse perked up sensing we were close to home, nuzzling at Tristan's shoulder as he tugged at a rope. Above us, a bell rang and the gate swung open.

"Welcome to Stronghold," he said. We went in, the gate closed behind us, and we stood in a roughly square courtyard.

The buildings inside the wall were log cabins. Chickens scratched around in the dirt, and a vegetable garden that looked like the recent rains may have come too late for it was marked out in one corner. Two more horses stood tethered at an open stable, and when Tristan unsaddled the horse, she immediately went to join the others, pushing her head into a bucket of water, drinking noisily.

"Where did you come from?" Tristan asked.

"West of here, Woomera," I said.

"Is it safe there?"

"No." There was no point in lying about it.

Tristan took us to one of the log cabins. It was quite spacious with a kitchen, living, and sleeping area to the right of the entrance. To the left was a blacksmith's shop complete with anvil, a brick fireplace, and a well-kept collection of tools. A blanket curtain hung along the back wall. Else jerked it aside and warily searched the back rooms. She found a long-drop toilet, food stores, and a pile of scrap metal. Though, she explained, not all in the same room.

CHAPTER 36

We ate rabbit stew with Tristan. He trapped rabbits and possums in the forest and grew vegetables irrigated with rainwater and his own waste. The setup was similar to the Moore Park community, but on a smaller scale. Then we slept, listening for the moans of the dead and hearing only the calls of owls and the hiss of possums in the trees. Before dawn we awoke to the smell of corn fritters and bush tea for breakfast. While we ate, Tristan started talking.

"We came out here all the time, the Medieval Celebration Society of New South Wales. We camped, and forgot about the real world for a while. When the epidemic started, we all came here. We brought our families and set up the defenses. A close-knit community of over sixty people, it worked out really well. We liked living off the land. We had the skills to do it. For some of us the end of the modern world was a chance to return to the world we truly wanted to live in." Tristan pushed some more sticks on the fire. "Then the evols came. We thought we were ready for them. We had built the wall, sharpened our weapons, and trained to fight. We were ready to defend what we had built."

I nodded. I'd heard versions of the same story before. People establishing a new society in the wake of the collapse of the old world, and then the undead come along and crash the party. Screaming, dying, chaos, panic, and the dream is over. Then the nightmare begins anew.

"We kept them at bay. We patrolled the forest, destroyed

the ones we found, and kept building. We were safe; people even had babies."

"I like babies," Else said, looking around with interest. "Where did they go?"

"Cholera. At least we thought it might be cholera. People living together, too many of them. Not enough water, the food was running out, and then people got sick. Some of them died. And . . ." Tristan's voice broke. "And fights broke out over what to do with them. Our doctor, he took care of the first ones. Before they came back. Then his wife died, she was sick with cancer he said. He'd nursed her the best he could for a few months but when she passed, he couldn't do it."

Else leaned forward, her eyes wide. "Then what happened?"

"She died in the middle of the night. Then she came back, she infected him. By the time the alarm was raised, they'd infected everyone else in the clinic." Tristan waved a hand towards one of the other log buildings.

"Twelve people infected, we had to slaughter them. Friends, family, children." Tristan shuddered. "It broke us, that night broke us. We were never the same after that. Within a week the first group left. Then others, all of them saying they would come back with help, or information or something."

"Well? Did they come back?" Else demanded.

"No," I said. "No one ever comes back."

"He's right, no one came back. Others died fighting the dead, or fighting amongst themselves. Some committed suicide, or got sick and died."

"How many did you put down?" I asked, like it mattered, or could give some scope to his pain.

"Fifteen, the last one this winter gone. A boy called Simon, died from a spider bite."

"Australia has over ten thousand species of spider, in seventy families. But only two can kill humans," Else recited.

"Not now, Else," I said. Tristan barely registered, still staring into the fire, seeing dead people.

I broke the silence before it became too uncomfortable. "You mentioned some armor we could use?"

Tristan shook himself. "Yeah, sure. Step into my office."

We went to the other end of the room. He took a short length of knotted cord and measured us. Arms, legs, and chests, all the vital bits that we didn't want chewed on.

After the measuring he gave me an old hoodie to wear. Then he picked up a pair of metal pants. "These are chain trousers, like long shorts; they tie off below the knee, so you will need a good pair of high boots to protect your lower legs." I stepped into the pants and Tristan attached a pair of leather straps like braces over my shoulders. Then he took a heavy shirt of chain mail out of an oil barrel. It still smelled of oil.

"Put your arms in here." I did and the mail slid down with a clinking melody, slithering against my body with a cold weight.

"It's heavy." I moved my arms and tried to imagine running in this. Else ran her fingers over the connected links.

"It feels smooth, like lizard skin."

"It will stop evol bites, swords, and any flying insect with a wingspan greater than eleven inches," Tristan said dryly.

"What about the plate mail?" I asked.

"You don't want that," Tristan said. "It's heavy and it requires training to learn how to fight in it. Worst of all you can't run while wearing it."

"Can you run in this?" I said moving from foot to foot, feeling the anchor weight on my shoulders.

"When a hundred zombies are on your arse, adrenaline will give you wings." Tristan finished strapping me into my new suit. He pulled a close-fitting chain-mail hood over my head and said, "Your hearing will be reduced, keep your eyes open."

I gave him a thumbs-up.

"You might need to help each other dress. It buckles here, and here. Drawstring around this collar, tie it off like this and tuck the ends in under the coif. That's the hood." Else watched intently and nodded.

I stood rustling slightly while Else got dressed. We selected helmets with grilled visors that covered the face. Fully kitted out, we went for a walk out in the courtyard. Else drew her sword and practiced moving with the added weight.

"She's good with a sword. Did you teach her?" Tristan asked.

I removed my helmet and pushed the coif back off my head. "Some of it. Mostly she's self-taught."

"Where are you going?" It was the question I'd been waiting for.

"Sydney."

"Why would you want to do that?" Tristan had been alone for months now. I'd met folks driven insane by solitude and fear before, and he seemed to be walking close to some kind of personal abyss.

"We have friends there in Moore Park." It was the explanation Else and I had practiced. We were going to join up with the Moore Park group.

"I . . . I can't leave here," Tristan said. "They'll come back. I told them all that I would stay here and wait for them to come back."

"Fair enough. If we find any members of the, ahh . . . Medieval Celebration group? I'll be sure to tell them you are still here," I said.

"Tell them to come home!" I stepped sideways, Tristan's beard flecked with sudden spit as he bellowed to the sky. "Tell them I've kept the place ready for them!"

"Sure thing, man, I'll tell them."

Else stopped fighting invisible enemies and watched us.

"Yeah, you go. You go and look for others, just like everyone else." Tristan stomped back into the cabin and slammed the door.

We helped ourselves to some supplies, a little corn meal, some dried meat, and a single canteen of water. I took a sword too; belting it on made me feel like an extra in a B movie. Unbarring the gate, we started walking back through the pine forest. The highway was in sight when the sound of hoofbeats caught up with us.

Tristan reined his horse in, fully armored, sword and shield gleaming in the morning sun. He raised his helmet visor and lifting his sword in salute he declared, "It is time for Sir Tristan to quest for the Holy Grail! I shall see you all in fair Albion!"

I half waved. Else thrust her sword to the sky. "Yay!" she yelled.

Tristan dropped his visor, kicked his horse, and cantered off through the trees.

"Wow, he is just perfect," Else declared.

The SUV waited for us, the carnage of the day before starkly evident in the bright sunshine. Birds foraging in the grass verge scolded but didn't flee when we walked past. The roar of the engine starting made us both jump a little and sent the birds leaping for the sky.

CHAPTER 37

We reached Sydney, driving up the highway all the way to Fairford Road where the mash-up of cars and wreckage clogged the arterial route like a heart attack. We suited up and walked the last few miles into the sprawling ruin of the city. Evols still wandered the streets so we crept around like teenagers coming in after curfew, all the old familiar terror coming back in a rush.

"There are so many of them . . ." Else whispered, her face grim.

"Yeah, and the ones to watch out for are the bastards smart enough to talk to you."

I watched for lights and signals that night, the patches of humanity that still shone in the darkness. They'd always been a reassurance when I traveled in Sydney, and a concern when those precious lights went out.

"We go that way." Else's study of the road maps made her more reliable than my own memory. On foot the path to Moore Park was long and twisted. I took detours, checking in on buildings I knew to be occupied, checking up on the people who eked out an existence behind the barricades. Every place had been abandoned, most now filled with trash piles that teemed with rats. More than once we found blood smears up the walls and the fly-blown remains of a few devoured corpses.

The evols weren't meant to do this. The city meat was protected by Tankbread; the geeks at the Opera House kept the supply coming and they left us alone. We left another gutted office building, the survivors torn to pieces or scattered and now roaming the streets hunting the rest of us.

I made Else pull her coif up and lace it tight before we stepped outside again. Wearing our armor and helmets we strode the streets of Sydney, a couple of crazy people in shark-proof suits. We avoided groups of evols, Else tugging on my arm, sensing them before I walked into trouble.

"They're hunting," she murmured as we lay behind a fence while a small crowd of them shambled past, moaning and stumbling into each other.

"The fuck?" I whispered.

"They're so hungry. They remember Tankbread, but they don't know what it is. They're hurting and they are so hungry."

"Fuck 'em." I stood up after the group passed. We climbed through car parks and shopping arcades. Broken mannequins and shards of glass crunched under foot. We slept that night in a penthouse suite atop an apartment building. The place had been redecorated. Someone had rescued and then copied famous works of art, re-creating them by finger-painting in streaks of shit smeared on the walls.

From the balcony I surveyed the night city. Fires lit the tops of various skyscrapers and I fancied I could hear singing. I took note of the locations, relieved that we were not alone in the city.

"What are they doing?" Else asked, curling her arms around me from behind, still oddly afraid of the heights we had ascended. She wouldn't step onto the balcony without clinging to me.

"They are singing, celebrating being human." We listened, snatches of song reaching us on the breeze.

"You never sing," she said.

"Nope, never had the knack."

Rats nested everywhere and it was easier to toss the mattress aside and sleep on the base. I woke up some time during the night; Else had snuggled in tight, but the walls were flickering orange and shadow. I lifted my head, and then rolled out of bed. Standing by the window, I looked out. A block away I saw a skyscraper engulfed in flames. The smoke, as black and thick as zombie blood, drifted from the fifteenth floor, spreading across the city. As I watched the blaze, I saw tiny figures falling from the windows, limbs spiraling as they plummeted. A cooking fire, or some source of comfort and light had been knocked over, and their sanctuary had become a trap. The way things were going, I thought, what the hell are the dead going to eat when we are all gone?

CHAPTER 38

I stand in a shallow boat, poled down the streets of Sydney, floating on a river of the dead. They move below me in numbers too great to count, in a slow circuit around Moore Park. Their flesh is in rags—it slides off their blackened bones and muffles their footsteps. They walk on a carpet of shed grey skin.

I step ashore at the sundered gates of Moore Park, where we fought against the legions of undead. Instead of Cerberus, three-headed watchdog of the underworld, the pregnant girl waits for me. Now she has three heads too: her round, blonde face; the tiny head of her unborn child, thrusting out at me from her torn belly; and the warpainted head of Josh mounted on her zombie killing stick.

They are going to be okay, I tell them. I'm going to save the world. Else is a cure for the evol plague. Three mouths open and scream that I'm too late. They are dead. The world is broken. This ground is no longer hallowed. This is a place where only the dead live and we are its ghosts.

I woke up screaming. Else leapt off the bed, ready to kill, and then kicked me in the ribs for scaring her like that. I wiped the sweat from my face, got my shit together, and we pulled out before dawn. Making our way down the seemingly endless rounds of stairs to ground level, we paused before stepping out into the silent streets. We waited, watching to see if any shufflers were taking an early morning constitutional.

"Moore Park is that way," Else said, her metal glove pointing past me. We started walking. Smoke from the burning office block wafted through the air like a stinking fog. It gave us cover, which meant it gave the dead cover, too. Buildings burned out of control in the city; the only thing you could do was stay away from the fire and look out for them coming down and showering the streets with rubble and falling glass.

The dead seemed drawn to the light of the fire. We went a city block out of our way to avoid a street congested with walkers and found more coming from other directions. Cutting through a decaying shopping center, we slipped out a side door and crept between cars along South Dowling Street. Evols wandered in loose groups and from there we ran for the green hills of Moore Park. The fences and barriers built up over years of living in a state of siege were intact and I'd nearly forgotten my nightmare until we came to the gate.

From the charred remains it was hard to tell what exactly tore the gate down. It could have been a battering ram, or a missile. Bits of bodies lay covered in dust and soot. Flies swarmed in angry clouds when we walked over the shattered remains. Else put her chain-mail sleeve over her mouth, sword held ready in the other hand as we walked into the park. The tents and shelters stood empty, flapping slightly in the breeze. A couple of dogs ferreted among the scraps of torn meat that littered the ground, and smoke drifted from the ashen remains of the few huts destroyed by fire. No one alive moved inside these walls.

I worked my way towards Josh's hut, refusing to accept that we might be two of the only people left alive in Sydney. Swords in hand, we advanced. The nearest dead rose up from the woman whose guts they feasted on and advanced towards us. Else cut the arm off the nearest evol. He grunted and stumbled, knocked off balance by the blow.

"Chain mail makes this harder," she muttered, embarrassed by the nonfatal wound. I finished the zombie, stepping up and smacking him across the throat with the sword I'd taken from Tristan's castle. His head fell back, opening up like a PEZ dispenser, and we were ready for the next two. I swung and carved a good chunk of skull out of the side of a male evol's head. His dead eyes rolled towards the wounded side and his hand reached up to grope at the black oozing mess leaking out of his brainpan. The second blow took the top third of his skull off and he dropped.

"I see what you mean," I said to Else. She adjusted her strikes and once again she cut the dead down with ruthless efficiency. Years have passed since I cut down an evol that I recognized, so I hesitated when Katie lurched up in front of me. I could see no recognition in her eyes, none of the fire that drove her thirst for revenge against the walking dead who destroyed her family, none of that casual contempt for the rest of us she had. Katie, I reminded myself, is dead. Destroying what remained would be what she wanted. I stabbed her through the throat with the sword before twisting the blade and cutting through the neck.

"More coming," Else warned.

"Run! Head to Josh's place!" I shouted. Else looked at me blankly, so I took off, our heavy mail clothing rattling as we ran. We could have stood and fought them for hours, protected by Tristan's chain mail. Killing zombies until our blades broke or we were smothered under a pile of hacked corpses. Running just seemed easier.

Josh's brick shed still stood in the center of the camp. We skidded to a halt under his drooping veranda and I opened the door. Stepping inside—Else right on my heels—we closed the door and put our backs against it.

"I've been waiting for you," Josh said.

"Josh, man am I glad to see you!" I felt truly elated. During our journey from Woomera to Sydney, talking to Josh again, explaining what we now knew to him, had been my focus.

He sat in a frayed wicker chair near the fire. Shelves of books stood behind him, and in the fireplace only cold ashes.

"You went to Woomera, you went all the way," he said.

"Yeah, we got there. And we got back." I stepped

forward. "Josh you aren't going to believe this--" Else blocked my way with her blade, her eyes intent on Josh.

"He's dead," she said.

"What?" I choked a laugh. "Don't talk shit, it's Josh."

He raised his head, the dark green sienna makeup now smeared, the black eye shadow deeper than usual, and the full color of his lips glowed fake.

"I have been waiting for your return," Josh said slowly.

"Josh . . ." A great weight crushed my chest, making it hard to breathe.

"I've held on, I've done everything I can. I enacted my emergency plan. It has two parts. It is my plan. Only to be used in emergencies."

"You're not making sense, man." I kept my sword ready. There would be almost enough space in here to kill him when we needed to.

"Apologies. Brain challenging. Think," Josh slurred slightly and then gathered himself. "Emergency plan phase one. Inject inhibitor agent. This will ensure high-functioning postmortem and allow for completion of phase two of emergency plan."

"What's phase two?" Else said.

"Destroy own brain," the zombie Josh said and lurched his arm up towards the side of his head. Else leapt forward, twisting the revolver out of his hand and stepping back against the fireplace.

"No, I need you," she said. "I need you to hear me and understand."

"You should be dead," Josh said, his head twisting to stare at Else.

"Woomera, we went to Woomera. I have a message from Doctor Wainright. You must listen."

"Wainright . . . the mouthpiece of the military aspects of the project. Cry 'Havoc' and let slip the dogs of war, that this foul deed shall smell above the earth with carrion men, groaning for burial," Josh murmured.

"Message follows, to Doctors Joshua Mollbrooke and Abraham Haumann, from Professor Richard Wainright,

PhD." Josh snorted at the title. Else ignored the interruption and continued speaking like she was reading from a transcript.

"Standing before you is the clone specimen provided by our colleague Doctor Haumann. Specimen received in poor condition, late-stage organ failure due to preprogrammed systemic failure and environmental factors, including malnutrition and dehydration. Utilizing our laboratory facilities we have managed to restore the specimen to full function. I have noted that Doctor Haumann has taken it upon himself to continue his work on immune system controls for control of GE virus factors. He appears to have made the breakthrough we postulated during our last weeks working together. To whit, this clone arrived with the requisite precursor elements in her physiology to create an antiviral blood plasma. I have completed the stem-cell manipulation required and she will be systemically operational within twelve days. Further course of action is as discussed. I look forward to seeing the results when she is introduced to the necrotic network. Yours sincerely, Doctor Richard Wainright, PhD, Combined Forces Project Woomera." Else took a long, shuddering breath and shook herself as if awakening from a trance.

"What was that about?" I said. Else shook her head, eyes wide with shock.

"It just came out of me, all those words. I remember hearing them when I was asleep."

"Hypnosis, subconscious implantation of message to be delivered to a target recipient," Josh said.

"Do you know what it means?" I asked.

"Yeah, it means you were too late to save me. But not too late to save the world." Josh convulsed, his mouth twisted in a pained grimace. His tongue, already turning grey, swiped over his rouged lips.

"Must control infection. Can't ohfuckjesus . . . stay, stay . . . focused . . . nngghhaa . . . " Josh exhaled like a live person. I took that as a good sign.

"We hypothesized about creating an antiviral factor. A

biological agent that could be introduced to the dead. Break the connections between them. Must be delivered to the… ohhhhhgodfuckme . . . delivered to . . . Adam. The alpha organism," Josh shuddered.

"You said it died? The first one you made, it died?" I looked from Josh to Else and back again, neither of them making any sense.

"Dead don't stay dead. Dead come back. Adam genetic source for Tankbread and mutated virus. Introduce refined Tankbread to Adam. Plasma. Kill the tree. Kill it at the roo— gaaaaaahhhhffunnnghhh! Root it out! It'll be hidden. Somewhere in the hhhhnngghhfuckme . . . the house. Look thereohhhggghhod . . . "

Whatever battle Josh was fighting against his own body he finally lost. The light in his eyes filmed over and he quivered with a final convulsion as his lips curled back in a hungry snarl.

I took the pistol from Else's hand and put it to Josh's forehead. There were no words. I fired, splattering his brains all over a shelf full of books that no one would ever read again.

CHAPTER 39

Else opened the door of Josh's brick shed and immediately slammed it shut again.

"Zombies?" I asked

"Uh-huuh!" She looked startled. "Lots and lots of them."

"Shit." I searched the room. Some tattered furniture, stacks of books, a filthy hammock nest of bedding, and a few cooking utensils. Armed with only the pistol and our swords, we were going to die in here.

I found a bottle, pulled the cork, and took a sniff. Alcohol, strong smelling. Tearing strips from a sheet I stuffed them down the bottle neck. "Find some matches, or a lighter, anything to make fire," I said.

Else rummaged near the fire and held up a silver cigarette lighter.

"Thanks." I took the lighter and flicked it alight. "Okay, now open the door!"

She pulled the door open and I stepped out under the veranda awning. Evols murmured and crowded forward. I touched the flame to the rag wick. Blue fire flared and I tossed the bottle into their midst. A dull wumph noise and the bottle exploded with a flash of light. The burning alcohol sprayed over the crowd, setting hair, clothing, and dry, dead flesh alight.

"Go!" I yelled and Else shot past me, her sword swinging as she went. We hightailed it out in the confusion and headed across the ruined campsite. The fire spread; evols don't move fast, even when they're on fire. These ones blundered into each other, tripping over the last of the tents and shelters, setting the remaining dry canvas ablaze. Thick smoke and searing heat filled the air. I kept my head down and ran, Else at my side, until we pulled up short, a wall of fire blocking our way.

"Go back!" I yelled and we ran down a path between two lean-tos. A moment later fire engulfed them behind us. Dodging between burning tents and immolated zombies we reached the fence. From there we headed around the perimeter of the inferno. The dead filled the gateway, drawn in by the heat and light of the sudden fire that blew hot embers at our backs.

"Can't go back!" Else screamed.

"Forward!" I yelled and we charged into the fray. Crashing into the front line of the advancing line of zombies, our swords rose and fell. Dead teeth snapped and tore at our chain-mail suits. We pushed them back, cutting through flesh and bone. The thick black ooze that their blood had become made the ground slick underfoot. Else howled, whirling and slashing. When we cut their legs out from under them, they crawled on severed stumps. When we hacked their reaching arms off, only their mouths remained. Gaping, hungry, and yearning to feed on our warm, blood-filled flesh.

Arms aching under the added weight of the heavy armor, I fought on. My sword caught deep in a woman's throat. I smashed my armored fist into a dead man's face. His bones crunched and I felt the alien stroke of his rotting tongue slithering hungrily through the gap between my glove and metal sleeve.

We fought to a standstill, cutting them down and fighting to stay on our feet as the dead dragged on us. Visions of my river Styx dream rose unbidden and the heat of adrenaline washed out of me with the cold flood of real terror. We were fucked. The dead forced Else to her knees. One of them with enough neurons firing to realize the helmet might come off pulled at her head. Three zombies tackled me in slow motion. I started to fall, yelling for Else to run.

Then silver flashed before my eyes and an evol's head flew off right in front of me. My steel helmet came off and I blinked my streaming eyes in the thick smoke. Tristan's horse reared, its hooves striking down like cleavers, crushing skulls and stamping the rotting brains into paste.

"For Albion!" Tristan roared as he rode down the teeming horde of zombies. His arrival distracted those attacking us, so we took advantage of the moment and fought our way clear of the clinging evols.

"Well met!" Tristan shouted from astride his horse. The heavy ball and chain weapon he favored whirred and hit. The spiked ball sang its own funeral dirge, like a bullroarer, as Tristan smashed rotting skulls.

A thousand pounds of angry horse and a rider skilled with melee weapons is a big advantage in any fight. We broke through the knots of zombies confused by the one-man cavalry charge. Tristan covered our rear, holding them back until we made it to South Dowling Street. We took shelter in the buildings opposite the park, waiting there and catching our breath until Tristan rode over the hill and came cantering down towards us.

"Sir Tristan!" I stood in the doorway and waved. He turned his horse and rode the animal right into the building with us.

"A magnificent battle!" He had his knightly accent back again.

"Yeah, it was quite something." I didn't want to play along.

"You saved us, brave Sir Tristan!" Else said. She didn't know enough to humor him; her adoration was genuine.

"It is my duty as a knight of the realm to give aid to all those in mortal peril, m'lady." He rose in his stirrups and bowed to her. Else executed a clumsy curtsey. I felt my gorge rising.

"For fuck's sake, enough pissing about. We need to keep moving." I wiped the shit off my sword and sheathed it, ignoring Else's hurt expression. "This is not a game. We almost died out there," I added, staring out through broken windows at the empty street.

"Yes but I came to your aid and we won the day," Tristan insisted.

"Bullshit! There are millions of evols out there. They don't care that you saved us, they only want to eat us, or make us like them. We have to find out if anyone's left alive at the Opera House. Until we get there, find Doctor Haumann, and he does his thing we haven't won shit!" I kicked an empty can, sending it careening off the walls. Nearly dying always puts me in a bad mood.

"We're alive," Else said, slipping her arm around my waist and resting her head on my shoulder.

"Yeah, but for how long? We have to get to the Opera House. We don't know if anyone's left alive in there."

Else pressed herself tighter against me, her fingers brushing against my neck.

"The restless dead will seek us out, I suggest we make haste," Tristan said. Like I hadn't been telling them that only a moment before.

"Sure, let's go." I kissed Else on the top of the head and she smiled, squeezing my hand. We slipped out of the ruined building. The sun was high in the sky now, the breeze had shifted and the smoke drifted downwind.

Last time we came this way Else hadn't learned to speak, we were on the back of a motorcycle, and all hell had broken loose at the Opera House. I chose not to share any of this with Tristan. The horse was hard to hide and when we encountered small groups of evols Tristan rode into them with gusto, weapons flailing.

"If everyone was like Sir Tristan, the evols would all be gone," Else said, watching him work.

"If everyone was like Sir fucking Tristan, we'd still be living in the Dark Ages. Come on, I'd like to get there before dark."

"Hey," she said to my retreating back. "Hey! What the fuck is your problem?"

I turned around. "My problem? You're drooling over the Tin Man and I'm busting my arse trying to keep you alive!"

"I'm not . . . drooling. What the fuck does that even mean?" Else stamped her foot in frustration, pulling her helmet off and pushing her coif back from her sweat-plastered head.

I ripped my own chain-mail hood off and threw it on the ground. "It means you like him. It means that everything I've done for you is worth nothing because as soon as some new guy comes along you think he is the best!"

"You're crazy!" Else laughed. "I just like the way he kills zombies!"

"What's wrong with the way I kill fucking zombies?!" I threw my hands up in the air and marched back to her.

"Nothing! He just . . . he's got a nicer way of doing it."

I got in her face, yelling and waving my arms. "You're a fucking moron! And he's completely fucking insane! He thinks he's a knight in King Arthur's court! He's going to get killed thinking he's fighting a dragon or some shit!"

Else's tanned face was pale with fury. She opened her mouth and then with a snarl she drew her sword and sprang forward, her body slamming against me as the blade flashed past my ear. Hearing a wet gurgling sound, I twisted to see an evol with one crusted-over eye socket, his teeth breaking on the sword blade rammed through the back of his mouth. Else twisted the sword and cut the spine. The zombie slid off her weapon and her arms curled around my neck. With tears welling in her eyes she said, "I don't love him."

"I don't love him either," I mumbled, and then I was kissing her. She didn't react for a long moment, and I felt a flush of stupid rushing up my neck. Then she kissed me back, her lips touching mine softly in an exploratory way. A soft whimper came from deep in her throat and her crotch pressed against me. I went hard, harder than I'd ever been as her mouth opened against mine. I heard a soft growl and opened my eyes. Evols, always turning up at the worst moments. I pushed Else back, her sword flicked around my head, and she used the momentum of her spin to decapitate a woman wearing broken glasses. We killed two more, stabbing them and chopping them into the ground.

"We'll talk about this later," I said. Else nodded, breathless and flushed from more than the fight.

"Where the hell did Tristan get to?" I started running. The chain-mail suit was heavy and hot and even without the coif I was sweating hard. The street had gone quiet, the dead crushed and still. We got to the end of the block, looking each way and turning in slow, searching circles.

His horse came into view around a rusting army tank. Walking slowly she snorted and flicked her head, reins trailing in the dirt. I made gentle clicking noises and caught hold of the animal, patting her neck and looking for Tristan.

"Here!" Else yelled and pulling the horse I jogged in the direction of her shout. I found Else crouched over the still form of Sir Tristan. He lay on his back surrounded by six destroyed evols. A broken piece of steel doorframe had burst through his chest and the wound was oozing thick blood.

"I am slain . . ." he whispered, red spilling from his mouth.

"No, you can get up. We can get you help." Else unfastened his helmet and slipped it and the chain-mail hood off his head.

"Easy, don't try to move," I said. I could see the metal spike through his chest was the only thing keeping him from bleeding out in seconds.

"One of those devils got under the horse, she reared and threw me, I landed badly." His voice had dropped to a whisper, his words clogged with blood. "Don't let me become one of them, there is no honor in such a soulless existence." He clutched at my hand, his eyes burning.

"Sure thing, Sir Tristan. I'll not let you suffer beyond death." It sounded weird to my ears but he seemed pleased.

"Thank you, my brave comrades. Never has a knight had such a fine squire, and a lady . . . truly the fairest in the realm . . . I bid you ave atque vale . . ." He sighed, his eyes closing. Standing up, I lifted his sword and took his head.

"Hail and farewell," Else whispered.

CHAPTER 40

I've eaten more horses than I've ridden, but Tristan's steed let me mount up and then only sidestepped slightly when I pulled Else on behind. It was nice not to have to walk for awhile.

We rode through a city where we seemed to be the only living beings left. A month ago life still clung on here with that determination of humankind to survive against all odds. Sure, some of us kissed dead-arse and others fortified themselves behind high walls and barbed wire with a siege mentality.

Then there were the ones like me, pledging allegiance to no group or philosophy. I didn't follow leaders, or join communes awaiting the arrival of the mothership, or the Americans or Jesus Christ in a chariot of fire. I just kept moving and surviving. Never planning any further than my next meal, my next safe place to sleep, and never allowing myself to believe in anything. I realized as I rode through the decaying streets of old Sydney that in spite of myself, I had found something to believe in: the warm-blooded girl who confused and terrified me with the way her mind devoured new information. Such a contrast to the total vulnerability and naivety she had when we met. With Else's head resting against my back, her arms linked around my waist, and the horse slowly plodding down the cracked blacktop, I finally understood that I did love her. I'd spent the years since the end of the world avoiding any kind of permanent arrangement because the ones you love die in this world.

Try not to screw this up, I told myself.

* * *

The Opera House stood shining in the late afternoon sun. The shipping container barricade was intact and the bus they used as a mobile gate still blocked the entrance.

"How do we get in?" Else said, wiggling tighter against my back and resting her chin on my shoulder.

"We can try through the botanic gardens, they have a farm up there." I kept my eyes on the streets and buildings. Where were the dead? The evols should be all over this place. Sydney had a population of over four million, and that many walking corpses meant you could always see some of them, but this street was deserted.

I turned the horse and we followed the wall around the green slope of the gardens until we found a place to get up off the road. The horse immediately started pulling her head down to graze. I let her do it, sliding Else down to the ground and then dismounting. The horse let me lead her, chewing mouthfuls of grass as we climbed the small hill.

"Peaceful, isn't it?" Else said, as we walked through the waist-high grass.

"Yeah, almost too peaceful." We came out on a wide path that led through the trees. Birds flew squawking from tattered skeletons at the sound of our approach.

"Mind the cow shit," I said as we walked. The livestock they kept up here seemed to be doing okay. Eating grass and waiting for the evols to milk them probably.

We passed gardens that showed signs of being tended until recently. Now weeds sprouted among the rows of fresh fruit and vegetables. I picked apples, oranges, and strawberries and we sat on the edge of the road, eating our first decent meal in a couple of days.

"When we have our place, I want a garden like this," Else said. "With all these trees and these things."

"Strawberries," I said.

"Strawberries, they are my favorite."

"You should try them with fresh cream and icing sugar," I said, eying a wandering cow.

"Cream from cows?" Else followed my gaze. "Can we catch one and kill it for the cream?"

"You don't have to kill a cow for the cream, you just milk them." I explained where milk comes from, and how it's extracted. Else burst out laughing. It was an infectious mood and, high on fruit sugar, we rolled around on the ground laughing till we cried. I guess the first person who ever thought of milking a cow got the same reaction from his friends.

We set off again, feeding the horse apple cores and leading her down the path. The cows were used to people, and we found a corral where two of them stood next to large plastic buckets waiting to be milked.

"No. Maybe later, on the way back," I said firmly. Something was not right around here, and I wasn't in the mood to try and milk a cow no matter how much Else sulked.

"Good-bye, horse," Else said when we unsaddled Tristan's steed and left her near a water trough. There were no guarantees anymore and we might not be coming back.

"Kangaroos can't breed with wallabies and horses can't breed with cows," Else stated as we set off through the long grass, passing grazing wallabies hopping around in the late afternoon sun.

"Is that right . . . ?" I was distracted; that old lizard hindbrain was pissing ice water down my spine again. I waved Else to silence and, dropping to a low crouch, I moved through the grass, passing buildings that had more recently been converted to stables and food stores. We stopped at the fence that bordered the wide-open terrace around the Opera House. Peering over the edge of the sheer bank, I could see the long pedestrian arcade was deserted. No living creatures moved and no evols either.

We headed along the fence line. The ground sloped down and we sat in the long grass looking out through the fence at the sail-inspired structures in front of us.

"Where did all the people go?" Else whispered.

"Dunno. Maybe they left?" Nothing obvious told us why they left. Did the evols kill everyone like at Moore Park? It made sense. The peace between the Tankbread producers and the zombies had collapsed the day we escaped from under the Opera House. Why would the dead leave anyone alive?

The wide steps with the sandbagged machine gun nests were unmanned. Sea birds shrieked and settled, tearing carrion strips from the few remaining bodies. A smell of salt and decay came on the breeze.

"Let's wait till dark and then we go in for a closer look."

Else nodded and slumped against me with a sigh. I crawled back into the long grass and made a nest. She crawled after me, stripping off her chain mail and curling up to sleep. I dropped my armor next to hers and lay there listening to the cows lowing and wondering what waited for us inside.

CHAPTER 41

I woke up to darkness and the ground sucking the warmth out of me. I sat up, shivering. Else kneeled nearby, sword in hand, staring out towards the fence, her face intense like a cat on the hunt.

Slipping forward on my elbows, I murmured, "What's up?"

"Evols," she said, her eyes steady in the darkness.

"You can see them?" I blinked and stared into the gloom.

"Can't you?"

"No, I can't see shit. It's dark." I drew my knees up to stand but Else yanked me down again. Now I saw them, three zombies, moving carefully, their clothes dark with fresh bloodstains. One still had a rifle gripped in his dead hand.

"They have guns now," Else whispered.

"Yeah, I recognize the one on the left. He was part of the house security force. Useless prick."

The patrol walked on. When they vanished around the corner, Else stepped out of the grass and headed into the open, running in a crouch.

"Shit," I muttered. Snatching up my sword, I scrambled after her. We were without any armor and had no protection should the dead get wind of our presence. Our only hope was that there might be survivors inside the soaring edifice of the Opera House.

I followed Else up the steps. She ducked down inside one

of the sandbag emplacements. I dropped in beside her.

"Guns," I said. "Cool." Firearms were scattered like discarded toys around the sandbag nest. I helped myself to a shotgun, loaded it, and stuffed my pockets with spilt shells.

"Where are the doors?" Else looked along the glass wall across the top of the steps.

"There, between those sandbags." We both glanced around. Seeing the steps were clear, we bolted. The glass door had been smashed. I pushed Else through the gap and crawled in after her.

Inside, the place was a mess. Potted plants lay shattered on the floor, shelving units were tipped over, and blood stained the desks and walls. I thought hard about where Charlie had led me last time I was here, through a door and down long corridors.

"Baby food," I said and set off to where the cartons lay spilled across the floor. Stepping carefully, we eased our way into the dark corridor.

"Doctor Haumann's lab was down here somewhere." I mentally ticked off the bathroom as we passed. A pool of dried blood spilled over the edge of the doorway, hanging in dark red icicles. Bullet holes dotted every wall and empty shells tinkled underfoot, threatening to send us skating with each step.

We saw no bodies. No walking corpses, and no chewed remnants of people. I held the shotgun ready and tried each locked door we passed.

One door stood open, a rack of guns spilling out into the hallway and a spray of blood fanned out across the opposite wall. "Looks like they left some for us."

I collected two submachine guns, matching the magazines on the floor to the ones already loaded into the guns and shoving them into my shirt. Else watched me shop. "Why don't we just stab and cut them?" she asked.

"Because guns fire bullets, and bullets can destroy an evol's brain from a safe distance."

"But they are so noisy," Else scowled at the weapons.

"Else," I said, shoving the SMGs at her. "It's likely you

are going to need to shoot some dead motherfuckers. Get used to it."

Else carried the SMGs and I accessorized with an ammo belt for a pump-action Mossberg shotgun and a heavy-bladed knife which I shoved in my belt. Three corridors later we stopped where a fluorescent light flickered beyond a door that had been smashed off its hinges. Long strips of torn flesh hung from the shattered door panels. It looked like a giant cheese grater. Something wanted to get into the laboratory beyond real bad. We crept into the room where I'd first met Doctor Haumann. Broken glass and spilled chemicals lay in a rainbow sheet across the floor. The mess crunched underfoot and the air had the acrid, metallic stench of spilt acid.

The door on the other side of the lab stood closed. I reached out to open it when Else spun around, her sword flashing into her hand. A filthy figure in a stained lab coat lurched back, his hands rising in surrender. I jerked the shotgun up and almost fired in fright. Blood and body juice wept through the broken crust on his ruined face. The flesh around his right eye had melted and the lidless orb bulged red and bloody. His left eye was swollen shut and deep pockmarks scoured his flesh down to the bone. The nose and cheeks were gouged, melted like in a fire, and he'd been pulling the tattered strips of his skin away, making his wounds bleed afresh and revealing the patchwork of his teeth. The geek reached out blindly towards us.

"Hel-bee," he whined through deformed lips. "Hel-bee." Else drew her arm back, ready to strike him down.

"Hang on, Else. Yeah, mate, we can help you. Tell us what happened here?"

"I'b burned, albaline . . ." His burst face and swollen tongue made it hard for him to pronounce his m's and k's.

"Alkaline breaks down proteins. Acid will burn you, a strong alkaline will dissolve you," Else said in her matter-of-fact way.

"We'll get you help, but first, what happened here?"

Through careful listening I made it out.

"Evols attacked the sanctuary. They destroyed so much. I don't know why. Doctor Haumann was alive last time I saw him. Charlie Aston too. I was too afraid to call out. I've been hiding here for weeks."

He cried a lot, dry hacking sobs, thick spittle and fresh blood oozing from his ruined mouth so much that my patience wore thin by the time we got what we needed out of him.

"Beese, hel-bee," he moaned again. I nodded at Else and stepped back. It took her two blows to decapitate him. I like to think he died after the first one.

Laying the shotgun on a bench I went over to one of the computers, more out of nostalgic curiosity than anything. I wiggled the mouse and the screen lit up, then it asked for a password or thumbprint identification.

"Else, bring me that guy's thumbs," I said. They needed a bit of cleaning, but his prints were intact. After a moment, we got the computer up and running. I clicked on folders at random, seeing nothing that meant anything to me.

"Wait, go back," Else said from behind my shoulder. "Open that one," her finger stabbed at a folder labeled "Poison Well." I double clicked.

"Just more geek papers on geek stuff," I said.

"Poison Well. I remember that name." Else clenched her eyes shut in concentration. "Before all of this, I sometimes remember things from when I was born. A man with white hair, said that Project Poison Well would be a success within twenty generations."

"Great, so what's Project Poison Well?" I asked.

"I can answer that question for you." We both jumped at the voice from behind us. Charlie-fucking-Aston, that bastard stood before us fresh faced, clear eyed, and thinking for himself. I lunged at him, but he stepped aside and casually threw me into the wall. Two evols holding guns stepped into the room and held Else at bay.

Smiling, Charlie continued. "Project Poison Well was Doctor Haumann's grand plan for the salvation of the human race. He engineered a mutated version of the Adam virus into an infection vector that would only attack reanimated cells, effectively destroying the risen dead and in time, eradicating the virus. He believed one day this antiviral would be available as a vaccine, so if any one inoculated by it were bitten, they would in fact infect the evol instead of the other way around."

"He told me he was close to saving humanity." I winced, shards of broken glass cutting into my hand where I'd fallen.

"Indeed he was, and I could not allow that to happen."

"Oh, so you're completely fucking nuts then?" I said, gingerly standing up.

"Not at all. I am however an absolute realist. Humanity has no future. The evols are the new dominant species on earth. If Haumann had been allowed to continue with his work, the future would be far less certain."

"Without his work we don't have a future!" I yelled and the evols shifted on their feet, shaking their heads in agitation.

"Humanity's light has gone out. Only the dying embers of that fire remain. Homo sapiens are facing extinction. The era of Homo necrosis has dawned." Charlie spoke with the calm certainty of the completely insane.

"So why are you still alive?" I clenched my fist, driving the jagged pieces of glass deeper into my hands. I watched the evols' noses twitch as blood dripped through my fingers.

"Because this is a time of transition. There is much still to be done. When my time comes, I will take my place at the right hand of Adam."

"Let me guess, you're going to wipe his dead arse?"

Charlie ignored the barb. "Tell me, how does it feel to have come so far and suffered so much, only to fail now? You got the Tankbread all the way to Woomera. Wainright helped you. He always was a special kind of genius. She's a primed weapon now, isn't she? Wainright made her a walking biological bomb. One bite of her tender flesh and we're all goners." Charlie shivered in ecstasy. "Dissecting her is going to be fascinating." He licked his lips; the idea of Else flayed open on a laboratory slab turned him on.

I gave a short laugh. "What's your secret, Charlie? The geek I saw a month ago couldn't throw people across the room."

"I have been preparing myself for the new world order. Stem cells, steroids, and some gene therapy. You should try it." He flexed his arms until his shirtsleeves split, the muscles bulging in obese cords.

"No thanks, I hear steroids make your dick shrivel." I lashed out with my palm open. My hand slapped Charlie right in the eye socket. The glass buried in my palm grated against my hand bones but Charlie shrieked as I burst his gloating eyeball.

The two evols moaned and convulsed at the sudden noise, their guns firing wildly. I ducked the spray of bullets and tackled Charlie to the floor. Launching from him, I threw myself to the bench where my shotgun lay. Snatching it up I turned, ready to fire, and saw Else standing, sword drawn over the still bodies of the two evols. Charlie had fled.

CHAPTER 42

Else bound my hand with bandages salvaged from the lab's first aid kit. "Is it true what he said?" I asked while watching the door.

"I guess, I mean I don't know." She wouldn't look me in the eye.

"If you let yourself get bitten, will your blood destroy the evol that bites you or not?" I asked.

"Yes!" she shouted and then started crying. "But to be really effective I would need to be eaten by as many as possible. I would need to die. Wainright, Mollbrooke, and Haumann knew that. They used you. They used you to get me to Woomera so he could add the missing gene tech to me."

I reached out and drew her close, holding her in a tight hug while she shuddered. "It's not going to happen, okay? I told you, we are going to fix this, then find a place somewhere and have babies and raise cows and grow crops."

She pulled back, her laughter shaking the tears from her cheeks.

"You and me, forever," I said and we kissed and it made everything worthwhile until Else broke away.

"I can't stop hearing them."

"Hearing who?" I asked

"Evols, there are so many of them here, a great booming chorus of voices. They are all whispering, but so many it sounds like shouting."

I frowned at the pained expression on her face. "We should get out of here. There's nothing left for us, no sanctuary anymore. We take the horse and ride like hell. Head north, up into Queensland, or Northern Territory. I've heard it's safe up there."

Else silenced me with another brief kiss. "No, I was created for a purpose. Maybe not by Sister Mary's god, but by men. I have to fulfill that purpose. One of the books I read, it was very confusing except for one line. The writer, Douglas Adams, said, "I seldom end up where I wanted to go, but almost always end up where I need to be." Else shrugged. "Destiny is what happens when we make choices."

"If you say so." I flexed my wrapped hand. "Else, why didn't you just shoot the bastards?"

"I thought I might shoot you by mistake." She took me by the hand and we left the lab, walking down narrow corridors strewn with trash and rotting food.

"In here," I said, and pulled Else into a dorm room. The place was untouched, beds neatly made and clothes still hung on the racks. I closed the door and wedged the nearest bed against it.

"What are you doing?" Else said.

"This," I answered and put my arms around her. She was getting good at kissing, and my balls had swollen up like blue coconuts since our first make-out session the day before.

She hesitated when I started removing her clothes, so I moved my hands to my own shirt. Shedding guns and ammo, I pulled the shirt over my head. I felt the grime and filth of our journey and the battles we had fought slipping away. Else whimpered in a deep throaty way and grabbed at my pants. Pulling the belt loose, she nearly tore my jeans down. I fell back onto the bed kicking my boots off.

Else arched her back, dropping her sword and guns, lifting her shirt over her head and exposing all of her long lean body to me for the first time. The sharp contrast between her tanned skin and the paler areas was the most beautiful thing I had ever seen. With a swift downward shove she slipped out of her jeans and crawled over me.

"How . . . ?" she whispered, her voice thick with need. I swallowed hard and put my hands to the back of her head, drawing her down for a kiss. She melted against me, the heat of my blood feeling cool against her fiery skin. Else moaned as our lips slid over each other, our tongues stroking as her hands worked over my body. Reaching between us she squeezed me so hard I grunted. Rolling over, I stretched her out along the bed and kissed my way down her neck. Else gasped as I touched her breasts with my lips and tongue.

I stroked my good hand between her thighs, feeling the heat and wetness. Trying to hold back and take this slowly, I stroked her gently with one finger until she bucked and thrust up against me.

"Ohhhh . . ." Else moaned, her eyes tightly shut and her mouth gaping open in a nearly silent howl. I teased her until she spasmed under my hand and cried out. Her head thrashed from side to side against the pillows. She took a moment to recover, breathing hard and reaching down to stroke my shaft.

"It goes inside me," she said and worked her butt down the bed until we lined up in the right position. I lowered my face to meet hers, kissing her as I slipped into that tight moist heat.

Else moaned into my mouth as I worked slowly, stroking in and out, pushing deeper. When my full length was buried inside her, we were both shining with perspiration. Else beamed up at me, her chest heaving.

"Faster," she said. "It feels good when you do it faster." I nodded and started thrusting. We arrived together, my whole body exploding into a nova of light and everything I was flooded into the beautiful woman underneath me.

I collapsed completely spent beside Else on the bed. My eyes closed as I waited for the blood to return to my brain.

"Can we do it again?" Else asked. I opened an eye and stared at her hopeful face.

"Sure," I sighed. "Any time you want. Except we shouldn't stay here too long."

Else frowned and rolled over to sit up on the side of the bed. She snatched up her T-shirt and roughly pushed her arms into the sleeves. I sat up, leaning on one elbow. "Hey," I said. "We have all the—" I stopped. Under Else's right arm was a brightly colored, round adhesive patch.

"What is this?" I reached out and stroked it with my fingertips. The color was a bright blue. No way it could change that fast.

"Donna gave it to me, when I was in the hospital. She said it might change color." Else lifted her arm and twisted to see the patch.

"Did she tell you what it meant?" A cold wind blew right through the ice cave of my gut.

"Nope." Else twisted harder, nearly tying herself in knots to see the patch. I reached out and ripped the adhesive off. Else hissed at the sting of it.

"It's nothing. Just means you are healthy, and one day you will make a great mother." I smiled at her until I thought my face would shatter.

CHAPTER 43

As we stalked through the dimly lit corridors of the
Opera House, I thought about Doctor Donna Preston. She
took a sperm sample from me, a nice fresh one, just the sort
of thing to inseminate a fertile female. I knew Donna wasn't
pregnant, but maybe she had knocked Else up with my
seed?

Else led us through unfamiliar corridors, up stairwells
clogged with human remains and through a warren of
empty passageways. The evols patrolled, but Else sensed
them before they saw us and we ducked into rooms, or
waited around corners and ambushed them. We stepped out
of the darkness, silently cutting them down with our swords
before moving on. We didn't speak. She knew what she
needed to do, and I couldn't tell her why she couldn't lose
her life to save the world. Without her and the tiny collection
of cells in her womb that would one day be our child, there
was no world. At least not one I wanted to live in.

"Wait," Else whispered and then peeked around the
corner of a wide gallery high above the ground. "Shit," she
muttered and pulled her head back.

"Problem?" I murmured and took a careful look. The
gallery was lined with evols. Soo-Yong, zombie master of the
Eastern Suburbs, strode like a general along their ranks.

"We're going to need to kill a lot of them," Else said.

"Best get started then." I flexed my arms and cracked my
neck. Lifting the shotgun, I took a deep breath.

Else reached up and kissed me, her eyes shining. "Let's fuck their shit up," she said and stepped into the gallery. Else leveled her guns and squeezed off the first rounds she'd ever fired. The SMGs barked and jerked up; the short burst of rounds split an evol in half from groin to shoulder. The glass windows overlooking the harbor exploded. I hurried after her. The shotgun boomed and a dead-head exploded. The ranks of zombies lurched forward with bared teeth and blazing hunger in their eyes. Else mastered the physics of automatic weapons in seconds, correcting her aim and scything heads off the dead in a long scream of hot lead.

Soo-Yong snarled and shoved the others forward, a shield of decomposing meat. Else's guns clicked dry; she dropped one and with her free hand reloaded. A dead woman lunged at Else's throat. The gun came up and the evol's head disintegrated as chunks of ceiling tiles rained down on our heads.

We fired until the guns burned hot and smoke clogged the air in a stinking cloud. Evols kept on coming, clawing their way up from wherever they were waiting to die at last at our feet.

Else abandoned her second gun and went to work with the sword. She danced and the zombies fell at her feet. I bludgeoned a teenager's face in with the butt of the shotgun and knocked him to the ground. With no time to reload, I drew my own sword and hacked his head off. We worked the crowd until only Soo-Yong remained.

"You not so bad dog," he said, his lips curling back in a snarl. "You came home."

"I came back to destroy every last arse-maggot one of you," I spat.

"You came back to die," Soo-Yong sneered. I spun my sword up over my shoulder and buried the heavy blade deep in his necrotic skull.

Else turned and raised her hands at a heavy wooden door. "In there," she said simply and pushed the door. I pulled her back.

"No, whatever is in there, it isn't your destiny. It isn't

anything that you need to die for."

Else struggled against my grip. "I have to!" she hissed. "Let me go!"

"There's another way." I checked the corridor; it was still clear. Taking the knife from my belt, I twisted Else's hand palm up. Taking the blade, I drew its edge across her skin. Blood welled up, thick and brighter than rubies. Else snarled, jerking back but unable to break my grip. I sank slowly to one knee. Else stared at me, her eyes widening in horror. Yeah, she'd gotten real smart during our time together.

"No!" she cried as I pressed my mouth to her wound, sucking and drawing the thick, rich blood from her wound and gulping it down. Else's other hand balled into a tight fist. She slammed it into the side of my head, knocking me across the corridor. I regained my feet, wiping the salt and copper taste of her from my mouth.

"This changes nothing," she growled, her teeth bared in fury.

"You're right," I said. "It doesn't change anything."

Her eyes flared bright with anger. I threw myself against the door, forcing it open. I heard Else scream. Slamming the door, I shot the bolt, locking myself in. I turned and saw a vision of hell laid out before me.

I had dreamed of a cave made of flesh. A living cathedral that pulsed and writhed. Except this wasn't my nightmare from Harris' train. This was real. The vast auditorium of the Sydney Opera House was overgrown with moving flesh in all shades of putrescence, from angry red to gangrenous black. Fumaroles of yellow pus swelled and burst, draining down over glistening green flanks that shuddered and pulsated. The dead filled the massive chamber, like the faithful attending church; they swayed and moaned, arms raised in supplication.

The door I had come through opened onto the highest gallery above the hall. Above my head, steadily growing tendrils of meat pushed across the ceiling and the air was thick with the cloying stink of rot and slow digestion.

I staggered forward, slipping on the foul plasma that seeped from the carpet of flesh underfoot. At the edge of the gallery I stared out into the wide space of the auditorium. The low moans of the living drifted upwards on the perfect acoustics of the hall. The survivors of Sydney and those who called the Opera House sanctuary lay embedded in hanging folds of quivering flesh around the walls. I watched horrified as a segmented tentacle, like a barbed and prehensile cock, slid out from the wall, the end of it splitting open revealing a bone spike glistening with dewy slime. The spike thrust forward and penetrated a writhing human figure. The tentacle pulsed and swallowed, sucking the shrieking body dry in seconds.

I looked away from the feeding and saw the stage for the first time. It wasn't a heart that hung there suspended by long ropes of animated meat. Instead it was a shape like a man. On the ground he would have stood close to eight feet tall. His body rippled with muscle, and every contour was perfect. The figure hung as if crucified, arms held wide, a massive fan of membranous webbing behind him. From this halo of skin ran tubes and lines like veins, all connected to the greater expanse that covered the floor and walls. The nutrients being sucked out of the living flowed back into him.

The door behind me shuddered under repeated blows and then exploded inwards. I lifted my shotgun, expecting a legion of evols. But Else came through alone. She staggered at the sight, looking past me at the figure suspending over the stage.

"Adam . . ." she croaked in horror, sagging into my arms.

"Yeah. The Alpha motherfucker. Haumann brought him here, kept him close so the evols would make peace. Half prisoner, half insurance policy. But I'd say he's grown beyond what they expected."

"He controls them. He sees what they see, knows what they know. All the evols, they are his vessels." Else groaned in sudden pain. "I'm grateful you can't feel it. His will is like an axe in my skull."

I opened my mouth to reply, and then the tumult of voices crashed over me in a roaring wave—the whisper of the locust swarm, swollen by untold numbers until it became a cacophony. The endless legions of zombies, the hive mind of the viral network driven by this one giant organism. Adam the spider at the heart of the dead web.

Else pulled herself up, her expression set hard. "I have to go down there. His hunger is so great he will take me, and my flesh will destroy him," she said.

"I hear them," I said. "I hear them!"

She searched my face. "You shouldn't have done that. We don't know what effect ingesting my blood will have on human physiology."

"It doesn't matter. I can hear them. Haumann's antiviral agent, the one that Wainright finished? That zombie-fucking bug that streams through your veins, it is in me. I am infected with the cure!"

Else grabbed me by my shirtfront and nearly jerked me off my feet. "No!" she snarled. "You promised me you would be with me forever! You do not die! You just don't!" The last came out in an angry shout, thick with tears.

"It must be destiny because I have no choices left," I said in the wake of a sudden calm that washed over me. "Else, you are pregnant. You are carrying our baby. If you live, our child will be the part of me that will be with you forever."

I kissed her, tasting her salty tears and feeling the refusal to let me go. I moved back and with Else holding my hands, I stepped up on the balcony rail and looked into her eyes.

"I love you, Else."

I floated, or flew as you do in dreams, over a writhing landscape of half-formed or half-digested corpses that wallowed within the dark gunk and slime.

The momentary illusion of weightlessness vanished and I plummeted into the thick sack of alien flesh that filled the expanse of the auditorium floor.

It did not burst and I did not plunge into it like a living hypodermic needle. I crawled through an undergrowth of gore and slime, the footing too unstable to stand. Through the translucent membrane lit by a green luminescence, I could see dissolving flesh melting off digested bones and feel the peristaltic contractions of the expanse of Adam.

The evols did not react to my presence among them. Instead they moaned and swayed, their legs rooted into the quivering earth like undead trees. I worked my way to the wall, holding on to hanging creepers of flesh to keep my footing and move closer to the stage.

"What do you think of my work?" A voice thick with pain and exhaustion came from the wall. I leaned out and stared upwards. Doctor Haumann. Mounted on the wall like a hunting trophy.

"I think you might finally win first prize at the science fair with this one, Doc."

To his credit, Haumann managed a smile. "Is he not magnificent? He will be their god, the source of all things necrotic."

"We made it to Woomera. Wainright made Else the weapon you wanted her to be."

Haumann gave a shuddering sigh, moving slightly within the imprisoning cocoon of stinking flesh that held him. "Thank you . . . Is she safe?"

"Yes, she's safe and I'm infected with your cure. I'm here to fuck things up."

Haumann nodded. "It is too late for us. But you can build the world anew. You can—" A tentacle burst through the meat wall and flowered in Haumann's chest. It ripped him open, shattering his ribs and spraying me with his blood. The feeler pumped, gorging itself on Haumann's corpse. Wiping the crap from my eyes, I drew my sword and moved on.

The stench grew so intense my brain stopped noticing. I slipped and crawled down the length of the huge room. Finally, grasping hold of a crusted-over rupture, I pulled myself up and lay gasping for breath on the undulating surface of the stage. The meat around me shivered and with a wet ripping sound a tentacle burst up between my legs. I scrambled back, expecting a bone spur to slam down and suck me dry. Instead the bulbous tip split open and a great rolling eye twisted to focus on me. It was unlike anything I had seen before. It spun slowly within that grey fleshy socket; irises of different colors peered out at me before it flexed and rolled again.

"Yeah, I'm here for you, motherfucker. This is your end standing here." My blood seethed and my skin felt like it might burst into flame at any moment.

"You have failed in your mission." Charlie Aston loomed up behind me. A misshapen fist the size of a football clubbed down on my shoulder. I dropped to my knees and rolled. Stabbing into the floor of undulating flesh with my sword, I pulled myself up.

"Hey Charlie, how's the eye?"

"I knew you were trouble," Charlie said. His face, already distorted with whatever jacked-up shit he'd pumped into his veins, was now made even more horrific by the weeping pit of his eye. "You showed up and Haumann was just going to hand over his first batch of antiviral Tankbread to you. Another day and I would have sabotaged the project. Killed them all. But that damn Soo-Yong made his move too early."

"Lucky me," I said. My shoulder felt like concrete and I took a moment to twist it, feeling something pop back into place.

"But you are all alone now, and your fate is going to be the same as all the others." Charlie pulled the remains of his shirt away. His body had mutated beyond mere steroid abuse. This was something alien.

"Adam's a growing boy. How do you like playing nanny?" I lifted my sword and grinned.

"He is beyond your understanding! He is a god!" Charlie's face swelled with an angry purple flush. Howling pure hatred, he sprang at me like an angry red gorilla. Everything slowed down to a frame-by-frame speed. I felt my eyes pound as absolute awareness flooded my senses. I took a step, dropped to one knee, and thrust the sword upwards with both hands. Charlie ran right into the blade.

The tip burst out through his back, catching on the enlarged bones of his spine. The sharpened steel twisted and then snapped. Charlie squealed and coughed, a great gush of blood bursting from his mouth. I lifted Charlie's head and showed him the jagged haft of the sword I still held. "Your god is dead," I said and rammed the rough end of the broken blade into his gaping eye socket all the way to the hilt. Charlie shuddered and slid to the floor.

Rising to my feet, I took a deep breath and looked out over the auditorium. The survivors of Soo-Yong's attack on the Opera House were all around me, entombed alive in this hideous organism. The few that were yet to be digested had already screamed until their voices broke. Only I remained to speak for them.

"Hey, arsehole!" I yelled up at the crucified giant. More tentacles erupted around me and they all sprouted the glistening bone needles. With a slow tearing sound, as if his chin had grown into his chest, Adam lifted his head and opened his large eyes.

"You missed one," I said and gave him the finger. Both hands. Fuck you.

CHAPTER 44

Else crouched by the growing pile of dry dirt. The man in the hole didn't look at her, he just kept shoveling and glancing at the fresh wallaby carcass stretched out by the woman's boot. He could smell the roasting meat already and it made his belly clench. Finally the man, whose name was Harcourt, judged the hole deep enough for its purpose. Climbing out, he stabbed the shovel into the dirt pile.

"Deep enough I reckon," he said, the hope clear in his voice.

Else stood up from her squat. "Lay him in there. Do it gently," she said. Harcourt wiped the sweat from his face with a filthy sleeve and hefted the cloth-wrapped body into the grave as carefully as he could.

"Fill it in," Else said, her voice cold. Harcourt hesitated only a moment. This woman was strange as anyone he'd ever met. She carried a sword on her back and moved like someone who knew how to use it. She'd found him checking his rat snares. Stepping out of the darkness she grabbed him by the throat. He'd offered up a prayer, figuring the damned evols had finally caught up with him. To Harcourt's surprise, she didn't kill him and only asked if he knew how to dig a grave. He nodded, there being no apparent benefit to saying no.

So now Harcourt found himself digging the final resting place for a corpse, a couple of days old by the smell of it. The woman left him working, saying she would be back with food as payment. Then she mounted a horse and rode away. He expected a can, maybe some dried rat. But an entire wallaby? Soon the hole was covered and Harcourt leaned on his shovel catching his breath. "I can make up a tombstone and put some words on it for you as well if you like," he said.

"Why?" Else glared at him.

"Because people should know there's a man buried here. A man who people cared enough about to bury."

"What do the words say?" Else asked.

"Ah, usually the name of the deceased, and well, I don't know what the date of his birth or of his passing are . . . so maybe just his name?"

"His name?" Else frowned.

"Yes, what was his name? For the tombstone," Harcourt said again.

"He never said," Else whispered and stared at the grave mound.

"Would you like me to say a few words, for the deceased?" Harcourt ventured after a long minute of silence.

"What words?" Else swiped at her tears like they were flies.

"It's customary to say some kind of farewell."

"Did you know him?"

"Uhh no, but it's what you do."

Else sniffed, wiped her nose with the back of her hand, and spoke to the mound of dirt. "You saved us all. Because of you the evols are lost and we can take back the world. You destroyed Adam; he sucked the life out of you and the antiviral infection in your blood. It melted him." Else's voice cracked and she sank to her knees, fists clenching handfuls of earth. "I want to hate you for leaving me. I want to hate you! But I can't! Why can't I hate you!?" she screamed at the burial mound with all the savagery of the grief tearing her apart inside.

"We can't hate the ones we love, at least not for long," Harcourt said. Else pressed her face against the dirt and howled. She wept. Curling into a ball she screamed her anger, her hate, and her love into the dirt, hoping I might hear her.

Now you know what I know. The Adam virus, the genetically engineered mutation, designed by Haumann, Mollbrooke, and Wainright to resurrect dead soldiers, mutated. Spreading through air, water, food, and soil. It's present in everything but lies dormant until the human host dies. After death, an awakening and the onslaught of unshielded understanding. The virus seizes that last spark of consciousness and creates an overwhelming flood through the senses. The dead see everything, they hear everything, they feel everything, and everything is hungry.

Focusing on just one thing for very long is almost impossible. Routines are soothing, well-learned patterns are reassuring. Noise, bright light, the hissing roar of living tissues — these things are too much. Until the dead feed and then it's like blowing your wad for about an hour. After that initial taste of living meat, the need to feed consumes everything.

With the destruction of Adam, the central mind structure collapsed and the evol mind network failed. Only now, as I lay here cloaked in dry dirt, hearing Else grieve above me, I walk through my memories and experience the scope of my growing awareness. The necrosis connection still exists. The engineered viral elements within my cells are sister to those of Adam, and they thrive still within Else and our unborn child. If I choose to use it, the evols will rise again.

I could reach out and touch Else, speak to her, comfort her. Yet if I use the power of the viral network to connect to her, I must open myself to the walking dead in their lost billions. The fading evols, who even now degenerate into the uncontrolled zombies we call the feral dead. I remain silent so in time they can be destroyed and Else can raise our child in a peaceful world.

I take some comfort in knowing that my story is one only the dead will ever hear.

###

14
BY PETER CLINES

Padlocked doors. Strange light fixtures. Mutant cockroaches. There are some odd things about Nate's new apartment. Every room in this old brownstone has a mystery. Mysteries that stretch back over a hundred years. Some of them are in plain sight. Some are behind locked doors. And all together these mysteries could mean the end of Nate and his friends. Or the end of everything...

PERMUTEDPRESS.COM

DAY BY DAY ARMAGEDDON
GREY FOX
BY BILL BRADDOCK

Time is a very fluid thing, no one really has a grasp on it other than maybe how to measure it. As the maestro of the Day by Day Armageddon Universe, I have the latitude of being in control of that time. You have again stumbled upon a ticket with service through the apocalyptic wastes, but this time the train is a little bit older, a little more beat up, and maybe a little wiser.

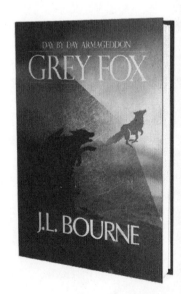

DEAD TIDE
BY STEPHEN A. NORTH

THE WORLD IS ENDING. BUT THERE ARE SURVIVORS. Nick Talaski is a hard-bitten, angry cop. Graham is a newly divorced cab driver. Bronte is a Gulf War veteran hunting his brother's killer. Janicea is a woman consumed by unflinching hate. Trish is a gentleman's club dancer. Morgan is a morgue janitor. The dead have risen and the citizens of St. Petersburg and Pinellas Park are trapped. The survivors are scattered, and options are few. And not all monsters are created by a bite. Some still have a mind of their own...

DEAD TIDE RISING
BY STEPHEN A. NORTH

The sequel to Dead Tide continues the carnage in Pinellas Park near St. Pete, Florida. Follow all of the characters from the first book, Dead Tide, as they fight for survival in a world destroyed by the zombie apocalypse.

BREW
BY BILL BRADDOCK

Ever been to a big college town on a football Saturday night? Loud drunks glut the streets, swaggering about in roaring, leering, laughing packs, like sailors on shore leave. These nights crackle with a dark energy born of incongruity; for beneath all that smiling and singing sprawls a bedrock of malice.

— PERMUTEDPRESS.COM —

TANKBREAD
BY PAUL MANNERING

Ten years ago humanity lost the war for survival. Now intelligent zombies rule the world. Feeding the undead of a steady diet of cloned people called Tankbread, the survivors live in a dangerous world on the brink of final extinction.

THE ROAD TO NOWHERE
BY BILL BRADDOCK

Welcome to the city of Las Vegas. Gone are the days of tourist filled streets. After waking up alone in a hospital bed, everyone seems to have fled, leaving me behind. Survival becomes my only driving force. Nothing was as it should have been. Things seemed to lurk in the buildings and darkest shadows. I didn't know what they were, but I could always feel their eyes on me.

PERMUTEDPRESS.COM

ZOMBIE ATTACK:
RISE OF THE HORDE
BY PAUL MANNERING

Voted best Zombie/ Horror E-books of 2012 on Goodreads. When 16 year old Xander's older brother Moto left him at Vandenberg Airforce Base he only had one request - don't leave no matter what. But there was no way he could have known that one day zombies would gather into groups big enough to knock down walls and take out entire buildings full of people. That was before the rise of the horde!

THE INFECTION
BY CRAIG DiLOUIE

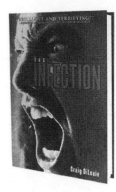

The world is rocked as one in five people collapse screaming before falling into a coma. Three days later, the Infected awake with a single purpose: spread the Infection. A small group—a cop, teacher, student, reverend—team up with a military crew to survive. But at a refugee camp what's left of the government will ask them to accept a dangerous mission back into the very heart of Infection.

PERMUTEDPRESS.COM

THE KILLING FLOOR
BY CRAIG DiLOUIE

The mystery virus struck down millions. Three days later, its victims awoke with a single violent purpose: spread the Infection. Ray Young, survivor of a fight to save a refugee camp from hordes of Infected, awakes from a coma to learn he has also survived Infection. Ray is not immune. Instead, he has been transformed into a superweapon that could end the world … or save it.

PERMUTEDPRESS.COM

THE INFECTION BOX SET
BY CRAIG DiLOUIE

Two full #1 bestselling apocalyptic thrillers for one low price! Includes the full novels THE INFECTION and THE KILLING FLOOR. A mysterious virus suddenly strikes down millions. Three days later, its victims awake with a single purpose: spread the Infection. As the world lurches toward the apocalypse, some of the Infected continue to change, transforming into horrific monsters.

THE BECOMING
BY JESSICA MEIGS

The Michaluk Virus has escaped the CDC, and its effects are widespread and devastating. Most of the population of the southeastern United States have become homicidal cannibals. As society rapidly crumbles under the hordes of infected, three people--Ethan, a Memphis police officer; Cade, his best friend; and Brandt, a lieutenant in the US Marines--band together against the oncoming crush of death.

PERMUTEDPRESS.COM

THE BECOMING:
GROUND ZERO (BOOK 2)
BY JESSICA MEIGS

After the Michaluk Virus decimated the southeast, Ethan and his companions became like family. But the arrival of a mysterious woman forces them to flee from the infected, and the cohesion the group cultivated is shattered. As members of the group succumb to the escalating dangers on their path, new alliances form, new loves develop, and old friendships crumble.

PERMUTEDPRESS.COM

THE BECOMING:
REVELATIONS (BOOK 3)
BY JESSICA MEIGS

In a world ruled by the dead, Brandt Evans is floundering. Leadership of their dysfunctional group wasn't something he asked for or wanted. Their problems are numerous: Remy Angellette is grief-stricken and suicidal, Gray Carter is distant and reclusive, and Cade Alton is near death. And things only get worse.

DOMAIN OF THE DEAD
BY IAIN MCKINNON

The world is dead, devoured by a plague of reanimated corpses. Barricaded inside a warehouse with dwindling food, a group of survivors faces two possible deaths: creeping starvation, or the undead outside. In their darkest hour hope appears in the form of a helicopter approaching the city... but is it the salvation the survivors have been waiting for?

PERMUTEDPRESS.COM

REMAINS OF THE DEAD
BY IAIN MCKINNON

The world is dead. Cahz and his squad of veteran soldiers are tasked with flying into abandoned cities and retrieving zombies for scientific study. Then the unbelievable happens. After years of encountering nothing but the undead, the team discovers a handful of survivors in a fortified warehouse with dwindling supplies.

PERMUTEDPRESS.COM

DEMISE OF THE LIVING
BY IAIN MCKINNON

The world is infected. The dead are reanimating and attacking the living. In a city being overrun with zombies a disparate group of strangers seek sanctuary in an office block. But for how long can the barricades hold back the undead? How long will the food last? How long before those who were bitten succumb turn? And how long before they realise the dead outside are the least of their fears?

ROADS LESS TRAVELED: THE PLAN
BY C. DULANEY

Ask yourself this: If the dead rise tomorrow, are you ready? Do you have a plan? Kasey, a strong-willed loner, has something she calls The Zombie Plan. But every plan has its weaknesses, and a freight train of tragedy is bearing down on Kasey and her friends. In the darkness that follows, Kasey's Plan slowly unravels: friends lost, family taken, their stronghold reduced to ashes.

—————— PERMUTEDPRESS.COM ——————

MURPHY'S LAW
(ROADS LESS TRAVELED BOOK 2)
BY C. DULANEY

Kasey and the gang were held together by a set of rules, their Zombie Plan. It kept them alive through the beginning of the End. But when the chaos faded, they became careless, and Murphy's Law decided to pay a long-overdue visit. Now the group is broken and scattered with no refuge in sight. Those remaining must make their way across West Virginia in search of those who were stolen from them.

—————— PERMUTEDPRESS.COM ——————

SHADES OF GRAY
(ROADS LESS TRAVELED BOOK 3)
BY C. DULANEY

Kasey and the gang have come full circle through the crumbling world. Working for the National Guard, they realize old friends and fellow survivors are disappearing. When the missing start to reappear as walking corpses, the group sets out on another journey to discover the truth. Their answers wait in the West Virginia Command Center.

PAVLOV'S DOGS
BY D.L. SNELL & THOM BRANNAN

WEREWOLVES Dr. Crispin has engineered the saviors of mankind: soldiers capable of transforming into beasts. ZOMBIES Ken and Jorge get caught in a traffic jam on their way home from work. It's the first sign of a major outbreak. ARMAGEDDON Should Dr. Crisping send the Dogs out into the zombie apocalypse to rescue survivors? Or should they hoard their resources and post the Dogs as island guards?

— PERMUTEDPRESS.COM —

THE OMEGA DOG
BY D.L. SNELL & THOM BRANNAN

Twisting and turning through hordes of zombies, cartel territory, Mayan ruins, and the things that now inhabit them, a group of survivors must travel to save one man's family from a nightmarish third world gone to hell. But this time, even best friends have deadly secrets, and even allies can't be trusted - as a father's only hope of getting his kids out alive is the very thing that's hunting him down.

DEAD LIVING
BY GLENN BULLION

It didn't take long for the world to die. And it didn't take long, either, for the dead to rise. Aaron was born on the day the world ended. Kept in seclusion, his family teaches him the basics. How to read and write. How to survive. Then Aaron makes a shocking discovery. The undead, who desire nothing but flesh, ignore him. It's as if he's invisible to them.

PERMUTEDPRESS.COM

AUTOBIOGRAPHY of a WEREWOLF HUNTER
BY BRIAN P. EASTON

After his mother is butchered by a werewolf, Sylvester James is taken in by a Cheyenne mystic. The boy trains to be a werewolf hunter, learning to block out pain, stalk, fight, and kill. As Sylvester sacrifices himself to the hunt, his hatred has become a monster all its own. As he follows his vendetta into the outlands of the occult, he learns it takes more than silver bullets to kill a werewolf.

PALE GODS
BY KIM PAFFENROTH

In a world where the undead rule the continents and the few remaining survivors inhabit only island outposts, six men make the dangerous journey to the mainland to hunt for supplies amid the ruins. But on this trip, the dead act stranger and smarter than ever before and the living must adjust or die.

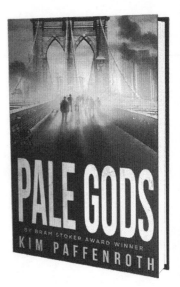

PERMUTEDPRESS.COM

THE JUNKIE QUATRAIN
BY PETER CLINES

Six months ago, the world ended. The Baugh Contagion swept across the planet. Its victims were left twitching, adrenalized cannibals that quickly became know as Junkies. THE JUNKIE QUATRAIN is four tales of survival, and four types of post-apocalypse story. Because the end of the world means different things for different people. Loss. Opportunity. Hope. Or maybe just another day on the job.

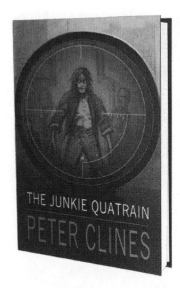

BLOOD SOAKED & CONTAGIOUS
BY JAMES CRAWFORD

I am not going to complain to you about my life.

We've got zombies. They are not the brainless, rotting creatures we'd been led to expect. Unfortunately for us, they're just as smart as they were before they died, very fast, much stronger than you or me, and possess no internal editor at all.

Claws. Did I mention claws?

PERMUTEDPRESS.COM

BLOOD SOAKED & INVADED
BY JAMES CRAWFORD

Zombies were bad enough, but now we're being invaded from all sides. Up to our necks in blood, body parts, and unanswerable questions...

...As soon as the realization hit me, I lost my cool. I curled into the fetal position in a pile of blood, offal, and body parts, and froze there. What in the Hell was I becoming that killing was entertaining and satisfying?

THE KING OF CLAYFIELD
BY SHANE GREGORY

On a cold February day in the small town of Clayfield, Kentucky, an unsuspecting and unprepared museum director he finds himself in the middle of hell on Earth. A pandemic is spreading around the globe, and it's turning most of the residents of Clayfield into murderous zombies. Having no safe haven to which he can flee, the director decides to stick it out near his hometown and wait for the government to send help.

THE KING OF CLAYFIELD 2
ALL THAT I SEE
BY SHANE GREGORY

It has been more than a month since the Canton B virus turned the people of the world into hungry zombies. The survivors of Clayfield, Kentucky attempt to carve out new lives for themselves in this harsh new world. Those who remain have been hardened by their environment and their choices over the previous weeks, but their optimism has not been extinguished. There is hope that eventually Clayfield can be secured, but first, the undead must be eliminated and law and order must be restored. Unfortunately, the group might not ever get to implement their plan.

THE KING OF CLAYFIELD 3
FIRE BIRDS
BY SHANE GREGORY

For weeks, he has fought the undead and believed that he was Clayfield's sole survivor. But when odd things begin to happen in the town, it becomes clear that other healthy people are around. A friend returns full of trouble and secrets, and they are not alone.

Something bad is coming to Clayfield, and there could be nowhere to hide.

INFECTION:
ALASKAN UNDEAD APOCALYPSE
BY SEAN SCHUBERT

Anchorage, Alaska: gateway to serene wilderness of The Last Frontier. No stranger to struggle, the city on the edge of the world is about to become even more isolated. When a plague strikes, Anchorage becomes a deadly trap for its citizens. The only two land routes out of the city are cut, forcing people to fight or die as the infection spreads.

PERMUTEDPRESS.COM

CONTAINMENT
(ALASKAN UNDEAD APOCALYPSE BOOK 2)
BY SEAN SCHUBERT

Running. Hiding. Surviving. Anchorage, once Alaska's largest city, has fallen. Now a threatening maze of death, the city is firmly in the cold grip of a growing zombie horde. Neil Jordan and Dr. Caldwell lead a small band of desperate survivors through the maelstrom. The group has one last hope: that this nightmare has been contained, and there still exists a sane world free of infection.

THE UNDEAD SITUATION
BY ELOISE J. KNAPP

The dead are rising. People are dying. Civilization is collapsing. But Cyrus V. Sinclair couldn't care less; he's a sociopath. Amidst the chaos, Cyrus sits with little more emotion than one of the walking corpses... until he meets up with other inconvenient survivors who cramp his style and force him to re-evaluate his outlook on life. It's Armageddon, and things will definitely get messy.

PERMUTEDPRESS.COM

THE UNDEAD HAZE
(THE UNDEAD SITUATION BOOK 2)
BY ELOISE J. KNAPP

When remorse drives Cyrus to abandon his hidden compound he doesn't realize what new dangers lurk in the undead world. He knows he must wade through the vilest remains of humanity and hordes of zombies to settle scores and find the one person who might understand him. But this time, it won't be so easy. Zombies and unpleasant survivors aren't the only thing Cyrus has to worry about.

MAD SWINE: THE BEGINNING
BY STEVEN PAJAK

People refer to the infected as "zombies," but that's not what they really are. Zombie implies the infected have died and reanimated. The thing is, they didn't die. They're just not human anymore. As the infection spreads and crazed hordes--dubbed "Mad Swine"--take over the cities, the residents of Randall Oaks find themselves locked in a desperate struggle to survive in the new world.

PERMUTEDPRESS.COM

MAD SWINE: DEAD WINTER
BY STEVEN PAJAK

Three months after the beginning of the Mad Swine outbreak, the residents of Randall Oaks have reached their breaking point. After surviving the initial outbreak and a war waged with their neighboring community, Providence, their supplies are severely close to depletion. With hostile neighbors at their flanks and hordes of infected outside their walls, they have become prisoners within their own community.

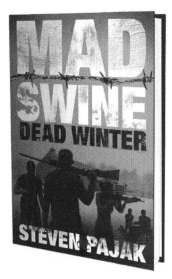

RISE
BY GARETH WOOD

Within hours of succumbing to a plague, millions of dead rise to attack the living. Brian Williams flees the city with his sister Sarah. Banded with other survivors, the group remains desperately outnumbered and under-armed. With no food and little fuel, they must fight their way to safety. RISE is the story of the extreme measures a family will take to survive a trek across a country gone mad.

AGE OF THE DEAD
BY GARETH WOOD

A year has passed since the dead rose, and the citizens of Cold Lake are out of hope. Food and weapons are nearly impossible to find, and the dead are everywhere. In desperation Brian Williams leads a salvage team into the mountains. But outside the small safe zones the world is a foreign place. Williams and his team must use all of their skills to survive in the wilderness ruled by the dead.

DEAD MEAT
BY PATRICK & CHRIS WILLIAMS

The city of River's Edge has been quarantined due to a rodent borne rabies outbreak. But it quickly becomes clear to the citizens that the infection is something much, much worse than rabies... The townsfolk are attacked and fed upon by packs of the living dead. Gavin and Benny attempt to survive the chaos in River's Edge while making their way north in search of sanctuary.

ROTTER WORLD
BY SCOTT M. BAKER

Eight months ago vampires released the Revenant Virus on humanity. Both species were nearly wiped out. The creator of the virus claims there is a vaccine that will make humans and vampires immune to the virus, but it's located in a secure underground facility five hundred miles away. To retrieve the vaccine, a raiding party of humans and vampires must travel down the devastated East Coast.

AMONG THE LIVING
BY TIMOTHY W. LONG

The dead walk. Now the real battle for Seattle has begun. Lester has a new clientele, the kind that requires him to deal lead instead of drugs. Mike suspects a conspiracy lies behind the chaos. Kate has a dark secret: she's a budding young serial killer. These survivors, along with others, are drawn together in their quest to find the truth behind the spreading apocalypse.

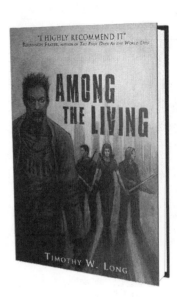

PERMUTEDPRESS.COM

AMONG THE DEAD
BY TIMOTHY W. LONG

Seattle is under siege by masses of living dead, and the military struggles to prevent the virus from spreading outside the city. Kate is tired of sitting around. When she learns that a rescue mission is heading back into the chaos, she jumps at the chance to tag along and put her unique skill set and, more importantly, swords to use.

LONG VOYAGE BACK
BY LUKE RHINEHART

When the bombs came, only the lucky escaped. In the horror that followed, only the strong would survive. The voyage of the trimaran Vagabond began as a pleasure cruise on the Chesapeake Bay. Then came the War Alert ... the unholy glow on the horizon ... the terrifying reports of nuclear destruction. In the days that followed, it became clear just how much chaos was still to come.

PERMUTEDPRESS.COM

QUARANTINED
BY JOE MCKINNEY

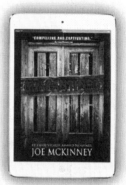

The citizens of San Antonio, Texas are threatened with extermination by a terrifying outbreak of the flu. Quarantined by the military to contain the virus, the city is in a desperate struggle to survive. Inside the quarantine walls, Detective Lily Harris finds herself caught up in a conspiracy intent on hiding the news from the world and fighting a population threatening to boil over into revolt.

PERMUTEDPRESS.COM

THE DESERT
BY BRYON MORRIGAN

Give up trying to leave. There's no way out. Those are the final words in a journal left by the last apparent survivor of a platoon that disappear in Iraq. Years later, two soldiers realize that what happened to the "Lost Platoon" is now happening to them. Now they must confront the horrifying creatures responsible for their misfortune, or risk the same fate as that of the soldiers before them.

Made in the USA
Charleston, SC
12 December 2013